The
Singles
Game

Lauren Weisberger has sold 13 million copies of her novels worldwide. She is the bestselling author of *The Devil Wears Prada*, which was published in forty-two languages and made into a hugely successful film starring Meryl Streep and Anne Hathaway. The hit sequel, *Revenge Wears Prada*, and her three other novels, *Everyone Worth Knowing*, *Chasing Harry Winston* and *Last Night at Chateau Marmont* were all bestsellers. A graduate of Cornell University, she lives in Connecticut with her husband and two children.

If you'd like to find out more about Lauren Weisberger and her books, join her online.

www.laurenweisberger.com
/lauren.weisberger
@LWeisberger
@laurenweisberger

Also by Lauren Weisberger

The Devil Wears Prada
Everyone Worth Knowing
Chasing Harry Winston
Last Night at Chateau Marmont
Revenge Wears Prada: The Devil Returns

The Singles Game

LAUREN WEISBERGER

HARPER

Harper
An imprint of HarperCollins*Publishers*
The News Building,
1 London Bridge Street,
London SE1 9GF

www.harpercollins.co.uk

A Paperback Original 2016
1

A catalogue record for this book
is available from the British Library

ISBN: 978-0-00-756924-3

Set in Meridien by Palimpsest Book Production Ltd,
Falkirk, Stirlingshire

Printed and bound in Great Britain by
Clays Ltd, St Ives plc

MIX
Paper from
responsible sources

FSC™
www.fsc.org
FSC˚ C007454

For Sydney, Emma, Sadie, and Jack
I love you all so much.

1

not all strawberries and cream

WIMBLEDON, JUNE 2015

It wasn't every day a middle-aged woman wearing a neat bun and a purple polyester suit directed you to lift your skirt. The woman's voice was clipped, British proper. All business.

After glancing at her coach, Marcy, Charlie lifted the edges of her pleated white skirt and waited.

'Higher, please.'

'I promise you, everything's in order down there, ma'am,' Charlie said, as politely as she could.

The official's eyes narrowed to a steely squint, but she didn't say a word.

'All the way, Charlie,' Marcy said sternly, but it was obvious she was trying not to smile.

Charlie pulled the skirt up to reveal the waistband of the white Lycra shorts she wore beneath. 'No underwear, but they're double-lined. No matter how much I sweat, no one will get a show.'

'Very well, thank you.' The official made a notation on her legal pad. 'Now your shirt, please.'

At least a dozen more jokes sprung to mind – it's like going to the gynecologist, only in workout wear; it's not just anyone she'll show her underwear to on the first date; et cetera – but Charlie held back. These Wimbledon people had been welcoming and polite to her and her entire entourage, but no one could accuse them of having a sense of humor.

She yanked her shirt up so far it covered most of her face. 'My sports bra is made of the same material. Totally opaque, no matter what.'

'Yes, I can see that,' the woman murmured. 'It's just this band of color here around the bottom.'

'The elastic? It's light gray. I'm not sure that counts as a color,' Marcy said. Her voice was even, but Charlie could hear the smallest hint of irritation.

'Yes, but I must measure it.' The official removed a plain yellow tape measure from a small fanny pack she wore over her uniform suit and gingerly wrapped it around Charlie's rib cage.

'Are we through yet?' Marcy asked the official, her irritation now readily apparent.

'Very close. Miss, your hat, wristbands, and socks are all acceptable. There is only one problem,' the official said, her lips pressed together. 'The shoes.'

'What shoes?' Charlie asked. Nike had gone above and beyond ensuring that her regular sneakers were modified to fit Wimbledon's stringent standards. Her usual cheerfully bright outfits had been changed entirely to white: not cream, not ivory, not off-white, but white. The leather around the toe cage was pure white. Her laces were white, white, white.

'Your shoes. The sole is almost entirely pink. That is a violation.'

'A violation?' Marcy asked in disbelief. 'The sides, back, top, and laces are entirely white, strictly to code. The Nike logo is even smaller than it's required to be. You can't possibly have an issue with the soles!'

'I'm afraid swaths of color that large are not permitted, even on the soles. The rule is a band of one centimeter.'

Charlie turned in panic to Marcy, who held up her hand. 'What do you suggest we do, ma'am? This young lady is due on Centre Court in less than ten minutes. Are you telling me she can't wear her sneakers?'

'Of course she must wear trainers, but according to the rules, she may not wear those.'

'Thank you for that clarification,' Marcy snapped. 'We'll handle it from here.' Marcy grabbed Charlie's wrist and hurried her toward one of the private training rooms in the back of the locker room.

Seeing Marcy rattled gave Charlie the sensation of experiencing turbulence on a plane. When you glanced toward the flight attendants for reassurance, it was almost nauseating to see them panicked. Marcy had been Charlie's coach since Charlie was fifteen, when she'd finally excelled beyond her dad's skill set. Marcy was chosen for her coaching acumen, of course, but also for the fact that she was a woman: Charlie's mom had died from breast cancer only a few years earlier.

'Wait here. Do some stretching, eat your banana, and do not think about this. Focus on how you're going to dismantle Atherton's game point by point. I'll be back in a minute.'

Too nervous to sit, Charlie paced the training room and tried to stretch out her calves. Could they be tightening up already? No, that was impossible. Karina Geiger, the fourth seed with the body of a refrigerator that earned her the unfortunate but mostly affectionate nickname the Giant German, popped her head into the training room.

'You're on Centre, right?' she asked.

Charlie nodded.

'It is a madhouse out there,' the girl boomed in a strong German accent. 'Prince William and Prince Harry are in the Royal Box. With Camilla, which is unusual, because I think they do not like each other, and Prince Charles and Princess Kate are not there.'

'Really?' Charlie asked, although she already knew this. As if playing Centre Court at Wimbledon for the very first time in one's career wasn't stressful enough, she had to be playing the lone seeded British singles player. Alice Atherton was only ranked number fifty-three but she was young and being hailed as the next Great British Hope, so the entire country would be cheering for her to crush Charlie.

'Yes. Also David Beckham, but he is at everything. It is not so special to see him. Also one of the Beatles, which one is still alive? I can't remember. Oh, and I heard Natalya say that she saw—'

'Karina? Sorry, I'm just in the middle of some stretches. Good luck today, okay?' Charlie hated to be rude, especially to one of the few nice women on the tour, but she couldn't stand the talking for even one more second.

'*Ja*, sure. Good luck to you, too.'

Karina passed Marcy on the way out, who had reappeared at the door with a tote bag full of all-white sneakers. 'Quickly,' she said, pulling out the first pair. 'These are a ten narrow, by some miracle. Try them.'

Charlie dropped to the floor, her black braid smacking the side of her cheek hard enough to hurt, and pulled on the left shoe. 'They're Adidas, Marce,' she said.

'I am really not interested in how Nike feels about you wearing Adidas. Next time they can get the sneakers right and none of us will have to worry about it. But now you'll wear what feels the best.'

Charlie stood up and took a tentative step.

'Put on the other one,' Marcy said.

'No, they're too big. My heel's slipping.'

'Next!' Marcy barked, tossing over another Adidas shoe.

Charlie tried the right one on this time and shook her head. 'I'm a little jammed up in the toe cage. And it's pinching my pinky toe already. I guess we could tape the toe and try it . . .'

'No way. Here,' Marcy said, untying a pair of K-Swiss sneakers and placing them at Charlie's feet. 'These might work.'

The left one went on easily and felt like it fit. Hopeful, Charlie slipped on and tightened the laces on the right shoe. They were clunky-looking and ugly, but they fit her feet.

'They fit,' Charlie said, although they felt like she was

wearing cinder blocks. She did a few jumps followed by a short jog and a quick cut to the left. 'But it's like wearing a pair of bricks. They're so heavy.'

Just as Marcy was reaching into the bag to pull out the last pair, an announcement came over the ceiling speakers. 'Attention, players. Alice Atherton and Charlotte Silver, please report to the tournament desk to be escorted to your court. Your match is scheduled to begin in three minutes.'

Marcy knelt down and pushed against her toes. 'You definitely have room in there. Not too much, right? Will they work?'

Charlie did another hop or two. There was no denying they were heavy, but they were the best of the three. She probably should try on the final pair, but she glanced up just in time to see Alice in her own all-white outfit walk past the training room and toward the tournament desk. It was time.

'They'll work,' Charlie said with more conviction than she felt. *They have to work,* she couldn't help thinking.

'Good girl.' The relief on Marcy's face was immediate. 'Let's go.'

Marcy slung Charlie's enormous racket bag over her shoulder and headed out the door. 'Remember, as much spin as you can. She struggles when the balls jump high. Take advantage of your height over hers and force her to hit high ones, especially on her backhand. Slow, steady, and persistent will win this one. You don't need excessive force or flash. Save that for the later rounds, okay?'

Charlie nodded. They were only just approaching the tournament desk and already her calves were feeling tight.

Was the right heel rubbing a little? Yes, it definitely was. She was going to get blisters for sure.

'I think I should try on those last—'

'Charlotte?' Another Wimbledon official, also clad in the same purple polyester skirt suit, took Charlie's elbow and led her the final ten steps to the tournament desk. 'Please, just a signature right here and . . . thank you. Mr Poole, both ladies are ready to be escorted to Centre Court.'

Charlie's and her opponent's eyes met for the briefest of seconds and they each nodded. Half nodded. The only other time they'd played before had been in Indian Wells two years earlier in the first round, and Charlie had beaten her 6–2, 6–2.

The entire group – Charlie, Marcy, Alice, and Alice's coach – followed Mr Poole through the tunnel that led to the most storied tennis court in the world. On both sides were enormous glossy black-and-white photos of tennis legends who had emerged victorious from Centre Court: Serena Williams, Pete Sampras, Roger Federer, Maria Sharapova, Andy Murray. Clutching the traditional trophy, kissing it; thrusting their rackets high into the air; pumping their fists. Exultant. Winners, all of them. Alice was glancing from side to side, too, as they walked toward the door that would take them onto Centre and thrust them onstage.

A hard squeeze on her upper arm from Marcy brought her back to the moment. She accepted her racket bag and slung it over her shoulder as though it weighed nothing, even though jammed inside were six rackets, a roll of grip tape, two bottles of Evian, one bottle of Gatorade, two outfit changes identical to the one she was wearing, extra socks, wristbands, shoulder and knee tape, Band-Aids, an iPod, over-the-ear headphones, two visors, eyedrops, a banana, a packet of Emergen-C, and the lone laminated photo of her mother that lived in the small zipped side pocket and attended every practice and tournament with Charlie.

Marcy and Alice's coach left to take their seats in the players' box. Although the two women walked onto the court at the same time, the audience cheered extra loudly for Alice, the hometown favorite. But it didn't much matter who they were cheering for: Charlie's pulse began to race in the exact same way it did before every match, big or small. Only this time she felt a tingling wave of sensation through her chest, a fluttering of anxiety and excitement so strong she thought she might be sick. *Centre Court at Wimbledon*. She allowed herself a quick look up to the stands, a moment to take it all in. All around her were crowds of well-dressed people standing and politely clapping. Pimm's. Strawberries and cream. Pastel suits. She'd played Wimbledon before, five glorious times, but this was Centre Court.

The words reverberated in her mind over and over again as she tried to will herself to concentrate. Normally, the routine Charlie performed when she reached her courtside chair was focusing: racket bag placed just so, water bottles neatly arranged, wristband put on, visor adjusted. She did all those things in the exact same order as always, but today she couldn't pull herself together. Today, everything registered when it should have disappeared into the background: the on-court anchorwoman repeating her opponent's name into the camera; the match announcer introducing the chair umpire; and most of all, the way her socks slipped into her sneakers, something that never happened when she was wearing her own shoes. She had enough experience to know that none of this was a particularly good omen – not being able to control your thoughts before play began usually didn't end well – but she simply could not block out all the stimuli.

. Warm-up was a blur. Mindlessly, Charlie whacked the ball to Alice's forehand and backhand and then fed her volleys and overheads. They each retreated to opposite sides to try a few serves. Alice was looking loose and comfortable, her lean legs moving fluidly around the court, her narrow, boyish torso twisting effortlessly to reach the ball. Charlie felt tight just watching her. Although the new shoes technically fit, they were making her arches ache and her right heel was already beginning to chafe. Again and again she willed herself back to the present, to the natural rush she felt every time she stroked the ball just so and it spun and bounced exactly where she'd intended. And then, suddenly, they were playing. She had lost the coin toss and her opponent bounced the ball on the opposite baseline. They'd done a coin toss, right? Yes, she thought so. Why couldn't Charlie recall any of the details? *Whoosh!* The ball whizzed past her left shoulder like a bullet. She hadn't even managed to make contact with it. Ace. First point of the match to Alice. The crowd cheered as madly as British etiquette permitted.

It took four minutes and thirty seconds for Alice to win the first game. Charlie had only one point to show for it, and that was because Alice double-faulted. *Focus!* she screamed to herself. *This whole match will be over before you know it if you don't get your damn act together! You want to flame out on Centre Court at Wimbledon without even trying? Only a loser would do that! Loser! Loser! Loser!*

The mental screaming and cursing worked. Charlie went on to hold her own serve and break Alice's. She was up 2–1 and could feel herself starting to settle. The queasy adrenaline that had troubled her before the match was morphing into that blissful state of flow where Charlie could no longer feel the irritation of her socks slipping or see the familiar faces in the Royal Box or hear the golf claps and quiet cheers of the infinitely well-mannered British audience. Nothing existed but her racket and the ball, and nothing mattered but how those two made contact, point after point, game after game, crisply, powerfully, and with intention.

Charlie won the first set, 6–3. She was tempted to congratulate herself, but she knew enough to recognize that the match was far from over. In the ninety seconds during the changeover, she calmly drank some water in small, measured sips. Even that took mental discipline – her whole body was screaming for huge, cold gulps – but she controlled herself. When she had rehydrated and taken three bites of a banana, she rooted through her racket bag and pulled out her backup pair of socks. They were identical to the ones she was wearing, and while there was no reason to believe they would perform any differently, Charlie decided to try. When she removed her old socks, her feet were a horror show: meaty, swollen, red. Both pinky toes were bloodied and the skin on her heels hung in loose, blistered rolls. The outsides of her ankles were covered in purple bruises from hitting the stiff tops and tongue of the leather. The whole of her feet ached as though they'd been run over by a bus.

The new socks felt like sandpaper, and it took every ounce of willpower to push her mutilated feet back into the shoes. Pain shot from her toes and heels, her ankles and arches, from the ball-of-the-foot bone that hadn't even hurt until that very moment. Charlie had to will herself to cinch the laces tight and knot them, and the moment she did so, the chair umpire called time. Instead of running high-kneed back to the baseline to keep loose and responsive, she found herself walking with a slight limp. *I should've taken some Advil when I had the chance*, she thought as she accepted two balls from a teenage ball boy. *Hell, I should have had the right shoes in the first place.*

And *bam!* That was all it took to open the floodgates of anger and, worse, distraction. Why on earth couldn't anyone have predicted that her shoes would be deemed inadmissible? Where were her sponsors at Nike? It's not like they'd never outfitted Wimbledon players before. Charlie tossed first one and then a second ball into the air to serve. Double fault. Whose responsibility was it anyway? She switched sides, offered a weaker-than-usual serve, and stood dumbly still as Alice blazed a forehand winner right past her. *Tennis players are superstitious. We wear the same underwear at every match. We eat the same foods, day in and day out. We carry good-luck charms and talismans and offer prayers and chant mantras and every other crazy thing to help convince whoever's listening that if only, please, just this once, we could win this lone point/game/set/match/tournament, it would really be so great and soooo appreciated.* Charlie's first serve was powerful and well placed, but again she was flat-footed and unprepared for Alice's return. She got to the ball but wasn't able to steady her stance enough to clear the net. Love–40. Was she seriously expected to wear someone else's shoes during her first match on Centre Court, the biggest, most intimidating stage on which she'd ever played? Really – shoes? She and her team spent hours selecting and fitting new sneakers when it was time for a change, but hey, here, just wear this random pair. They'll be fine. What do you think this is, Wimbledon or some-thing? *Whack!* The anger coursed through her body and went straight to the ball, which she hit at least two feet past the baseline, and just like that, she had lost the first game of the second set.

Charlie glanced toward her box and saw Marcy, her father, and her brother, Jake. When Mr Silver caught her looking, he broke into a reflexive smile, but Charlie could see his concern from where she was standing on the baseline. The next several games were over in a flash, with Charlie only managing to hold on to one. Suddenly Alice was up 5–2 and something inside Charlie's head snapped to focus: *Oh my god. This is it.* She was about to lose her second set on Centre Court to a player ranked thirty spots lower. To play a third set right now would be hell. It was simply not an option. The infinitely polite British crowd was downright raucous by their standards, with light clapping and even the occasional cheer. Forget the blisters, forget the brick-like shoes, forget the raging anger at all the people on her team who should have prevented this from happening. None of that mattered now. *Hit hard, hit smart, hit consistently,* she thought, squeezing her racket tightly and releasing, something Charlie often did to relax herself. *Squeeze, release. Squeeze, release. Forget the bullshit and win the next point.*

Charlie won the next game and then the game after that. Once again she settled down, forced her mind to think of nothing but stroking the ball and winning the point. When she tied up the second set at 5–5, she knew she would win the match. She breathed deeply, evenly, summoning huge reserves of mental strength to tune out the pain that was now radiating from her feet up her legs. Cramping. She could deal with that, had a thousand times before. *Focus. Hit. Recover. Hit. Recover.* In an instant it was 6–5 in the second set and Charlie had to secure only one more game to win it. It was so close now she could feel it.

Alice's first serve was high on spin but low on speed and Charlie jumped all over it. *Winner!* Her next one was much harder and flatter, and Charlie smashed that one straight down the line. They rallied back and forth a few shots on the next point before Alice dropped one just over the net. Charlie read it early and set her body in motion, running as fast as her legs would take her toward the net, her racket outstretched already and her entire upper half bent forward. She could get there, she knew she could. She was almost there, literally within inches of connecting the very top part of her racket head to the ball, only needing to give it a little tap to get it back over the net, when her right foot – feeling like it had a five-pound bag of flour attached to it – slid out from under her like a ski. Had she been wearing her own light, properly fitted sneakers, she may have been able to control the slide, but the heavy, blocky shoe flew across the grass court as though it were a sheet of ice, and it pulled Charlie with it. She flailed gracelessly, tossing her racket so she could use both hands to break her fall, and then . . . *pop.* She heard it before she felt it. Didn't everyone? It was so damn loud the entire stadium must have heard that awful popping sound, but on the off chance they missed it, Charlie's scream caught their attention.

She hit the ground hard, like a kid falling from a top bunk. Every millimeter of her body hurt so much it was nearly impossible to ascertain where the awful popping sound had originated. Across the net Alice stood watching Charlie, a sympathetic expression carefully arranged on her face. Pushing her palms into the impeccably manicured grass, Charlie tried to hoist herself to sit but her wrist folded in like paper. The chair umpire held her hand over the microphone and leaned forward to ask Charlie if she needed a medical time-out.

'No, I'm fine,' Charlie said, her voice barely a whisper. 'Just need a minute to get myself together.' She knew she had to pull herself up and get back into position. She could take a medical time-out, but it was practically cheating: unless a player was actually bleeding all over the court, it was generally thought that they should suck it up. *Suck it up*, she thought, giving herself another little hoist. This time she felt the pain that shot up her left palm, straight through her wrist, and into her shoulder. Two more points to even it out. *Suck it up. Stand up and win your match!*

The spectators began to clap for her, tentatively at first and then more enthusiastically. She wasn't the favorite, but those Brits knew their sportsmanship. Charlie raised her right hand in a gesture of thanks and reached forward across the grass to get her racket. The exertion made her head spin, and more pain – this time from her foot or ankle or shin, it was impossible to tell – shot up her leg. *Those f'ing shoes!* she yelled to herself, the panic beginning to set in. Was she seriously injured? Would she have to withdraw? *Dear god, what was that awful sound and how hard is it going to be to rehab? The US Open is only eight weeks away* . . .

The umpire's voice interrupted her thoughts, and the sound of her own name snapped her back to reality. 'I am granting a three-minute medical time-out for Ms Silver. Please set the timer for . . . now.'

'I didn't request a medical time-out!' Charlie said peevishly, although her voice clearly wasn't carrying. 'I'm fine.'

In an effort to ward off the head trainer, who was fast approaching her, Charlie swung her legs beneath her body and summoned every last ounce of energy to push herself to stand. She made it upright and was able to glance around her, to take in Alice's barely detectable smile and the umpire's careful observation of the televised match clock, ready to pounce the moment the time-out was over. In the front row of the Royal Box, Charlie could see David Beckham checking his cell phone, her injury of no interest whatsoever to him, and then to the right, in Charlie's own box, the panic-stricken look of concern on Marcy's face; she was leaning so far into the court from her seat that it looked like she might fall. Her father and Jake wore matching grave expressions. All around her people chatted with good cheer, took sips from their Pimm's, and waited for the match to resume. The trainer was standing next to Charlie now and had just reached his cool, strong hand to her throbbing wrist, when, without any warning at all, the whole world went black.

2

the love department

The very first thought that crossed Charlie's mind when she awoke from surgery on her Achilles' injury was: *I'm done. Finished. Like it or not, it's time to retire, because there is no returning from this injury.* It felt like someone had run over her right foot with a car, built it back up using a paring knife, and laced it together with rusty wire and some rubber cement. The pain was indescribable; the nausea, overwhelming. She had thrown up twice in the recovery room and once in her hospital bed.

'It's just the anesthesia,' a portly nurse clucked, checking Charlie's gauges and screens. 'You'll feel much better soon.'

lauren weisberger

'Can you hook up one of those morphine drips? To keep her quiet?' Jake asked from his chair underneath the window.

The nurse didn't answer. Instead, she told Charlie she'd return with a tray for dinner and left.

'She loves me,' Jake said.

'Clearly.' Charlie felt a wave of nausea wash over her and she grabbed the kidney-shaped puke bin.

'Should I, like, hold your hair?'

Charlie coughed. 'I'm fine. It passed.'

She must have fallen asleep, because when she woke up, the sky through her tiny room's window had darkened and Jake was chewing an In-N-Out burger.

'Oh, hey. I ran out for some decent food. I have an extra burger here if you can stomach it.' Jake dunked two fries in a little tub of the special sauce and popped them in his mouth.

Charlie was surprised when she felt a pang of hunger. She nodded, and Jake unpacked a cheeseburger, fries, and a Coke on the tray next to her bed. He placed a straw in the soda, yanked open a few ketchup packets, and pushed the swinging tray in front of her.

'This right here is pretty much the only benefit to rupturing your Achilles' and having to drop out in the first round of Wimbledon on Centre Court in front of the entire world, just as you're about to win the match,' Charlie said, stuffing the burger into her mouth one-handed, since her left arm was in a cast from thumb to elbow. The first bite was almost orgasmic. Ever since the Bloody Mary she'd gulped on the flight home from London to California in preparation for her surgery at UCLA, Charlie's only consolation had been the food.

'It might be worth it?' Jake asked through a full mouth.

'I listened to a TED Talk the other day about the founders of In-N-Out. Do you know it's family owned, and they plan never to sell or franchise it?'

'Fascinating.'

'No, it really is. I bet you haven't noticed that they discreetly print Bible citations on their cups and burger wrappers?'

'I most definitely did not.'

'Well, I thought it was interesting.' Charlie had no idea what it meant, but she noticed the bottom of her Coke cup said JOHN 3:16.

Jake rolled his eyes. 'Dad told me to tell you he'll be back as soon as he's finished. There was a special event at the club tonight, some fund-raiser, so they had him teaching clinics back-to-back. I had to promise a thousand times I wouldn't leave your side for a second.'

Charlie groaned. 'I am so getting babysat around the clock, aren't I?'

'You are. He's convinced you're going to wake up thinking your career is over and throw yourself off the nearest bridge. Or I guess you would have to walk in front of a train. There aren't really bridges around here . . .'

'What's it to him? Don't you think he'd be happy if I stopped playing? How many trillion times has he said that tennis is no way to live your whole life?'

'Many trillion times. But he knows you want it, Charlie. He's a good enough dad that he can hate the whole idea of something and still support his kids because we want to do something. Like you turning pro, and me sleeping with men. I think it's fair to say neither thrilled him, but he got on board. He's good like that.'

They ate the remainder of their burgers in comfortable silence while Charlie tried to imagine what her father was doing at that moment. He'd been teaching at the Birchwood Golf and Racket Club for more than twenty years. They'd moved to Topanga Canyon from Northern California when Charlie was three because the club promised her father more responsibility and better pay than his job coaching boys' tennis at an elite boarding school. A few years later he was promoted to head pro, and now he ran both the tennis and golf programs, despite knowing little about golf. He spent most of his time checking inventory and hiring pros and smoothing over small tiffs with members, and Charlie knew he missed the actual teaching. He still taught the occasional lesson, most often the old-timers and small children, but at sixty-one he couldn't keep up with the teenagers or young professionals who moved fast and hit hard. No one acknowledged it, but the lesson requests had shifted to the younger teachers and Mr Silver most often found himself in the pro shop or the club's main office or even the stringing machine. If tonight were like the other charity events the club hosted, her dad would be feeding balls at the children's clinics that served as day care while the parents donned their best black tie and nibbled canapés in the dining room that overlooked the ninth hole. He never complained, but it made Charlie despondent thinking of him leading a game of offense-defense with a group of eight-year-olds while his peers drank and danced together inside.

'Why do you think Dad still does it?' Charlie asked, pushing her tray away. 'I mean, he's been there, what? A quarter of a century now?'

Jake raised an eyebrow. 'Because he never went to college. Because he's proud and will never take a dime from either of us. Because he was, by all accounts but most of all his own, a womanizing asshole during his pro years until he met Mom, and by the time they had me, it was too late for him to go back to school. You don't need me to be telling you any of this.'

'No, I know. I guess I just mean, why hasn't he ever moved? Ever since Mom died, we don't have any real ties to the area. Why not try somewhere else? Arizona or Florida? Marin? Mexico, even? It's not like he has some great life in LA that he would miss so much.'

Jake looked down at his phone and cleared his throat. 'I don't know that places are lining up to hire a sixty-year-old pro with a few years' experience on the tour forty years ago. One who – I hate to be blunt about it, but let's call a spade a spade – sleeps with every single woman who shows up for some help with her backhand. Birchwood treats him pretty well, all things considered.'

'I think I just threw up in my mouth.'

Jake rolled his eyes. 'He's a grown man, Charlie.'

'Do you think he's happy?' Charlie asked. 'I mean, I know he's had every opportunity to get married again and has clearly not chosen that route, but does he *like* his life?'

Their father had worked around the clock to support them both, to give them every opportunity that their far more privileged classmates had enjoyed: summer camp, music lessons, annual camping trips to national parks. And of course the tennis lessons. He'd taught them both to play from the time they were four. Jake soon lost interest, and Mr Silver never pushed him. Charlie, on the other hand, was a natural: she loved her tiny pink racket, the running and balancing drills, the tube she used to help pick up balls. She loved filling those little paper cone cups with icy water from the Gatorade cooler and scraping the clay off her sneakers with the floor-mounted rolling brush and the way the tennis balls smelled when she cracked open a brand-new can. But most of all she loved her father's undivided attention, how he focused entirely on her and his face lit up every time she flounced onto the court with her ponytail braid and purple striped sweatpants. The look that was usually reserved for whatever woman he was dating at the time, a seemingly endless cadre of middle-aged divorcées stuffed into too-tight and too-short dresses, who would hang on his arm and offer Charlie insincere compliments about her bedroom or her braids or her nightgown before following her father into the night in a cloud of potent perfume.

Not that they were all like that. Sometimes the women were younger, not yet mothers themselves, and they would talk to Charlie and Jake in high-pitched voices like they were zoo animals, or bring them thoughtful but age-inappropriate gifts: a stuffed koala bear for Charlie when she was fifteen; a Heineken beer koozie for a seventeen-year-old Jake. There were women Mr Silver met at the club, women he met at the Fish Shack down on Malibu Beach where he'd been going for twenty years and knew everybody, women who were just passing through Los Angeles on their way from New York to Hawaii or San Francisco to San Diego, and who somehow, someway, always found their way to the Silver house. Charlie's dad never expected his kids to offer anything more than a friendly hello over French toast in the morning, but he also never seemed to consider that it wasn't the healthiest of examples to march an ever-changing parade of one-night stands through family breakfast. A handful of them stuck around for a few weeks – Charlie had the most vivid memories of a very kind, exceedingly skinny woman named Ingrid who seemed genuinely interested in both Silver kids – but mostly they vanished quickly.

Tennis was when Mr Silver focused entirely on Charlie. It was the only time he wasn't working, or fishing, or chasing his latest lady interest, as he liked to call them. When they walked out onto the court at Birchwood – almost always at night under the lights, when the paying members were home with their families – Mr Silver's attention narrowed to a laser beam of light that warmed Charlie the instant it focused on her. It was the one thing that hadn't changed after her mother died: the obvious delight he took in teaching Charlie the game he loved. All those years had been a labor of love for him, from the time she'd followed him like a duckling around the court as he demonstrated the baseline, the alleys, the service line, and no-man's-land, to the very first time Charlie took a game off him fair and square when she was thirteen and Mr Silver whooped so loudly a grounds-keeper came to make sure they were okay. Nothing got in the way of their lessons: not Charlie's mother's death nor the women who kept him company in the years that followed. He taught Charlie everything she knew – strokes, footwork, strategy, and of course sportsman-ship – straight up until she won the sixteen-and-under Orange Bowl at age fifteen, the Grand Slam of junior tournaments, and Mr Silver insisted he'd taken her as far as he could.

Jake stretched his arms overhead in the chair beside her and let out a loud exhale. 'Like his life?' He rubbed his chin with his forefinger and thumb. 'I think so. He's slowing down at work, yes, but not in the love department.'

'The *love department*?' Charlie reached behind her head to adjust her pillow. 'That's just plain gross.'

'Oh, come on, Charlie. Twenty-four is old enough to acknowledge that your father is a man whore. There are worse things.'

'Like what?'

'Like your mother being one.'

Charlie couldn't help a small smile. 'Fair point.'

Her phone pinged. She turned to grab it so quickly from the night table that her foot twisted ever so slightly and pain shot up her leg. *You playing new haven?* the text read. Marco.

She smiled despite her pain and the fact that, no, she was not playing the Connecticut Open – nor the US Open, nor any of the Asian tournaments in the rest of the summer and fall. She'd be lucky if she were ready for Australia in the new year.

Hey! Just out of surgery. Rehab to follow. Fingers crossed for australia january . . .

Pobrecita! Sorry, bella. u ok?

'You got a guy you're not telling me about?' Jake asked, looking suddenly interested.

Thanks! Good luck in cincy. Miss you! she pecked out with her thumbs and then regretted the moment she hit 'send.' *Miss you*? She didn't even realize she was holding her breath, willing him to text back, until Jake spoke again.

'Hello? Charlie? Seriously, ease up on the phone a little. You look like you might crush it.'

She relaxed her grip. Still nothing.

'Wanna watch something? I brought the cable to hook up my iPad to the room TV, so we can watch a *Shark Tank* if you want.'

Another ping. This one had only two letters, the only ones that mattered: *xo*.

Charlie put aside her phone and, unable to wipe the grin off her face, said, 'That sounds great. Cue it up.'

'Come on, Charlie. One more! You're not such a complete pussy that you can't do one more, are you?' Ramona screamed. No one else in the rehab gym even blinked.

Charlie was lying prone in a leg-press machine, but she couldn't bring herself to push against the weight bar with only her injured right foot, as Ramona had requested. Instead, she cradled her broken wrist against her chest and used her healthy foot to assist the injured one. Ramona swatted away her left leg. 'Trust it!' she yelled. 'The Achilles' has been fixed, but you're never going to strengthen it if you don't fucking *trust* it!'

'I'm trying, I swear I am,' Charlie breathed through gritted teeth.

Ramona smiled and slapped a meaty, masculine hand on her own tree-trunk thigh. 'Well, try harder!'

Charlie smiled despite her pain. Ramona and her filthy mouth were the only redeeming parts of what was starting to feel like endless physical therapy. She completed three more just to prove she was tough before collapsing in a heap on the blue mat.

'Good. You actually did decent work today.' Ramona gave Charlie a playful kick. 'Same time, same place, tomorrow. Bring your A-game,' she called over her shoulder as she headed to her next client, a Lakers player who was rehabbing a shoulder injury.

'Can't wait,' Charlie muttered as she pulled herself to standing.

'Great job today,' Marcy said as she followed Charlie to the locker room. 'You're really showing huge improvement only five weeks in.'

'You think? It feels like it's taking forever.' Charlie stripped off her sweaty shorts and T-shirt and wrapped a towel under her arms.

Marcy led the way to the hot tub and took a seat on the bench while Charlie gingerly lowered herself into the steaming water.

'You're doing it exactly right and according to schedule. It's no small thing to come back from a ruptured Achilles' and a fractured wrist in six months. Really five if you count the training you'll need for the Australian Open in January. Most regular civilians would have trouble with it, not to mention a professional athlete who needs to compete at elite levels. Patience is key here.'

Charlie leaned her head back. Eyes closed, she flexed her feet to allow the Achilles' to stretch in the heat. It ached, but the shooting pain to which she'd grown accustomed immediately after surgery was thankfully gone. 'I can barely imagine walking without limping again. How am I going to jump and turn and lunge on it?'

Marcy's neat blond ponytail was so thick and precisely tied that it barely moved as she rested her elbows on her knees and peered at Charlie. 'Have you considered the possibility that it may take longer? That perhaps Australia isn't completely realistic?'

Charlie opened her eyes and looked at Marcy. 'Frankly? No, I haven't. Dr Cohen said it was possible to make a full recovery in six months, and that's exactly what I plan to do.'

'I hear you, and I respect that, Charlie. I just think it could be wise to talk about a game plan if for whatever reason that doesn't happen.'

'What's there to discuss? I'm going to work my ass off and hopefully be ready for Australia in January. If that's absolutely impossible – like, I'll damage it even more if I try to play – then of course I'll have to wait a bit longer. What's the worst-case scenario? Starting with Doha in February? It's not ideal, but if I have to do that, I will.'

Marcy was silent. She clasped her hands together.

Charlie made little circles in the water with her right hand while taking care to keep the cast on her left arm dry. She thanked her lucky stars each and every day that it wasn't her playing arm; all the doctors assured her it wouldn't affect her backhand. 'What are you so nervous about?'

'Nothing, it's just . . .' Marcy's voice trailed off as she looked down at the wet tiled floor.

'Spit it out. Seriously, we've known each other long enough that you don't have to mince words. What are you thinking?'

'I'm just wondering . . . It's my job to consider all the possibilities, to think through any possible complications or unexpected . . . you know.'

Charlie felt a little wave of irritation rise, but she took a deep breath and forced herself to sound neutral. 'And?'

'And, well, I think we should at least have a conversation – as hypothetical and unlikely as it is – about what things look like if this injury turns out to be more . . . intractable.'

'You mean if I can't recover from it?'

'I'm sure you will, Charlie. Dr Cohen is the best, and he's certainly seen this before. But of course every person is different, and all bets are off when you're talking about someone who needs to perform at your level. It's a lot more complicated.'

'So what are you saying? Because I think I understand, but I can't quite believe you're suggesting it.'

It wasn't so unheard-of that the women argued – they spent more than three hundred days a year together – but it was usually about mundane things: assigned seats on the plane, when to meet for breakfast, whether to watch *House Hunters International* or *Property Brothers*. But suddenly this conversation felt fraught with something Charlie couldn't quite identify.

Marcy held up her hands. 'I'm not suggesting anything more than we consider all the possibilities. If you are one of the small but real percentage of athletes who can't make a full recovery from this very serious injury, I think we need to talk about that.'

'I see.'

'Charlie, don't be like that. I believe in you. But some things are out of our control.'

'This isn't one of them,' Charlie said quietly.

'I know you think that, and trust me, no one hopes

you're right more than I, but there is a very real possibility that an injury like this could be . . . lingering.'

'Career-ending. You may as well say it; it's what you mean.'

'Fine. I will say it, then. Career-ending. Now, we are both hoping against hope that it's not true for you – and it probably won't be – but it *is* something we should talk about.'

Charlie hoisted herself from the water. Marcy handed her a towel. Charlie didn't feel the least bit self-conscious about her nudity, even now, even despite their conversation – it was like being naked in front of her own mother. Once again she wrapped it around herself and sat next to Marcy on the bench.

'I disagree. I really don't want to talk about it.'

'Okay, but I think—'

'And if we're being completely honest with each other, I'm upset you're even considering it.'

Marcy cleared her throat. 'It has nothing to do with my opinion of you, or your game, or your ability to overcome this. It's statistics, Charlie. Nothing more, nothing less. Some people will come back from this, and some won't.'

'So what's the alternative?' Charlie asked as she wiped away a sweat rivulet that ran down her forehead. 'Give up? Is that what you're saying?'

'Of course not. We need to see this through. Hopefully everything will be fine.'

'Fine? That's our big goal? For everything to be fine?' Charlie knew she sounded peevish, but she couldn't help it. The irritation she'd felt mere minutes before was quickly becoming outright anger.

'Charlie.' Marcy's voice was quiet and controlled, just like her. Just like Charlie, too, until the dreaded fall at Wimbledon had come along and blown up not just her ankle but her entire life. The last few weeks had been the longest stretch since she was four years old that she hadn't so much as picked up a racket. Always she had wondered what it would be like to have a break, take a real leave from tennis, live a normal life. Now she knew, and it was awful. Granted, going to rehab and lying on the couch in her father's house wasn't exactly like sipping margaritas on a Caribbean beach, but Charlie had been astounded to realize how much she missed playing. She was eager to get back. More than eager – desperate – and the last thing on earth she needed to hear was her trusted friend and coach suggesting that maybe tennis wasn't really in her future.

'Marcy, I want to make something very clear here: I *will* come back from this injury. I *will* get into the top ten. I *will* win a Grand Slam. And I need you to believe that. I'm twenty-four, Marce. Not old, but certainly not getting any younger. If I'm ever going to make it really big, it needs to be now. Not in two years. Not in three. Right this very moment. I've worked too hard to give up on myself now, and I hope you won't either.'

'Of course I'm not giving up on you! No one believes in your potential more than I do. But part of being a professional is being able to have honest and rational conversations about the reality of a situation. That's all I'm trying to do here.'

'You're assuming that I'm going to quit over my injury because you did over yours,' Charlie blurted out, and instantly regretted it.

Marcy flinched as though she'd been hit but didn't lose her composure. 'You know that was an entirely different scenario.'

It was Charlie's turn to be quiet. Was it so different? Marcy had torn her rotator cuff not once but twice. The first time she'd chosen rehab instead of surgery, and the injury hadn't healed entirely. By the time it happened a second time, it was potentially too late for surgery to do much good. She should have at least tried it – all the doctors thought so – but instead, at age twenty-seven, Marcy had announced her retirement.

'If you say so.'

'If I say so? Charlie, they put my odds of making a full recovery, enough so I could play again, at ten percent. Meanwhile the surgery could possibly have done more damage than good, and the rehab was going to be a year or more. Where exactly was I going with news like that? Not up in the rankings, that's for sure.'

They'd walked back into the air-conditioned part of the locker room, and Charlie was starting to shiver. She grabbed another towel and draped it over her shoulders before turning and looking Marcy straight in the eye. It felt exhilarating to speak so plainly, so directly – it was something she almost never did. 'I need you to push me right now, to tell me that I'm going to come back from this stronger than ever. Not question whether or not I'll ever play again,' she said softly.

'You know that's not what I'm doing.'

'But that's how it feels.'

'We obviously have a lot to talk about. We'll figure this all out, sweetie, I promise, but I have to run. I'm meeting Will at Dan Tana's. It's our anniversary tonight.'

Charlie looked up. 'It is? I didn't even know he was out here with you.'

'Yes. It was a good excuse to steal a long weekend away. We both fly back to Florida tomorrow.'

'Well, wish him a happy anniversary for me.'

'Everything's going to be fine, Charlie. Not fine – great. You're doing a stupendous job with the rehab here, you really are. I'll be back in three weeks to check in on you, and in the meantime, I'll be prepping everything behind the scenes to get you all set for Australia in January. Sound good?'

'Sounds good,' Charlie said, although their talk had made her feel queasy and cold all over.

They each leaned forward and Charlie kissed Marcy's cheek. 'Have fun tonight.'

'Thanks. I'll talk to you tomorrow.'

Charlie watched as Marcy walked to the door and let herself out. She took a quick shower and then pulled on white jeans and a tank top. After checking to make sure she was alone in the locker room, she dialed Jake's number.

When he picked up, she heard the rumble of people talking in the background. 'Where are you?' she asked.

'One guess.'

'Are you stalking that instructor again? What was his name? Something ridiculous. Herman?'

'Nelson. And if you would take just one class with him, you'd be converted forever.'

'You know how I feel about spinning. And that one class you dragged me to at SoulCycle almost killed me.'

'You're a professional athlete, Charlie. It's a bunch of

THE SINGLES GAME

Wall Street guys who drink too much and moms who don't eat enough. You were fine.'

'That's not what I meant and you know it. But listen, do you have a second?'

Charlie listened as Jake high-fived someone and then called out a good-bye, and she pictured him wrapping a towel around his neck and ducking out onto the busy New York sidewalk.

'Okay, I'm all yours. What's up?' He was still out of breath, and she shuddered, wondering if he'd done back-to-back classes.

'You remember how you told me that Todd Feltner was retiring? When was that? Two months ago?'

'Yeah, about that. He announced it right before Wimbledon. Said he's done everything he's wanted to do, so he was going to take some time off before figuring out his next step. Why?'

'Because I want to be his next step.' Charlie surprised herself with the confidence she heard.

'Come again?'

'I want to hire Todd Feltner, and I want you to help me make it happen.'

Her statement was followed by silence.

'Charlie? You want to tell me what's going on here?' There was a twinge of concern, if not outright panic, in Jake's voice. He wasn't only her brother, he was her manager, and there was no more significant decision in a professional tennis player's life than who would coach her.

'Look, I have to meet Dad soon, so I don't have time to explain everything. But suffice it to say that I've been having doubts about Marcy for some time now. And today

33

those doubts crystallized. Do you know what she said to me?'

'Tell me.'

'She asked what my Plan B was for when my Achilles' doesn't heal and I can't play ever again.'

'Why would she say that? Dr Cohen has every expectation that it's going to heal completely. Does she know something I don't?'

'No, not at all. She was just what-iffing. Over and over again. She was almost insistent. I don't have to tell you what that does to my mental game, do I?'

Jake's silence confirmed he understood.

'I have been supportive when she's expressed that she doesn't want to travel so much anymore because of the fertility treatments. It's not easy for me or best for my career that she's not at all the smaller tournaments, but of course I understand why she needs more time right now. I have tried not to blame her for the fall at Wimbledon, but you and I both know that it was her responsibility to make sure my shoes were cleared for play ahead of time. The fact that I was forced to wear someone else's sneakers is insane. And look what happened.'

'Mm-hmm,' Jake said. Charlie could tell he was listening very closely.

'But the one thing I can't live with is the doubt. Breaking my wrist, blowing out my Achilles', and being forced to leave the tour for six months is hard enough. It sucks beyond description. But having my own coach wondering if I'm ever going to recover enough to play again? To *insist* we talk about what happens if I don't heal? I can't get past that.'

'I hear you,' Jake said. 'I really do.'

'That doubt is poison. Every time I look at her from now on, I'm going to know she doesn't think I can do it. Maybe there *is* a chance I won't recover, won't ever play again at the elite level. But I sure can't afford to be thinking that. Not now. And my coach can't either. I love Marcy, you know I do. She's been like a mom to me all these years. But I'm almost twenty-five, Jake. Hardly ancient, but running out of time if I really want to achieve something here. And I do. Want to achieve something. I know I can't play forever – and I don't necessarily want to – but I want all the years of sacrifice and hard work to pay off. I want to win a Slam, and it's becoming clearer every day that Marcy is not going to be the one to take me there.'

'I don't disagree with you,' he said quietly. 'But Feltner? You really want to go down that road?'

'I know he's supposed to be a jerk of epic proportions. I've heard all the stories. But he's the best, hands down. And I want the best.'

'He's never coached a woman before.'

'So maybe he's never met the right woman! You were the one who told me he's bored in retirement. He's so young! What's he doing, sitting around Palm Beach all day, working on his tan? Can you get him on the phone for me? I just need five minutes, and I'm going to convince him that he should work for me.'

'Of course I can get him on the phone, but I think the chances of him accepting are slim. And I don't imagine that having Todd Feltner as your coach is all kittens and sunshine, Charlie. I support you a hundred percent – if you want him, I'll do anything I can to help get him – but please don't delude yourself into thinking that he's some sort of dreamy unicorn ride to the top of the rankings. He's a killer, plain and simple.'

Charlie smiled. 'So I've heard. Get us in touch, okay? I love Marcy with all my heart, but I have to do what's best for my career. I want him to be *my* killer.'

3

not even the good stuff

BIRCHWOOD GOLF AND RACKET CLUB, AUGUST 2015

Charlie twisted her wet hair into a bun and hobbled as quickly as she could manage to her Jeep. It would take at least fifteen minutes to drive to Birchwood, and she was supposed to be meeting her father at that very moment. She barked out a quick voice text apologizing and saying she was on her way, and threw the car into gear. As soon as she pulled out of the parking lot, her phone rang. Figuring it was Jake calling her back, Charlie hit 'talk' on her steering wheel without checking the number. A strange man's voice boomed through the car's speakers.

'Charlotte? Charlotte Silver?'

'This is she. May I ask who is calling, please?' *Way to sound like a nine-year-old,* she thought. It was the phrasing her mother had insisted upon every time she answered the family's phone.

'Charlotte, this is Todd Feltner.' Charlie was stunned into silence. She'd told Jake minutes earlier that she wanted to talk to Todd and figured it would be days, if not weeks, before it actually happened.

'Hello, Mr Feltner. Thanks so much for getting in touch. Jake said you might possibly be—'

'I heard you're freshly out of surgery.'

Charlie was thrilled he had called, and she tried not to think about how abrasive he sounded after only ten seconds.

'Yes. I still have months to go before I'm ready to play again, but I'm getting there. I'm actually leaving rehab as we speak.'

'Why?'

Charlie actually glanced at her phone, resting on the passenger seat beside her, as though it might reveal something about Todd's strange call. 'Why? What do you mean?'

'Why are you bothering to rehab it? Maybe I'm confused, but I heard from your brother that you popped your Achilles'. I had a player in 2006 with that exact same injury, and he never recovered from it. And he didn't also have a wrist injury, which I understand you do?'

The nerve! If it had been anyone else on the line, Charlie would have calmly told him it was none of his business and disconnected the call. But she couldn't get past the fact that Todd was a living legend: more total Grand Slam wins for his players than any other coach; more players ranked number one; a reputation for bringing players back from injury, addiction, mental breakdowns, and even chemo to play better than ever. If men's tennis had a celebrity, a magician, and a guru all rolled into one, it was Todd Feltner.

Charlie cleared her throat. 'I did have an uncomplicated wrist fracture, yes. But thankfully it was my left wrist. They expect it to heal entirely and not affect my backhand at all. The cast is nearly off.'

'You have a beautiful one-handed backhand,' Todd said. 'Clean and powerful, every bit as good as your forehand. Rare for a woman. Rare for anyone, actually.'

'Thank you,' Charlie said, feeling herself swell with pride. 'That means a lot coming from you.'

'Which is why it's such a shame you'll probably have to give it up. Not completely, mind you, but certainly at the highest echelon of competition. You may get those bones and tendons all fixed up by the best orthopedist money can buy, but mentally it's going to fuck you up. I've seen it so many times before.'

'I don't know why you'd say that,' Charlie said, choosing her words carefully. 'You coached Nadal after that devastating knee injury and he went on to win the US Open. One year later!'

'Are you comparing yourself to Rafael Nadal?'

Charlie could feel her face redden. 'No, of course not. But you of all people know that players recover from injuries all the time, and they come back to play their best tennis ever. I know it'll be challenging, but it's not impossible. And I'm willing to work for it.'

Charlie checked her mirrors and merged onto the

highway. She could feel her own heart racing faster. Who did he think he was, calling her like that just to tell her that she was destined to fail? But more than that, did it mean it was true? If both Marcy and Todd Feltner thought she'd never come back from this injury, was she fooling herself to think she could do it?

Todd cleared his gravelly throat. 'Well, just some friendly advice from someone who knows: Save yourself the heartbreak and think about retiring early. You'll go out gracefully, at your peak. What were you ranked pre-injury? Twenty-two? Twenty-five? That's damn good, better than most players can even dream. Bow out now, take good care of your injuries, and you'll be able to play non-professionally for the rest of your life. Hell, you may even get to have a family if you call it quits now. Not many of the other girls can say the same thing.'

Charlie gripped the steering wheel in her now-sweaty hand and promptly forgot all about Todd Feltner's qualifications and accomplishments. Jake was right: this was not going to work. She kept her voice calm and steady as she said, 'Listen, Mr Feltner. I don't know why you're saying such awful things to me, but let me make something very clear: I will come back from this injury. I will get into the top ten. I will win a Grand Slam. I even think I can be number one. Do you want to know why? Because I'm not a quitter like that big baby you once coached, Mr Feltner. I did not leave high school every day at noon to train for six hours and do my homework by the light of the glove compartment on the way home from tournaments to *give up*. I didn't miss movies and trips and proms and hanging at the mall and sleeping in and getting drunk and kissing boys to play *round-robins* at my local country club. And speaking of country clubs, I didn't ask my father to work day and night teaching rich middle-aged women and spoiled kids and rude bankers so I could *bail* the first time something got a little challenging. And I sure didn't leave UCLA – the best year of my life – to *quit*. So while I have incredible respect for what you've accomplished in our profession, and I was planning to ask if you would consider coaching me, I will kindly ask that from now on you keep your opinions to yourself. I'm sorry if I wasted your time, Mr Feltner, but I made a big mistake. You and I are clearly not a good fit.'

'Charlotte? Don't hang up.' Todd's tone was firm but she could hear it was conciliatory, too.

'I've said all there is to say.'

'*I* haven't. Let's just say that you've convinced me.'

'I'm sorry?'

'I'm sold. On coaching you. I was worried you didn't have the fire to back up those gorgeous strokes and that pretty face, but I can see now that you do. I'm yours.'

Charlie was stunned into silence. Todd Feltner wanted to coach her? None of this made sense.

'And call me Todd, for chrissake. You want it badly, and only I can give it to you. You know it, and I know it. We should meet in person to finalize details, and I'll actually be flying through SoCal next week on my way to Hawaii, so I'll have my secretary call to set it up. Good talk, Silver. We're going to kick some ass together.'

The phone disconnected. Charlie was so shocked she had to slam on the brakes to keep from rear-ending the car in front of her. She drove like a grandma in the far

41

right lane for a mile or so before she voice-prompted the Bluetooth to call Jake's cell.

'You are not going to believe who I just spoke to,' she said without saying hello. She could tell from the ambient street noise that Jake was walking to the subway from SoulCycle, where he would take the 1 train up to Harlem, change and shave, and head into the office.

'Hmm, let me think about it. Can't possibly be Feltner himself, considering I got off the phone with him four minutes ago and he said he was calling you right away.'

'You didn't even warn me!'

'When Todd Feltner agrees to call someone right away, I'm not going to be the one to ask him to hold on while you and I have a little powwow about it. You sounded pretty damn sure this was the right choice when we hung up ten minutes ago. How did it go?'

'He said he would coach me.' Charlie barely believed the words as she said them.

'He what?'

'Coach me. Todd Feltner said I convinced him, that I had the fire, or what it takes, or something like that. I can't remember exactly, but he was a complete dickhead and then I sort of told him off – politely, of course – and then he said he was convinced.'

'Oh. My. God.'

'Are you really so surprised? I'm almost offended.'

'Charlie, are you sure that's what he said? Are you sure it's what you want? I mean, I can see the appeal, I really can, but this guy is no joke.'

The truth was, Charlie had been taken aback by Todd's harsh tactics and abrasive manner. He was clearly the very opposite of Marcy, whose quiet calmness was something that had reassured Charlie for nearly a decade. But she was ready for a change. No, it was even more than that – she needed it.

'I'm not going to lie, Jake, he sounds like an animal – and of course I'm going to take some time to weigh it – but I think this is one of those opportunities that can truly change my life. This might even be *the* opportunity. We can't be so blind that we can't see the big picture here. The way I see it, I have possibly just been given a chance to go from good to great. From a winner to a champion. Do you care if I'm a champion? No. Does Dad? Of course not. I know you'd both love me if I wanted to retire tomorrow and become a hairdresser. But *I* care, Jake. More than I can even explain. This might be my shot, and I'm wondering if I'd be insane not to take it.'

'He is the absolute best,' Jake said quietly.

'He's even better than that. I hate to state the obvious – and it's a sorry testament to women in sports, to be sure – but it's practically an honor to think that he'd take on a woman when there are dozens of top men who would hire him in a heartbeat.' It was sad but true: male players typically made more prize money, drew bigger audiences, and commanded higher endorsement deals, and in turn, everyone wanted to work with them.

'What's next?' Jake asked. 'How did you two leave it?'

'He's coming to LA. We're going to meet. You'll come, too, right? I can't do this without you.'

'Of course,' Jake said without hesitation. 'I'll buy a ticket as soon as you say the word.'

Charlie eased the Jeep onto the exit ramp and slowed

at the stop sign. She was less than a mile from the club when she suddenly remembered who she was meeting. 'Don't say anything to Dad, okay? We both know how he's going to feel about this, so I don't want him to know until I'm absolutely certain.'

'Roger that. I've got to run, C. Call me when you're done with Dad. And, Charlie? I hear what you're saying. I think it could be an incredible opportunity.'

'Thanks, I appreciate that. Keep your fingers crossed for me, okay?' She pressed 'end call' just as she pulled up to the club's valet stand.

'Hey, Charlie,' called out the club's director of operations from his perch overseeing the teenage valets. 'How's the foot?'

She eased herself out of the SUV and waved. 'Getting there,' she said, handing over her keys. 'My dad inside?'

'Yes, he said he'd wait for you at your table.'

She thanked him and limped toward the restaurant. The maître d' led her to the far-right corner of the dining room, where the best table in the house looked out over the spectacular ninth hole. Before Charlie turned pro, neither she nor her father had ever sat at that table – her father had barely ever eaten in the guest dining room. Since her success, they were both now treated like royalty.

'Sorry I'm late,' she said as she gingerly lowered herself into the chair. The Aleve hadn't kicked in yet, and the postsurgical pain combined with the rehab muscle ache left the whole area throbbing.

Her father leaned over to kiss her cheek. 'That's okay. It's not so terrible sitting here looking out the window, especially on a day like this. How was rehab?'

Even at sixty-one, Mr Silver had a full head of hair. It was beginning to gray around the temples, prompting plenty of eye-roll-inducing 'silver' puns from her father, but Charlie thought he was as handsome as ever. His tan was deep but he'd somehow avoided the leather-skinned look that afflicted so many men who'd spent lifetimes in the sun, and his eyes were still startlingly green or blue, depending on the color of his shirt. Granted, he'd added a few extra pounds around his midsection – and he'd started wearing dorky outfits that included brown leather belts paired with knee-length shorts – but his mostly fit six-foot-three frame compensated for a lot, and clearly none of his lady friends seemed to mind the extra weight or the lack of fashion sense.

Charlie yanked at the waistband of her white jeans, which had gotten noticeably tighter over the last couple of months. 'Ramona is a taskmaster. But I do think she's good.'

'She's the best, everyone agrees.' Mr Silver coughed. 'Charlie, there is something that—'

'I reached out to Todd Feltner. He wants to coach me,' she blurted out before even placing her napkin on her lap. She wasn't planning to breathe a word about her conversation with Todd, but the familiarity of the club where she'd practically been raised combined with her father's warm hug and kind eyes had opened the floodgates. She regretted it the minute she said it.

'Pardon?' Her father looked up, his expression alarmed. 'Todd Feltner, the men's coach?'

'Men's coach no longer. He wants to coach *me*, his first and only female player. He thinks I have what it takes.'

'Of course you do; you don't need that jerk-off to tell you that,' her father said sharply. He took a deep breath and made what appeared to be a concerted effort to calm down. 'Sorry, I'm just surprised.'

Charlie reached across the table and touched her father's hand. 'I know Todd doesn't have the greatest reputation as a person, but as a coach . . . well, he's the best.'

Mr Silver took a sip of water. 'Do you know how many fines he's paid the USTA for his outbursts? You remember what he did to Eversoll, don't you? It was caught on camera if you need a refresher. He's a loudmouth, and he's abusive to his players. Why on earth would you want to work with someone like that?'

'I'm not looking for a friend or a manager,' she added, her temperature rising.

'Last time I checked, you had a coach.'

'I still do, and you know how much I love Marcy.'

Her father pulled his hand back, gently but with intention. 'She shifted you from the juniors to the pros. She's skillful. Gracious. And not to put too fine a point on it, but she happens not to be an asshole. The tennis world is full of them, and Marcy is one of the most genuine, honest people I've ever met. I don't know about you, but that means a lot to me.'

Charlie felt a quick flash of anger. 'It means a lot to me, too, Dad. *Obviously*.'

They both smiled at the teenage waiter who brought them their identical grilled chicken salads, no tomatoes, dressing on the side. Charlie knew her father would have ordered the steak sandwich with fries if he'd been dining with anyone else, and she appreciated his show of support.

'Does he understand your game? Your strengths, weaknesses, personality? Does he have the right relationships with tournament directors and tour officials and board members? Does he have a proven track record for helping you improve your game? Focus on strategy and court management? Protect you from all the business noise that's better handled by others? Can Todd Feltner help plan the optimal travel and training schedule to maximize performance without sacrificing sanity?'

Charlie forced herself to take a deep breath. Her father played professionally for less than three years, over four decades ago. Why was he being so tough on her? Charlie chewed her food slowly and stared at her plate.

'I'm surprised to hear you're even considering firing Marcy and hiring Feltner,' her father said.

'I want to win,' Charlie said finally. 'And I think I need a change to do it. Marcy has been my coach for almost ten years now. I was fifteen when you hired her to work with me.'

'You'd just won the Orange Bowl. As a fifteen-year-old! You'd far outpaced my coaching ability by that point.'

'I'm not criticizing. She was a great choice for me then. But let's be honest with each other: you didn't hire her because she was the best possible coach available. You chose her because she was young and easily influenced, and you knew that she wouldn't go around your back to pressure me to turn pro.'

'Charlie, this is all water under the bridge. And I don't think there's any denying that Marcy was perfect for you at a really vulnerable age in—'

'I agree, Dad. She was perfect. Literally, perfect. Only

twenty-eight herself, just retired due to the shoulder injury, and sweet. More like a big sister than some intimidating middle-aged ogre who was going to make me hate the game. I appreciate that, I swear I do. I think she was an excellent choice. I still do.'

'But?'

'But I've been on the tour for years now – I've played all the tournaments, traveled to all the places. I've steadily improved with Marcy, there's no denying it, but I'm starting to think it hasn't been fast enough. I'm almost twenty-five! Do you know how many women won their first major titles at twenty-five or later? Ten. In the entire Open Era! Ten. And that's not even considering the fact that I'm recovering from an injury so bad the press is saying I'll never win a big tournament again. Even Marcy suggested as much.'

'You've gotten to the quarterfinals of Australia and the French Open – twice. You've reached the semis at Indian Wells and Singapore. I hardly think you're doing a shabby job.'

'That's not what I'm saying and you know it. I want to win a Slam. I've trained my entire life for that, and now it seems like I have an opportunity to work with someone who might be able to take me there.'

'I just don't know that—'

'All other things being equal, if your goal was to win a US Open in the next two years, who would you hire? Marcy Berenson or Todd Feltner? With no consideration for their style of coaching or likability or whatever else we're throwing in there.'

Her father was silent.

'Yeah, me too,' Charlie said quietly.

'That doesn't necessarily mean he's the right choice for you,' Mr Silver said, taking a sip of his beer.

Charlie met his gaze. 'It sounds like Todd's not the right choice for *you*,' she said.

Mr Silver peered at Charlie.

'There's more than winning, Dad, of course I know that. Every year the women's tour becomes more and more focused on fitness. Fifteen years ago, if you lifted for an hour a day, you could expect to outlast most of your opponents in a tough three-setter. All that's changed now. Women spend almost as much time on fitness training as they do on the court, and Marcy's not totally up to speed on that. I've told you before that she's not willing to travel as much, and that's been difficult, too.'

'She's trying to have a baby, Charlie. I know you understand that.'

'Of course I understand that! She's still a friend, Dad. She and I spend more time together on a weekly basis than pretty much anyone else. I was one of her bridesmaids when she married Will! And it's natural that he doesn't want her to travel so much. Forty-some weeks a year is hell, especially when you're going through in vitro. I get it, I really do. I hope more than anything she'll be able to get pregnant. But then what? You think she's going to want to hop on planes every three days and head to Dubai? Shanghai? Melbourne? Toronto? London? And when she very understandably doesn't want to travel like that – or can't? I know I sound callous here, but where does that leave me?'

Her father nodded. 'It's one of the risks of hiring a female coach. But I like to think we stick by our friends when—'

'I'm not sure why you're doing this to me.' Charlie's voice was almost a whisper.

'We're just having a conversation, Charlie.'

'It doesn't feel like a conversation, Dad. It feels like one giant shaming. We haven't even mentioned what happened at Wimbledon. Ultimately she was responsible for the shoes. She's slowed down a lot lately trying to get pregnant. And you should have heard the conversation we had about my future just this morning.'

The waiter, a local high school kid who, according to her father, was headed for a tennis scholarship to a Division I school, removed their salad plates and replaced them with small bowls of mixed berries.

'It sounds like your mind is made up. I may not agree with you, but I support you in whatever you decide,' Mr Silver said, scooping some whipped cream onto his berries.

Support me so long as I agree with you, she thought. And although Charlie hadn't been certain that hiring Todd was the right move, it had become much clearer as she'd outlined all the reasons to her father, whether he liked them or not.

'Yes. My mind is made up,' Charlie said with more conviction than she felt.

'Well, okay, then. We agree to disagree.'

They were the exact same words Mr Silver had used more than five years earlier when, during the summer before her sophomore year, Charlie had decided to turn pro. Charlie had always understood that finishing four years of college and competing at the top levels of the women's tour were mutually exclusive, and of course so had Mr Silver – but her father's disapproval had bordered on outrage.

Charlie was about to point out that their conversation was following a familiar pattern, but she was saved by Howard Pinter, the owner of the club. Howard was rotund and bald and spoke with a spittle-spraying lisp and he always wore suspenders that looked like they stretched painfully over his enormous midsection. Howard loved them both, and told them every chance he could, especially now that Charlie was famous.

'Peter. Charlie! Why didn't I know you two were having lunch here today?'

'Howie,' her father said, already on his feet. 'Good to see you.' The two men shook hands.

Charlie moved to stand, but Howard pushed down gently on her shoulder. 'Please sit, dear. Are you both enjoying lunch? Will your friend be joining you, too?'

At first Charlie thought Howie was asking her, but then she noticed the expression on her father's face. *Shut the hell up,* it said as he looked directly into Howie's eyes. Never in her life could she remember her father giving someone such a look of . . . what? Panic?

Whatever it was, Howie got the message. 'Forgive me, I'm all confused. You know how it is at my age: I'm practically addled. I'll tell you, I can barely remember how to dress myself every day. Can you believe there was a time I used to know the name of every kid who worked in the pro shop or the kitchen? Now I'm lucky if I remember who my own children are.' He forced a laugh.

As quick as the anger had flashed across her father's

face, it was gone. 'I'm just filling Charlie in on all the club gossip,' he said, smiling.

Howard dropped into a seat at the table with surprising agility. 'Ooooh, tell me, tell me. No one tells me the good stuff anymore. You think I care who's bickering about court assignments or about the golf course maintenance? Hell, no! I want to hear who's screwing each other in the coat closet!'

They all laughed, and Charlie was relieved that her father seemed able to lighten up, but she couldn't help her lingering feelings of irritation. The three of them chatted for a few minutes, with Charlie filling Howard in on seemingly juicy but totally benign tour gossip: rumors of Natalya's dating a famous quarterback; the billionaire Saudi who'd reportedly offered seven figures to each of the top three men's players to play a single match with him at his compound in Jeddah; the number-five-ranked woman who had just failed a surprise doping test. He clapped his hands together and grinned. *That's not even the good stuff,* Charlie thought. She wondered how he'd react to the Todd Feltner news. Or, for that matter, the fact that she was casually hooking up with the hottest male player on the tour. She smiled to herself just thinking about it.

'Okay, I'll leave you two to your lunch,' Howard said, looking at Mr Silver. There was an uncomfortable beat of silence. Howard cleared his throat and pushed his chair back. 'Well, if you two will excuse me, duty calls. I'm sure some bored housewife is berating one of my locker room staff as we speak. Charlie, always a pleasure. You come visit us more often, you hear?' He bent down to kiss her on the cheek; Charlie willed herself not to wipe away the lingering wetness.

'Thanks for coming over to say hi, Mr Pinter,' she said. 'And no blabbing those tour secrets, okay?'

He belly laughed like Santa Claus and ambled away. Charlie turned to her father.

'What's he talking about? What's the good news? And who's your "new friend"?'

'It's not a big deal, Charlie. It's just that Howie arranged for me to move into one of the three guest cottages they keep at the far end of the property – near the lap pool? They're quite nice.'

'The cottages that were built in, like, the early nineteen hundreds? Do they even have heat? Why on earth would you want to live in one? I don't think anyone has actually stayed in one of those in decades!'

'They're a bit rustic, yes, but think of how much time I'll save not having to drive back and forth from Topanga every day. The traffic has really—'

'And what about *our* house? Mom loved our house!' Charlie didn't mean to bring up her mother right then, but she hadn't ever imagined a day when her father would sell her childhood home. After all, it was the last place her mother had lived. It was where she had died. It seemed unfathomable he would ever leave it.

'I know she did, sweetie. We all love it. But you have to understand that things change, situations change. I just don't have the time or the energy to take care of something that size at this point in my life.'

'So you'd rather live *here*? You already spend too much time here.' Charlie could feel her rising panic. 'This is about money, isn't it?'

Her father met her gaze. 'This is not about money.

That is absolutely none of your concern, do you hear me?'

'Why else would you do this? I don't understand why you won't let me help! What does any of it mean if I can't help my own family?'

'I'm still your father,' he said sharply. Then, softening: 'No one understands more than I just how much you have to invest in your career. A sizable salary for your coach, and all the travel for both of you and Jake, and I'll refrain from imagining how much more Todd Feltner will require than Marcy. You need to invest in yourself, Charlie.'

'I just don't understand why you'd move—'

He held up his hand. 'Enough. It's going to be great for me to downsize and lose the commute. Yes, it will be hard, too. But it's time.'

Charlie forced a smile despite the sinking feeling in her stomach. 'Okay, then. Maybe we both have to agree to disagree.'

4

the twenty-third-best girl

The FOR SALE BY OWNER sign may as well have been trimmed in Christmas lights, because it was the very first thing Charlie saw every time she looked out her bedroom window. It had been two weeks since her father had announced his intention to move onto the Birchwood property, and still she could barely process it. The three-bedroom bungalow set back a bit off Topanga Canyon Boulevard was less than idyllic – the curving driveway had long ago crumbled into loose rocks and the exterior desperately needed a new paint job (not to mention new doors and windows), but what her childhood house was lacking in curbside appeal, it more than made up for in memories: the Sunday night barbecue dinners on the back patio surrounded by the woods; riding her bike with Jake to Topanga State Park and stopping for Cokes on the way at the roadside gas station that had since turned into an organic market; helping her mother tend the window boxes of impatiens they would plant each year. Her family had never been one to throw lots of parties or host loads of guests, but Charlie remembered a mostly happy childhood in that house, a home that her mother loved and cared for with great joy, the place where she had closed her eyes for the final time. It was fitting that Charlie had barely changed her childhood room – right down to the Justin Timberlake posters – and that she still considered it her home because really, why would she pay rent somewhere else when she traveled eleven out of twelve months? What did not fit was the idea of her father selling this piece of their shared history and moving into a guest cottage. On Birchwood's property. In the *Palisades*. She shook her head just thinking about it.

On the ESPN app on her iPad, she was watching a biopic on the complicated life and times of Todd Feltner's coaching career. She fast-forwarded through the beginning years that showed Todd growing up on Long Island and playing first singles for Great Neck North. She bypassed his time playing singles at the University of Michigan, his short-lived stint in the Morgan Stanley training program, and his discovery while on vacation in Florida of a thirteen-year-old tennis prodigy who was making extra money caddying Todd's golf game. Something about this child – Adrian Eversoll – so inspired Todd that he left his much-maligned desk job, moved to Tampa, and set about learning everything he needed to coach a young kid with a gift before launching him to the world number one in eight short years, despite not having any professional tennis experience himself. The coverage included plenty of scenes of Todd screaming at and berating Adrian and, later, other men he'd coached to the top. In one particularly unnerving US Open semifinal, tournament security had forcibly removed Todd from Adrian's player box after he'd cursed the player so loudly and profanely that the television cameras couldn't even broadcast the outburst on live TV. But then, minutes later, another scene: Adrian hoisting that champion's trophy high above his head, kissing it, as the world cheered. Charlie watched, barely breathing, almost able to *feel* the weight of that trophy, hear the crowd roar its excitement, smell the sweat and the gritty Queens air as she was declared the best. Despite herself – despite Todd's downright frightening fireworks display – she knew then and there that she wanted it. She wanted him.

As though he were already tapped into the private recesses of her mind, her phone rang and a young girl with a high-pitched voice said, 'Charlotte Silver? I have Todd Feltner on the line.' Charlie felt her pulse quicken and tapped the pause button on her iPad.

'Charlotte? Todd Feltner here. Pardon my French, but I'm done dicking around with text messages. I fly into Long Beach on Friday at noon. I'm turning around again and getting on a flight to Hawaii at eight, and I'd rather not come to the boondocks, so what do you say we plan to meet in the lobby of the Standard Hotel downtown? I'll give you my dog and pony show and you can run down your whole list of questions and we'll get this knocked out. Two o'clock?'

A million things raced through her mind. Charlie didn't like how presumptuous he was. But she took a deep breath, remembered Jake's urgency and her own burgeoning excitement, and said, 'Two o'clock it is, Mr Feltner. I'll plan to see you there.'

'Grand!' he said, managing to make it sound sarcastic. 'And it's Todd. "Mr Feltner" makes me think of my father, and if you'd ever had the pleasure of meeting that winner, you'd know that's a pretty shitty thing.'

'Todd, then,' Charlie said. Before she could feel awkward, Todd announced his assistant would confirm the details by email and hung up.

She texted Jake *It's on* with the time and place, and turned off her phone.

When Charlie walked into the Standard wearing jeans and a fitted blazer, she was deliberately fifteen minutes early. Relieved to have a little time to order a glass of sparkling water and get her notes in order, she assured herself nothing would deter her from her list. She'd neatly printed no fewer than nineteen bullet points – some questions, some conversation topics about which she wanted to hear his thoughts – on a sheet of light-blue stationery. But when she walked over to the hostess stand in the lobby restaurant to request a table, Todd bellowed from his banquette near the back bar. 'Silver! Over here.'

Todd didn't stand when she reached the table. 'Sit,' he said, waving his hand at the remaining seats. 'You don't care if I call you Silver, right?'

'Actually, I prefer Charlie,' she said, claiming the chair that was farthest from Todd even though the view it afforded was directly of the wall. 'You're here early.'

'Todd Feltner rule number one: if you're not early, you're late.' His laugh was a cross between a guffaw and a scoff. Charlie couldn't decide which she disliked more: his asinine 'rule,' or the fact that he was talking about himself in the third person.

At only five foot ten, his strength as a college player came exclusively from his muscular shoulders and immensely wide, powerful thighs, lending him the strange look of being nearly as wide as he was tall. Now that he was well into middle age, the muscled, tanklike physique had been refashioned into a pear shape: nearly atrophied shoulders and upper body ballooning out into an enormous ass and belly, all of it perched on pale, skinny legs.

'What are you having?' Todd asked, pushing a menu in her direction.

A woman wearing leather pants and high-heeled booties appeared at their table, and it took Charlie a moment to realize she was their waitress. She glanced at her phone and saw it would still be thirteen minutes until Jake arrived, maybe more.

'Um, just a cup of coffee for now, please,' she said. She intended to order lunch but wanted to wait for Jake.

'Decaf,' Todd barked. Both the waitress and Charlie turned to look at him. Did he want a decaf himself, or was he demanding one for Charlie?

'For her,' he clarified.

Charlie forced herself to smile. 'Thank you, but no, I

prefer regular.' She turned to the waitress. 'Full caffeine, please. Extra, if you have it.'

Todd laughed, the snake tongue darting at full speed. 'Enjoy it now, sweetheart. You work with me and you can kiss it good-bye, right along with everything else that's remotely enjoyable. But we'll get to that.'

Charlie knew if Marcy were there instead of Todd, they would have already ordered club sandwiches and fries and would be cracking up over the latest celebrity gossip. Charlie was wracking her brain to come up with some benign small talk to fill the time when Jake appeared like a vision before them.

'I hope I didn't miss anything,' he said, leaning over to kiss Charlie's cheek. Todd didn't stand for him either, but Jake walked around the table and clapped him on the back. 'Todd, great to see you. Thanks for making time today.'

Charlie was always a little surprised to see her big brother looking so professional. His crisp white dress shirt highlighted his tan complexion, and his whole look – European-cut navy suit with no tie, expensive watch and shoes – screamed successful Hollywood talent agent. No one would have ever guessed he lived in a walk-up studio apartment in Harlem – or that his one and only client at the sports agency where he worked was his own sister.

They hadn't even ordered food before Todd clapped the table and said, 'None of us have a lot of time here, so let's cut right to the chase. Silver – uh, Charlotte – you're a damn good player with a lot of potential. But so far that's all it is. You've been on the tour now for nearly five years and you have no Slams, only two major singles titles and a ranking that's never gone above twenty-three. You also just had surgery. I'm sure plenty of people have recommended you retire.'

'With all due respect, Mr Feltner, being the twenty-third-best female tennis player on earth isn't too terrible,' Jake offered. Charlie shot him a grateful smile, but the sound of Todd's fist meeting the table again startled her so much she almost knocked her coffee over.

'Wrong answer!' he all but screamed, his tongue going a mile a minute. 'Was that what you used to dream about as a thirteen-year-old who was winning all the tournaments you entered, who showed incredible perseverance and determination and who cleared her path of opponents like a fucking *lawn mower*? To be twenty-third-best? I don't think so. I sure hope not, because that is not the attitude of a champion. You think Steffi Graf used to hope and pray she could be ranked in the twenties? Or Evert or Navratilova or Sharapova or either of those Williams sisters ever turned to their coaches or their daddies or the mirror and said, "Gee, I hope I can be the twenty-third-best girl someday?"' This last part was said in a hideously high-pitched imitation of a female voice. 'Please. Spare me.'

Charlie burned with shame – and something else. Todd Feltner was right. She *did* want more. She didn't want to be a footnote in tennis history, not after all her hard work. 'You've made your point,' Charlie said quietly.

'If I'm going to come out of retirement to coach a *girl*, I am only going to do it for one who has the killer drive. Are you the one, Charlotte Silver? Do you have the taste for blood? Or are you happy to flounce from court to court in your little white tennis skirt with your cutesy braids and smile so big and wide that everyone just adores you?'

Todd flipped open a magnetic screen cover on his fifteen-inch iPad, turned it to face Charlie, and began to swipe through images of Charlie through the years. Always the braid. Always the smile. Always the runner-up.

'We are sitting here right now because *I* think that beneath the sweet-little-girl exterior you really, really want to make it to the big leagues. To the top ten. To the Slam title. And personally I'm here because I think you have the best fucking one-handed backhand I've ever seen on a chick – er, a girl. You have an instinctive understanding of your placement on the court – trust me, you can't teach that – and, at least from what I can see on tape, the mental toughness to come back when you're down. That, Charlotte Silver, is why we're here.'

Charlie tried not to smile. Todd Feltner *had* homed in on her areas of strength, quite accurately in her mind. He'd done his homework. Still, the sequence of photos showing her as a friendly and happy dilettante had been devastating.

'If we do this thing, first and foremost, you're going to have to lose the sensitive-girl crap. Like, right now I can see your eyes watering. We all can't be worrying about your feelings every second or no one's ever going to get anything done. I'll talk straight to you and you talk straight to me. No bullshit, okay? Secondly, we need an image overhaul. We'll take steps to banish the sweet girl in braids and replace her with the fierce, ballbusting competitor that other players fear and respect. We'll employ an image consultant, since that's clearly not my area of expertise, but one I do think is important in this case. She can advise us all on hiring the right PR people, stylists, social media consultants, what have you, who will get you all straightened out. I don't want this to concern you too much – I will be in charge of your practice and travel schedule, and I guarantee you that none of this bullshit edges out what's really important: namely, your game. It's important, but ultimately, no one is going to give a shit what you're wearing if you're not actually winning.'

Charlie nodded. Todd sounded crude, yes, but also fair.

'We will immediately hire a full-time hitting partner.' When Charlie opened her mouth to protest, Todd cut her off by raising his hand. 'I know you're going to say you don't need one, that it's perfectly adequate to hit with the other girls for warm-ups and practice, and I'm here to tell you you're wrong. Dead wrong. And don't give me the whole I'm-only-number-twenty-whatever-I-don't-deserve-my-own-full-time-hitting-partner BS. It's a chicken-or-the-egg thing, and I've seen too many times how players' games go through the roof when they have someone good on staff with them all day, every day, working them over. It's non-negotiable.'

'Okay,' Charlie said. She'd thought that same thing so many times but couldn't justify the costs. She wasn't winning enough to hire a full-time hitting partner and then pay for his travel as well.

'I'm okay with you using tournament physios and trainers, so long as I can see that your fitness is improving and you're sticking to the programs they set up for you. Also, a nutritionist. Not forever, just until you drop ten pounds from the lower body and build up your shoulders a little more. That won't be a huge deal, but I'm not going to lie, Charlie: it's going to cost money. The good news is, you'll be winning more, and this up-front cash outlay is going to feel like pocket change if we all do our jobs right. You hearing me?'

Charlie was trying hard not to focus on the ten-pounds comment. He was right, of course; it just wasn't easy to hear. She nodded.

'Your brother will oversee the business end of things, like securing a big endorsement deal – something in addition to Nike, whose terms we will renegotiate once you break into the top ten – and from there? Let's just say the path is lined in gold.'

Todd folded his arms across his chest and gave Charlie a smug smile while Jake nodded beside him. In all the years she and Marcy had worked together, they'd never had a meeting resembling this one. Everything they worked on was directly related to Charlie's game: perfecting her slice, getting her more comfortable at the net, tweaking the spin on her second serve, adjusting the placement of her approach shots. When they weren't actually on the court, she and Marcy were usually laughing in player dining or exchanging copies of *US Weekly* on a flight or binge-watching HGTV in random hotel rooms all over the world. Never had there been any mention of Charlie's 'image' beyond the importance of good sportsmanship. Marcy expected Charlie to take responsibility for her own healthful eating, which included lots of fresh fruit and vegetables, protein, and heavy carbs before matches; she consulted regularly with the tournament trainers to create good work-outs, but she wasn't standing over Charlie with a clipboard and a stopwatch, enforcing any sort of regimen. They were coach and player, first and foremost, but they were also dear friends, confidantes, and occasionally – when Charlie grew weary of the travel or depressed by the solitude of the sport – more like mother and daughter.

'You're right about not dreaming of being twenty-third in the world. And you've analyzed my strengths on the court fairly. I want to win, Mr Feltner. Todd. I want to come back stronger and better than before. You really think you can get me there?'

Across from her, Todd met her gaze. 'I brought Nadal back from a horror show of a knee injury. I got Adrian Eversoll four Slams. I coached Gilberto to the number one spot, and he was a pussy before he met me. My currency is *winning*.' He glanced at his watch. 'Oh, shit, I have to run. Listen, think it over and get back to me by the end of the week. We can do great things together, Silver,' he said, looking at Charlie. 'Hah, gotcha! Just kidding. *Charlie*.'

Jake laughed. Charlie forced a smile.

'Just one more thing to toss on your plate. If I'm going to do this, you need to be free and clear. Don't call me to accept until you've cut ties with that lady coach of yours. *Capisce?*'

Todd stood up and opened his billfold, but Jake waved him off. 'Please, this is on us. Thank you so much for taking the time to come meet with us. We'll talk everything over and get right back to you.'

Todd gave them both a little wave, either not noticing or not caring that Jake had stuck his hand out across the table. 'You've got what it takes, kid, and I know how to make sure you reach that potential. Whatever you decide, I'll be in your corner from now on. Peace.'

Charlie watched him barrel out the door.

'That was amazing!' Jake breathed, looking after Todd as though Michael Jackson had just left their table.

'I didn't get to ask him all of my questions,' Charlie muttered.

'I think he pretty much covered it, don't you? I mean, the difference between Todd Feltner and Marcy Berenson is unambiguous, you know? They are just operating in different universes.'

Charlie couldn't disagree. 'I want him,' she said. 'I'm pretty sure I hate his personality, but I love his plan and his fire and can-win attitude. Besides, I fully acknowledge that this is one of those fork-in-the-road situations, and there's the potential for me to seriously regret not seizing this opportunity. Living legends don't walk into your life every day asking to coach you.'

Jake held up both hands in a sign of resignation, just as the model waitress brought out their food.

'Do you serve champagne here?' Jake asked.

The woman looked at him like he was deranged. 'Of course.'

Jake didn't seem to notice her tone. 'Terrific, we'll take two glasses, then.' He looked at Charlie and grinned. 'It sounds like we have something to celebrate.'

Charlie had just finished setting the kitchen table for two when the phone rang. It took her a minute to realize it was the landline.

'Hey, Dad,' she said into the ancient receiver.

'How did you know it was me?'

'Who else would be calling here?' she said before she

realized it wasn't exactly the kindest way to put it. 'I just meant, I'm sure all your lady friends call your cell.'

'Charlotte, I'm sorry for the late notice, but I won't be home for dinner tonight after all.'

She waited, but her father offered no further explanation.

'Hot date?'

'Last-minute plans.'

Charlie had planned to serve a nice, semi-homemade meal and ask calmly and confidently for Mr Silver's support in hiring Todd. She was going to do it regardless, but the whole thing would feel so much better if she knew her father was behind her. 'I was going to cook for you.'

'Thanks, sweetheart, but why don't you go ahead. I won't be home until later. Or tomorrow.'

'Tomorrow?' Charlie asked, incredulous. Her father never, *ever* went out on dates when she was home, never mind slept over at some random woman's house. She made a mental note to ask Jake if there was someone special.

'I have to run now,' he said in answer. 'Love you,' and he hung up.

Charlie pulled a frozen garlic bread from the freezer and scanned the package for heating instructions. Just as she popped it into her father's surprisingly sophisticated toaster oven, Charlie's phone rang.

It was Marcy. As soon as Charlie had gotten home from her meeting with Todd, she'd emailed Marcy to ask about dates for a visit. Marcy lived in St. Petersburg, Florida, and it had been forever since Charlie had been to her home. The WTA offices were located nearby, and Charlie planned to meet with officials about her coaching change at the same time. It was going to be a truly hideous conversation, but Charlie knew it had to take place in person. On Marcy's home turf. At the very minimum, Charlie owed her that.

Charlie made herself answer the phone. 'Hi, Marce!' she said brightly. Even though the two of them communicated daily, it was almost always by text or email.

'Hey, Charlie. How are you?'

'Um, pretty good. Ramona was her usual charming self today. But I have to admit, she knows what she's doing. My wrist is a non-issue now, and I really feel like the foot is getting a little better each day. There's no pain anymore; now it's just building up the strength.'

Marcy had visited twice during rehab, but her IVF process and Charlie's inability to play yet made it silly for her to shuttle back and forth more often.

'I'm so happy to hear that,' Marcy said now.

'Yeah, she's been great.'

There was an awkward pause. Then Marcy said, 'Charlie, I hope you won't mind me being direct, but we've known each other long enough that we can be honest with each other, right?'

Instantly, a small, hard knot formed in Charlie's throat. 'Of course,' she managed to choke out, hoping she sounded normal.

'Why do you want to come see me in St. Petersburg this week?' Marcy's voice was calm and curious, but Charlie thought she could hear a twinge of suspicion.

'I told you, Marce, it's been forever since I've been there. I'm feeling better now and could use a break from the scene around here. I'd love to see you and Will, and of course I can swing by the WTA offices and maybe hammer out some—'

'You said you'd be straight with me, Charlie.'

Marcy was right, she deserved honesty – but this was not a conversation Charlie wanted to have over the phone. As difficult as it was going to be, Charlie was determined to do things the right way.

'Charlie, I don't want to make this any harder for you than I am guessing it is. And maybe I'm waaaay off here, so I'm going to ask you a straightforward yes-or-no question, and I'd really appreciate it if you could be honest.'

'Okay . . .'

'Do you want to come down here so you can fire me?'

Charlie's silence was all the confirmation Marcy needed. 'I thought so,' she said quietly.

The word 'fire' was so abrasive-sounding, so clinical, that Charlie wanted to argue with her, but there was no denying the truth in the question. Instead, the knot in her throat grew tighter, and it loosened only as the tears began to stream down her cheeks.

'I'm sorry, Marcy. I wanted to have this conversation face-to-face,' she said, hating herself for letting it all unfold this way.

'I know you did, Charlie. And I appreciate that, I do. But we've never gotten hung up on formality before, so we shouldn't really start now. I didn't want you to have to drag yourself across the country just to tell me something I already suspected.'

'You did?' A sob escaped and Charlie clamped her hand over her mouth.

'Yes. I know you haven't been happy that I haven't

wanted to travel as much in the past year. You clearly know that Will and I are trying to get pregnant, and I'm sure you wonder how that's going to affect you.'

'No, Marcy, it isn't—'

'You don't have to apologize. It's natural. This is your career; I certainly understand your concerns. I've had a lingering feeling that you blame me for what happened at Wimbledon. We both know that was a fluke – and you were points away from winning that match – but I do accept that I played a role in that entire debacle, and I'm sorry for it.'

'Marcy, please, if you'll just—'

Her coach's voice was strong and steady. 'My only wish is that we could've been more open about these things. Actually put them out there and addressed them before you felt the need to look elsewhere.' Then, after a beat: 'My father-in-law is currently in LA on business. He's a pretty big tennis fan, as you might imagine, and he saw you and Todd meeting in the lobby of the Standard. It wasn't hard to piece it all together from there.'

Charlie felt like she'd been punched. 'I'm sorry, Marce. The timing was so weirdly coincidental. I'm coming back, he wants to come out of retirement . . .' She didn't know quite what else to say.

'He has quite the reputation.'

'I know. I haven't hired him yet. I, uh, I wanted to talk to you first.'

Marcy cleared her throat. 'I appreciate that, Charlie. Your trying to come down here and everything. I just . . . I just hope you know what you're getting yourself into.'

Charlie didn't know what to say, probably because she

didn't really know what she was getting herself into. It was all starting to feel very real.

Marcy cleared her throat. 'Look, I don't want this to end badly. I can imagine this isn't easy for you either, and I want you to know that, first and foremost, we're friends. It's been an honor coaching you these last years, but more than that, I've felt privileged to get to know you as a person.'

'Marcy . . .' Charlie couldn't disguise the sounds of her crying.

'You deserve the best, C. You work hard for it, always have. So while I wish this all could have ended differently, yes, I hope you know I'll be cheering you on from the sidelines. With that Achilles' all healed and the Todd Feltner Midas touch, there's no saying how far you'll go . . .'

Charlie couldn't speak now, and hated herself for it.

'I've got to run,' Marcy said, sounding as sorry as Charlie felt. 'This isn't good-bye, okay? We've got plenty of business stuff to sort out over the next couple of weeks – put me in touch with Todd's assistant and I'll make sure the transition goes smoothly – and plenty of personal stuff, too. Hey, you still have that hideous chiffon dress you borrowed for that banquet, remember? Don't think you can just *keep* that ugly thing.'

They both laughed. It was hollow, but it helped, at least momentarily.

'Marcy? I'm sorry. I've loved working with you all these years. I wasn't planning – I didn't even think – I, just . . . I'm sorry.'

'I know. I am, too. Talk soon.' And before either of them could say another word, Marcy disconnected the call.

Charlie stared at the phone in her palm for a few seconds. Even with all the flights and the anonymous hotel rooms and the cities and countries, Charlie usually didn't feel alone. It was strange, this sensation of being adrift somehow without one of the only constants in a life that was defined by movement and change.

Ready or not, she thought, just as she smelled the burning and the smoke alarm sounded from the kitchen. *Here we go*.

5

connecting rooms

MELBOURNE, JANUARY 2016

The sound of a vibrating cell phone woke Charlie from a deep sleep, and she pulled it under the heavy down duvet where she was hiding from the air-conditioning. Who said only Americans wanted AC? The Australians seemed to like it just fine.

'Hello?' Her voice was raspy, as though she'd smoked a pack of cigarettes. Which, needless to say, she had not.

'Charlotte? What the *fuck* are you doing?' Todd boomed through the speakerphone that Charlie had accidentally turned on in her fumble for the phone. 'It's already seven and I'm standing alone on the court.' He sounded livid, which was really nothing new, and yet it made Charlie anxious every time. Like she was always doing something wrong.

Charlie pulled her phone away to look at the screen. 'It's only seven, Todd. Our practice time isn't until eight,' she mumbled, already swinging her legs to the floor. She glanced at her right foot and breathed a sigh of relief when it looked completely normal. Of course it would look normal – both the Achilles' tendon and the fractured wrist had healed completely months earlier – but examining the areas had become habit.

'Get your ass out of bed. Did you watch the tapes I left you last night? I ordered an egg white omelet to your room, it should be there in ten minutes. I want you on-site in thirty minutes. You think Natalya is lounging in bed, watching TV? That's not what top players do. And remember, if you're not early, you're late.' Without waiting for a response, he hung up.

If you're not early, you're late. Charlie bit the inside of her cheek.

There was rustling from the other side of the bed. Charlie had almost forgotten Marco was there until he said, 'Did you tell him you are not lazy, just very tired from fucking?'

'No, I didn't tell him that,' she said, swatting him across the chest.

'It is always good to tell the truth,' Marco said, pushing himself up on his elbows. 'What? You are looking at me and thinking I am, how do you say, Adonis? Yes, I have this problem with women all the time.'

Charlie laughed, but she knew Marco was hardly kidding: he was freaking gorgeous. He knew it, she knew it, the entire female population of planet earth knew it – at least, anyone who had tuned in to watch a men's tennis match in the last five years and had caught a glimpse of Marco changing shirts between sets. That ten-second flash of bare chest had garnered Marco Vallejo a *People*'s Sexiest Man Alive award. His perfect body was splashed on billboards all across the world showcasing underwear, sneakers, watches, and cologne, and he regularly walked red carpets with actresses and musicians and models. His ranking hadn't slipped below number four in three years. Having last won the US Open in a breezy three-set final, he was favored to win the Australian Open. He'd made millions in winnings, tens of millions in endorsements, and kept homes or flats in countries all over the world. It was widely agreed upon that Marco Vallejo was one of the greatest players of the Open Era. And he was in Charlie's bed.

There was a knock on the door. Charlie glanced around and, not finding any of her clothes or even a robe, yanked the sheet out from under the duvet and wrapped it around her chest. 'Just like the movies,' she muttered, pulling the door open.

The room service waiter couldn't have been a day older than nineteen. He sneaked a glance at Charlie, clearly nude under the sheet, and flamed red from his neck to his hairline. He glanced toward the bed, where the rumpled sheets and pillows confirmed everything, but Marco was much too experienced to get caught in such an amateurish way. Years of sleeping in strange hotel rooms with different women had taught him all the tricks, and even now Charlie wondered how he'd made it from the bed to the bathroom without anyone noticing.

'Good morning, er, Ms Silver. I have an egg white omelet with mushrooms, onions, and spinach, hold the feta. Fruit instead of potatoes. A large decaf Americano with skim milk. And some ice water. Is there anything else I can get for you?'

'Decaf? Really?' By now Charlie was familiar with Todd's no-caffeine policy, but she found it newly annoying each time he instituted it.

'That's what the order says. Would you like me to bring you regular?' the boy asked, his eyes darting, afraid to settle on any one detail.

'No, no, it's fine,' Charlie said, despite meaning the very opposite. She'd been officially signed on with Todd since last August, and the nearly five months of rehab, training, and strategy had gotten her exactly where he'd promised: strong and confident, ready for the Australian Open. It was true Marcy never would have asked her to give up coffee. Hell, Marcy never would have had her dieting. But she couldn't argue with her newly flat stomach and toned thighs, nor her more muscular arms and improved cardio-vascular fitness.

Charlie signed the check and, after tipping the still-red server, closed the door. 'You're safe to come out,' she called to Marco.

He emerged from the bathroom with his wavy hair wet, wearing nothing but a towel. 'I have a practice court at eight,' he said. 'What about you?'

'Same,' Charlie replied. 'Sorry, Todd ordered my breakfast so there's nothing here for you. You want me to call and add some oatmeal or something?'

'No, I am meeting Coach in player dining in twenty

minutes, I'll just eat there.' He cinched the towel tighter around his waist. His six-four stature and two hundred pounds of sheer muscle made his Mediterranean complexion almost an afterthought. Almost.

She checked her phone for the time. 'We got lucky again that the doping people didn't show up at six this morning. One of these days we are going to get caught together.'

Three hundred sixty-five days – regardless of where in the world she was or what she was doing there – Charlie was required to provide an address where she could be found, in person, for one hour in every twenty-four-hour period. She could choose whether that hour was noon or four in the afternoon or eleven o'clock at night, and she could change it every day, but the scheduling tended to get so confusing and so disruptive that nearly all the players provided their hour from six to seven each morning. It was early enough that they wouldn't be anywhere else yet but late enough that it wasn't a total devastation sleep-wise if the testers actually did show up. Which they did, sometimes as often as eight or ten times a year. Then again, some years they didn't show at all. You just never knew.

'So long as it's for sex and not for steroids, I don't mind,' Marco said, pecking her on the lips and grabbing his room key. ''Bye, gorgeous. Play well.'

'You too,' she said, although she knew they wouldn't ever talk about either of their respective matches. 'Good luck.'

He opened the connecting door between their rooms. 'This is very convenient,' Marco said, grinning. 'I might just request this arrangement from now on.' He stepped through the door and closed it again from the other side.

Charlie pressed her eyes closed. A scene from the night before flashed into her head: it was right around eight-thirty, and she had just changed into her nightshirt and ordered some mint tea from room service. She was still high from her first-round win earlier that day and a cele-bratory dinner with her father and Jake, who had arrived in Melbourne just in time to see her match. Lights-out was at ten, which would give her a solid nine hours of sleep before her seven a.m. wake-up. Nine hours was ideal, eight was acceptable, seven was challenging, six was a colossal disaster: this she knew from experience. Over the years Charlie had become a disciplined sleep machine. With the mint tea, a white-noise machine, and an eye mask and earplugs, she could sleep anywhere: player lounge, flight, tournament car, hotel, host home. Throw in a little melatonin for the worst of the jet lag and she was good. It had taken years of fine-tuning to perfect the sleeping, but it was crucial to the program and she made it a priority.

A repeat episode of *Scandal* had just begun. Charlie climbed under the covers with her mug and a copy of *US Weekly*. Better to watch Olivia and Fitz hash out another week of 'I love you but I can't be with you' than think one more minute about tennis. Her mind kept flashing back to critiques Todd had made after her first-round match ('Stop being so fucking tentative! You're a big girl, get that body of yours up to the net and hit the damn ball! Until you put some genuine effort into developing more than a serviceable second serve, you're going nowhere!'), but right then she forced herself to focus on the TV. Livy's clothes. Fitz's commanding presence. And, during commercials, back to the magazine for pics from Angelina and Brad's latest adventures in New Orleans. She'd just begun to relax when she suddenly heard music playing in an adjacent room.

Quickly, she dialed the front desk. 'Hello? Hi, I know it's not even nine, but I thought I was on a player-only floor.'

'Yes, Ms Silver. That's correct. Is there anything we can do for you?' The male receptionist was friendly but clearly tired of dealing with tennis demands.

'Well, I hear music coming from the room next to mine. One closer to the elevator. It's blasting now. Like, thumping bass. Can you call the room and ask them to turn it down? Or preferably off?'

'Certainly, Ms Silver. I'll remind the room's occupant of the twenty-four-hour quiet rule for players.'

'Thank you,' Charlie said. She put the phone down and listened. The walls were thin enough that she heard the volume lower for just a minute as a phone rang in the adjacent room, but a moment later it was blasting even louder than before. Enrique Iglesias? Seriously?

Throwing the covers off, Charlie marched into the hallway and pounded on the door of the room. Guaranteed it was going to be some fifteen-year-old kid who'd won a wild card into the tournament and had no idea what protocol was on the player floor. She was raring to go with her whole planned monologue when the door swung open and Marco grinned at her.

'Charlotte Silver,' he crooned in what could only be described as a hot dirtbag accent. 'Look who came to visit.'

He was, naturally, wearing only boxer briefs and a leather bracelet with a fishhook clasp. A smoky scent – weed?

79

candle? incense? She couldn't quite tell – wafted from the room, and the horrid dance music emanated from the nightstand iPod speakers. A sheen of sweat covered his entire gorgeous body.

She felt her face grow red. 'Marco? Hey, sorry to . . . interrupt. I didn't know it was you. Obviously. I mean, I had no idea you were in this room, and I never, ever would've knocked if I'd known that you were, um . . .'

It wasn't every day you accidentally interrupted someone you'd previously had sex with while he was currently having sex with someone else. What was the protocol for that? Charlie had no idea, but she was certain she wasn't supposed to be standing there (still!) to register a noise complaint.

Marco threw his head back and laughed. Charlie only noticed how his abs contracted. 'Charlie, Charlie. Come in,' he said, motioning inside the room.

A threesome. She had been trying her best to be open-minded about casual sex with Marco (her best friend Piper's voice was always in her head: 'Loosen up! You only live once! This is the twenty-first century, no one cares anymore!'), but a threesome was just not happening.

'Sorry, I've got to get to sleep. Just wanted to ask if you wouldn't mind turning the music down, but no worries. I have earplugs.' *I have earplugs?* she yelled at herself. *Why don't you just say you carried a watermelon?*

Charlie reached her own door at the exact same moment she realized two things. One, she'd locked herself out. Two, she was wearing only a nightshirt that just barely covered her butt – and no underwear.

'Now you have to come in,' Marco said. 'Come, you can call the front desk from here.'

It turned out that Marco wasn't stashing some groupie model in his room. He was merely doing a series of push-ups and sit-ups to obnoxious musical accompaniment. 'And I dance a little, okay? I admit it,' he said with the cutest, most devious smile Charlie had ever seen.

He offered her water from the minibar while they waited for a bellboy to come up with a key. Marco motioned for her to take a seat on the bed, but she couldn't manage it without exposing her entire naked crotch. And so they both stood, making small talk about the availability of practice courts and other insipid topics. When they heard a knock at the door and Marco bade her good night, she was almost offended he hadn't made a move. The last time in London right before Wimbledon had been incredible, hadn't it? Sure, it had been six months, but he'd texted her a bunch while she was rehabbing her injury. He must have moved on, she thought, trying hard to convince herself that she didn't care. She was a modern woman, capable of handling a casual fling without feeling like her entire self-worth depended on hearing from him again. But just to be safe, Charlie bolted back to her room and threw on a lacy thong. She couldn't change into cuter pajamas without looking like she was trying too hard, but she could make a few minor, hopefully unnoticeable adjustments: mouthwash, clear flavored lip gloss, scented moisturizer. A swipe of the brush through her hair and, okay, fine, maybe a quick little session on her bikini line with the tweezer. It wasn't the easiest thing to keep perfectly groomed when you were on the road forty-five-plus weeks a year. Back under the covers and pretending to watch her show, Charlie was just starting to feel ridiculous and wholly rejected when she heard a knock on the door that adjoined both their rooms. Which of course she answered.

It had been an insanely fun night, and although she knew she would eventually be exhausted from staying up way too late, right now she felt pretty terrific.

Charlie ate quickly and gulped her bland coffee. Someone from the front desk buzzed up to let her know that the car had arrived to take her to Melbourne Park. She pulled on a pair of spandex shorts, a sports bra, and a sweatshirt, pausing only to slip her feet into rubber flip-flops. Her racket bag was prepacked, of course, with everything she needed for a day of training and practice: she may have stayed up a little too late last night with Marco, but she never, ever forgot to pack her bag.

Charlie settled into the backseat of the Lexus SUV and stretched her legs. The sex had been good, yes. Okay, it had been great. It always was with Marco, which was part of the problem. They'd known each other for years already, having met as juniors when they were both sixteen, but they didn't sleep together until earlier that year, when Charlie had lost in the early rounds of Indian Wells and Marco had been eliminated before the semis. Coincidentally, both had taken an exceedingly rare night off from training before the next tournament and checked in, completely separately, to the Parker Méridien in Palm Springs for some solo decompression time. Charlie had been reading a magazine in the spa, waiting to get called in for her massage, when she heard a man say her name.

Hesitatingly, almost grudgingly, she lifted her gaze. The last thing on earth she wanted was to be recognized by some tennis fan who wanted to chat about her less-than-stellar performance the day before. Or worse, someone she actually knew, so that she would be forced to make conversation and ask all about their life and then – god forbid – have dinner together and catch up. She was shocked when she glanced up to see Marco Vallejo smiling across the spa's quiet room, wrapped in a robe so small it barely cinched closed.

'Hey, gorgeous,' he said, his smile literally stopping her heart.

Charlie somehow managed to keep her cool. They'd known each other forever, yes, but had not spent any time together alone. Certainly not undressed alone. 'Hey,' she said, praying she sounded more casual than she felt. 'You doing hot stone or aromatherapy?'

After their treatments, they met for dinner, which was flirty and fun, and then, at Marco's suggestion, took a bottle of champagne to the deserted outdoor pool. It had been three months, maybe more, since Charlie had had a drink, but she didn't hesitate when Marco poured her a glass. One turned into two and two into three, and before she knew what was happening, they were naked in the deep end of the pool, treading water and staring up at the night sky. It felt like she was in someone else's body entirely, another girl from a novel or a film without a care in the world, someone who laughed and winked and pushed her shoulders back with confidence. The champagne buzz was incredible, heightened by its rarity and the sensations surrounding her: the glow from the stars above; the completely free feeling of wearing nothing binding or constricting; the way the warm water enveloped her entire body when she floated on the surface and the quickness with which her nipples hardened the instant they hit the cold desert air. It felt like every neuron was firing double-time.

They swam until they were both shivering and hopped into the hot tub, where they finished the champagne by passing the bottle back and forth. Neither had thought to organize towels before stripping down, so they ran back to Marco's poolside casita room naked, freezing, clutching their clothes and laughing like teenagers. Not that either of them had had many chances as teenagers to do anything crazy or reckless. Charlie helped herself to a robe in the bathroom. By the time she came back out, Marco had lit two candles by the bedside, wrapped some sort of sarong-like fabric around his waist, and pointed the remote control at the gas fireplace. A perfect fire roared forth from the fake logs.

'Well, what do we have here?' he asked, opening the minibar. Out came two mini bottles of Absolut and a can of tonic.

'Are you serious?' Charlie asked with mock surprise. 'Tonic? Do you know how much refined sugar is in tonic water?'

This cracked them both up, at least until the cocktails were mixed. It was an almost inconceivable act, this casual drinking of alcohol: she knew that, until that night, neither of them had consumed more than a single drink at a time in months.

Marco lowered himself onto the floor in front of the fireplace and motioned for Charlie to join him.

'I so wish this were bearskin,' Charlie said, stroking the chevron flat weave beneath them.

Marco gently but firmly pushed her down to her back. He climbed on top of her and pressed his chest against hers. 'I will make you forget about the rug.'

In twenty-four years Charlie had never had a one-night stand. She'd made out with other players at junior tournaments, but hadn't actually lost her virginity until she'd met Brian her freshman year at UCLA. Since then, she'd been with only a handful of guys, and they'd all fallen somewhere in that nebulous place between casual fling and committed relationship: she had dated them, yes, but there was never a discussed exclusivity, probably because she was never in one place more than a few nights at a time. Or at least that's what she always told herself. If she were being honest, she often did wonder why men fell all over themselves declaring their love for her but vanished as soon as they got a real glimpse of the non-glamorous side of her lifestyle. Wondered if she were just using her travel schedule as an excuse for why she hadn't had a real boyfriend in six years. Wondered if she would ever meet someone who was interested in getting to know her beyond how she looked in a tennis skirt and how she had performed at the previous tournament. And most of all she wondered if it were even possible to have a normal relationship as long as she always put tennis first.

But that night Charlie wasn't wondering at all. That night she was tipsy and free and making out with the most famous men's tennis player in the world. Or, at the very least, the best-looking. He kissed her neck and ground himself into her; they rolled, their arms around each other, alternately kissing and laughing and kissing again. When Marco magically pulled out a condom and raised his eyebrows, Charlie didn't even have to think before nodding.

'Miss Silver?' The driver's voice interrupted her delicious memory. It took Charlie a minute to remember where she was.

'Mmm?'

'We're here. Are you okay with the entrance closest to the locker room?'

'Yes, that's great, thanks,' Charlie said. She squeezed her legs together as though the driver knew what she'd been thinking.

She yanked her racket bag out of the car and thanked the driver again. Holding her lanyard credentials out for at least another half dozen people to check, Charlie tried to bring her attention back to practice. The first round had gone easier than she'd expected – easier than she had any real right to expect – but it would be foolish to assume it would happen again. All the girls these days were capable of beating one another at any given time, even the lower-ranked or unseeded ones. And of course her bracket had gotten exponentially harder now that her own ranking had fallen so precipitously after her slip at Wimbledon: her injury had kept her out of the entire hard court summer season and all of Asia in the fall, and her number thirty-six ranking showed it. She had come so close to the chance of playing a Grand Slam as a top seed, and then *bam!* Blown up by a pair of shoes.

'Excuse me? Would you please sign my hat?'

Charlie looked up to see a girl of twelve or thirteen standing outside the women's locker room. She had a credential around her neck that read PLAYER GUEST, and

Charlie knew immediately she was a coach's daughter. None of the male players would have a child that old, and almost none of the female players had kids, period. This girl spoke with a quiet Australian (South African?) accent. It looked like she'd been waiting there for days.

'Me?' Charlie asked, actually pausing to look around. A handful of kids here and there asked for her autograph after every match, but they were usually the dedicated tennis fans who collected signatures from each and every player, regardless of who they were or how they played.

'You're Charlotte Silver, right?'

Charlie nodded.

'I love your braid so much!' the girl exclaimed before looking embarrassed. 'And I saw you the other night on *First* and you totally rocked it.'

'You saw that?' At Todd's insistence, Charlie had agreed to guest host an episode of *MTV First* to 'help raise her profile with the tween crowd.' The show's stylist had dressed her in a pair of painted-on leather pants, a low-cut silk tank, and those thousand-dollar studded Valentino sandals that she'd seen in every magazine. She'd danced and lip-synched and cracked up right along with the teenage hosts and, yes, were she to be honest and a little bit immodest, she *had* rocked it. Todd had referred to the whole thing as 'getting her feet wet.' Charlie was actually a little excited – the night had been fun – but she was relieved, too, to get back into her regular tennis dress, her comfy sneakers, and her standard pink ribbon-woven braid.

'Yes! I loved it. Here.' The girl handed her a Sharpie and a powder-blue hat that read AUSTRALIAN OPEN in rhinestones.

Charlie scrawled her name across the side and said, 'There you go, sweetie.'

The girl beamed. 'Thank you so much. My father coaches Raj Gupta and he never does anything cool like you.'

Charlie laughed. 'What can I say? Girls are just better.' She reached for the locker room door. 'Thanks for coming to see me.' She and the girl slapped a high five and Charlie all but skipped into the locker room.

When she came back out, Todd was waiting for her. 'You look chipper,' he said, grabbing her racket bag. Whenever the two of them walked together anywhere, Todd insisted on carrying the bag. It was less chivalry than a fear she might strain something, and although she found it a bit demeaning – Charlie was, she was pretty sure, stronger – she relented.

'This sweet little girl totally recognized me and asked in the cutest way if I would sign her hat. She'd been staking out the locker room just waiting for me.'

'Get used to it,' Todd said, walking briskly through the stadium's underbelly hallway toward the practice court exit. 'With the image overhaul we're rolling out, you're going to be the Beyoncé of women's tennis.'

As if to punctuate his declaration, a handful of teenage boys stopped talking and turned in unison to check out Charlie as she and Todd walked past.

'See?' he said, unable to hide his smile. 'So . . . is that the *only* reason for your shit-eating grin this morning?'

Alarm bells went off instantly. How could Todd possibly know about Marco? Neither one of them had ever so much as flirted in public. They didn't talk at player parties, or give more than an obligatory nod toward each other in the lounge or player dining. Charlie had told only Piper about Marco, which was low-risk from a confidentiality standpoint: having only played college tennis with Charlie, Piper was completely removed from the whole professional circuit. Instead, she was happily ensconced in a fabulous bungalow near Venice Beach with her boyfriend, who was a doctor, and her interior design company was beginning to get all the right attention. Piper was thrilled to hear the juicy details, but there was no way she would broadcast them to anyone. Charlie knew for a fact that Marco had told no one. They were never late for practices or matches. Except for that random first night in Palm Springs, they never drank or partied. Both of them took great care to keep their occasional trysts under wraps: neither wanted the attention from the media or, arguably worse, their fellow players, should the news get out. Besides, it wasn't like they were dating. It was all very occasional. Very casual. It was what Charlie had come to expect from the kind of guys she met, and Marco was certainly no exception.

Charlie walked through the gate that Todd held open and headed straight for the seats by the umpire chair. She kicked off her flip-flops, pulled on socks, and began to methodically lace her sneakers. 'What other reason could there be?' she asked, trying to keep her voice light.

'Oh, I don't know. Maybe an extra-enthusiastic *hola* from a certain Spaniard?'

In her shock Charlie completely forgot to play it cool. 'How did you know about that?'

'Well, well. So something did happen. I hoped so, but I wasn't sure.' Todd's self-satisfied smile was unsettling.

'You *hoped* so? What does that mean?' What she wanted

to say was *My sex life is really none of your business*, but iron-
ically she still felt like they didn't know each other well
enough to be so direct.

'Start stretching,' Todd said, checking his watch. 'Dan
will be here in ten minutes and I want you ready to go.'

Immediately Charlie dropped to the court and began her
usual routine of hamstring and calf stretches. 'Seriously.
Why would you hope something happened with Marco?'

He began to laugh. 'I can't think of anything better than
you and Marco as a couple. All that shiny black hair and
those blue eyes and long, tanned limbs? He's the fucking
king of men's tennis and you can be his queen. It's like
Steffi and Andre getting together, only with two gorgeous
people. Tennis royalty. Just think of the magazine covers.'

'Weren't you the one who explicitly prohibited me from
dating? Who said that if I wanted to play seriously again,
I had to promise no relationships?' Charlie had almost
laughed when Todd spelled this out during their hiring
negotiation: she'd been flattered he even thought a
boyfriend possible. Clearly he didn't realize what her last
five years had looked like.

Todd pushed on her lower back as she folded chest to
thighs and pressed both her palms into the ground. 'Who
said a damn word about relationships? I'm talking dating.
Or whatever you want to call it. Showing up and leaving
events together. A red carpet here and there. Some full-
length feature articles on how well matched you two are.'

'How romantic,' Charlie said drily, although even his
definition of a fake relationship sounded pretty damn
great.

'You both travel too much to maintain anything real,

you know that. I know that. And Marco most definitely knows that. But smile for the cameras when you're already in the same place, hold hands, show off those bodies, and whatever you choose to do behind closed doors is your decision. So long as it doesn't interfere with your training. Just no sex the night before a match, okay?'

'You want me dating Marco because it's good for my image?' Charlie asked, incredulous.

'I want you dating Marco because it's *great* for your image,' Todd corrected. He checked his phone. 'Where is that kid? He's two minutes late.'

Charlie wanted to ask Todd if he knew about her and Marco's history and the fact that last night wasn't the first time, but she didn't want to reveal anything he might not already know. Deciding to fish a little, she said, 'Why Marco? He's not the only good-looking top-ten player.'

Todd motioned for her to begin stretching her upper body. 'That's true. But he's definitely the most high-profile. And let's just say I had a feeling you would . . . how should I put this? Hit it off.'

'What's that supposed to mean?'

'Exactly that. And I was right. A simple request to the hotel for connecting rooms, and it sounds like you two took care of the rest. Of course, that's none of my business, but I have to say, you do look to be in good spirits this morning.'

'You did not!' Charlie said, almost unable to process what he had just said.

'Oh, I sure did. Dan! Over here, you're late!'

'Sorry,' Dan said, glancing at his watch. 'It's only a minute.'

lauren weisberger

Todd glared at him but thankfully spared them both the whole 'If you're not early, you're late' spiel, and they all took their positions: Dan and Charlie on opposing baselines, Todd at the side, holding on to the net.

'Other side!' Todd barked the moment they each began to bounce in place.

Charlie sighed and jogged to the sunny side of the court. Todd insisted she always practice on the side with the worst conditions – sun, wind, shadows – since she wouldn't have the luxury of choosing during a match.

Dan hit a few easy forehands and backhands to warm her up, but within five minutes he was whacking them hard and fast. It always amazed her how a guy an inch shorter could hit the ball so much harder than she could. She was still getting used to having a hitting partner. Marcy, as an ex-pro, had always acted as both coach and practice partner, and even in her late thirties could still give Charlie a run for her money. Dan was twenty-three and had recently graduated from Duke, where he'd played first singles. At Todd's insistence Charlie had hired Dan to travel with her, and she could definitely see her game improving from hitting against a man every day. In the couple of weeks they'd been practicing together, Charlie was already better at returning deep baseline shots.

They spent most of the practice working on Charlie's famed one-handed backhand. Todd thought she wasn't being aggressive enough with it after her injury, and he was right. At one point he yelled at her for slicing the ball one-handed. 'Lazy!' he screamed. 'Your wrist is completely rehabbed. If there's something you need to tell me about how it feels, then do it. If not, start moving those fucking feet!' It went on like this for nearly three hours: Charlie scrambling, pushing, lunging, sliding, twisting; Dan returning every shot like a backboard; Todd screaming until his voice went hoarse and sweat slid down his brow. 'Is this what I signed on for?' he yelled over and over again. 'Is this really the maximum of what you've got? Because that's goddamn pathetic!'

When she was finally allowed a break, Dan filled her water bottle and said, 'He's pretty tough on you.'

Charlie glanced at Todd, who'd moved to the other side of the court to take a call, and said, 'Yes. But it's good. I need it.'

Dan cleared his throat.

'What? You don't think so? I had the nicest coach on earth before him, and look where it got me. Twenty-three. Todd may not be the fuzziest guy around, but he's the best.'

'That's for sure. Hasn't he coached more players to Grand Slam titles than anyone else?' Dan took a deep swig of water; not that he looked like he needed it – he had barely broken a sweat.

'Sure has. He took Adrian Eversoll from obscurity to winning three Slams in a year. I'm the first woman he's ever agreed to coach,' Charlie said with pride.

'Cool. That's cool.' It was obvious Dan thought the exact opposite.

Charlie's phone buzzed with a text.

What the hell time is it there? Call me. I have news.

Can't call. Tell me now. Charlie smiled. Piper was constantly getting into trouble and there was little Charlie enjoyed more than living vicariously through her. They rarely saw each other, but it never seemed to matter: they always picked right up where they'd last left off.

Not a chance, ho. Call me.

Who u calling a ho? Just bc I had random sex w/M last night after we bumped in 2 each other in the hall?

I love it! I've finally convinced u?

Would u kick him out of bed?????

Fair point. Call me when u can.

'Charlie! Stretch it out and meet us at the car in twenty. Dan, come with me,' Todd barked, already halfway to the facility. Without a word, Dan dropped his cup in the garbage and trotted after Todd. Charlie glanced at her watch and tried to see if there was enough time to call Piper but decided to wait until she was back at the hotel. She used a towel to mop off her forehead and neck and did some cool-down stretches. The late-morning heat was just starting to pick up, and almost without thinking, Charlie sprayed all her exposed skin with another layer of SPF 70. Most of it slid right off her forehead and into her eyes. Wrinkles were inevitable – the tour schedule literally chased the sun around the globe for eleven months out of every twelve – but Charlie had read somewhere that 70 percent of professional athletes who mainly practiced and played outside got skin cancer by age fifty. Marcy had always been a lunatic about keeping Charlie protected with hats and specialty face sunscreens and loose SPF practice clothing, but Charlie hadn't been so diligent about it now that she was with Todd.

She wanted to text Marcy a picture of herself and her giant bottle of La Roche-Posay with some idiotic caption that she knew would make her laugh, but of course she couldn't do that. When her phone rang again, she was momentarily convinced Marcy had read her mind and called to say hello, but Charlie knew without even looking at the screen that it was impossible: you didn't fire someone and then chitchat like girlfriends.

'Hello?' She held her breath while waiting for the response. Of all the difficult parts traveling so much entailed – airports, delays, jet lag, strange hotel rooms, difficulty maintaining a functional relationship, to name a few – one of the most annoying was essentially sacrificing caller ID. It almost never worked in foreign countries, so answering every call was a crapshoot.

'Charlie? It's me.' Jake's voice sounded like it was a million miles away instead of five.

'Hey, I'm heading in for a shower. What's up?'

'Just wanted to make sure we're all still on for dinner tonight. Is Dan coming? I know Todd is. I need to know how many to make the res for. Heads up, Dad wants to celebrate your birthday tonight.'

'Hmm, I think it's just us – you, me, Dad, and Todd. Dan made it pretty clear that when he's not working he's doing his own thing. Unless there's a special someone you want to bring? Being that it's my birthday celebration and all.'

Charlie draped a clean towel across her neck and walked off the court. Natalya Ivanov, the statuesque Russian currently ranked number one in the world, jammed her body past Charlie at the court's entrance. The girl's racket bag slammed into Charlie's thigh with a serious *whomp*.

'Excuse me,' Charlie said as nicely as she could manage.

'What? Are you talking to me?' Jake asked.

'No, not you. Just bumped into someone walking off the court. No big deal.'

Infuriatingly, this made Natalya laugh. 'Why don't you worry about manners, and I'll worry about winning.' She leaned in so close when she said this that Charlie could smell her shampoo.

Before Charlie could come up with a single response, Natalya turned and followed her coach and hitting partner onto the court, already chatting with them in a glamorous mixture of French, Russian, and English.

'Oh, I hate her so much!' Charlie hissed into the phone, rubbing the reddening scratch across her thigh. 'Why is she so nasty? I ignore the bait. But she's always such a bitch to me.'

'Natalya, I'm guessing? Good. Channel that anger and use it to beat her. I'd like to see the two of you in the finals together. So would the entire world, and certainly all of your endorsers.'

Charlie felt her fingernails dig into her palms. The finals. Of a Grand Slam. Against Natalya. She would do anything – anything – for that opportunity. All those years of practice and training, lifting and sweating and sacrificing – it would all be worth it if she had just one chance to beat Natalya in front of the whole world. There, she admitted it.

Charlie could still clearly remember the first time she met Natalya. Charlie had competed all over the western part of the United States, but her father hadn't yet hired Marcy to coach her and travel with her beyond their home region. Natalya had been training for years at one of the Florida academies, but her manager mother wasn't pleased with the instruction she was receiving, so she moved Natalya to a small, prestigious academy near Sacramento. The very first time they played each other was a fourteen-and-under tournament where both girls had made it to the semis, and Charlie was floored to see Natalya blatantly cheating on her line calls. There were no line judges or umpires for most junior tournaments, just a whole lot of talk about sportsmanship and honesty and integrity. Natalya won that day, and she proceeded to win every match the two of them played for the next two years. Finally, with Marcy's support, Charlie filed an official complaint to the tournament director of a sixteen-and-under the girls were playing in Boulder, Colorado, and an official was dispatched to the court. Charlie won that day for the first time, and it didn't take much to recall the look of hatred Natalya had flashed her as Charlie held the tournament trophy high.

A rivalry had been born, at least according to Natalya. Charlie hated the conflict, completely refused to engage. Her mother had always insisted she take the high road, so she tried her best to stay out of the girl's crosshairs, to kill her with kindness, to maintain a polite, professional distance whenever possible. But Natalya didn't make it easy: she bad-mouthed Charlie every chance she got; she tried to hire away Marcy; she hit on any guy in whom Charlie showed the least bit of interest. It wasn't only Charlie Natalya attacked – she was nasty and vindictive to everyone on the tour – but she was especially ruthless with the attractive women around her age, especially when a particularly good performance threatened her clear number one ranking.

'Charlie? You there?' Jake asked.

The sound of his voice jostled her back. 'What? Yes, sorry. I have to run. I'm meeting Todd soon for a strategy lunch and then I have lifting from one to three. I'm hoping to cram in a massage before heading back to the hotel. Dinner's at six?'

'Roger that. I'll make sure Dad knows. He's wandering around downtown Melbourne right now, practicing his Crocodile Dundee accent on unsuspecting shop owners.'

Charlie forced a laugh, which caused Natalya to turn around and glare. 'Quiet on the court!' she shouted from the opposite baseline.

'Don't worry,' she said under her breath as she strode toward the car. 'I was just leaving.'

6

no more little miss nice girl

A guy wearing a Euro-tight suit descended upon Charlie the moment she walked through the door. 'Charlotte! We're so happy to have you join us!'

Charlie wracked her brain trying to place him. Was he the husband of a player? He seemed gay, so it was unlikely, but you never really knew these days. A colleague of Jake's from Elite Athlete Management? A friend of Todd's? Someone she'd met a dozen times before, who would surely be offended when she didn't remember his name?

'Hey, great to see you, too!' she said with way too much

enthusiasm. She prayed she wouldn't have to introduce him to anyone.

'Great first match!' His enthusiasm met her own. Still no hint.

'Thanks, I definitely got lucky. Fingers crossed for tomorrow.'

'Yes, you're playing tomorrow afternoon? We'll get you out of here in no time.'

'That would be great . . .' Okay, so he definitely worked at the restaurant. Todd's assistant had booked the table at Botanical weeks earlier: he insisted on eating at the trendiest restaurants in every city they visited. 'Better optics,' he always said when Charlie asked why they just couldn't go somewhere low-key.

'Your father and brother are already seated. Todd isn't here yet, but he called to say he was on his way.'

If you're not early, you're late, Charlie couldn't help thinking. 'You know Todd?' she asked. This wasn't the least bit surprising, but Charlie didn't know what else to say.

'Honey, that man has brought every player to eat here since we opened. All the greats. They come to celebrate wins and they come to cry into their sparkling waters when they lose.'

'Wow. I had no idea.'

Charlie followed the still-nameless maître d' through the modern leather and steel dining room. She noticed a large party in the corner, a mixed group of Slovakian male and female players with their coaches, but pretended she didn't see them. When they reached the table, Charlie was relieved to see her dad and Jake already seated.

'Happy birthday, sweetheart,' Mr Silver said, standing

to embrace Charlie. He smelled of the same subtle after-shave he'd been wearing for as long as Charlie could remember. And tennis. That combination smell of new tennis balls and sunshine and Har-Tru clay that every man who spent his life on or near the courts seemed to emanate from every pore. He smelled like home.

'Thanks,' Charlie said, hugging him tightly. 'But it's not until next week.'

'Well, we thought we'd celebrate tonight because we're all together. It's a double celebration – first big match back.'

'Twenty-five sounds old, doesn't it?' Charlie accepted the seat her father had pulled out for her and turned just in time to see Jake shake the maître d's hand and him slide a piece of paper into Jake's pocket.

When the man wished them a good meal and left, Charlie turned to Jake. 'Did he just slip you his number?'

'Mind your own business,' Jake said.

A busboy appeared and poured them all water from a carafe. Jake drank his down in one swallow and asked for more.

'Isn't there a more modern way to do that? Can't he, like, beam it to your phone, or find you on some location-based app where he can see your pecs before committing?' Charlie poked her brother.

'You're charming.'

'I'm just saying, the gays are usually very cutting-edge with these things.'

'Okay, okay, let's all calm down,' Mr Silver coughed, yanking on his already unbuttoned shirt collar. No one had been more supportive (or less surprised) when Jake came out in college, but Charlie's father still grew suddenly quiet and uncomfortable with any direct references to Jake sleeping with men. Which naturally delighted both Jake and Charlie to no end.

'Greetings, Silver family,' Todd boomed to the table. His designer jeans and blazer did nothing to disguise his bulk. All the sun had weathered his face prematurely, making him look at least a decade older than his forty-four years, and his eyes were always rheumy, watery. In the most reptilian way, he both blinked and licked his lips almost constantly. While his appearance had always repulsed Charlie, now that he was her coach she found it comforting. In a world of overwhelmingly – almost unnaturally – attractive people, it was nice to have someone around who wasn't blindingly gorgeous. Someone who didn't flirt with her or let his hand accidentally on purpose brush against her ass or make crass jokes or ogle other women. Granted, he had actually arranged for her room to connect with Marco's in the hope they would sleep together, but in the grand scheme of inappropriate behavior toward a female player from her male coach, Todd was downright dreamy.

Both her father and Jake stood to shake Todd's hand.

'Hello, Mr Feltner,' Mr Silver said formally. Nothing about her father was formal or stuffy, but he'd acted awkwardly around Todd from their very first meeting.

'Call me Todd! Peter. Jake. Charlotte. Great to see everyone.' He took a seat and immediately motioned for the waiter. 'Gentlemen, can I interest you in some tequila? They have a great selection.'

Charlie tried not to smile as both her father and her brother nodded. Her father drank beer and Jake preferred vodka, but no one wanted to speak up.

'Excellent. We'll do the six-flight tasting, please,' Todd said to the waitress. Her father blanched. Jake stared at the table. 'And a sparkling water with a lemon for the lady.'

Lime, Charlie thought, but she, too, kept quiet.

There was a moment of silence before Jake seemed to wake up and said, 'Well, let's jump right in, folks. Exciting things are happening with Team Silver, so let's run through them. Todd, why don't you start?'

Charlie was pleased Jake had taken control of the dinner. When she'd officially hired him as her agent/manager a couple of years earlier, all the tongues had wagged. Amateur move. Momagers were for tween movie stars, not highly trained professional athletes. There were dozens of agents around the globe – experienced, savvy men and women – who had literally been fighting to sign Charlie, and when she'd gone with Jake, only twenty-six at the time and barely past the assistant stage, they'd all rolled their eyes in collective objection. It had taken some time and a few missteps, but it was worth it to Charlie to have someone on her team whom she could trust beyond question, someone who had no agenda beyond what was best for her. And now it seemed especially crucial with Todd at the helm.

The waitress returned with their tequila flights, and everyone ordered. After each had sipped their first taste – and Todd downed his – Todd cleared his throat.

'So, status update. First and foremost, I just got the official report from Charlotte's exam last week at HSS, and Dr Cohen confirms Charlotte's right foot and left wrist are entirely healed. The scans were all perfect.'

Jake and her father clapped while Charlie did a mini bow at the table.

'Dino, the physio I highly recommend, is the best. If he can get Federer through his shoulder injury he can get Charlie through anything. Ideally, he'd travel with us to all Slams and Premier Mandatory tournaments. Of course, that will cost.' Todd made a sweeping motion with both hands. 'I leave that decision up to you.'

'The physios they provide at tournaments are usually very good,' Charlie offered. 'You even said so yourself in our first meeting in LA.'

The new team Todd had put together was great but expensive. There was money coming in, certainly, from both winnings and endorsements, but it felt like it was hemorrhaging, too. Between Todd, Dan, and Jake, Charlie now had three full-time people on staff and paid everyone's room, board, and travel – in addition to her own – while on tour.

'You get what you pay for,' Todd said, flopping back in his chair as though the depth of everyone's idiocy was exhausting.

'Definitely something we can discuss further, although if Charlie is comfortable using the tournament physios, I'm inclined to try that route first and use Dino on an as-needed basis,' Jake said with more confidence than Charlie knew he felt. 'What else can you update us on?'

'Well, as you all know, I've developed an entirely new approach for Charlie. Thanks in large part to the good work you've done with her, Peter, her foundation is solid. Great ground strokes, comfortable playing the baseline. Service is very solid and her net game is among the strongest of all the girls.'

The use of the word 'girls' rankled her, but again, Charlie kept quiet.

'In my opinion, Charlotte needs to be focusing all of her energy and attention on her mental game. You can be a decent player with strokes like hers, but she'll never be a winner without better mental toughness. No more sweet little Charlie with the big smile and the apology for everyone.' His voice went up a few octaves to a grating imitation of a female. '"So sorry for hitting it wide. Sorry for walking in front of you. Sorry, it's actually my turn for the practice court." *No más*, people. From here on out we'll be working on a mental makeover, if you will. I want aggressive. Go-getting. Intimidation. You think the men are walking around apologizing for everything and hugging each other? Hell, no! And the girls shouldn't be either.'

Todd took another taster from the flight, sniffed it, and threw it down his throat. The entire table watched as his tongue encircled his lips.

Mr Silver glanced toward Charlie, but she wouldn't meet his eyes. Todd was right. She was too nice. 'I hear you,' Charlie said. 'I could definitely be more aggressive.'

'You think? 'Cause *I* sure fucking do. No more Little Miss Nice Girl with the pink ribbon and the big, toothy smile. This is serious business with serious stakes, and it's time you acted like it.'

Charlie's father cleared his throat. 'I respect everything you're saying, Todd, and to an extent I do agree. But do you think it's wise to expend so much energy on trying to change Charlie's personality? Call me old-fashioned, but I still see some value in sportsmanship – especially in a sport like tennis.'

Todd smacked the table. 'Of course! I'm not advising her to be a *bitch* out there, but trust me when I say it wouldn't be the worst thing either. The girls today, they're tough. They've got muscles like men, they hit the ball hard, and they'll do whatever it takes to win. Just look at the ones on top – they're hot *and* tough. Real competitors, all of them. *That's* what I'm talking about.'

Charlie was relieved when the waitress returned with their dinners. She'd ordered the salmon because she'd eaten it the night before her first-round win. It was stupidly superstitious and of course no better than reading tarot cards or avoiding sidewalk cracks, but she couldn't help herself: she would eat salmon every single night until she lost. She'd also wear her ponytail in a braid with a ribbon woven through it, drink exactly two mugs of mint tea after dinner, and turn off the lights at ten on the dot. *How would sex with Marco fit in?* she silently wondered. She had slept with him the night after her win, so technically speaking, she should probably do it again . . .

'And what about fitness?' Charlie's father asked between bites of his steak.

Todd chewed, swallowed, and polished off another shot of tequila. 'What about it?'

'Well, Marcy felt like that was a major way forward for Charlie. That it was easier even a few years ago to be reasonably in shape, but that the women's game has evolved lately to become so much more about strength and fitness.'

'Why do you think I have her on the new eating plan? She's a knockout, don't get me wrong, but we still need to shave off a few more pounds. Long, lean, strong. We'll get there.'

Charlie took a sip of her sparkling water and stared at her plain grilled fish and side of greens. She was permitted specific carbs on match days – steel-cut oatmeal, whole wheat pasta, certain protein bars – but practice days were a drag. When had it become normal to listen to a group of people discuss her weight and her body right in front of her? The only thing weird about it was that, two official matches into Todd's regime, it didn't seem weird anymore.

'Well, I think she looks great exactly the way she is,' Charlie's dad said, and Charlie could feel herself blush. 'I meant more from a stamina perspective.'

It had probably been only two or three years after her mother died when Charlie had found two books in the glove compartment of Mr Silver's car: *Raising Daughters with Dignity and Respect: A Parent's Guide* and *The Single Dad's Primer on All Things Girl*. Page corners were turned down and paragraphs were highlighted, and her father had even made some notes in the margins, things like 'Don't always compliment appearance, compliment innate qualities,' and 'Always tell her she's enough just the way she is.' She'd cried for nearly thirty minutes that day, sitting alone in the driver's seat of the beat-up Jeep Wrangler that had always embarrassed her, and wondered where he'd found those books. The thought of him shopping the local bookstore, searching for something – anything – that could help him navigate the overwhelming task of raising two kids alone, could make her throat close to this day.

'Of course she looks great!' Todd all but sang. 'You gotta trust me on this. I got Adrian down from two hundred to below one-ninety and what happened? He won Roland-Garros that year.'

'Yes, but Charlotte's weight aside – which, for the record, I personally think is perfect – and focusing again on fitness: Marcy felt strongly that more off the court and in the gym could really pay dividends from the perspective of—'

'With all due respect, Peter, I'm not Marcy.' Todd had set down his fork and turned to look at Charlie's dad. 'Of course Charlotte needs to be fit. But that won't mean shit without the whole package. Yes, her backhand's great, blah, blah. Again, not enough. She needs a body that can cover the court and not give out during tough, hot three-setters and killer strokes, but then what? Attitude, that's what. Does she want it? Does she really, really want it? Does she want it so bad she can fucking *taste* it? If the answer is yes, then Charlie needs to show that. It's not enough to show up: she's got to stomp all over her opponents. And that's what you've hired me to help her do.'

Charlie threw her father a grateful look for not reminding the table that Todd was certainly not his choice.

'Wusses don't win Slams. It's the same in tennis as it is in life: nice guys lose. It took some time, but we roughed Adrian up a little, got him fired up and ready to win, and guess what? He started winning. That farmer fucking teddy bear. *All the time. Everything he entered.* Because when he walked onto that court, his opponents knew, could feel, that he wanted nothing more in life than to crush them. And there's real value in that.'

'Definitely,' Charlie said. She wasn't sure she agreed entirely, but there was no arguing with Todd's record. And where, exactly, had Marcy's insistence on fairness and good manners gotten her? A double injury and a loss in the rankings, that's where.

'To new strategies and bright futures,' Jake said, holding up his glass. Jake may have still been learning the ropes, but he'd known his entire life how to defuse an awkward situation, and never before had it come in so handy.

Charlie reached for her sparkling water while her father held aloft his still-full tequila snifter, and they clinked with Jake and Todd.

'To Charlotte, who's going to take her new badass self and trample the competition. Starting with that whiny little Croat tomorrow,' Todd said with a grin.

'How about to a very happy twenty-fifth birthday? May this be your best year yet,' her father said, smiling at Charlie.

'It's your birthday, kid? I didn't even realize. Happy, happy,' Todd said, taking another slug.

Charlie didn't bother correcting him or telling him the actual date. It wasn't hard to see her father despised him and, yes, he was no Marcy, but Charlie knew – she just knew – that Todd Feltner was exactly what she needed. She was nearly twenty-five years old, in the best shape of her life, and had never made it to the finals of a Slam. It had to be now.

'We can discuss the rest of the image stuff another time,' Todd said, scrolling through something on his phone. 'There's already a lot of food for thought.'

'"Image stuff"?' Mr Silver asked, eyebrows raised.

'The new Charlie needs a hotter look. Sexy and glamorous – don't worry, we're not going for dykey here – just a lot more sophisticated than this whole little-girl-with-braids-in-tennis-dresses thing she's got going on. Hard to take someone seriously when they perpetually look like they're twelve. Especially with a bod— a figure like Charlie's. It's practically criminal not to take advantage of it.'

Even Todd must have noticed the murderous look on Mr Silver's face, because he rushed on. 'Don't worry for a minute: Charlie's entire focus will be on tennis, perfecting both her physical and her mental game. I've got good ideas for the image stuff – the clothes, hair, publicity, that kind of bullshit – but I'll make certain Charlie will expend only the bare minimum of energy on it. I'll get people lined up to take care of it all. She'll only have to think pace, accuracy, intimidation. And *winning*.'

It felt like the entire table was deeply relieved when the waitress came by holding a plate of chocolate cake with a lit candle in it. Her father and Jake began to sing, but Charlie, feeling embarrassed in front of Todd, waved them off.

Usually she liked to take a minute and think, really will her wish into existence, and then blow out the candle with her eyes clenched shut to ensure it would come true, but she could feel Todd's impatience. She blew out the candle without wishing for anything at all and turned to Jake.

'We should really get going,' she said, and Jake understood immediately that she wanted dinner to be over.

'No time for coffee, I'm afraid,' Jake announced. 'Mandatory player party already started and Charlie needs to put in some face time before lights-out.' Jake accepted the check, signed the receipt, and slipped the corporate card into his wallet.

'Thank you for dinner, Silvers. It was enlightening as always,' Todd said, rising before anyone else. 'Charlotte, meet me in the lobby tomorrow morning at eight. I'll send breakfast to your room at seven-thirty. Light practice for two hours and an early lunch. Get some sleep.'

Charlie nodded, making a mental note to be ready for breakfast by seven and in the lobby by seven-thirty as Todd strode out. Her father came around the table to embrace her.

'Trust me, Dad. I know what I'm doing, and Todd is the best. He really is,' she said into his chest.

'Of course I trust you. I just don't like how tough he is on you. I know I'm only your old man, and admittedly I'm a little biased, but I happen to think you're pretty great just the way you are.'

'He's going to get me where I need to be,' Charlie said fiercely, hoping more than anything it was true. 'Marcy couldn't do that.'

'Marcy got you to twenty-three. I would say that's doing it.'

'But she was a pushover! And as a result, I was a pushover. Not to even mention the fact that I lost at Wimbledon because she screwed up on the clothing details.'

'Everyone screws up, Charlie. God knows I did in every imaginable way all those years I was raising you two. You don't fire good people for one mistake,' he said softly, reaching for her hand.

Charlie yanked it away. 'I can't possibly be the best there is with a coach who isn't pushing me every minute of every day.'

'Well, it looks like you've chosen the right guy for that.

I don't claim to know much about professional tennis anymore, but common sense says that it's great strokes, fitness, and dedication that wins tournaments. Not outfits or endorsements. Or intimidation, for that matter, which sounds to me like a different word for being a jerk.'

'Yeah, well, when five of the guys you've coached win Grand Slams, then I guess you can tell me what you think. But until then I'd say Todd knows what he's doing.'

Her father recoiled like he'd been slapped.

'I'm sorry,' she whispered.

It was her father's turn to pull away his hand. 'No, you're right. It's not my place.'

'Of course it is, Dad. I shouldn't have said that. No one has done more for me than—'

Jake clapped a hand on each of their shoulders, looking like he'd just returned from winning the lottery. 'Ready, Charlie? Let's do a quick drive-by at the player party. Dad, I called a taxi to take you back to the hotel.'

'Wait, can we talk about this for just a minute? Dad, I really didn't mean—'

'Come on, guys. It's after eight. Lights-out at ten doesn't leave us a lot of time.' Jake ushered them both toward the door, and Charlie tried not to notice that people in the restaurant were watching her.

Mr Silver leaned in to kiss Charlie's cheek. 'Happy birthday, Charlie. I'm sorry for butting in. It's just your old man looking out for you. But you don't need it. You've always made the best decisions for yourself, and I know you will now, too.'

As their car pulled away, Charlie turned around to see her father watching them through the back window. She distinctly remembered his unabashed delight when, at four years old, she seemed to have a knack for the game. In the first couple of years, he had actually brought her to the clay courts where he'd taught since age twenty-two and pushed her. When Charlie wanted to spend afternoons with her classmates swimming at the town pool or climbing on their swing sets instead of at the club, Mr Silver would lecture her on the rare gift she was receiving by starting so early. She had her whole life for pools and playdates, he'd say, but you only ever got one chance to learn the fundamentals, to develop your swing and game at such a young age that it all became second nature, that once you had honed those skills, neither time nor competition could take them away. Over and over he said, 'You have a talent. You must see where it takes you.' And although there were times when young Charlie grew weary of more hours spent on the court, she also loved hearing the admiration in her father's voice. He never said it to Jake, and he never talked about the other kids he coached at the club with anywhere near the level of respect with which he spoke about Charlie. She loved the way he examined her form and shopped with her for equipment and spent hours devising drills and lessons to best teach the skills he thought she most needed.

In elementary school, his demands grew greater: first he required one, then two, then three hours a day of practice. Charlie rarely played with friends after school, never took ballet or joined a soccer team. She loved tennis, she truly did, but the monotony of it began to wear on her. Charlie's mother often tried to intervene – and sometimes even went around her father's back, inviting two or three of Charlie's classmates over to play with her in the basement or watch movies in the family room – but Mr Silver always found a way to get her back to the court. It went on like this for years, this strange arrangement where he continually pushed her to practice and Charlie both loved and resented him for it, and it might have continued straight into her adolescence if it hadn't been for her mother playing the ultimate trump card: her deathbed plea to Charlie's father that he take a step back and offer more support and less instruction. Her mother had requested it and made her father repeat it: Charlie, and Charlie alone, would decide if she wanted to play tennis. That late-October afternoon when she was eleven, with its Indian summer heat and heartbreakingly blue skies, was not only the day Charlie lost her mother: it was the day her father stopped pushing her once and for all.

Charlie didn't notice she was crying until she felt Jake's hand on her shoulder.

'What's wrong? Is it Dad? Don't mind him, he isn't himself lately.'

'I was awful to him,' she said. Charlie wiped tears away and looked at her brother. 'What do you mean?'

'Charlie, he's fine. Everything's fine. You need to focus right now on your match tomorrow. Are you feeling good?'

'I'm feeling fine. That seems to be the operative word these days.'

'Don't be nasty. Dad's here to watch you win this tournament because he loves you and you're the center of his universe and you always will be, even if you say something obnoxious over dinner one time. Can you move on?'

Charlie dabbed her eyes and tried not to smudge her mascara. 'Yes.'

'Good. Now, I wasn't going to say anything until after the Open, but I am super-close to closing a deal for you. A big deal.'

'You are? How big?'

'The biggest yet.' Jake's grin was unmistakable.

'Mercedes?'

'Bigger.'

'Ralph Lauren?'

'Bigger.'

'What's bigger than Ralph Lauren?'

'You want to guess or you want me to tell you?'

'I thought you were talking to the Ralph Lauren people,' Charlie said. 'They were all excited to sign an American, but you were trying to clear it with Nike to make sure there would be no overlap on court. Am I making this up?' Charlie tried to keep up with all the things Jake was pursuing on her behalf, she really did, but there were always so many details.

'Swarovski.'

'Swarovski? Are you serious? You're not serious.'

'Dead serious.'

'They've never signed a tennis player. You told me that yourself!'

'I did indeed. They've never found someone they thought was glamorous enough. But they really like the new Charlie rollout that Todd and I have planned. The whole new public image: stronger, more confident. You, just more fabulous. They probably think they can get a bargain, too, because your ranking slipped post-injury, but I obviously won't let that happen.'

The car pulled up to the Park Hyatt just as Natalya

stepped out of a red Lamborghini convertible. She was wearing a red beaded Valentino dress, low-cut in the back and exposing easily an entire foot of naked thigh, paired with five-inch sparkly silver sandals.

'That works,' Jake said with admiration.

'Do you see how long her hair got? Overnight? Who the hell can maintain extensions on tour?' Charlie whispered. 'I'm lucky if I can wash it.'

'Charlie, Charlie, Charlie. So naive.' Jake placed his hand protectively on the small of her back and guided her toward the red carpet. 'She brings her own hair and makeup when she travels.'

'She does not!'

Jake guided her past the small cluster of photographers who were busy snapping Natalya. They'd almost made it inside when she heard her name. When she turned around, Natalya was smiling at her with the warmth of a feral cat.

'Charlotte! I wasn't expecting to see you here,' Natalya said with a laugh.

Charlie inhaled slowly and reminded herself to stay calm. 'Oh, well, since it's a mandatory player party, and I am, in fact, a player . . .'

Natalya's smile narrowed. 'Maybe you'll find a man tonight. Stranger things have happened!'

It was all Charlie could do not to shout her news about Marco. It would almost – almost – be worth it just to see the reaction on Natalya's face. But before she could come up with a response, she felt Jake give her a little push to the side.

'Hi, Natalya,' Jake said, reaching out to kiss her cheek. 'It's good to see you.'

Natalya turned her gaze to Jake, making no effort to disguise her blatant appraisal.

'Why, hello,' she purred flirtatiously.

He likes men! Charlie wanted to scream.

Natalya brushed back a handful of fake blond hair and gasped. 'I'm being so rude! Have you met my date yet? Benjy, this is Charlotte Silver and her brother, Jake. Charlotte and I have known each other since we were wee little ones playing as juniors. She's on a comeback after a huge debacle at Wimbledon last year. How are your injuries, by the way?'

Charlie was spared responding when Natalya's date stepped forward and thrust out his hand. 'Benjy Fuller, pleasure to meet you,' he said. He was just as tall as most of the male players, somewhere in the six-foot-four or six-foot-five range, but he must have weighed at least forty or even fifty pounds more. His sandy brown hair was cropped short and tight and his shoulders nearly bulged out of his sport coat. And then it hit her. This wasn't just any huge guy named Benjy: standing before her was the legendary starting quarterback for the Miami Dolphins, a man who had broken nearly every QB record in his eight-year, two-time Super-Bowl-winning career.

'Benjy Fuller?' Charlie said, her mind racing. 'Wait, today is Wednesday in Australia, so it's Tuesday in Miami . . . Aren't you playing on Sunday? How can you be here right now?'

Benjy laughed as Natalya clung protectively to his behemoth arm. 'A football fan, huh? Love it.'

Natalya giggled. Her dress sneaked up even higher. 'He's such a sweetie! They have a bye this week so he got an extra day off. I sent a plane for him and he came all this way for just two nights! I'm a lucky girl, no?'

Benjy patted Natalya's nearly naked backside. 'I can sleep more on that plane than I can at home. Couldn't pass up the chance to come wish this girl good luck in person. Watch her kick some butt.'

More giggling and groping ensued.

Charlie glanced down at her own dress, which now felt more like a small shower curtain, and said, 'Well, that's just so great. We've got to head in now. Nice meeting you, Benjy. And good luck, Natalya.'

Natalya pursed her heart-shaped lips and leaned over to peck Charlie on the cheek. She smelled of expensive perfume. 'You have some spinach or something between your teeth,' she whispered ever-so-sweetly. 'Thought you'd want to know.'

And without another word, Natalya and Benjy waved to their crowd of admirers and swept into the party.

'She's hideous,' Charlie said, stepping through the door Jake held open for her. She rooted around her mouth with her tongue but didn't feel anything between her teeth. Still, she pulled a mirror from her bag to check. 'If our lovely dead mother hadn't insisted a thousand times that I be kind and polite to everyone, I might have killed her already.'

'Yep, Natalya's pretty awful. But Benjy's even cuter in person than he is on TV.'

From the relative safety of the bar, Charlie surveyed the room and noticed all the players clustered in tight little groups around the room. A handful sipped wine or beer – the men, mostly, and even then Charlie knew they'd only have a single glass – and they divided themselves up primarily by nationality: Italians with Italians, Spaniards with Spaniards, Eastern Europeans together despite the fact that they all spoke different languages. It was a universally gorgeous group. Although there were exceptions, the men tended to be well over six feet tall with small waists and broad shoulders, while the women had legs a mile long and not an inch of cellulite. Everyone had blindingly white teeth and thick hair and dressed like they were spending the night at the VMAs. Trainers and coaches and massage therapists and agents and managers and tournament officials all mingled about, looking decidedly less fabulous, but by comparison they only heightened the overall attractiveness quotient of the players. Charlie instinctively scanned the room for Marco, but he was nowhere to be found.

Jake handed her a glass of Pellegrino. Something or someone seemed to catch his eye. 'Hey, you okay by yourself for a few minutes? There's someone I have to say hello to.'

'Take me with you. This isn't exactly the friendliest pond for solo swimming.'

'I'll be fine,' Jake laughed, walking away.

'I meant me!' But he had already vanished into the crowd.

She resisted the urge to pull out her phone and stand in the corner. She said a few hellos to players who passed by, but she couldn't seem to get in the party mood. The player parties had been so much more fun when she was younger. At nearly every one, she'd find herself on the dance floor, flirting, chatting up some of the more outgoing players and their friends. It had been exciting to meet people from all over the world and hear their stories, one of the things she loved most about playing professionally. But lately Charlie felt awkward: perched on a barstool, making small talk with the usual crew, biding her time until she could get back to her hotel room to read and unwind. After five years on tour, the faces were mostly familiar now, and the dancing was best left to the teenagers. Plus now there was Marco. The men's and women's tours didn't always overlap – they were only in the same place less than half the time – but when they did, Charlie couldn't stop thinking about him, wondering if they would see each other, when, where, and how.

She could count their rendezvous on one hand: the first spectacular time in Palm Springs, followed immediately by an even better round two at the Miami Open; there had been a torturous few weeks until the men's and women's tours overlapped again in Madrid; a very fun night before the next tournament began in Rome; and then the night of the player party before the French Open, which, incidentally, Marco had gone on to win. The next time they were in the same place at the same time was a month later, the fateful Wimbledon where Charlie had crushed her Achilles', only a day after she and Marco had hooked up at Richard Branson's lavish pretournament party. At his estate. In a bathroom, to be precise. Their hookups almost always took place in the lead-up to a tournament or its very first days, since once competition ramped up, neither of them wanted the distraction. Charlie was starting to feel an almost Pavlovian response to mandatory player parties: in her mind, they were now associated with sex with

Marco. At all the tournaments where only the women were playing, she found herself so much more relaxed. There had been no mention of Marco and any women either in the media or through the usual player gossip circuits, but that didn't mean much: Marco could be at the tournament and quietly sleeping with anyone – a grown daughter visiting her coach father on tour; one of the PR women for the men's tour; any of the trainers or nutritionists who worked with the players; or, likeliest of all, any one of the hundreds of female tennis groupies in each city who turned out to the player parties and tournaments in extension-swinging, stripper-smelling, stiletto-wearing droves. Charlie could vomit just thinking about it.

'You look so happy,' Karina Geiger said as she approached Charlie.

Charlie laughed. 'Thrilled. You can tell?'

As usual, Karina had flouted the tour's instructions to dress up for the party and was wearing a pair of sweatpants and a zip-up hoodie. 'Hey, I think I owe you a welcome back, *ja*? Your first tournament since . . .'

'Wimbledon. First round.'

'*Ja*, right, I remember. All better now?'

Charlie nodded. 'According to the experts, everything is fixed.'

'I am glad you are back. How is your draw? I cannot remember which bracket you—' She was interrupted by a petite brunette – attractive, if not actually pretty – who came and planted a kiss right on Karina's mouth.

'Hallo, *süsse*! I want you to meet Charlotte. She is not a bitch, a rare thing for the women players. Charlotte, this is my girlfriend, Annika.'

The two women shook hands. 'Nice to meet you,' Charlie said.

There was a commotion at the other end of the bar, and all three women turned in time to see Natalya and Benjy dirty dancing in the middle of a huge circle of admirers. She was bent over at the waist, her hands nearly touching the floor, and he was grinding into her from behind, one arm holding her around the middle and pressing her against his pelvis. 'Single Ladies' blared from the speakers and the whole room began to clap in unison.

'She always is so . . . how do you say . . . classy?' Karina said. 'A true lady on and off the court.'

Charlie laughed. 'The stories I could tell you . . .'

Annika said, 'Those I would like to hear one day. Come, Kari, let's get something to eat.'

They waved good-bye and Charlie watched as they walked toward the buffet of sushi and assorted noodle salads. Once again she scanned the room, instinctively searching for Marco before she even realized what she was doing. Irritated with herself, she pulled out her phone to stare at something – anything – and realized she had never gotten back to Piper.

You still up? What time is it there? I don't even know what day it is. I want the dirt, she texted.

An answer pinged back immediately. *Ronin and I engaged. Down on one knee. Giant rock. The whole nine.*

What?? Serious? Charlie felt a strange flip-flop feeling low in her chest. It was hardly a surprise – they'd been dating for nearly a year – but still. Piper was getting *married*? Meanwhile, Charlie was standing alone at a bar in Melbourne, wondering about the next time she might have super-secret sex with a guy who probably had ten other girls just like her stashed in cities all over the world.

Totally serious. V. excited. Can't wait for you to hang w/him more. Feel like you barely know him.

What I know, I love!!!! Charlie wished she could delete a few of the exclamation points after she hit 'send.' *I'm so happy for you.*

Have to run. Luv u, honey. Good luck tom. xoxo

Mwwah! Congrats again. More tom. '

Charlie stood, staring at the chain of Piper's texts until Jake appeared at her side.

'Everything okay?'

'Piper and Ronin got engaged,' Charlie said.

'Good for them. Is she happy?' Jake asked in his couldn't-care-less voice.

'Yes.'

'So what's your problem with it?'

'I don't have a problem with it.'

'Charlie. Come on.'

'No, of course I'm happy for her. Why wouldn't I be? It's just – when your best friend is about to get married, and you are still completely single and sleeping alone in different hotel rooms every night, it makes you consider your own life, you know?'

'I'd say you have the better end of the bargain. They're pretty nice rooms, and it's not like you never go out with anyone. Maybe soon you'll even tell me who your secret affair is with.'

Charlie looked up. Jake grinned and took a sip of his drink.

'Excuse me?'

'You heard me.'

'I don't know what you're talking about.'

'Oh, save it, Charlie. I know you're seeing someone. Todd knows you're seeing someone. Hell, even Dan probably knows it. I'm sure you think you're being super-stealthy and everything, but we're not blind. All the secret texting and phone stashing and those you-might-die-if-you-don't-locate-him-*right-this-second* looks you keep flashing around this party? Please. All I need to know now is who. It won't take long. You'll break or the tennis gossips will give it up. No one can keep a secret on this tour. We both know it.'

Charlie couldn't even articulate why she hesitated telling Jake about Marco, especially since she generally tortured Jake with the level of detail when it came to other guys. But she knew it didn't take a shrink to identify her own ambivalence: the combined shame and excitement of having a secret affair, the lack of a label making clear their relationship, the thrill of sneaking around combined with the torment of not really knowing what they had. She wasn't ready to hash it over and hear opinions just yet, especially those of her overprotective brother.

'Whatever you say, big brother.' Charlie kissed Jake on the cheek. His beard still felt strange to her lips. 'I'm going to head back to the hotel. Todd's been leaving match tape for me to watch every night, and he quizzes me on it the next morning. Plus, I'm tired and I need to be focused for tomorrow.'

Jake nodded. 'Okay, be that way. Sleep is a good idea. Come on, I'll walk you out to the car.'

'No, I'm good, thanks. Stay and have a drink for me.' Charlie squeezed his arm. 'Thanks for everything, Jakey.'

Charlie ducked out of the bar and grabbed the first tournament car in the queue. And then she did what she had never, ever done before. Without thinking about how it might come across, or how he would respond, or what it might mean for either of their matches the following day, Charlie pulled out her phone and scrolled through her 'recents' list until she found Marco's name. Before she could convince herself what a terrible idea it was on so many different levels, she wrote, *Room 635, headed back now. Meet me there.* She powered down her phone and slipped it into her bag. It was done.

7

america loves a makeover

SOUTHERN CALIFORNIA, FEBRUARY 2016

'This is bliss,' Piper groaned, and Charlie smiled into her face cradle.

'So you won't hate me forever that I'm missing your engagement party?' Charlie asked. She almost sighed in pleasure as the masseuse kneaded her hamstrings with the perfect amount of pressure.

'Massages go a long way to making me hate you less. I would suggest buying me a package of these if you really want to stay friends,' Piper said.

The girls were facedown on side-by-side tables in the Couples Suite at the Four Seasons Santa Barbara spa. The shutters were pulled open to the sound of the waves, and although the air was crisp, the February early-morning sunshine warmed the room. The heated tables, roaring fire, and hot paraffin wraps around their hands and feet added to the cozy feel.

Charlie laughed. 'Noted.'

'Any chance you can come afterward to help me look for shoes? I'm finally caving and buying a pair of platform sneakers.'

'I wish. Todd's already waiting for me. We have a lunch "strategy meeting" at the Ivy. My exhibition match is at three, and it's followed by a full-two-hour practice. I'm going to have to ask permission to pee this afternoon. Unfortunately, shoe shopping is off the table.'

'Won't it be strange to go back? Like, as a professional now? I think just walking on those courts would give me a full-on anxiety attack.'

'Well, you spent a lot more time there than I did,' Charlie said, and then regretted the way it had come out. 'Sorry, I didn't mean it like that.'

'No, you're right. Four long years. The weirdest part is, I don't miss it for a single second.'

'Why would you? You didn't like it.'

'Hey, it got me out of my fucked-up house, didn't it? And we wouldn't have met if I hadn't played, so it wasn't all bad.'

It felt like the ultimate of ironies that Charlie, who had never spent time at any of the prestigious tennis academies – something of a rarity among top-level players – had turned pro, and Piper, who had spent her entire childhood and adolescence at one, couldn't care less about the game. When Piper first told Charlie about how her parents had shipped her to the Bollettieri academy in Florida when she was nine, Charlie almost didn't believe her.

'You must have been so good,' Charlie said, her eyes wide when Piper told her this during their first meal together in the freshman dining hall at UCLA. *Could you even dress yourself when you were nine?* Charlie wondered. She could barely remember.

'Good at what? Tennis?' Piper's laugh was joyless. 'Outside of the fancy day camp they'd sent me to the previous summer, I'd barely picked up a racket. They told all their friends they were sending me there to "cultivate my talent," but that's only because it looked way better to ship your nine-year-old off to a prestigious tennis academy than to another standard-issue boarding school. But that's really all it was, at least for me.'

Piper had explained how super-rich families from all over the world dispatched their children to these tennis academies as a sort of high-end, year-round babysitting service. For six figures a year, sons and daughters of Saudi royalty and European financiers and Texan oilmen and South American entrepreneurs could guarantee their children would learn English, complete school requirements, get trained by the best coaches in the tennis world, and never need to come home for much longer than a week at Christmas and two during the summer. Plus it sounded good to tell their friends their kids were 'training at Bollettieri' side by side with the kids who showed genuine tennis potential and had been sent to the academy because their coaching needs had actually surpassed whatever was available to them in their home countries. What no one expected, of course, was that every now and then a few of the rich kids who were there for the 365-days-a-year babysitting actually turned out to be decent players. Piper was one of them.

She had played doubles her first three years at UCLA and singles her final year, although she never ranked higher than number four on the team. Charlie was ranked number one from the day she arrived on campus until she dropped out to turn pro a year later, but somehow things were never competitive between them. Maybe because it was obvious that Piper wasn't committed to tennis. She showed up for required practices and seemed to enjoy matches, but she would never, ever attend optional early-morning lifting sessions or extra weekend hit-arounds like the rest of them. Piper stayed out late and dated a million different guys and took weekend trips with her non-tennis friends. Charlie didn't even *have* any non-tennis friends. The few times they'd discussed it, Piper was always a little vague. 'I love tennis,' she'd say with a laugh. 'I love drinking and traveling and dating and sleeping and reading and shopping, too. I'm certainly not going to give up my life for a *sport*.' Even today, Piper played only once a week with a group of ex-college players who hit better than 99 percent of casual players but who looked at tennis as merely a hobby, something to cram in between work and social life. A good workout and some fun. It was impossible for Charlie to imagine.

'Coach Stephens is gone now and I've never even met the new guy. I don't know anyone anymore,' Charlie said. Her massage therapist asked her to turn over on her back and then draped a lavender-scented beanbag across her eyes.

'Whatever. At least it got you to LA. How long has it been? Two months?'

Charlie was glad she'd insisted on the spa day, but it couldn't make up for all the missed time. She exhaled slowly and said, 'Tell me more about Ronin. Why him?'

Charlie could hear the smile in her friend's voice. 'Why him?' she laughed. 'Because he'll have me.'

'Oh, please. Half of LA would have you, Pipes. Hell, half of LA *has* had you . . .'

'Easy, tiger. I'm not the one whose fuck buddy just happens to be—'

'Piper!' Thankfully, her friend realized that she shouldn't finish her sentence. While it wasn't especially likely the masseuses knew who Charlie was, she didn't need gossip about her and Marco – especially gossip that included the phrase 'fuck buddy' – splashed across the internet. No, thank you.

'Ronin. Tell me everything.'

'Everything? Well, let's see. He grew up in St. Louis, although his family moved a lot when he was a kid.'

'Where's he from originally?' Charlie asked.

'I just told you. St. Louis.'

'No, I meant where are his parents from?'

'You mean because he's Asian? He can still be Asian and from St. Louis, you know.'

'Oh, save it, please. I meant because he has an accent. Or is that something you never noticed?'

'His parents are from Japan. He was born there and spent large parts of his childhood there. But he's an American.'

'Got it. American. With a defensive fiancée. Check. What else?'

Piper laughed. 'Sorry. It's just my mother is such a blatant racist. She's obsessed with the fact that he's of Asian descent. Like, really can't wrap her mind around it and wants to talk about it all the time. I guess I'm just sick of having it be at the center of every freaking conversation.'

'Your mother would be uncomfortable if you brought home a Catholic. Or a brunette. It's the cross you bear being the liberal-minded daughter of rich WASPs.'

'True. So anyway, you know he's an ER doctor—?'

'The doctor who just wants to surf all day, right?'

'There are so many boards in our garage right now, I can't even count. When does someone get too old to be doing the whole stoner-surfer thing?' Piper asked.

'Apparently not at twenty-nine. He must be so psyched about your parents' place in Maui . . .'

Piper laughed. 'Totally. If only he could figure out how to ditch my parents. They're going more and more frequently now that my dad retired. Last time we were all there together my mother actually said something about not knowing that "people of Oriental descent" surfed. It was as lovely as you might imagine.'

It was Charlie's turn to laugh. 'Just give her lots of half-Asian babies and she'll shut up.'

'It's funny, I tried to explain to her that Ronin also has a mother who wasn't super-thrilled with our relationship – this poor woman has been hoping her whole life for a sweet Buddhist girl who could cook a decent bowl of udon noodles, and she got stuck with an atheist Protestant *Mayflower* chick whose family has more cases per capita of alcoholism than the whole of the Betty Ford clinic – but you don't see *her* complaining. Nope, just brought me right into the fold and taught me how to assemble a halfway decent bento box. My mother doesn't understand that to save her life.'

Charlie immediately tried to imagine what it would look like to be able to introduce her mother to her future fiancé. Her mom had missed it all, of course: Charlie's first period, the prom, the college dorm room, the first time competing in a Grand Slam. Charlie's parents had eloped in the late eighties when her mom found out she was pregnant with Jake, so they never had an official engagement or a proper wedding. Maybe that was why Charlie felt increasingly uneasy as friends started to get married off?

The sound of a chime brought Charlie back to the massage. 'I'm finished now. Please take your time sitting up and getting dressed,' her therapist was whispering. 'We'll wait outside.'

'That was great,' Piper said, rubbing her eyes. Even with pillow indentations across her cheek and bloodshot eyes, Piper looked like a supermodel. She shrugged on a robe as Charlie tried not to stare.

As if in answer, Piper raised her eyes in Charlie's direction and said, 'You're looking great these days.'

Charlie rolled her eyes. 'Uh-huh. That's why Todd can't shut up about these last five pounds.' Charlie grabbed her thighs in both hands. 'Wanna trade?'

The girls walked out of the suite and toward the locker room. 'You think Marco Vallejo is thinking about anything except how hot you look as he mounts you every chance he has? Seriously, Charlie. Enough with the ugly duckling complex. You may have been a little thicker a few years back, but you're officially hot now. I just want to hear how you're handling this whole casual sex thing. Because the Charlie I know isn't exactly a sleep-around kind of girl.'

'Well, there's a first time for everything, I guess.'

'From everything you've described, he's not your boyfriend. He's not even really your friend. You have to be okay with that for it to work. Are you okay with it?'

'Of course.'

'You're not!'

'I have to be. That's definitely the arrangement.'

The girls took their snacks to the patio outside, where they sat down in front of a small wood-burning fire.

'I don't have *feelings* for him,' Charlie said quietly, realizing the truth for the first time. 'I just like having someone.'

'He's way better than just *someone*,' Piper said, taking a sip of tea.

'You know what I mean.'

'I do. I know it gets lonely traveling that much. You're gone all the time. You have nothing even resembling a normal life. And historically you're a serial monogamist. Trust me, I've thought about it a lot. Ronin and I talk about how hard it must be for you all the time.'

Charlie turned to look at Piper. 'Seriously? Those are your words of wisdom? "My fiancé and I talk all the time about how epically fucked-up your life is"?'

Piper reached over and gave Charlie's arm a poke. 'Shut up, you know that's not what I mean. It's all coming from a place of concern.'

'Oh, good. That makes me feel much better.'

'Well, it should. I *do* worry about you. Maybe having a

boyfriend wouldn't be the worst thing in the world. Maybe you and Marco should try actually going out to a movie or dinner or something normal people do. Have a conversation. Tell him about yourself. Ask him questions. He must have some interest outside of tennis. Maybe find out what it is . . .'

'Can you even imagine what the media storm would be around that? If we went out on a real normal-people date? There would be cameras everywhere.'

'Oh, come on, who cares? Two consenting adults who both just happen to play the same sport start to date? Is it really so scandalous?'

Charlie thought about this. When Piper put it that way, it was true: it didn't sound so crazy. During the handful of times they'd hooked up and gone to great lengths to keep it quiet, it hadn't even really occurred to her that the secrecy might not be necessary. What was the worst thing that could happen? They would try dating and it wouldn't work? So what? A few reporters would ask some annoying questions about it, a couple of talking heads would give big 'I told you so's the same way they do whenever relationships between professional athletes – or actors or musicians or anyone in the spotlight – failed, and who cared? Why had they been so determined to keep things quiet? Who, exactly, was it benefitting?

'You're right,' Charlie said, slowly nodding.

'What?' Piper feigned an incredulous expression.

'What is the big deal if we do start dating for real? Like you said, he's one of the only guys in the world who understand where I'm coming from.'

'Plus he's magnificent.'

'So long as we both understand that our careers come first, I don't see why it couldn't work.'

'Not to mention that he's spectacular-looking.'

'I mean, I haven't had anything resembling a serious relationship since . . . my god . . . college. Brian was the last one.' Charlie gazed skyward as she calculated.

'Have we talked about how great his hair is?'

'The few-month fling with the tennis journalist? Not my finest moment. But at least he was a nice guy.'

'Even his name is sexy.'

'Oh, and the downhill ski racer I met on the flight to Monaco. Talk about competing schedules.'

'Would you think it's weird if I told you I fantasized about his abs?'

'Christ, Piper. I'm pathetic! Do you realize it's been since my freshman year in college that I've had a relationship longer than a few months? I'm twenty-five years old. And practically a virgin.'

Piper smiled and patted Charlie's hand. 'Let's not get carried away here. You've dated. You're just not . . . what's the best way of saying this? The best picker. And you have some challenging circumstances, what with your whole lifestyle and all. It doesn't mean all hope is lost.'

'Thanks.' Charlie looked down at her phone. 'Oh, I've got to run. I have to be back in LA in an hour and a half. If there's traffic, I'm never going to make it.'

'Love you, C. Thanks for a great day. I'm now only half pissed off you're missing my engagement party.'

Charlie kissed Piper's cheek. 'See? Money *can* buy friendship. An important lesson.'

'That may as well be my mother's mantra. Nothing I

135

haven't heard from the cradle.' Piper wrapped a cashmere infinity scarf around her neck, and for the thousandth time Charlie wondered how her friend was so effortlessly chic. 'And don't forget to buy yourself something nice for Valentine's Day, okay? I would suggest chocolate, but since you're on a starvation diet, maybe jewelry. No tennis crap!'

They waved good-bye and Charlie handed the valet her ticket. She found herself wishing again she could stay the night and party with the rest of their college friends, but she needed to be back in LA by four. She eased her rented Audi convertible onto the 405 and turned the music up. It was that perfect kind of winter day that only Californians understood: high sixties, warm sun, cool breeze. Literally the kind of day for which they invented convertibles. Near Malibu, she calculated that she was fine with time and moved over to the PCH: it would take longer, but it was worth it to drive along the water. Charlie switched the XM station to the Blend and sang along with Rachel Platten and Taylor Swift and Ed Sheeran until her throat felt raw and her eyes were tearing from the wind. How many times had she driven the PCH her freshman year? She and Brian would go for drives on Sunday afternoons and bicker over the radio: she always wanted top forty; he always wanted anything else. She had even told him she was leaving school – and him – to turn pro at the Fish Shack in Malibu.

Brian knew with a wisdom exceeding his nineteen years that a long-distance relationship with someone who'd be traveling three hundred days a year was unrealistic. The breakup was miserable. It took only a few months on tour for Charlie to see that maintaining a relationship was actually impossible only for the women. For the men it was a totally different world: they had girlfriends who traveled with them, dressed in designer jeans and high heels with perfect hair and makeup each and every day so they could stretch out like kittens in various players' lounges all over the world, waiting for their hot, sweaty men to walk off the court. Four out of the top five ranked men in the world were married. With children. It had taken Charlie's breath away when Marcy had once pointed that out, followed quickly by the number of women married in the top twenty: one. And the number in the top twenty with children? Zero. Men weren't exactly lining up to follow their player girlfriends all over the world, keeping their hotel beds warm at night and breakfasting with them at six a.m. in cafeterias from Dublin to Dubai, waiting to hug those sweaty, exhausted women when they finally left the court, alternately elated or enraged, depending on the day. The couple of men who did give it a go for a little while didn't last long: coaches and male players and even other female players whispered about their lack of jobs and their abundant free time, calling them pussy-whipped and losers and mooches. But the various models and actresses and anonymous pretty things who traveled all over to support their boyfriends? Everyone seemed to understand they were just doing what the men needed.

The car in front of her came to a screeching halt and it was all Charlie could do not to rear-end the massive black Suburban. She had mindlessly followed the nav through Malibu and Santa Monica and across Brentwood and the leafy streets of Beverly Hills to the Peninsula, where the Suburban pulled in right ahead of her.

A text pinged on her phone. Todd. *Thirty minutes, Ivy, Robertson. Don't be late.*

She tapped back a single letter, *k*, and handed her keys to the valet. Two porters were busily unloading trunk after trunk of coordinated Goyard luggage from the depths of the Suburban, and Charlie couldn't help but linger on the sidewalk to see which celebrity would emerge. From the looks of the bags, it was likely a Kardashian. Possibly a Rihanna- or Katy Perry-type pop star. Definitely not an A-list actor, judging by the sheer amount of baggage. This person had packed the whole house and was here to stay. Just as she was about to give up and walk inside, the driver removed a Wilson racket bag the size of a Great Dane from its perch atop the passenger-side front seat. Hanging from it was a soda-can-sized 'charm,' a diamond-encrusted owl with emerald eyes and a lipstick-lined beak and long eyelashes that Charlie knew were made from actual rabbit whiskers. She would recognize that gaudy owl anywhere.

'Look who it is!' Natalya crowed to Charlie from the backseat of the Suburban. Every single man, woman, and child who either worked the valet line or was waiting in the parking area of the Peninsula Beverly Hills stopped reading their texts and looking for their keys and wrangling their children and turned to watch the six-foot-tall blonde, in shorts so minuscule everyone could make out the neon pink underwear, languidly slide down the side of the car. Charlie swore she could hear a collective sigh when Natalya's sandal landed safely on the pavement.

'You're sweet to wait for me. Here, grab this.' Natalya thrust a Goyard-logo-covered train bag into Charlie's arms. 'Thanks, darling.'

Shocked to see Natalya in Los Angeles a full four days before they were both set to play Indian Wells in Palm Springs, Charlie unthinkingly followed her into the lobby.

'What are you doing here?' Charlie asked as Natalya showed her ID to the front desk person. It occurred to Charlie that she, too, should be checking in, but she couldn't remember if she'd left her purse in the car or if it was on the valet cart.

Natalya leaned in close enough for Charlie to catch a pleasant whiff of vanilla-scented perfume. 'Benjy just played in the Pro Bowl in Hawaii. He's meeting me here tonight for a little . . . R and R. What about you, Charlie? Another night hunkered down with your team? It must get lonely with only your coach and your brother for company.'

Charlie's pulse quickened.

'You really should think about getting yourself a man,' Natalya said, pulling her phone out. 'What about that new kid on the men's tour, the one from Philly? He'd probably sleep with you.'

A picture flashed in her head: Brett or Brent or something, nearly six five, with gangly limbs and acne. Sixteen, maybe seventeen years old at the most. It was followed quickly by a visual of Marco soaked in sweat after a match, the Dri-FIT of his T-shirt literally sticking to his muscles, headband holding back his thick black hair. Then his smile, the one she'd only seen him flash for her privately . . .

Natalya's laugh snapped her back. 'Oh, wait, I think he already has a girlfriend. Don't worry, I'll keep thinking.'

Usually it was her mother's voice she heard, reminding her to take the high road, be polite, rise above the conflict.

Charlie tried hard to follow the advice, she really did, but today it was Todd's voice that reverberated in her head. *Mental toughness. No more sweet girl. Stop being a doormat. Do you think Natalya sits around every day wondering how to make more people like her? You shouldn't either!*

The elevator doors began to close, but they slid open again when Charlie stuck her hand between them.

'What are you doing?' Natalya snarled, all of her fake niceness evaporating in an instant.

'Watch yourself,' Charlie said in a voice so low it could have been mistaken for a growl.

'How dare you even—?'

Charlie threw the train bag that she'd been holding in a dumbfounded shock through their entire run-in straight into Natalya's arms, who caught it with a loud *oomph*.

'I hope you have a great time with your boyfriend tonight, Natalya,' Charlie said, leaning in through the doors she held open. She was pleased to see that Natalya looked downright afraid. 'Because I'm coming for you. I may not beat you next week, or the week after that, but mark my words: it's going to happen. And I am going to love every second of it.'

With that, Charlie stepped backward out of the elevator and watched Natalya's mouth hanging open as the doors swept shut. She glanced quickly around the lobby to make sure no one else was watching and then she allowed herself a small, satisfying fist pump.

As she swung open the white picket fence and let herself into the Ivy's front porch area, Charlie heard the unmistakable clicking of cameras and flashbulbs. All at once, a crowd of paparazzi had gathered in a small swarm on the sidewalk, and with them a group of young, highly groomed Sunday afternoon shoppers. Not knowing what was happening, Charlie froze.

A moment later she felt Todd's hand on her back. 'They're not here for you yet, sweetheart. But they will be soon.'

Charlie felt herself flush, first with embarrassment, followed quickly by annoyance. 'I didn't think that,' she huffed, following him to a round table on the patio. She took a seat facing the street and saw what all the commotion was about: Blake Lively and Ryan Reynolds, pushing their daughter in one of those strollers that cost as much as a used car.

'Seriously, feast your eyes, Charlie, because that is exactly what it's going to be like for you when Meredith does her thing.'

'Are we talking about me already? Good, that's exactly how I like it.'

The woman standing in front of their table was in her mid-thirties and only five feet tall because of her heels, but it was the mane of cascading red curls that caught Charlie's attention.

'Your hair is amazing,' Charlie breathed, before remembering they hadn't even been introduced.

'You think? Mostly I hear that I look like Little Orphan Annie,' Meredith said, yanking on a red lock.

'I was thinking more like Merida from *Brave*.'

Meredith laughed. 'I like you already. I'm Meredith Tillie, and you are obviously Charlotte Silver.'

'It's really nice to meet you,' Charlie said, finally remembering to stand and shake Meredith's hand.

Todd motioned for everyone to sit just as his phone rang. 'Get to know each other,' he barked, heading for the picket fence.

'He's just so charming, isn't he?' Meredith asked, and batted her eyelashes like a Southern belle.

'Adorable. Truly.'

The women smiled at each other. Maybe Todd's whole image makeover idea wouldn't be quite as terrible as Charlie had been anticipating. Meredith seemed likable. They each took a sip from the fruit smoothies the waiter had brought, and Meredith explained how she'd gotten started in the business, moving from FIT into a design house, PR firm, crisis management, and now her own image consultation company. Charlie couldn't imagine having six careers before age thirty. Or even two.

'Who have you worked with?' Charlie asked.

Meredith smiled coyly. 'Well, I sign a lot of NDAs, as you might imagine, so no specifics, but let's see. There was the woman who left Scientology after decades, and she hired me to take her from cult whack-job to respected author. The teenage pop star who got knocked up at seventeen while hooked on meth; she's now the face of L'Oréal and about to appear on an upcoming season of *Dancing with the Stars*.'

'Wow, is she really? I know exactly who you're talking about.'

'No names, please,' Meredith said with a raised hand. The other she tapped on the table in concentration. 'Who could forget the actor who broke into the biz by giving blow jobs to every movie exec in town and unfortunately developed a bit of a reputation as a male hooker? We reworked some things with him and he was just featured on the cover of *GQ* as the embodiment of a twenty-first-century Renaissance man – speaks Mandarin, volunteers at a women's shelter, dates a Victoria's Secret model, blah, blah, blah. Oh, and the revered mother of four and highly respected politician who must have been the only woman in all of history with a debilitating gambling problem? I mean, seriously, a female blackjack addict? It's ridiculous. Anyway, it took a lot of hard work, but I just got her elected for a second term. So you see, it's a mix.'

'What's a mix?' Todd asked as he wedged his pear-shaped bottom into the petite chair between the two women. He waved his hand at a busboy and asked him for a martini.

'My clients. I'm giving Charlotte a little background.'

'She likes when you call her Charlie,' Todd said.

'She can call me whatever she wants,' Charlie said.

'Relax,' Todd crooned, flipping through the menu. 'Don't get bitchy. Everything's fine.'

'At the risk of sounding rude, I am a little stressed-out. Being that I don't have a gambling problem or a meth addiction or a penchant for prostitution, I'm not sure what's so horrible about me that it warrants Meredith's services.' She turned to Meredith. 'Forgive me for saying so – and you certainly seem nice enough – but I think this is a waste of everyone's time.'

Meredith and Todd glanced at each other.

Todd rolled his eyes. 'Of course you're not some crack-head. No one's suggesting anything of the sort. But let's be real here. We need—'

'I think what Todd is trying to say is that, yes, I am probably overkill for what we're trying to accomplish here.

You don't need me to tell you you're great just the way you are – pretty girl, sweet as they come, stellar reputation, hard worker, great potential, huge crowd-pleaser. Plus your background – poor girl from the wrong side of the tennis tracks who lost her mother so early – plays really well with fans. It's all great, Charlie. But if we can make it even better – and trust me, we can – it's only in your best interest to do so.'

So there it was. Charlie's whole persona, neatly summarized for public consumption by a complete stranger. She would have been upset this woman invoked her mother's death so casually if she weren't so shocked by the entire summary, a little glimpse into how the world perceived Charlie.

Todd must have been able to see the distress stamped plainly on Charlie's face. 'Don't go getting all pissy, Charlie. This sport of yours isn't just a little hobby. This is a huge industry, with all sorts of opportunities, and pardon my French, but you'd be an asshole for not taking your piece.'

Meredith cleared her throat and shot Todd another look. 'It might be easier if you think about the fact that everyone, regardless of their career, has a public persona and a private one, right? We aren't here to tamper with your private life or change who you fundamentally are as a person. But it's naive to think that your public persona can't – or shouldn't – be manipulated to maximize the benefit to you.'

The waiter appeared and began to lower a bread basket onto the table, but Todd barked, 'Get that out of here!' Not missing a beat, the man tucked it under his arm and took their order, looking unsurprised when they all requested the exact same salad.

Charlie waited for him to leave and said, 'Okay, my public persona needs some "manipulating." Can you be more specific?'

With this, Meredith's smile was beneficent. 'Of course, darling. Keeping in line with Todd's plan to make you more aggressive and confident on the court, we would do our best to mirror that boldness off the court. To that end, we'd like to do away with Charlie as Good Girl and make you into . . . are you ready for this? The Warrior Princess.'

'The what? Oh, come on.' Charlie laughed.

Neither Meredith nor Todd cracked a smile.

'It's brilliant, Charlie. It'll give you a rock-solid identity that fans and media alike can attach to. And let me tell you, it's exactly what you need.'

'The *Warrior Princess*? You're serious?'

Meredith continued as though she hadn't heard Charlie. 'First, we'll eliminate the brightly colored tennis dresses in favor of something darker, sexier, edgier. We'll lose that childish ribbon you weave through your hair. We will work with great hair and makeup people to update your look – without affecting your performance, of course. I'll bring in a stylist to help redo both your look on court, which is the most important, but also overhaul your off-court wardrobe for player parties, inter-views, charity events – really anywhere you'll be seen. You'll need a quick session with one of our media trainers so you can better control your own message, but we'll be doing all the behind-the-scenes work to get the media clamoring to cover you. Your brother is already hard at work securing an additional endorsement deal, one that would add a little interest, a little seduction, to the usual sporty brands everyone represents. Overall, there is very little to do.'

Charlie's eyes widened. Very little? Meredith had just outlined an entire image overhaul that required a bulleted list and no fewer than five people to execute it.

Todd took a slug of his drink. 'Remember your promise that you were going to lose the sensitive-girl crying crap? We're way ahead of the game here, Charlie. In your five full years on the women's tour, you have remarkably never done a single fucked-up thing that we need to undo. No scandals to clean up. All peaches and cream. So we reverse engineer this.'

Meredith nodded. 'It's true. It's a lot easier going the other way, weaving in some intrigue and interest, than it is trying to expunge years of bad decisions.'

The waiter set their salads in front of them. Todd shoveled a forkful into his mouth before the women picked up their silverware.

'I told her you're fucking Marco,' Todd said through a mouthful of food.

Charlie inhaled sharply. 'My own brother doesn't even know!'

Meredith placed a warm hand on Charlie's. 'I'm a vault. Todd told me because it's definitely something we can use to our advantage. I already have—'

'Wait a minute. I am not using my . . . situation with Marco as some sort of image thing.' Charlie couldn't bring herself to use the word 'relationship' to describe whatever it was she and Marco had between them.

'Of course we understand that's not why you're involved with him,' Meredith crooned soothingly. 'But we'd be remiss if we didn't honestly acknowledge that this particular preexisting relationship could have a great deal of value to all of us.'

'It's not a relationship,' Charlie said, despite herself. 'It's actually not something I want to talk about.'

Meredith nodded knowingly, her red curls bouncing in agreement. 'Understood. For now, let's all agree to keep this between us. You can trust me, Charlie. We'll just see what happens. Perhaps things will develop naturally between you two, and you'll be ready to raise the profile on this a bit more. We can take it a day at a time.'

Todd took a big swallow of martini and licked his lips. 'Can you even imagine the optics on that one?' he asked as if Charlie weren't sitting right there. 'I mean, these two young hardbod— er, athletes, both of them hot stuff on and off the court? My god, it would be a media shitstorm. The good kind. Even when I coached Adrian and he dated that supermodel – this would eclipse that.'

Charlie looked to Meredith in a panic. 'I already said it: bringing Marco into this is out of the question. It's not like he's my boyfriend, or that we even really have a . . . It's more like an understanding, and even that's not totally spelled out.' She knew she was rambling – and more so, that she didn't owe them any explanations about her love life – but she couldn't stop. 'It could be over tomorrow for all I know. I don't even know what "it" really is, so there's no way I'm going to—'

'Charlie. I'm reading you loud and clear. Marco is off-limits. Whatever you have is your business. We'll respect that. For now.'

'Thank you,' Charlie said, hating that her embarrassment

147

was spelled out for everyone to see in the warmth of her cheeks. She took a small bite of salad and a sip of her Pellegrino as she tried not to think about what the 'for now' really meant.

8

hitting like a girl

'Welcome back,' a girl in a UCLA sweatshirt called to Charlie as she, Dan, and Todd made their way through the crowds gathered to watch the match.

'Thanks for coming home!' came another voice.

Charlie smiled and waved to the students. She was only a handful of years older than most of them, so why did she feel like she could be someone's mother?

UCLA had heavily promoted the charity exhibition match as promised – all the viewing stands were packed with a crowd ten-deep behind them. Charlie did a quick calculation and was thrilled with the amount of money

149

they would be raising for metastatic breast cancer, the kind that had killed her mother swiftly and ruthlessly.

At charity matches, coaches were allowed on court, so Todd escorted Charlie. As demanding as Todd was, Charlie felt some comfort having him there. It was one of the most challenging aspects of the sport: the solitude. No matter what was happening on that court, Charlie dealt with it alone. During a match, Charlie had only two things to depend on: the condition of her body and the toughness of her mind. Off the court wasn't much different, since the girls were so competitive. She had Piper and Jake and her father – but confidants were otherwise rare. After so many years of training combined with the insane travel schedule, the prevailing attitude was that no one was looking for friends. The girls from smaller, non-English-speaking countries might stick together a bit more out of necessity, but everyone else mostly went it alone. It was the only thing Charlie didn't love about her sport, but she knew she was still better off than athletes from other sports whose coaches gave them three minutes to prove themselves before directing them back to the bench.

'Charlie? Charlie Silver?' a woman's voice called from behind her. Charlie turned around and scanned the faces through the fence, but she didn't recognize anyone. The voice sounded timid, like the woman didn't want to interfere, but also oddly familiar.

'Charlie? Over here.'

It took Charlie a few seconds to locate the source, but when she finally saw the woman who was waving at her, Charlie almost dropped her racket.

'Eileen?' she asked, more to herself than to her mother's long-lost best friend.

'It's me!' The woman laughed, her nose scrunching up. 'Not that you can probably tell with all this gray hair.'

It was true, the neat gray bob instead of the dirty-blond ponytail had initially thrown Charlie off, but now that she was looking, Eileen had otherwise barely aged.

'I can't believe it,' Charlie said, walking toward the fence. 'It must be, what, twelve years since we've seen each other?'

Charlie hadn't meant it as a criticism, but Eileen visibly recoiled. 'I'm sorry,' she near-whispered, not even noticing all the students who were listening.

'No, I didn't mean . . . just that it's been a long time since . . . we saw each other. That's all.'

Eileen leaned in, grabbed Charlie's hand. 'It was wrong of me to leave you and Jake and your father like that. I was just so . . . overwhelmed. And I was having problems with my – Well, anyway, you don't want to hear all this now.' She dropped back again. 'I work as an executive assistant to the dean of admissions, and, well, I heard you were on campus today, so I thought I'd pop by and say hello . . .'

'Silver!' Todd's voice hit her like a shovel. 'Enough gossiping. Get your ass over here!'

On the court, Dan was doing hamstring stretches while Todd paced back and forth. She held up her pointer finger.

'Go, I don't want to interrupt. I just – I just wanted to say hello. And congratulate you on your tremendous accomplishments. Your mother would—' Eileen stopped herself, as though remembering that she didn't really have the right to invoke Charlie's mother when she'd dropped out of all their lives so soon after her death. 'Anyway, good luck today.'

'Silver! Right now!'

Charlie pressed her hand to the fence and did her best to smile at Eileen. 'Sorry, I have to run.'

'No, of course. Go. I have to get back to work, but it was, um, it was *so* good to see you, Charlie. It really was.'

Charlie turned around to wave once more on her jog back to the baseline, but Eileen had already vanished into the crowd. Charlie pulled a ball from under her skirt, dropped it, and smacked it to Dan's forehand. She felt a little ridiculous for bringing her hitting partner to a college charity match, but Todd had insisted the day not interfere with her competition schedule. Which meant there would be a full-length, official practice following the exhibition match. She tried not to think about how sore her body would be after four straight hours of tennis and instead focused on loosening her muscles and warming up her limbs. The crowd oohed and aahed appreciatively as Charlie slammed overheads (Dan kindly lobbed her easy ones) and lunged for layup volleys. Afterward, as she sipped water on the sidelines, her opponent walked onto the court.

Charlie got up to introduce herself to the girl, a petite phenom from China who was UCLA's current number one, but Todd clamped his hand around her wrist. 'Wait for her to come to you,' he said under his breath.

'Seriously?' Charlie asked, watching the girl wave to her friends. 'She's a kid.'

'She's an opponent and you need to practice treating

her like one,' he growled. 'Are you a fucking debutante or an athlete?'

'I really can't be hard-hitting and friendly?' Charlie asked. 'I'm obviously going to kill her. I'd like to at least be gracious about it.'

Dan stood off to the side, shaking his head. As a man, was he incapable of understanding why Charlie wanted to put the girl at ease? Or did he agree with Charlie that Todd was going overboard?

'Hi, I'm Yuan. Thanks so much for coming today. My aunt has breast cancer, so I'm especially honored to play for your same cause. It means a lot to me that you accepted my invitation.' Yuan smiled widely at Charlie, who couldn't help but smile back.

'It's my pleasure,' she said, meaning every word. 'My mother died from breast cancer when I was eleven, so I understand where you're coming from. I'm glad you asked me.' Charlie could feel Todd glaring at her, but she ignored him.

Every year the number one singles player at UCLA could choose a charity for the Celebrity Exhibition and invite a celebrity opponent. Because it was LA, most of the players chose actors or musicians, which didn't make for particularly great tennis, but who wouldn't want to see Bradley Cooper running all over the court in shorts and no shirt, sweaty and grinning and playing to the crowd? Last year she'd read Reese Witherspoon had been invited to play. The first year Charlie had gotten to choose the celeb, she didn't hesitate for a second: Martina Navratilova graciously accepted and, even though she was thirty-five years Charlie's senior, managed to take a set off her before Charlie beat her in the next two. It had been the most thrilling match of her entire life, playing against a living legend. Charlie was light-years from Navratilova in terms of record and experience, but she hoped Yuan felt a tiny bit the same way.

'Don't give her more than a game in either set,' Todd whispered in her ear as Charlie adjusted her headband.

'I'm not "giving" her any games,' Charlie said.

'Double bagels is humiliating.'

'Not as humiliating as knowing someone's handing you a game.' She was almost relieved when Yuan played nearly perfect tennis and took a game off Charlie in the first set and two from her in the second. The girl was petite, but she was mighty. And the students went crazy cheering for both of them.

'That was awesome, thank you,' Yuan said as they shook hands.

'You hit beautifully,' Charlie said. 'You ever think of joining us?'

Yuan looked taken aback. 'Turning pro? Me? No way.'

'You're definitely good enough,' Charlie said, collapsing into the courtside chair beside the net. 'Better than I was when I played here.'

'Thanks, that's nice to hear. But I want my degree. I want to study medicine and go home to China one day to practice. Tennis is great, and I love it, but it's a means to an end.'

'I hear you,' Charlie said, suddenly feeling awkward. She never felt her college dropout status more acutely than when someone else pointedly and confidently made the choice to finish her degree.

Todd came over to the girls and clapped Yuan on the shoulder. 'Good match. You probably could have gotten another game off Charlie if you'd taken a few more risks, especially with your serve, which isn't half bad. When you're playing someone so much better, it's not enough just to keep the ball in play.' He turned to Charlie. 'You, on the other hand, were lazy!' he all but shouted. 'You were dragging ass on the baseline, and we're going to fix that right now. Meet me on Court Six in ten minutes for practice. I sent Dan to pick up some protein, but no dinner until we're finished.'

The girls watched as he picked up Charlie's racket bag and walked off the court.

'And that is why I don't play professionally,' Yuan laughed.

'Oh, you get used to it. Without hours of classes a day, there's plenty of time for practice. It's not so bad,' Charlie said, although she knew that wasn't at all what Yuan meant.

'Anyway, thanks again. And good luck the rest of the season. I'll totally be cheering for you!' Yuan gave Charlie a hug and bounded off the court, no doubt headed for a hot shower and then probably a night spent with friends, either at a movie or studying, maybe even a college bar. Charlie watched her wistfully.

Dan was waiting for her on Court Six with a prepacked box he'd picked up at Starbucks containing a hard-boiled egg, some apple slices, and a stale biscuit with a packet of peanut butter. She downed the box of chocolate milk first, not even bothering to use the straw, and then devoured everything else.

'Thanks,' she said. 'That was lifesaving.'

'Anytime. I was going to get you a latte, but Todd would have put a bullet in my head.'

Charlie did a snort laugh. 'Yeah, probably not worth the murder risk. But thanks for thinking of it.'

'You looked great out there,' Dan said, motioning toward the first court. 'I mean, uh, your game looked really solid, and I think you're making a lot of progress with—'

Charlie's phone rang. The caller ID was a jumbled bunch of run-on numbers, which only meant it was someone – anyone – calling from abroad. Charlie gave Dan an apologetic look and answered the call.

'Charlotte?' The voice and accent were unmistakable, despite the fact that she had never before spoken to him on the phone. Was that possible? In nearly a year? Only texts and emails and Snapchats, but never a real, live, actual conversation?

'Marco?' she heard herself ask, although of course she knew who it was. Next to her, Dan recoiled. She knew she was being rude – she'd interrupted him, after all – but this was *Marco*. 'Where are you?'

'Hi, hi. I am calling from Rio. You are in California, yes?'

'Yes, I just finished an exhibition match in LA. I'll be here practicing until I head to Palm Springs . . .'

He remembered, didn't he? Where they'd first hooked up a year earlier after that bottle of champagne and the skinny-dipping? That chevron print rug in front of the fire? Breakfast together the next morning right in the restaurant because they were all alone and had nothing to hide? Charlie wondered what he would think of the fact that she now had an image consultant who was champing at the bit to tell the world they were sleeping together 'for the optics' of it.

'Yes, that is why I call. To let you know that I had to pull out of Indian Wells. I won't see you next week.'

To say Charlie was disappointed was an understatement – in her mind, she'd already set the stage for round two, and it looked a whole lot like their first meeting – but another part of her was delighted that he even thought to call her before she'd read the update on the daily news digest sent out by the ATP. Was it a high bar for a guy with whom you were having sex? Not exactly. Did she sort of hate herself for being *grateful* that the man she was sleeping with had picked up the phone for the first time in a year? Yes. But she reminded herself that this was what casual looked like.

'Is it the shoulder?'

'*Sí*, it is strained. Nothing so serious, but the physios are advising two weeks of rest so I do not do more damage.'

'Ugh, I'm sorry. Are you staying in Rio?'

'No, I am going back to Madrid tonight to stay with my parents. But I wanted to make sure I will see you in Miami?'

'Miami? Yes, of course. Miami.' She glanced at Dan, who was clearly trying to listen without appearing like he was listening.

'Charlotte? I am sending you kisses. I must go now, but I wanted to tell you that I miss you.'

Charlie gripped the phone so hard it almost slipped from her hand. 'I mi—' She remembered Dan at the very last second. 'Same here,' she said. 'Keep in touch.'

She was still staring at the phone in disbelief when Dan said, 'It's okay, Charlie. I'm not going to tell anyone.'

157

'Tell anyone what?' she snapped. 'There's nothing to tell.'

Dan shrugged. 'Whatever you say. In case you haven't noticed, I do travel with you pretty much every day of every week. I've known for a long time. So has Todd. We're not blind. But it's none of my business. I just wanted to reassure you that I haven't – and would never – breathe a word to anyone else.'

'You're right, it's none of your business. Whatever you think you know, you don't.'

Dan held his hands up. 'Loud and clear.'

They both watched as Todd walked toward them, phone pressed to his ear, looking extremely displeased.

'Move, people!' he shouted, and it took a beat for Dan and Charlie to realize he was yelling at them.

The practice that followed was brutal. Charlie could barely concentrate: the combination of the fatigue from the match she'd just played, the call from Marco, and the ensuing weirdness with Dan resulted in Charlie's making Todd even more furious than usual.

'Where the hell are you?' he screamed. 'You look like you're here, but you're not mentally present. Where is your concentration right now? What are you thinking about, getting your nails done? A little shopping? Maybe a facial? Buy yourself something pretty? I, CHARLOTTE SILVER, NEED YOU TO FUCKING FOCUS!'

Charlie could feel her face redden. She tried not to notice the gathering crowd around her court, all of whom could hear every word Todd yelled.

Dan drilled her backhand. For just a moment, Charlie thought she felt a small twinge in her left wrist.

'Low to high!' Todd barked.

It went on like that for two hours: Dan slamming shots at her; Todd screaming like a deranged lunatic; Charlie trying desperately to move her feet, turn her shoulders, hit low to high, follow through, switch her grip, get light on her feet, keep her eye on the ball. Charlie was bouncing on her toes at the net, trying to volley even more aggressively than she normally did. She wasn't allowed a break until she'd successfully returned ten in a row. After a half hour, her record was six. Dan smashed another one straight down the line, and Charlie didn't even get her racket on it.

'Where the *fuck* is your head?' Todd yelled from the sidelines. 'Are you blind? Drunk? Or just lazy?'

Charlie knew enough not to answer him, instead lunging for the next three and actually managing to hit a winner on the fourth. 'Does that count?' she asked, staggering over to the sideline for water.

'Get back out there,' Todd growled, snatching away her water bottle before she could reach for it. 'You haven't earned your break yet.'

Charlie nodded and sprinted back to the baseline. She wanted to kill Todd, but she knew this was how he operated. Charlie had known it going in: Todd liked to break his players down and rebuild them into winners. Champions. So, despite being exhausted and thirsty and feeling like she wanted to sit right down on that hot court and cry, she got back up on her toes. She bounced and moved and dived, circled back for overheads to smash crosscourt and hurried back to pick up drop shots. By some miracle she returned nine net shots in a row, and finally – finally! – she didn't psych herself out on a relatively easy backhand volley, putting it away with more finesse than power, a pretty shot that hit the perfect angle.

Todd nodded. That was as close to approval as he would ever get, but to Charlie it was as though he'd skywritten his congratulations.

'Pretty freaking great, huh?' she said, nudging him with the head of her racket. 'Admit it, you're impressed.'

'I'll be impressed when you win Indian Wells next week and Miami after that. Until then, I want you aggressive. You're still too tentative. You're hitting like a girl.'

'I *am* a girl,' Charlie said.

Todd glared at her.

'Natalya isn't remotely masculine, and she's ranked number one,' Charlie said, scrambling to follow Todd off the court. Dan followed behind them, carrying both his racket bag and Charlie's.

The crowd of students clapped for her when she walked off the court, a towel draped across her neck. Sweat rivulets ran down from her forehead.

'You know she's ranked, like, among the top women in the world, right?' one girl said to her friend, who appeared impressed.

'She's smokin',' Charlie heard a guy half whisper to someone, although she pretended she hadn't heard.

'If you're into man thighs,' his friend replied.

'Dude, she can hear you!'

'What? I'm not saying anything I'm sure she doesn't know. Great hair, great rack, but big legs. It happens.'

'Your friend's right,' Charlie said loudly to the second guy. He looked like he wasn't a day older than seventeen, with hairy arms and a skimpy goatee. 'I can hear you.'

'Ignore 'em, Charlie. You rock!' a voice called from somewhere in the crowd, which had parted for her to pass.

Charlie flashed a quick smile of thanks, but she had to run to keep up with Todd as they walked toward the locker rooms.

'Natalya is tough as nails and doesn't let anyone get away with anything. That's what I'm talking about,' Todd said as he led them past the crowd. They were alone now, just the three of them, but still Charlie noticed students staring at her as she walked past.

She lowered her voice. 'I work my ass off day and night. I haven't had a cookie or a burger or a goddamn drink in longer than I can remember. I'm on that court and in that gym longer than anyone you can possibly—'

Todd cut her off. 'I take no issue with your work ethic. It's decent. And your strokes are mostly there. They're not perfect, but you've got more god-given natural talent than anyone deserves, and that one-handed backhand of yours is a fucking blow-away. What you don't have – and what you very badly need if you have any hope of making the super-big leagues – is the mental focus. Not news, is it? I told you as much when we first met. I know you want it – I wouldn't have agreed to work for a girl if I didn't see at least that – but wanting it and fucking *going for it* are two different things. I need Cutthroat Charlie. Brutal Charlie. Step-on-Your-Own-Mother-to-Get-Ahead Charlie. It's my job to get her here. It's your job to use her – and win with her – once I've created her. Think you can do that?'

The 'working for a girl' comment aside, it was the most complimentary Todd had ever been. Charlie tried not to smile. 'Yes,' she said. 'I know I can.'

'Good. Get some dinner and a solid nine hours. Tonight I'm leaving you coverage of a match between Ivanov and Azarenka from a couple of years ago. I want you to pay particular attention to the way the two women interact as they're preparing to play, switching sides, et cetera. It's clear as day they want to fucking kill each other, and I think it's damn good inspiration. I'll see you at the gym tomorrow at seven-thirty sharp.' He walked off without saying good-bye to either Dan or Charlie.

'Hey, you want to grab some food? I was reading about a great ramen spot right off campus, and I promise not to tell Todd . . .'

It sounded appealing – the restaurant, the food, Dan's easy company – but she couldn't make herself say yes. She had that strange jittery feeling she got after losing a match or downing a double espresso, uncomfortably amped up and exhausted at the same time.

'Or I can certainly be persuaded to hit up the In-N-Out in Westwood. I mean, that's never a bad option either.'

Charlie looked him in the eye. 'Actually, I think I'm going to take a rain check tonight. Just eat in my room and get to sleep early. I want to make sure I'm not coming down with anything . . .'

'Sure, yeah, no problem,' Dan said quickly.

'Sorry, I just . . . I just need to—'

'It's totally fine. Have a good night, okay?' He immediately turned to walk away before remembering he was carrying her racket bag. 'Oh, here. Do you want me to drop this by your hotel? I don't mind.'

'No, not at all. But thanks.' The awkwardness was palpable.

Charlie waved as Dan trotted off, feeling both guilty and relieved. She was about to head into the locker room before remembering that she was free and clear and would be so much happier soaking in a long bath in her luxurious hotel room. It was a little over three miles from the campus to her hotel, and although Charlie had planned to walk across Wilshire Boulevard and maybe take a quick detour to window-shop Rodeo Drive, she made a game-time decision to jump in an Uber. At the hotel, she walked into the restaurant to request that a salad be brought up to her room and promptly ran smack into Brian, her ex-boyfriend from freshman year.

'Charlie Silver,' he said. It wasn't a question or a statement so much as a declaration.

He was not wearing hiking boots or a fleece vest or those army-green cargo pants that zipped off to become shorts. No sexy two-day stubble. No longish hair. He didn't even really smell the same: Charlie couldn't detect a hint of sweet smoky pine, as though he had just returned from fighting a forest fire. Instead, this grown man wore a suit. And not just any suit, but one that was tailored enough to hold its own on the streets of Paris or Barcelona. He was clean-shaven and fit, and although there wasn't so much as a crinkle around his green eyes, he looked older, more mature.

'Brian.' She wasn't at all surprised to see him, nor was his new clean-cut appearance any sort of shock. He never updated his Facebook account, from what she could tell – obviously she checked every now and then – but he regularly posted pictures on Instagram, which of course she followed. He and Piper also kept in touch, so Charlie already knew he returned to LA often to recruit on campus, that he was currently living in Chicago, and that his girlfriend, who looked like Jenna Bush's doppelgänger, had recently moved into his apartment. And despite her knowing all this, tonight was the first time she'd seen him since the summer after her freshman year.

Brian grinned. 'What are you doing here? Doesn't your dad still live in Topanga?'

Charlie could feel her cheeks redden. Naturally she felt guilty for staying at a hotel instead of at her father's. Leave it to Brian to home in on that in half a second. 'Oh, you know, I played an exhibition match tonight, and the school offered to cover my room so I wouldn't have to drive back late . . . I was just on my way to shower . . .' She remembered only then that she was still wearing her soaking wet practice clothes and took a step back in case she smelled. God forbid she ever ran into an ex wearing actual clothes – no, she had to be clad in head-to-toe sweat-wicking fabrics with her greasy hair tied off into a messy bun. A red and bumpy chin from some sort of adult-onset acne. And probably bad breath.

'Well, you look great,' Brian said automatically, because he couldn't possibly mean it.

'I look like Courtney Love on a bender. Maybe worse,' Charlie said.

Brian laughed. 'Listen, do you have time for a quick drink or a coffee or something?' He glanced at his watch. 'I have a work dinner at nine, but I'm free until then.'

She froze for a second. The last thing Charlie wanted to do was make small talk or, worse, hear about Brian's new girlfriend. The bath in her room was calling to her, as was dinner under the covers with HGTV for company.

Brian must have seen her hesitation. 'Come on, fifteen minutes. For old times' sake.'

She couldn't think of an excuse fast enough – she clearly wasn't headed anywhere the way she was dressed – and it had been forever since they'd seen each other.

Charlie nodded. 'I can do fifteen minutes, but then I really have to get upstairs. Should we sit here?'

The waiter came to their table. Charlie ordered a club soda with lime, and Brian sheepishly asked for the spiked pink lemonade. 'With an umbrella, if you can,' Charlie added. 'He really likes those.'

It wasn't nearly as awkward as it should have been, this acknowledgment of an old inside joke. But it was quickly followed by an acutely uncomfortable silence.

'So . . .' they both said, and laughed.

'So . . . congratulations on everything. Seriously, Charlie, what you've done is incredible. What are you now? Top twenty? Higher? It's really terrific.'

Charlie tried not to look too pleased.

'Oh, thanks. It feels good to break into the top twenty, definitely. I was injured at Wimbledon last year, and it's been a long road back. I hired a new coach, and he has me on a whole new program, so things are hopefully headed in the right direction.'

'Eversoll and Nadal's old coach, right? Aren't you the first woman he's ever worked with? Very impressive.'

So he was following her career. Interesting.

'How are you feeling?' Brian asked. He quickly added, 'The injury, I mean. Are you all better?'

'Yes, I think so. Physically it's all rehabbed and everything checks out. Mentally it's harder. I don't want to hesitate ever to lunge or slide or turn at a sharp angle, so it's learning to trust that it really is as good as new. The wrist is completely, totally better, but the foot still haunts me sometimes. Just in my head.' She cleared her throat and was about to ask Brian what kind of job brought him back to LA, but he leaned forward in that active-listening way he'd always been so good at and asked, 'What's it really like being on tour? Is it as glamorous as it seems to us mortals?'

She'd been asked this same question no fewer than a thousand times by a thousand different people, and she always gave similar, canned responses: *It's tough but I love it; work hard, play hard; the travel gets taxing but getting to play a sport I love every day makes it all worthwhile.* But something about the way Brian furrowed his brow in concentration and peered at her, obviously waiting for a real answer, made her pause.

'It can be hard,' she said quietly. 'It's a different hotel every week. No place feels like home. I don't really have a normal life, you know? Probably the hardest part is being away from . . . people I care about. I don't see my dad as often as I'd like, and it's not easy to keep in touch with friends. It can definitely be . . . well, thank god Jake travels with me a lot of the time now.'

Brian nodded. 'I bet it takes a toll.'

'I'm not complaining, I hope it doesn't sound that way. It's just tough sometimes to stay close to people because I'm not at all in charge of my own schedule. I could be at a tournament for two weeks if I'm winning or knocked out the first day – everything is last-minute and it makes it just impossible to plan anything in advance. But it's all good right now. I'm starting to feel like it's all coming together.'

The waiter brought their drinks. Brian held his up and said, 'To reunions. It's good to see you, Charlie.'

Charlie clinked his glass with her own. 'You too!' she said, a bit more cheerily than she'd intended. 'I've been blathering on and on, and you still haven't told me anything. You're in Chicago now, right?'

'Yeah, I moved there a couple of years ago. Winters aren't so easy after LA, but I'm adjusting.'

'Did you move there for work?'

'Yep. I work for an environmental consulting group. We help companies go more green, and I'm actually in LA to do the first-round interviews of graduating seniors. We hire a handful of new grads every year. UCLA has such a great program that the company likes hiring here.'

'Corporate America, Brian! The green version, yes, but still. Your pot-smoking, Phish-following, nineteen-year-old self would never have believed it.'

He laughed. 'I'd be lying if I said the occasional joint didn't get smoked, but not all that often anymore. My girlfriend doesn't like it. Phish either. We mostly listen to tortured singer-songwriters and alt-country. We are walking cliches.'

'It happens,' Charlie said with a shrug. 'So tell me about her. What's her name?'

Brian lifted his gaze to check and make sure Charlie wasn't being snarky or weird. Satisfied, he started right in, and as soon as he did, Charlie wished he would stop.

Almost instantly, Charlie tuned out as Brian described

Finley, and how totally coincidental their meeting was, and how they hit it off almost instantly. The more animated Brian grew, the fewer words Charlie processed: registered nurse, stuck in an elevator, Santa Fe, big dog (small dog?) named something irritatingly cute, five brothers and sisters, marathons. It wasn't tremendously nuanced, but it was far more than Charlie needed to create the image in her mind of a sporty Finley (*Finley*?) with her cute blond bob, keeping her cool while stuck in an elevator after coming home from a run with her Bernese mountain dog (dachshund?) to a brunch filled with look-alike siblings who all brought homemade oatmeal and French toast and other high-carb foods that Finley could eat ad infinitum and never gain weight. Oh, and she was a porn star in bed, but the private kind, of course, the girl who loved and craved sex constantly with her committed man but no one else, because he was the only one who'd ever made her feel comfortable enough to access her secret inner sex goddess. It was all right there, tied up with a neat little ribbon, suddenly making Charlie despise this girl she didn't know.

'She sounds really great,' Charlie said with no inflection whatsoever. She wasn't jealous, exactly – more bored, and tired, and wanting to escape.

'Yeah, she is.'

'That's great,' Charlie murmured.

They finished their drinks. Charlie felt like she did an adequate if not spectacular job of feigning interest in the rest of their conversation, which was basically an information download on both their families. When Brian politely asked if she'd like anything else, it was all Charlie could do not to bolt straight to her room without another word.

Their good-bye hug was stilted, the kind where each person subtly pushes the other while half embracing, and it was only once the elevator doors shut, cocooning Charlie in a blissful embrace of silence, that she finally exhaled. Her anxiety returned for a brief minute when she found a plastic bag containing two DVDs hanging from her door-knob – Todd's promised tape of some hyperaggressive Ivanov–Azarenka match she needed to memorize – but she tossed it aside and turned on the bath.

Ex-boyfriends are better on Instagram than in real life, she thought as she stripped down and lowered herself into the steaming hot tub.

Her phone pinged.

Great seeing you tonite.

He couldn't possibly mean that, could he? Not with all the weird silences and oversharing and awkward hugs. Not to mention the inimitable Finley warming his bed and brightening his life.

You too! she pecked out.

Another ping. She reached back to the bathroom vanity to silence her phone, but it wasn't Brian this time.

Hey gorgeous! What day r u going to miami? Want to make sure I am there waiting 4 u . . .

Grinning like an idiot, Charlie forced herself to power down the phone without responding. She could almost hear Todd telling her to act like a winner, not a beaten-down puppy dog. Fine, then. She would let Marco wonder what she was up to and get back to him in the morning. Juvenile? Yes. Effective? Undoubtedly.

She sunk into the bath, the hot water washing over her shoulders, and envisioned her reunion with Marco. He may not have responded to her late-night invitation in Australia, but he had forwarded her that funny viral *Saturday Night Live* video just last week, hadn't he? And when she'd replied to tell him that she thought it was hysterical, he'd written back *xoxo*. Clearly, this wasn't the stuff of Shakespeare, but at least he'd been thinking about her, too. Maybe he'd even had a similar epiphany: they had a great time together, the sex was undeniably fantastic, they understood each other's time commitments and limitations, and they had tennis in common. Other famous people dated each other all the time – just look at Natalya and Benjy. So long as they were disciplined enough to stay focused and keep their priorities straight – which she absolutely knew they both were – then why shouldn't they have a relationship?

Brian who? She closed her eyes and inhaled the scent of the lavender travel candle she'd lit and placed beside the tub. *He's all yours, Finley darling. All yours.*

9

the warrior princess does not wear flats

MIAMI, MARCH 2016

When Charlie walked through the connecting door to her room at the Four Seasons Miami, she was surprised to see a fully dressed and alert-looking Jake sitting on her bed. Unless important business called, he tried never to get up before eight. Or even better, nine.

'Is everything okay?' she asked, her mind flashing to her father. 'Is it Dad?'

'He's fine. Everyone's fine. You want to tell me where you were at six in the morning? It doesn't look like the gym, I'll tell you that much.'

Charlie glanced down: she was wearing admittedly minuscule boy shorts adorned with tiny embroidered roses, one of those drapey yoga sweatshirts that fell sexily off her shoulders and dipped down in the back to the top of her butt, and a pair of Ugg scuff slippers. Anyone with eyes could easily see she was wearing neither underwear nor bra. In three strides she walked to the bathroom and grabbed the robe that hung behind the door. Cinching it around her waist, she said, 'It's none of your business! Why don't you tell me why you sneaked into my room in the middle of the night?'

'You missed your drug test,' Jake said, raking his hand through his hair. 'They waited for twenty minutes even though they're not obligated to, and then they left. They called my office to declare it, and my office called me.'

'Shit.' Charlie slumped into the desk chair.

'It's only a warning this time, Charlie. But next time you're automatically suspended, regardless of the outcome.'

'I don't believe this! What are the chances they'd choose today?'

'The chances? I'd say they were pretty damn high. We're in Miami! You think the testers would rather show up at six a.m. in Qatar or Florida? I mean, seriously, Charlie.'

She smacked her own thigh. *Stupid!* In her excitement at jumping into Marco's bed, she'd forgotten all about the one-hour window she'd provided for the doping officials to test her.

'Enough of the sneaking around. I've known forever now you've been sleeping with someone. Why won't you just tell me who it is? A player? Coach? Not that hitting partner of yours, is it? He *is* cute.'

'Dan? He's a baby.'

'He's two years younger than you. That hardly qualifies as scandalous. It's barely even interesting. Are you telling me you haven't even noticed that he has a crazy six-pack? That detail just eluded you?'

Actually, it hadn't eluded her. Dan was a bit thinner than she may have liked, and an inch shorter than her, but the abs made up for it. And who wouldn't notice the great teeth and nice, easy smile?

'Dan is very good-looking, yes,' Charlie said. 'But we've barely spoken in the few months we've been working together. He slams balls at me, says "Yes, sir" to Todd, and then beelines off the court the second practice is finished. I'm sure he's a perfectly nice person, but I am not sleeping with Dan.'

Jake gave an exasperated sigh. 'But we all know you're sleeping with someone. Who is it? Leon? Paolo? Victor? It's Victor, isn't it? I heard he just broke up with his girl-friend. He reminds me of Brian. The whole hippie-dippie thing.'

Charlie grinned. She was enjoying this. 'I'll have you know, Brian went from hippie-dippie to total prep practi-cally overnight. And you really think Victor's my type? I should be insulted. Especially since I just so happen to be having a very fun fling with Marco.'

She waited, almost holding her breath, excited for Jake's reaction.

He stared at her.

'Marco? Marco who?'

'How many freaking Marcos do you know, Jake? Think about it.'

'Marco Acosta? Isn't he Leon's massage therapist? Or does he work for Raj now? I can't remember.'

'Jake!' She punched his arm.

He furrowed his brow. 'There's Roger's business manager, but I thought he went by Marcello. I see him at tournaments sometimes. Isn't he married?'

'I could kill you.'

'Just tell me.'

'I shouldn't have to. This is ridiculous.'

'What's ridiculous is that you're sleeping with Roger's married business manager and he's, what? Twenty years older? More?'

'Marco Vallejo, you jerk.'

Jake's lower jaw dropped open.

'Marco *Vallejo*?' he whispered.

'The one and only. What, is it really so hard to believe he'd sleep with me?'

'Yes!'

'Thanks. You really know how to make a girl feel good.'

'I can't believe it. You're having an affair with *Marco Vallejo*?'

'Okay, this is getting insulting. Or is this where you tell me you're sleeping with him, too? Haven't you always kind of figured that was going to happen? One of these days we'd fall for the same guy . . .'

He finally closed his mouth. 'I'd sleep with him in a second. Who wouldn't? But no, I'm sorry to report I'm not . . .'

'Well, I am! Just did, in fact.' Charlie smiled devilishly.

'Oh my god. He's spectacular. He's been the one all along? The one you've been sneaking around with, thinking none of us noticed? How could you *not tell me*?'

'The first time was last year, after Indian Wells. But it—'

'Last *year*?'

'Do you remember when I took that night alone in Palm Springs? He was there, too, and, well . . . anyway. Then we saw each other here and there . . . and then again in Australia. It's all been very casual. You know what the schedule is like, and now it's times two. But it's certainly not anything official.'

'Sounds to me like it's something.'

'Yes, well, it's . . . open. Casual.'

'So you've said. Like, fifteen times now. And you're fine with that? I'm finding all this hard to believe.'

Charlie considered this. 'I wouldn't say it's my absolute first choice, sneaking in and out of each other's hotel rooms like we're cheating on our spouses. But it's okay for now. And things actually seem to be picking up a little. Don't get me wrong, I don't think we're racing to the altar, but he's starting to act like he likes me marginally more than all the other girls he may or may not also be sleeping with.'

'That's really beautiful.'

'Don't judge, Jake! You can see firsthand that normal relationships are practically impossible for me. What's *your* excuse, by the way? Seriously, so long as we're talking about this, why are you the only celibate gay guy I've ever met?'

'Charlie . . .' His voice was low, warning.

'No, really. How long ago was it that you brought home Jack? Two years? And what's been going on in your love life since then? A whole lot of nothing. Unless you're some sort of secret MVP on Grindr and I don't know about it, it seems to me like you shouldn't be the one talking. For someone who professes to want *children* one day, you've got a lot of work to do in the romance department.'

Jake held up a hand. 'Two totally different things. I do meet guys. I just don't feel the need to tell you about every failed first date I've ever had. Yes, I'm looking for a committed relationship, and it turns out that's about as easy to find in the twentysomething gay world as it is for professional female tennis players. But we're getting off topic here. Who else knows?'

Charlie thought about this. 'I don't think he's told anyone, and I sure haven't. Except for Piper. And Todd, although that wasn't my choice. Oh, and Dan, too. And now you.'

'You told *Todd* and not me?'

'Oh, grow up, Jake.' Charlie cinched her robe tighter, enjoying this more than she thought she would. 'Marco did actually ask me if I wanted to go to the player party together tonight. So that's interesting.'

Jake collapsed into the desk chair as though an actual bullet had entered his body. 'You're lying.'

'I am not. He just asked right now. As I was leaving.'

'And what did he say, exactly?'

'"Charlie, would you like to go to the player party with me tonight?" It was pretty straightforward.'

'Oh my god. Are you ready for this?'

'Ready for what? I didn't say yes yet. I told him I'd text him when I knew my plans.'

'Wow. I'm surprised. You're better than I thought.'

Charlie smiled. 'Thanks. I admit I thought it was ludicrous to play manipulation games when Piper suggested it, but this whole hard-to-get act seems to work. He totally wants me more.'

'Piper is the queen. Was. But you were just telling me how casual and "open" this whole arrangement is.'

'True. But I think by asking me to tonight's party, he may want to go public. And you're the first person I've been able to tell.'

'I'm in shock.'

'I know. And I'm trying not to be offended. Anyway, I think going public could be a good thing. Obviously Marco and I have a lot in common, not the least of which is our schedule. Maybe this thing with him can be different.'

Jake sighed. 'He *is* different, C. He's about a trillion times more high-profile than anyone you've ever dated. Yes, he seems like an okay guy. Certainly not the relationship type, but I'll defer to you on that one. I just hope you know what you're getting yourself into.'

'Even you have to admit it's perfect timing.'

Finally, Jake cracked the smallest hint of a smile. 'For the rollout? Yeah, it would be pretty great. We're all prepped and ready to start here, in Miami. Todd can give a few pre-interviews to get the press warmed up, and I'm in talks with *Vogue*. It *is* actually ideal timing.'

There was a knock at the hotel door.

Jake glanced at Charlie. 'Your friend come back for round two? Or would that be three?'

'Don't be *vile*.' Charlie smiled, walking nervously toward the door. Two waitresses pushing a table-sized cart greeted her by name and, in synchronization so perfect it looked rehearsed, poured two cups of coffee, then two cups of ice water, and removed the silver platter covers with a flourish. They vanished nearly as quickly as they had arrived.

'He's nothing if not efficient,' Charlie murmured, spearing a slice of cantaloupe from the fruit plate.

'Todd did this? How did he know I'd be here?' Jake asked, eyeing the second egg white omelet with mushroom and spinach.

'He didn't. He was hoping you'd be Marco.'

With this, Jake looked like he might pass out. 'He arranges breakfast for both of you?'

Charlie nodded. 'He makes sure we have adjoining rooms. Trust me, no one will be happier to hear that I'm going to the party with Marco than Todd.' She took a bite of omelet. 'What am I going to wear?'

'That's been all worked out. The stylist Meredith hired can't get here until tomorrow, but she sent ahead some great options for you to try. I can tell already the Thakoon dress is the one. You're going to have to start wearing heels. Nothing too crazy, no stilettos – I get it, I really do – but at least two, three inches.'

'Not happening,' Charlie said, sipping her coffee.

'Happening. The Warrior Princess does not wear *flats*.'

'Wait, can we get back to *Vogue* for a minute?' Charlie interrupted.

'You're American and hot and starting to win. They want an interview.'

'Why now? I was winning before Wimbledon, and no one seemed to care that much. Not like they care about Natalya.' Charlie sipped her black decaf coffee and wondered if she could call down for an order of pancakes.

'Natalya is a Russian and gorgeous and ranked number

one. She can work a red carpet better than Angelina Jolie. She exclusively dates celebrities. She's a controversial bitch. And she has one hell of a team working every detail for her. She's an inspiration, Charlie. But Todd and I think you can do even better.'

'I refuse to be a controversial bitch. You know that. I just don't think it's—'

Jake held up a hand. 'I know. Kisses and sunshine. No one's asking you to be as nasty as she is, but you should be seen as stronger. Tougher. What we've all been talking about.'

'So you agree with Meredith's whole image rollout?'

'I do. I think it's very well conceived. You stay true to yourself as a decent person, but you present as a fighter. A warrior. You just fought back from a devastating injury, a spectacle on Wimbledon Centre Court, and we think the public is going to eat it up. The Warrior Princess is who they want.'

Charlie felt something stirring inside, a frisson of excitement. Or terror. She couldn't be sure, but she needed a moment. 'I'm kicking you out now. The car is picking me up in thirty minutes and I need a shower.'

'I'll see you at the site later this afternoon. We good?'

Charlie headed toward the bathroom. 'All good,' she called behind her as she did a little skip. She felt no uneasiness, even after the drug test debacle. She was too excited by the idea of the Warrior Princess arriving at the player party on the arm of the hottest male player on tour. She liked the sound of that.

10

red carpet make-out

MIAMI BEACH, MARCH 2016

'Charlie! Over here, look here!'

'Marco, turn this way! Smile!'

'Charlie, who are you wearing? Charlie, over here!'

Charlie heard the screams before they even stepped out of the tournament Escalade in front of South Beach's Zuma restaurant. Stepping onto the blue carpet that stretched from the street to the restaurant and was lined on both sides with paparazzi, Charlie was pleased to discover that she felt like a model walking the runway. Jake had been right: the black Thakoon dress, with its long sleeves, cold-shoulder cutouts, and sexily open back, was a winner.

Paired with the three-inch snakeskin sandals she'd grudgingly agreed to, Charlie's already long legs looked like half
their regular width and double their natural length. She
had agreed to forgo her usual time-saving ponytail for an
in-room blowout, and even Todd had nodded his approval
at the long, dark waves that tumbled down her back.

Marco grabbed her elbow and leaned in to whisper in
her ear, 'I was going to apologize for it being such a zoo,
but I think they're here for you.'

A hush fell over the jumble of photographers and
onlookers as each person came to the obvious conclusion:
his mouth was awfully close to her ear – *was it on it?* Was
there something going on? Were Marco Vallejo and Charlotte
Silver *dating*? A general titter spread among the crowd.

Suddenly, it occurred to Charlie that Meredith was right:
the crowd would go nuts if they knew she and Marco were
dating. Or hooking up. Or whatever they wanted to call
it. He initiated their arrival together, so it certainly wasn't
like he was trying to keep the whole thing under wraps
anymore . . . Maybe Meredith and Todd and Jake were
right. Maybe it was time. And before she could talk herself
out of it, Charlie turned to Marco, grabbed him around
the neck, and pressed her lips to his. She felt a momentary
stab of panic, and possible regret – had she seriously miscal-
culated? – but then Marco was kissing her right back.

The crowd went crazy.

'They're kissing! Do you see that?'

'Oh my god, did you know they're together? I didn't
know!'

'When did *that* happen?'

'They're making out! It's perfect – look at those two!'

And even: 'Can you imagine what their babies will look like?'

'Can you imagine how their babies will hit the ball? With genes like those?'

They pulled apart and smiled at each other. Charlie thought she could see a hint of respect in Marco's expression – perhaps a glimpse of approval of her boldness? Charlie inhaled deeply. It was a perfect March evening in Miami. Balmy air that carried the scent of tropical flowers and the ocean. The sky was streaked with shades of pink and orange as the sun set behind a row of swaying palm trees. The warmth of Marco's hand on her back felt wonderful. She looked all around, trying to savor the moment, but Isabel, a publicist from the Women's Tennis Association, swooped over to rescue them. 'Follow me, you two,' she said. Was that a smile Charlie detected? *Yes, it certainly was.* Isabel was clearly delighted.

The onlookers continued to catcall and cheer as Charlie and Marco, now holding hands, made their way through the tall double doors. Not that the gawking stopped then: nearly everyone assembled inside had made their way to the front of the room to check out the commotion.

'Hi,' Jake said, walking up to them. The grin on his face was unmistakable.

'Jake, you've met Marco Vallejo, right? Marco, this is my brother, Jake Silver.'

Marco's eyebrows crinkled adorably. 'Hello, Charlotte's brother.'

'Do you two know each other?' Charlie turned to look questioningly at Jake, but he was grinning like a lovestruck teenager.

'Good to see you, man,' Marco said.

'Charlie, you look gorgeous!' Isabel said. Gushed. Bubbly was a good quality in a publicist, and Charlie had always liked her the most of the whole team, but the girl was sounding downright manic. 'Who are you wearing? Dress and shoes and jewelry? I'll be getting calls all night asking . . .'

A few of the men's players had closed in on Marco and moved him toward the bar, where he was now standing in the middle of a circle of gigantic, beautiful men, already telling a funny story. When he caught Charlie looking at him, he rolled his eyes and flashed those ridiculous dimples. It was all she could do not to run to him.

'Charlie? The dress?'

'What? Oh, sorry. Yes, the dress is Thakoon, is that how you say it? And the shoes are Louboutin,' she said, trying not to mangle the pronunciation.

Isabel smiled.

'I know, I'm hopeless if it's not made out of Drymax,' Charlie said.

Jake looked her up and down. 'You look great, C. I'm glad you went with it.'

Isabel nodded furiously in agreement. 'I heard *Vogue* went well today. They are terrific, aren't they? Just so professional!'

'Yes, well, they definitely have the fashion thing down,' Charlie said. The photo shoot earlier that day had been a surprisingly fun time – great music, cool clothes, a handsome photographer, and an entire team of people doting all over her, doing her hair and makeup and choosing jewelry and accessories, all the time telling her how beautiful she looked. What wasn't to like? In addition to Charlie there had been a professional swimmer, golfer, and soccer player, and the spread was going to highlight how these female athletes (all attractive, all blond except for Charlie, and all with less than 10 percent body fat) looked great in their skirts/swimsuits/cleats but could shed them all for slithery bias-cut silk sheaths or beaded mermaid dresses or frothy princess gowns and look even better. The shoot had been more glamorous than most of the others Charlie had done, where she was typically posing in a tennis skirt, sneakers, sleeveless top, and wristband. Usually, the only variables were her hair (in a braid, a ponytail, or down) and whether she was holding her racket in some faux swinging motion or keeping it resting against her leg, right below her jauntily pressed-out thigh. She'd done local fashion magazines and *Sports Illustrated* and a cool spread in *GQ*, but this? A *Vogue* shoot meant zero spandex; heavy on the makeup and labels; super-skinny editors racing around in sky-high heels; clouds of cigarette smoke and bottles of champagne. It had felt way more like a fun afternoon at a fabulous friend's house than another grinding work obligation.

'So . . . I hate to pry – it's none of my business, of course – but inquiring minds will want to know . . .' Isabel was blushing. Poor thing. She actually *did* hate to pry, which was one of the reasons Charlie liked her the best. A non-prying publicist was the rarest breed of all.

'We planned to come together tonight, yes,' Charlie said.

Isabel tucked the front of her brunette bob behind one ear. 'I see. So, not to put too fine a point on it, but would

184

it be fair to say you two are . . . dating? Together? I'm just not sure what to tell people when they ask.'

Jake opened his mouth and Charlie could tell he was about to make some crack about yesterday's walk of shame. She shot him a death look and turned back to Isabel. 'You know? I don't think we've defined it yet. But it's probably fair to say we're seeing what happens.'

'Got it,' Isabel said, nodding furiously. Her phone buzzed and she looked down at the screen. 'Looks like word is already out.' The girl held the screen up for Charlie to read. The text was from Annette Smith-Kahn, the president of the WTA, and it read: *Silver/Vallejo? For real? Please say yes.*

They all laughed.

'She's upstairs right now entertaining some of the local South Florida VIPs,' Isabel said. 'And I can guarantee you, she's very, very happy about the two of you "seeing what happens."'

'I should probably go up and say hello,' Charlie said. 'Jake, come with me?'

The next two hours were happy chaos. Charlie made the rounds and chatted with a bunch of the WTA staff, players, the usual mix of Miami celebs (all the Housewives, Marc Anthony, Tiger Woods), and of course Marco. They were treated like royalty, the king and queen of the palace ball, and Charlie couldn't deny it was the most fun she'd had at a player party, ever. Miami was historically better than most, but typically the parties included overly healthy food, loud music, local tennis groupies, and the same rotating cast of characters. Attendance was mandatory, after all, but everyone wanted to depart for the hotel for a good night's sleep as quickly as possible. 'Tennis players may be hot, but they sure as hell aren't partiers,' Piper always said whenever Charlie dragged her to another player event. But tonight, despite her nerves for her early match the next morning and the slightly overwhelming amount of attention, Charlie was having a terrific time.

'I have asked for my car,' Marco said, leaning in close to her. 'Do you want to leave with me?' They were sitting next to each other on a banquette, sharing a plate of sashimi. Charlie was drinking her usual Pellegrino; Marco had enjoyed one beer when they first arrived and then promptly switched to club soda.

'Arriving and leaving together?' Charlie said flirtatiously. 'What will people think?'

'I do not care what they think,' he said gruffly, and Charlie could feel the flutter in her belly.

She ran through the calculations. It was already a few minutes after nine. By the time they said their good-byes and reverse-walked the red carpet and made their way back to the hotel, it would be ten o'clock. Even a quick visit to Marco's room would take a minimum of an hour, and she knew she'd need some wind-down solo time in her own room before she'd even be able to think about sleep. Considering her match was called for nine the next morning, and she'd already requested a wake-up call at six and a backup at six-fifteen, she knew what she had to do.

'Sorry, I'd love to. But I'm playing first tomorrow. I'm going to hitch a ride back to the hotel with my brother.'

'Your brother? That does not sound like fun.' His lips curled into a boyish pout and Charlie nearly leaned in to kiss him right there.

'No, it's definitely not. But you know what will happen if we go home together.'

Marco slid his hand between the banquette and Charlie's thigh and squeezed just so. 'I do know . . .'

She groaned. Not audibly, she hoped, although it did seem like a few of the players sitting at the next table turned to look. Just as Charlie stood to look for Jake, Natalya appeared. She was wearing Charlie's identical Thakoon dress, only Natalya's was a spectacular shade of fuchsia, and she must have had it altered to dip lower at the cleavage and rise higher on the thigh. Her shoes were some sparkly confection with at least five-inch heels, another player no-no: undue stress on arches and ankles from stilettos? It was unheard-of. Except for Natalya.

'Charlotte! Is that you in there? I didn't recognize you without the usual floral thing. How *très chic* we are, no? Matchy, matchy!' Natalya trilled, her Russian accent stronger tonight than usual. She turned to Marco and all but purred, 'Hello, darling. Looking very handsome, as always.'

'Natalya, where's your boyfriend? I just read he might be traded to Buffalo. That sucks! You must be devastated.' Charlie said it with as much faux sympathy as she could muster.

Natalya's eyes narrowed to slits. 'This is the life of a professional athlete, no? Go where they tell you. We can't all be lucky enough to be screwing someone who plays our own sport.'

Charlie beamed. 'Yeah, I definitely recommend it,' she said. 'It's just so much more convenient. But I'm happy you met Benjy. Everyone always talks about what meatheads football players are, but he seems like a really nice guy.'

'Where is he tonight?' Jake asked as he walked up beside Charlie. 'I assumed he'd be here, since we're in his home city.'

Natalya turned to glare at Jake. 'You think he wants to come to another of these parties? I'll see him later.'

Marco stepped in the middle of the awkward threesome. 'Ladies? Jake? I'm saying good night,' he said. He kissed Natalya's cheek and followed it up with a peck on the corner of Charlie's mouth.

'That must be your cue, too,' Natalya said to Charlie, waving expansively. 'Don't you two just make the cutest couple. Couldn't have planned it better if you tried.'

'What's that supposed to mean?' Charlie asked.

But Natalya had already turned to greet a bevy of college-aged guys who were on the tour as hitting partners for the women. Dan had been invited to the party but, as always, he declined.

Jake pulled gently on Charlie's arm. 'You sure you don't want to ride back with Marco?' he asked.

'I'm sure. I'm playing first thing tomorrow. Let's go.'

Jake hesitated, and Charlie peered at him. 'Jake? You have something going on, don't you? Who's your target?'

He snorted, and Charlie couldn't help but smile. Her brother always looked his most handsome in one of his fitted dark suits with a white shirt open at the neck. He wasn't conventionally gorgeous like Marco, but his height combined with his obsessively excellent grooming – neat, trendy beard; perfectly maintained tan; longish hair professionally trimmed every twenty-one days – made him attractive to men and women alike. When he wasn't working, Jake tended toward skinny-fit jeans with cash-mere hoodies. Oversized black frames and one of his million pairs of vintage Nikes kept him looking like he could be anyone from a trendy gay Chelsea guy to a cool, youngish Park Slope dad. Charlie wondered yet again why he wasn't dating someone terrific.

'Target? Aren't you sweet. Like I have to attack someone to get him into bed.'

'Not exactly what I said, but hey, if that's how it is . . .'

Charlie followed Jake's gaze to Natalya. He was studying her intently as she air-kissed the starstruck college boys who flocked to her whenever and wherever they had the chance. Even from across the room, it was hard not to watch her.

'She's enough to make you think women aren't so bad, huh?'

'Oh, stop it, Charlie!' Jake snapped. He was headed toward the door before Charlie could respond, and she didn't think she could have been more surprised if he'd turned around and punched her. Nothing upset Jake, ever. Certainly not Natalya Ivanov.

They rode back to the hotel together in silence. Charlie patiently waited for him to apologize or explain, but when they walked into the lobby, he muttered that he'd see her at the site the next day and disappeared into the elevator without waiting. She peeked into the lobby bar, hoping to bump into Marco while knowing full well that he was already in his room and probably asleep, before heading to her own room and getting undressed. She set her phone alarm and confirmed her wake-up call with the front desk and then climbed under the covers and turned off all the lights. She lay perfectly still on her back, arms and legs outstretched, palms facing up, and breathed. Four counts inhale and four counts exhale, until she felt her entire body begin to relax. It had been a great night, better than she'd even expected. She and Marco were officially a couple, at least as far as the public knew. Inhale, exhale. Her new coach had her on track to climb the rankings, and it seemed to be working. Inhale, long exhale. Her opponent the next day would be tough, because at this level they all were, but Charlie felt a rare calm and a complete confidence that she would soundly beat the girl and go on to advance in the tournament. Inhale, exhale. Everything was in alignment. This was her time.

11

bedazzled

KEY BISCAYNE, MARCH 2016

The Key Biscayne players' lounge boasted a huge roped-off patio flanked on all sides by palm trees and giant windows. As the early-morning light poured in, Charlie once again thought how lucky she was to have a career that followed the sun.

'All my men await, I see,' Charlie said, nodding hello to Dan and Todd and kissing Jake on the cheek.

'Why are you just staring at your phone like an asshole?' Todd yelled at Dan while staring at his own phone. 'Take her bag to the locker room and tell the attendant we'll be ready for a stretching room in ten minutes.' Dan reached

191

over for Charlie's racket bag and immediately headed downstairs.

The lounge, usually packed with players and coaches draped across the leather couches, staring at their phones and iPads, was virtually empty this early: only Gael Monfils and his coach sat in the corner, drinking what looked like hot water and lemon, and a teenage girl that Charlie recognized as a wild card was asleep on a chaise longue wearing sweats and a pair of hot-pink Beats headphones. The flat-screen TVs mounted on nearly every vertical surface showed mostly empty courts. Some doubles players were warming up on Court 4, and Charlie's opponent was beginning to stretch on Court 7, but otherwise all was quiet.

'She's here early,' Charlie said, nodding to her opponent on the screen.

'You would be, too, if you were ranked in the seventies. She knows she's going to lose, but be ready for her to put up a good fight. Watch the drop shots. She's surprisingly skilled with them,' Todd said, never looking up from his phone.

'You feeling a little better today?' Charlie asked Jake. He, too, was staring at his phone.

Both Jake's and Todd's devices beeped.

'They're ready for us,' both men simultaneously announced.

'Who's "they"?'

'Meredith's girl. She's here and all set up.' Jake stood and hoisted his Jack Spade man purse over one shoulder.

'Excuse me – what?'

Todd and Jake had already reached the door that led to

the women's locker room. 'Her name is Monique, and she's got your new outfits and everything else you'll need,' Jake said, holding the door open for her.

'Can someone speak English here, please? I agreed to a stylist for off-court help. Not for what I wear to play.'

Todd motioned toward her outfit. 'I'm no fashion guy, but even I know that doesn't scream Warrior Princess. Or anything good.'

'This is what I have to wear,' Charlie said, motioning down toward her turquoise and pink tank dress and co-ordinating undershorts. 'I have two backups in my bag plus approved socks and sneakers. Or did you forget that my contract requires this?'

'That's all been worked out,' Todd said. Again his phone beeped.

'Worked out how? What's going on?' Charlie stood, hand on hip. As a signed Nike athlete, Charlie was contractually required to wear the clothing that Nike provided for her in the color and style of Nike's choosing. She could make the occasional request, which they usually did try to honor – preferring a built-in sports bra to a shirt that required a separate one; feeling more comfortable in a dress rather than a top and skirt; wanting thicker straps on her tank top versus skinny ones or, worst of all, short sleeves – but that was pretty much all the input she got. All the Nike-signed women would wear different variations of the same color every tournament, and there really wasn't too much you could do about it. Turquoise and neon pink wouldn't have been her colors of choice, but so long as it was comfortable and it fit, which it admittedly always did, she'd long ago stopped wishing for more control.

'Monique is freelance, and she's dressed everyone. She happened to already be in Miami this week for a *Harper's Bazaar* shoot,' Jake said, scrolling through his work BlackBerry. 'Nike gave me written approval for a rebrand, and they messengered over some options first thing this morning. They're willing to let you break ranks with the color coordination in favor of better publicity. Monique is waiting in there to put it all together.'

Jake yanked open the locker room door and Todd motioned for Charlie to walk ahead. 'Just go. And do what she says.'

Charlie flashed the guard her credentials and walked into the carpeted locker room that no one except players – not coaches or physios or friends – was permitted to enter. Charlie immediately wondered how Monique had managed it.

'Charlotte? I'm Monique. Yes, I can see you are every bit as tall as they said. I really didn't believe them.'

'Didn't believe who?' Charlie asked.

Monique had taken over the entire stretching area off the changing room. There was a portable garment rack stuffed with hooded sweatshirts, warm-up pants, tennis dresses, skirts, tank tops, and T-shirts. Off to the side was a folding table overflowing with undershorts, sports bras, socks, and various sweatbands. Strangest of all, every single item was black.

'Your coach. Your brother. *Wikipedia*. Six feet tall? So few of even the models these days are that tall. But don't worry, I sized accordingly.' Monique finally stood up. She was surprisingly unkempt, but in that fabulous, bordering-on-homeless-looking way: stringy, waist-length platinum hair with three inches of black roots; silky black harem pants with elastic around the waist and ankles; a messy tangle of silver and gold and leather chain necklaces; a men's V-neck undershirt topped with a weathered moto jacket; and chunk-heeled snakeskin booties that could, oddly, work for both prostitutes and grandmothers. The pièce de résistance was a diamond-encrusted platinum infinity ring that wrapped around and between all four fingers of her left hand, rendering her entirely dependent on her left thumb and right hand for even the simplest of tasks.

'I'm an athlete, not a model,' Charlie said, trying to keep her voice light. 'Plus, Nike has my measurements down to the millimeter. They custom-make all my outfits. They know my sizes.'

Monique laughed. Not nicely. 'Yes, well, there wasn't time for that today. Kissing Marco Vallejo last night changed the rollout schedule, so we're doing the best we can on short notice. We'll patch it together for Key Biscayne and then – where are you next? Acapulco? – we'll have it done right.'

There was so much to dissect that Charlie didn't even know where to start. '"Patch it together"?'

'Come here, we don't have a lot of time. Don't you have to be, like, carb-loading or something at eight?'

'Breakfast? Yes, I do try to eat that.' Charlie walked over to the garment rack and began looking through the clothes. 'Why is everything black?'

'Warriors wear black.' Monique didn't look up. She was busy pairing a top and skirt together.

'I actually prefer dresses,' Charlie said. 'I get distracted when I'm wearing a tank top and it twists up when I serve. What about this one?'

'Hmm,' Monique murmured. She sounded supremely uninterested. 'My, there's really not a lot of variety in tennis wear, is there? Here, I want you to try this.' She held up a relatively innocuous plain black tank and a straight skirt.

'*No one* wears black,' Charlie said, panic rising. 'This is tennis, not a nightclub.'

'Try it on.' Monique's voice was calm but firm: there would be no more discussion.

Charlie stripped completely naked and stood tall: shoulders back, hips out, strong and confident and proud. She hoped to make her new stylist at least a little uncomfortable, but Monique didn't seem the least bit surprised. Instead, she slowly moved her gaze from Charlie's feet up to her face, coolly examining every inch of her naked body.

'Lovely,' she declared after a long moment, during which Charlie was irritated to discover herself feeling awkward. 'Really just so much better than all the starving models. Beautiful stomach, real boobs, some curve around the hips. Some might say the thighs are too strong, but I think they work for you. And your ass is to die for. How do you keep it so high?'

Charlie felt her cheeks go hot. 'I can't decide if I want to kiss or hit you right now. Both, I think.'

Monique threw her head back and let out an addictive laugh. 'Then I know I'm doing something right. I *like* you. You'll work. Just trust me, okay? You're going to kill it.'

Charlie nodded. When Monique directed her, she tried on the tank top and the skirt. Both were supremely basic, pieces she'd worn thousands of times, the only discernible difference from the literally hundreds of skirts and tanks she owned being that they were black.

'Mmm, turn around. Okay, I like the little flare here, but we definitely need to take the length up.' She yanked upward on Charlie's bra straps, causing both her breasts to give a little bounce. 'Good, I like that. I'll just do a little work here and . . . here.' She placed a couple of safety pins, scrawled a couple of notes in a little red Moleskine, and turned to look at Charlie. 'Okay, get back in that hideous turquoise thing and go have some breakfast. When can you be back here? Twenty minutes?'

Charlie nodded.

'I'll have everything ready by then.'

'You're going to alter them? It's comfortable the way it is!' Charlie didn't mean to whine, but there was no way she was letting this woman – this *stylist* – screw up her comfort level on the court. She was a tennis player first and foremost – not, as Monique had so subtly pointed out, a fashion model. Wimbledon and the shoe debacle of 2015 were still fresh in her mind: there could be no more wardrobe malfunctions. Not one.

'Go. Leave me. I don't have much time,' Monique said. She reached into a gigantic canvas tote bag and pulled out a sewing machine.

'Is that seriously a—?'

'Go!'

Minutes later Charlie left the locker room. Jake and Todd immediately descended on her to ask a million questions, but Charlie insisted she was going to reserve judgment until she was dressed. She ordered oatmeal with almond butter and sliced bananas with a side of two hard-boiled eggs from player dining and tried her best to watch her iPad. Earbuds in. Completely ignoring her brother and coach. Concentrating on the latest *This Old House* was far better than focusing on her building anxiety over her upcoming match, so she chewed slowly and methodically and silently. The moment she finished, she headed back to the locker room.

'Sorry, I know that wasn't long but I have to get dressed now. Like, this second. I'm not cutting short my practice time just to—'

Monique held up her hand. 'I'm finished. Come here.'

Charlie walked over to Monique's makeshift workshop in the stretching room and noticed two other players watching them from the lockers. Charlie could see why. In the barely twenty minutes she'd been gone, Monique had somehow managed to sew a thin band of black leather along the bottom of the skirt.

'Oh my god, you did this? Wait, when did you do this? And how? Monique, they look awesome, but there is absolutely no way I can wear leather on the court. You understand that, don't you?'

Monique snorted. 'Stop talking and get undressed. Right now.'

'But it's leather.'

'Leather *accents*,' Monique corrected. 'Naked. Now.'

Charlie glanced up at the wall clock. She needed to be on the court in ten minutes if she wanted to fit in her entire stretching and warm-up regimen. Acutely aware that the two other players were watching her every move, she once again stripped out of her turquoise dress. First, she pulled on a pair of the black undershorts that Monique handed her; they were the same ones she usually wore, and she didn't even notice until Monique pointed it out that these now had a *C* and an *S* embroidered in a glittery fabric on her ass. One on the left butt cheek and one on the right, to be more precise. And yet, they didn't feel any different.

'Your skirt flips up, what, a million times each match? And the entire stadium is staring at your ass, am I right?'

Charlie nodded.

'It's probably the main reason men watch women's tennis,' Monique announced with authority. 'We'd be downright remiss if we didn't take care of this branding opportunity.'

'Amen, sister!' one of the players called from her locker. They weren't even pretending not to watch. 'I'd like some ass branding, too. Do you have any more letters in there?'

Everyone laughed, including Charlie. She covered her bare breasts with her hands and gave a little flounce in front of the mirror. As predicted, her skirt flew up and her silver initials were on full display.

'Here, now this.' Monique handed her the black Nike sports bra she'd tried on earlier, only now this one had crystals studded across all three intersecting back straps.

'What, do you, like, bring your own BeDazzler?' Charlie asked, dumbfounded. She pulled the bra over her head and was relieved to see that the stud backs were covered underneath in a silky-soft fabric. Nothing felt any different than usual – better, even.

'Yes.'

'I was kidding!'

'I'm not. It's an actual BeDazzler, from the infomercial

in the early nineties. I have two backups from eBay just in case. I would die without it. Here, put the tank on.'

Monique had taken the standard Nike tennis tank and cut a personal pizza-sized hole out of the back – just large enough to reveal Charlie's toned shoulder muscles and the rhinestones that now decorated her sports bra.

'That looks really good,' Karina Geiger called out, and gave Charlie a thumbs-up. 'Maybe I'll try it, too,' Karina guffawed as she ran her hands down over her large, squared-off hips.

'Thanks.' Charlie smiled. She had to admit, she agreed. Without being asked, she pulled on the tennis skirt. Though the leather was obvious to the eyes, there was nothing but that silky-soft fabric touching her skin. It looked badass but felt great.

'How did you do this?' she asked Monique. 'You're magic.'

Monique waved her off. 'Here, just your hair now.'

'I wear my hair in a braid. It's non-negotiable!' Charlie all but screamed. The outfit looked and felt amazing, but the braid had to stay. Over the years, she had tried it all – sweatbands, ponytails both high and low, buns of every size, even down for one particularly horrid five-minute stretch – but nothing felt comfortable on the court except a single long braid. Tied off at the crown and again at the bottom with simple elastics, often with a colored ribbon woven throughout for color. Sprayed with L'Oréal Elnett to contain flyaways. And if it was exceptionally hot, topped with a stretchy, thin headband. Here she would not – could not – be flexible.

'I know I can't fuck with the braid,' Monique said, rolling her eyes. 'Here, use these first.'

Charlie accepted the two sparkly hair ties and stuck them both between her lips. She gathered her dark waves up into a ponytail at mid-height and tied it off. It took only another ten seconds to weave her thick, wild ponytail into a wide braid and freeze the flyaways with some hairspray. 'There,' she said, feeling her head and braid to make sure everything was in place. 'That's how I like it.'

'You wear a headband sometimes, right? Or a visor?'

'I'll wear a sweatband when it's really hot out, but only because the front pieces of my hair fall out of the pony-tail and stick to my forehead. No visor. No hat. I don't like the shadows they throw on my face: it screws with my depth perception of the ball. Sometimes reading the spin, too.'

'Uh-huh,' Monique muttered. She couldn't have sounded less interested. 'Just work with me on this one, okay?'

The two other girls had finished in the locker room and left. Charlie wondered where her opponent was. They would be called to the court in less than five minutes. Was it possible she was already out there?

'Work with you on what, exactly? I'll admit, I had my doubts – and I'm still not sure it's a great idea to play in ninety-degree heat wearing all black – but I do think I look great.'

'It's all sweat-wicking and Drymax and all that crap,' Monique said, rooting around in her giant Goyard tote. 'Don't get hung up on the black thing. And you can see for yourself that neither the leather nor the rhinestones will get in your way. It kills me, but I admit this is one of the very few times it's important to consider function as well as fashion. Come here.'

Charlie had just finished lacing up her sneakers – they were exact replicas of her usual shoes, just entirely in black and dotted with swirling rows of crystals – and she stepped toward Monique.

'Close your eyes.'

'No makeup. It's a total disaster when I sweat and—'

'No makeup. Now close your eyes.'

Charlie obliged. She felt Monique gently pull something over her head, taking care not to mess up her braid, and then secure it with two bobby pins. 'Perfect!'

Charlie's eyes flew open. Monique led her over to the full-length mirror in the dressing area, and Charlie could only stare at herself.

'I know it's a little unconventional, but I really think it makes the whole—'

'I love it,' Charlie whispered. She reached up to touch the small and impossibly delicate cluster of jewels right above her hairline. The little crown was sparkly yet elegant, and it was held in place by one of Charlie's stretchy black sweatbands that nearly entirely blended into her hair.

'Good, you should.' Monique nodded. She appeared satisfied and perhaps a bit relieved.

Charlie fingered a line of minute purple stones that came together in a small heart shape, right toward the center. 'Amethysts. My mother's birthstone,' she whispered.

'Yes, your brother clued me in to that. The rest are colored and clear Swarovski crystals, as are all the crystals adorning your sports bra and sneakers. Their people will be thrilled.'

Charlie moved her eyes from her studded sneakers to her shortened, leather-trimmed skirt, checked out her sexily opened-up tank and bedazzled sports bra, and finally came to rest on her little headband crown, which, if she wasn't seeing it in person, she would have sworn it sounded tacky at best and hideous at worst and thought: *Yes. This works.*

'Go!' Monique said.

Charlie threw her arms around the surprised stylist. Monique hesitated for a moment but then hugged Charlie back. 'Whoa, okay, so you like it. Great.'

'I love it.'

'Excellent. It will only get better when we aren't so rushed. Kick some ass today, okay?'

Charlie thanked Monique and practically skipped the entire way to the players' lounge.

Dan was the first to look up from his novel when she walked in. 'Damn,' he breathed, allowing his eyes to move from her legs to her head. 'You look hot.'

He must have instantly felt embarrassed for his brazen assessment, because he mumbled an apology, but Charlie was delighted. 'You think?' she asked, doing a little turn. 'It's good, right?'

'It's better than good,' Dan said. 'It's freaking amazing.'

Todd walked over holding a take-out cup of coffee. He used his free hand to grab Charlie's upper arm and pull her in a semicircle while he examined her like a cut of meat. 'Now, *that's* what I'm talking about,' he said. 'Edge. Some sex appeal. A big, fat middle finger to those pretty little dresses you're always running around in.'

'So you like it?' Charlie asked, although she already knew the answer.

'Hell, yes, I like it. It says "Fuck me" and "Don't fuck with me" at the exact same time. What's not to like?'

'You have a real way with words, you know that?' Charlie said, and although she knew she should've been offended by his vulgar appraisal, she couldn't help but relish the praise – especially from Todd.

Charlie looked around to show Jake, but when her match was announced on the overhead speaker, Todd turned and put both hands on her shoulders.

'Listen to me very carefully,' he said, his face mere inches from hers. She could smell the coffee on his breath and see the silver fillings in his back teeth. Charlie tried not to cringe. 'We've already talked strategy. You know how to crush this girl. Use this match as a chance to practice being a *complete fucking bitch.* She's nothing to you – just a speck of meaningless dirt you're going to send right back into oblivion after you stomp all over her six-oh, six-oh. Understood?'

Charlie opened her mouth to say something, but Todd held up his hand.

His face came in even closer. 'You are a goddamn warrior, Charlotte Silver, and warriors *win*. What they do not do is hug their opponents or ask after their mommies or hope and pray that everyone adores them. Do you understand me?'

'Yes,' Charlie said.

'What are you?' he asked.

'A warrior.'

'And what do warriors do?'

'They win.'

'And what are you going to say to your opponent when you see her on the court in four minutes?'

'Nothing.'

'That's right – nothing. *Not one goddamn word.* She's as good as dead to you, do you understand? You have bigger things to worry about than how she's feeling today. Like beating her so badly she'll want to quit forever. *Capisce?*'

'*Capisce.*'

'Now go. And don't come back to me if you lose this match, Silver.'

Todd turned around and stalked toward the other side of the lounge where Charlie knew he would fix another huge coffee and then find his way to her player's box.

Dan raised his eyebrows at her. 'Well, that was . . . something.'

Charlie saw the disapproval in his expression, but for once she didn't let it make an impression. Yes, Todd was intense, but whether it was Todd's pep talk or her make-over, she felt every bit as tough as she looked. Was it possible a new look could create confidence? Charlie wouldn't have thought so before. But now she looked down at her all-black fabulousness and knew the answer was *Hell, yes.*

12

hot new couple alert

'Can I get you anything else?' the pool attendant asked, his young face smiling and eager.

Charlie pulled her earbuds out and thought for a second. 'Another iced coffee would be great. Decaf,' she forced herself to say. When he walked off, she glanced around to make sure she was still the only one by the pool – not particularly surprising, considering it was eight in the morning – and pressed play on her iPad.

The ESPN announcer was Chris Evert, one of Charlie's heroes. She and John McEnroe were commentating on a highlights reel from the tournament in Key Biscayne.

She fast-forwarded through the men's coverage, stopping only to admire Marco's set point (a twenty-rally tiebreaker in the fifth set, when he'd come back after losing the first two sets to win not only the match but the entire tournament – she especially liked when he threw his racket high into the air and fell onto both knees, leaning over to kiss the court), and then skipped around through the women's matches until she found her own. Her first-rounder against Deanna Mullen of Canada had been the blowout Todd had demanded. Charlie had beaten her 6–0, 6–0, in a thirty-nine-minute match that left the poor girl in tears by the end. It wasn't a surprise to anyone – Charlie was by far the favorite in the match, as the higher-ranked player – but she'd never beaten anyone so soundly in her entire professional career. Jake credited her new Warrior Princess outfit for giving her the extra competitive edge; Todd insisted it was his advice to Charlie beforehand not to talk, look at, or otherwise socialize with her opponent. She waved them both off, laughing and saying it was sheer skill and determination, but she wondered if they were right. She felt fierce in her black outfit, with everyone staring admiringly: she wanted not just to beat her opponent but to crush her. When the girl choked back tears of humiliation at the end of the match, Charlie instinctively headed toward the net to say something comforting, but one sideways glare from Todd in the player's box stopped her in her tracks. She could hear his refrain in her head: *You're a warrior. Warriors don't hug their enemies.*

Her second-round match had gone much like the first, enough to prompt Chris Evert to wonder if this wasn't some sort of new and improved Charlotte they were seeing. 'It's like she's an entirely different player,' Chris's voice narrated over a point where Charlie smashed a winner down the line. 'We don't usually see this hyperaggressive, go-getter style of play from Charlotte Silver.'

'I hate to be the one to talk about the elephant in the room, but is she wearing diamonds?' McEnroe asked.

'Crystals,' Evert laughed. 'Swarovski, from what I've been told. You heard about her new endorsement deal? She's the new face of Swarovski crystal worldwide. I don't want to speculate too much on figures, but I think it's safe to say that this young woman will be wearing a crown pretty much every waking moment of every day.'

'Kudos to this girl's PR team,' McEnroe said. 'It's not easy to upstage Natalya Ivanov, but Charlotte Silver's doing that. Charlotte's the clear fan favorite now.'

Chris added, 'This girl went from cute and competent to sexy and killer, literally overnight.'

A clip of Charlie hitting balls into the stands after her quarterfinal win played, and she had to admit that the new look was striking on camera. Even though she lost in the semis – to Natalya, of course – nearly everyone agreed that Charlie was the one to watch.

'Is it, like, totally sexist or chauvinistic or whatever to suggest that sucking face with the number one male player in front of the entire world is helping her cause a little? Or am I a total jerk for saying that?' The camera flashed back to McEnroe and Evert sitting side by side in a viewing box above the court.

Evert laughed. 'I could probably think of another way to phrase that, John, but, no, I don't disagree with you.

Charlotte Silver and Marco Vallejo are the best couple in professional tennis since Steffi and Andre.'

'Or you and Jimmy? Let's not forget about that,' McEnroe said.

The reel cut to Natalya's tournament-winning final game, where she confidently served out the match 40–love and won the final point on an ace. Both commentators admired her serve, but Charlie noticed they sounded significantly less interested in Natalya than they normally did. Less interested than they sounded in Charlie.

'Here you are, miss,' the waiter said, setting down the iced coffee. He was clearly trying very hard not to stare at Charlie's body. He was failing.

'Thank you.'

He lingered, and Charlie wondered if she needed to tip him that very moment, but he only said, 'I don't mean to bother you, uh, Ms Silver, but I saw you play at Key Biscayne and . . . wow. You were great.'

Charlie shielded her eyes as she looked up at him. He was around eighteen, tall and lanky with an oversized nose and a smattering of freckles. His white polo shirt read VICEROY ANGUILLA and was tucked neatly into crisp navy shorts. He was no Marco, but he was cute in a young kid sort of way.

'Call me Charlie! Are you a tennis fan?' she asked with a smile. 'I wouldn't imagine there would be much interest around here.'

'Oh, no, just the opposite. The island has a lot of terrific players. I actually teach the team at the local high school. It's volunteer, of course – they don't have any money even for uniforms – but the kids are really into it.'

'Amazing. I would have loved to come see it. This is pretty much my only free hour of the visit, but maybe if I can sneak away later . . .'

'That would be awesome! The kids love you so much, and I'm sure they'd be so—'

'What's up, gorgeous?' Marco slid into the chaise longue next to Charlie. His shoulders and waist created a triangle of tanned and muscled perfection. His swim trunks sat low on his pelvis, almost too low, exposing a near-indecent trail of hair that climbed up over his washboard stomach straight to his perfect innie belly button. The trunks were not loose.

'Hi,' she said, or at least tried to. *Get control of yourself,* she thought. The previous night had been the first time she and Marco requested adjoining rooms right at check-in and didn't care who overheard. Neither of them wanted to spend the night yet – sleep was too important – but it had been refreshing not to have to hide.

Marco shielded his eyes and looked at the young pool boy. 'Hey, can I get a strawberry banana smoothie with a scoop of protein powder? My coach left a canister of the right brand with the chef, so check with him. Thanks, man.'

The boy's face flamed red, and he took off in nearly a sprint.

'He's really a nice kid. He was just telling me how he volunteers to—'

'Yes, nice kid. Listen, pretty girl, I saw you have a practice court at eleven, and I was hoping I could switch with you.'

Charlie yanked on her bikini top. There was a little metal

plate holding the two cups together, and it was burning hot from the sun. If she wasn't careful, she'd have double *T*s for Trina Turk literally burned into her chest. 'What time do you have?'

'I am at four. The last one. But I want to get it over with so I can have some time by the pool today.'

'Sorry, I can't do it. With the shoot starting at sundown, I'll need to be in hair and makeup by then. Maybe someone else can switch?' Charlie pushed her sunglasses up on her head and stared out over the azure sea. She could barely believe she'd been invited on this shoot. And with Marco? In Anguilla, no less? The whole thing was insane.

'Oh, come on,' Marco wheedled. He slid his hand under her bikini top and cupped her in his hand. Instead of feeling good, it pulled the already burning metal doodad against the underside of her breast, where it seared her flesh. She pushed his hand away.

'Stop! We're in public,' she whispered, hating the way she sounded.

'In case you haven't noticed, the public is very happy to watch us fool around,' Marco said with that devilish grin that always made her stomach flip-flop. 'What do you say? You take four and I'll get you a massage. My treat.'

The pool boy returned, and Marco accepted the smoothie without saying thank you. He took a long pull on the straw. 'Good enough,' he declared.

'Thank you so much,' Charlie said to the boy, overcompensating with a huge smile. 'I think we're good now.'

'Yes, Ms Silver,' he said before once again bolting.

Charlie turned to Marco. 'I can't do it. I've got the court from eleven to twelve-thirty. Dan is all lined up and Todd will be with us via Skype. After that there's lunch and then lifting.' Charlie glanced at her watch. 'Why don't you ask Natalya? I saw on the sign-up sheet that she has the court at nine.'

'Forget it,' Marco said, obviously irritated. He dropped his smoothie on the side table hard enough that some splashed over the edge and stood up. 'I'll see you later. I've got a lot to do.' And without a kiss or a smile or a farewell, he started to walk away.

'Seriously, Marco? You're mad because I won't switch practice times with you?'

She knew he heard her, but he didn't stop walking. Moments later he disappeared inside the poolside restaurant.

Charlie sighed and placed her earbuds back in. Practice courts at tournaments were hard enough to negotiate – there was a whole stressful system based on a mysterious combination of ranking, seniority, timing of matches, and the aggressiveness of one's coach in bullying the schedulers – but today wasn't like that. There was one court at the hotel designated for their use and there were six players invited to the Tennis's Hottest Players spread featured annually in *Vanity Fair*'s June issue. They each got ninety minutes of court time and were expected to work out meals and lifting schedules on their own, with the plan that the shoot would take place during 'magic hour' that evening, the short window of time just before sunset when the light was at its most perfect.

Charlie turned back to her iPad and surfed some more. She clicked through some Instagram photos of Piper and Ronin at a fund-raising party at Ronin's hospital. All the

other wives were wearing typical DVF wrap dresses in
varying prints or black pants with a jewel-colored silky
top; Piper was swathed in a leopard-print romper with
sky-high studded heels and her hair piled wildly atop her
head. She was the only person Charlie had ever met who
could pull off fuck-me red lipstick at all times of the day
or night without ever looking like a hooker. Charlie smiled
and picked up her phone.

*Saw your pics from the lupus benefit. Very respectful of the
cause. I was impressed.*

The three dots flashed for a few seconds before the
message came back: an emoticon of a hand giving the
finger.

*No, seriously, I saw those heels at a peep show joint in Times
Square a few months ago. Very chic.*

This time, Piper replied with a picture of her own bitmoji
holding up her middle finger.

*Love you, too. Did I mention I'm in Anguilla? They pronounce
it Ang-gee-lah. Just thought you should know.*

*If you weren't screwing the hottest guy on the planet, I'd be
forced to point out what a huge, raging loser you are.*

*Yes, well. I am screwing the hottest guy on the planet. Who
now calls me his gf, btw.*

*I am going to have to work extra hard as your maid of honor
to upstage the two of you. I might start planning now.*

Hahahahah not so fast!

Charlie put her phone down and noticed her heart was
pounding. Of course Piper was kidding, but the mere
mention of marrying Marco made Charlie nauseated,
excited, and anxious all at once. It had only been ten days
since they'd gone public, but she supposed you could count

the whole year they'd been sleeping together as some-thing . . .

An email from Isabel, the WTA publicist, popped up on Charlie's iPad and she opened it.

Dear Charlie,

Please find enclosed the roundup of last week's events. I've included all the mentions, stories, interviews, spottings, blind items, and photographs that include either you, Marco, or both of you since the night of the player party in Miami. Congratulations! This is truly tremendous reach, and we are always appreciative of the chance to draw attention to our sport. I hope you're enjoying the VF shoot. I'm in constant contact with their people, but please do let me know if I can be of any further assistance.

All the best,
Isabel

Below the note were three dozen links, which at first glance included everything from *US Weekly* to *O, The Oprah Magazine*. Page Six had a juicy tidbit insinuating rumors that she and Marco had been having an affair – 'in various luxe hotel suites all over the world' – for over a year now; *Gawker* featured a rambling sexist exploration on why female tennis players were, in their words, 'pretty much the only attractive professional women athletes on earth,' with especially derogatory commentary aimed at female basketball players and swimmers; *E! Online* had dug up a dozen photos of both her and Marco as junior players, and paired them with lots of empty, breathless copy lines like 'Meant to be!' and 'Fated from birth!' across their website.

Most online magazines and blogs featured the photograph now dubbed 'The Kiss': some zoomed in to make it look like a sneaked paparazzo shot and others blurred the background using Photoshop so you couldn't quite tell that Charlie and Marco had pecked while walking a red carpet in front of hundreds of people, but they all sent the same message: Hot New Couple Alert.

Charlie turned off the iPad and tucked it in her beach bag. Lowering the lounge chair to flat, she stretched her arms overhead and felt the early-morning sun hit her body. It had all happened so fast. New coach, new look, new boyfriend, new aggressive style of play. And just in case there was any doubt it had been the right call, there were the tangible results to consider: a semifinal finish at a Premier Mandatory tournament, a bump in her ranking, and more media attention in the last week than Kate Middleton had gotten with her second pregnancy announcement.

When she woke up a half hour later, it felt like she'd been asleep all morning. When was the last time Charlie had been relaxed enough to fall asleep poolside? Hell, when was the last time she'd even *been* poolside? Of all the fabulous hotels she stayed in, all the exotic cities and far-flung countries, she rarely ever saw anything except the airport, the tennis site, and the inside of her hotel room. Occasionally she'd have dinner at a great restaurant or attend the player party at a fun nightclub, but all of these five-star places with the best chefs and the prettiest clientele could be anywhere. If it weren't for the jet lag and the passport stamps, Charlie could barely ever remember if she was in Hong Kong or Shanghai, Melbourne or Auckland. One time she'd written a group email update to Piper, Jake, and her father and told them about what she'd seen out of her window on the drive from the Abu Dhabi airport to her hotel; it had taken her father replying to ask if she wasn't playing in Dubai that week before she realized he was right.

Her phone read 9:08 a.m. Normally Charlie hated running, but it was widely acknowledged among players as the only way to squeeze in a little sightseeing: it counted as a workout, and you got to see a bit of local flavor at the same time. She headed back to her room to change, and although the private plunge pool on the balcony of her oceanfront suite nearly dismantled her motivation, she changed into shorts, laced up her sneakers, and tucked a twenty-dollar bill in her sports bra in case she found a place to buy some water. Meads Bay beach was nearly empty when she jogged down, only a couple of families with young children sitting in the shallow surf, and they gave her tired waves as she ran by. Her feet hit the sand rhythmically and her breath started to come faster. Despite her fitness level, she could never manage more than a seven-minute mile for any real length of time, but she settled into a comfortable pace and focused on taking in the salty air. In a few minutes Charlie was running past another resort, not nearly as luxurious as the Viceroy, but nice enough and filled with happily shrieking children. In another half mile or so the beach ended abruptly with an understated PRIVATE PROPERTY sign affixed to an imposing gate. Behind it, lush vegetation rose seemingly out of the sand to mask a stucco mansion: only the shingled roof was visible above the palm trees.

Veering off the beach onto a paved sidewalk, Charlie followed the path out toward a village road. To her left was a sprinkling of cottage houses, a church, and what looked like a schoolhouse. She turned right and ran toward a village with a charming little pedestrian area dotted with local shops and restaurants. There were a few tourists poking around with their telltale sunburns and oversized straw bags, but mostly the customers were Anguillan: old ladies bustling about with sacks of plantains and school-children in crisp uniforms finishing their breakfasts. A little donut shop at the end of the strip advertised bottled water, so Charlie jogged over.

'Hey!' she heard a familiar voice say from somewhere behind her.

Charlie stopped, her heart doing little flip-flops. Had Marco followed her? Was he here to apologize?

When she turned around, it took her a moment. 'Dan? What are you doing here?'

He sat in a green plastic chair, an espresso cup in front of him. Shielding his eyes from the sun, he looked up at Charlie and said, 'I could ask you the same.'

Charlie mopped a stream of sweat from her forehead and then awkwardly wiped her wet palm against her shorts. 'I was just out for a run. Figured it was my only chance to leave the hotel and look around a little.'

'It's pretty nice, huh?'

'The hotel? It's gorgeous.'

Dan laughed, a hearty laugh with crinkly eyes and his face turned to the sky.

'I'm going to get a bottle of water. Do you want one?' she asked him.

He motioned to the cluster of three empty chairs at his table. 'Why don't you join me? We don't have to be back for another forty minutes or so. They have the most killer coffee. Even better than Turkey.'

Charlie glanced around helplessly. Why did she suddenly feel so uncomfortable? And then she realized: she'd never been alone with Dan. She barely ever spotted him off the court, to the point where Jake often wondered aloud where he went and what he did. It seemed Dan was not interested in hanging out if he wasn't on the clock. Other women befriended their hitting partners – some were even rumored to sleep with them – but Dan clearly wanted no part of any of it.

'No pressure, Silver. If you don't want a coffee, I won't be offended.' Another smile, this one a little bit mocking.

Charlie took the seat directly across from him. An Anguillan man appeared almost instantly.

'She'll have a double,' Dan announced.

Charlie opened her mouth to protest that Todd didn't allow caffeine, but Dan held his hand up. 'Trust me, Silver. Your secret is safe with me.'

'Thank you,' she said, clasping her hands together. 'So, what brings you here?'

'You do, actually.'

'No, I mean here. This village.'

Dan shrugged. 'I just went out for a walk this morning and ended up here. I heard the food was good on the island, but I can't believe I didn't know anything about this coffee.' He looked so peaceful, so collected. He was wearing a pair of khaki shorts and a vintage surfing T-shirt and sneakers.

'Do you do that a lot?'

'What? Go walking?' Dan asked. 'You know, I guess I do.'

'Is that where you always are when we're not hitting?'

He appeared to think about this. 'Yeah, I guess so. It's my chance to see things, you know?'

The waiter reappeared and placed espresso cups in front of Charlie and Dan and a miniature pitcher of steamed milk in the middle.

'Here, do it like this.' Dan poured the milk into Charlie's cup and popped in a single cube of white sugar.

'Todd will have your head for that,' Charlie said, her voice singsongy and teasing.

'Well, screw him, then,' Dan said. And then, a beat later: 'Sorry, I didn't mean that.'

Charlie laughed. 'So it all comes out! I had no idea.'

'No, it's not like that,' Dan rushed to say, looking more agitated by the second. 'I didn't mean that. I respect Todd as a coach, and I owe him a lot for this gig. For picking me.'

Charlie reached across the table and placed her hand on Dan's. 'Hey, slow down. You were kidding. Todd can be a huge jerk. I get that. I'm not going to run off and tell him anything, okay? Don't worry.'

Dan stared at Charlie's hand for a long, awkward moment. She yanked it back to her lap.

'Sorry,' he said.

'You don't have anything to be sorry for!'

'It's just that I'm really grateful for this job, even if he is . . . difficult sometimes.'

'Difficult?' Charlie shrieked. 'He's a first-rate asshole. But that stays between us.'

Finally, a smile.

'So, when you say you "owe him for this gig," am I to interpret that to mean there was competition? Because Todd showed me a video of you hitting one day – I think it was your final year at Duke in a match against UVA, if I'm not mistaken – and he was all, like, "This is *the* guy. I got him and he's going to change your life."'

'Yeah, I'm not sure that's exactly how it went down, but it's nice of you to say that,' Dan said.

'I'm serious! He was insistent it be you, and only you.'

They each sipped their coffee and Charlie tasted instantly that Dan was right: it was insanely good.

'So what were you doing when Todd called you? You were two years out of college, right?'

Dan nodded. 'I was back home in Marion, in Virginia, working for my family's hardware store. I was playing some local tournaments but, man, it was depressing.'

'You never thought about turning pro? First singles at Duke is pretty impressive.'

He shrugged. 'It's not that I never thought about it, but it didn't really seem like an option. There was no extra money growing up for lessons or coaches or anything, so I pretty much taught myself. The whole point was to get a full ride to college, which I did, so I certainly couldn't leave once I got there. I was good, yes, but I'm not sure I was good enough to go the distance. I couldn't risk it. The guaranteed degree was way more valuable than the small possibility I could make any real money playing tennis. At least, that's what I tell myself,' he said with a smile.

'And then Todd called . . .' Charlie let her voice trail off.

'And then Todd called. He said I was perfect for the position, but I think the truth is that my price was right.

No one else would have done it for practically free—' He stopped, clearly horrified. 'I didn't mean it like that. My god, I can't keep my mouth shut today.'

'I knew the salary wasn't a lot, but Todd told me that was the going rate,' Charlie said quietly. Why hadn't she paid more attention to this when it was all happening?

Dan waved her off. 'Stop. Please. I'm not doing this for the money. I'm doing it because it's probably my only chance to travel the world and see these incredible places before I go back to Virginia and take over the store for good.' He coughed. 'And if we're being completely honest here, I'm doing it because I think you're a fucking awesome player with incredible talent and potential, and I want to be there when you win your first Grand Slam. Because I know you're going to, and I also know it's going to be the first of many. I would have been crazy to turn this down.'

'You think so?' Charlie asked. It was all she could do not to hug him.

'I fucking know so.'

'You say "fuck" a lot,' Charlie said. 'I didn't know that about you.'

Dan grinned. He glanced at his watch. 'Come on, Warrior Princess, we have to go. Practice courts wait for no one.'

He dug for his wallet, but Charlie said, 'I've got this.'

'What, you think I'm so poor I can't buy us some Caribbean coffee?'

Charlie rolled her eyes. She liked the new cursing, joking Dan. 'No, I'm just thinking it's fun to have an excuse to pull money out of my bra.' And she plunged her hand into her shirt.

Dan averted his eyes, but it didn't stop him from saying

flirtatiously, 'Best reason I can think of. Come on, Silver. I'll race you back.'

'Oooooh, you think you can beat me just because I'm a girl? I run a seven-minute mile choking for air like no one's business.' Charlie left the entire twenty on the table and finished the last sip of coffee. The caffeine felt like a transfusion of pure life. 'Now, move your ass!'

Dan sprinted forward, and, laughing, Charlie ran after him to catch up.

13

tennis royalty

DANIEL ISLAND, SOUTH CAROLINA, APRIL 2016

'Aarrrgh!' Charlie screamed as her racket connected with the rising ball right at the sweet spot. It sailed back, barely clearing the net, before landing so close to the baseline that Charlie wasn't sure it was in. She rarely grunted – she thought it a gross and unladylike strategy some of the women used to distract their opponents – but this time it had been a purely biological response to hitting the ball with every ounce of her strength. The shrieking grunt had escaped her lips involuntarily. She was horrified but had to admit it felt good.

'Thirty–love,' the female umpire announced into her microphone from her raised courtside chair.

223

'Challenge!' Karina bellowed, pointing a sizable hand toward the line. 'That was out!'

'Ms Geiger has challenged the call. We will review the point,' the umpire declared.

Charlie's heart pounded from the exertion and excitement. They'd been playing for two and a half hours already, and she was two points away from winning the entire tournament in Charleston. She took deep inhales through her nose and exhaled through her mouth, walking slowly to keep her legs loose. When she glanced toward the player box she saw her father, Jake, Dan, and Todd all turned away from her, their attention directed at the mammoth overhead screens, waiting for the replay to begin.

Slowly, ever so slowly, the camera focused on Charlie's shot: it sailed over the net, making a near-perfect arc on its path to the baseline. There, just before it landed, the camera zoomed in so only the ball and a few inches of the baseline tape were visible. In the slowest of slo-mo, the ball inched its way toward the line and *tap!* A tiny sliver of the ball's underside grazed the very back of the tape. A shadow-like graphic of the slo-mo camera confirmed it: there had been one centimeter – perhaps less – of overlap between the ball and the baseline. But that's all she needed. She pumped her fist at the same time the crowd cheered. Todd sprang to his feet and raised both arms over his head and screamed, 'Yeah, Charlie! Now, *finish* this!'

'The score shall remain thirty–love,' the umpire announced calmly. 'Karina Geiger is out of player challenges.'

Karina slammed her racket against her leg hard enough to hurt and shouted, *'Mach es dir selber!'*

Trying to stay calm, Charlie walked to the line and motioned to the ball girl, who immediately ran over and proffered two balls. Charlie tucked the first one in the leg of her black undershorts. The second one she bounced rhythmically one, two, three times and then tossed in the air. The late-afternoon Charleston sun was blinding, but she'd practiced in enough bright sunshine to stay focused on the ball. She watched it rise toward the sky, and then at the perfect moment, just as the ball was reaching the peak of its ascent, Charlie launched both feet off the ground, extended her right arm from behind her back to over her head, and went after it with the strength of her entire body.

The ball landed in the inside corner of the service box but Karina never even got near it. An ace. The radar screen at the back of the court registered the speed of the serve: 103 miles per hour. The crowd roared.

'Forty–love,' the chair umpire announced. 'Match point.'

'Charlie! Charlie! Charlie!'

'Quiet on the court, please,' the woman said sternly, but the crowd ignored her.

Charlie's opponent looked like she was in physical pain, which she likely was: the match time was now an official two hours and thirty-eight minutes. The girls had split the first two sets, each winning one in a tiebreaker, and now the third set score was 5–4. They were both drenched in sweat, breathing hard, and beginning to feel the onset of what they knew would be hours of killer leg cramps. The temperature was ninety-one degrees.

Match point, match point, match point, Charlie repeated over and over in her mind before breathing deeply to calm herself and stay focused. If she couldn't harness and control the adrenaline surging through her body, she'd be at risk of blowing the whole thing: her hands would start to shake, her legs would wobble, her concentration would break. Drawing in long, deep inhales, she forced herself to examine the strings on her racket while she tried to slow her heart rate.

The ball girl reappeared. Charlie accepted a towel and mopped her brow. She plucked one ball from the two the girl held at eye level and slowly, deliberately walked over to the baseline. This was it. This was where it ended, where Charlie claimed her third-ever career singles title at a Premier-level tournament. When she glanced across the net right before throwing the ball into the air, she saw Karina standing at the baseline. Instead of being in position to receive Charlie's serve, the girl was doubled over with her head between her thick knees. Not injured or sick, from what Charlie could tell at that distance, but taking an extra few seconds to catch her breath and slow the pace.

The rules of the game dictated that Charlie, as the server, had to wait until the receiver was ready, but they also stated that the receiver had to be ready within a reasonable amount of time of the server being ready. Karina knew Charlie would never serve the ball until she was ready; Charlie knew Karina knew, and she also knew Karina was deliberately messing with the pace to throw her off. Icing the kicker. Karina was probably betting on the fact that the chair umpire would never call a delay of game on a match point, not to even mention tournament point. She was clearly using psychological warfare to try to wrest any little advantage out of a nearly lost match. It was shitty and unsportsmanlike and it was working: Charlie could feel herself growing angrier and angrier as she stood at the line, bouncing the ball over and over, waiting for Karina to look up and acknowledge she was ready to continue play.

As her opponent stretched her arms toward her toes, Charlie glanced toward the stands. Todd stared back at her as though he'd been willing her to look up. 'Serve the ball,' he mouthed.

Charlie's eyes widened. It was clear what he was saying, but how could she? She looked to the chair umpire, who seemed unfazed, and then back to Todd. His eyes had narrowed; he was glaring at her. 'Now!' he silently screamed.

It was one of the things Todd was always harping on in their training sessions. These women were not your family, they were not your friends, they were not even your acquaintances: they were your enemies. They walk onto that court and spend every moment trying to undo your concentration, overpower your strokes, outthink your strategy, and crush your intention. They employ every advantage they possibly have, and if you want even the smallest chance of beating them, you need to play the game, too. Like a competitor, and not like the girl who's trying to win Homecoming Queen. Charlie hated this lecture, but it was clear – at least in this moment – that Todd was right. Her opponent wasn't losing sleep over good sportsmanship. Why should Charlie?

Without another thought, Charlie steadied her feet at the baseline, bounced the ball one time, and tossed it in the air. Out of the corner of her eye she could see Karina react and stick her racket out toward the ball, which went flying out of bounds. It was exactly what Charlie was hoping for: so long as the receiver attempts to return the ball, she was considered ready to receive.

For a moment no one realized what had happened, but then the chair umpire leaned forward into her microphone and announced, 'Game. Set. Match. Tournament. Congratulations to Charlotte Silver on winning the 2016 Volvo Car Open,' and the crowd went wild.

Charlie immediately threw both arms into the air and let out a whoop. The sound of the crowd cheering on Center Court combined with her coursing adrenaline made everything clearer, louder, and more pronounced. This was it. She could feel it. This win would surely catapult her ranking into the top ten and improve her seeding for the upcoming French Open. It would signify to the top women that she was a serious contender. This win would thrill the Nike people, confirm to Swarovski that they'd signed the right woman, and no doubt encourage other possible endorsement offers to come forward. Charleston wasn't the biggest tournament of the year, but it was prestigious. First place there was the real deal.

After Charlie had reached up to adjust her tiny crystal crown, she turned to her player box. In the front row, Todd, next to a rep from the WTA, was beaming. Jake was taking pictures of the scene with his phone. He flashed Charlie a huge grin and motioned for her to smile for the camera. On Jake's right was an empty seat where Dan had been sitting just moments earlier. *Where has he run off to already? He couldn't take an extra ten seconds to congratulate me?* she thought with irritation. But it was her father sitting in the row behind them, an otherwise empty row of four seats, that gave her pause. He was the only one still seated, his hands folded in his lap, his phone nowhere to be seen. Instead, he watched Todd and Jake celebrate with a slightly sad expression. Was he shaking his head? Charlie craned to see better. When her father caught her eye, he smiled, but it was devoid of any happiness. And she understood immediately.

'I, uh, I think she's waiting for you,' the ball girl murmured to Charlie as she motioned across the net. There, standing with her feet hips' width apart and her racket pulled tight across her midsection, was Karina. The girl stared at Charlie with unbridled hatred.

As Charlie walked toward the net, Karina's gaze remained fixed. 'You are not just a slut, but you are a cheater, too,' Karina whispered.

Charlie reeled back like she'd been hit. She'd never heard the usually affable Karina speak this way. 'Excuse me?' she asked, hating her shaky voice.

'I thought you were different, but I was so wrong.'

Charlie stood dumbstruck. Had this girl, who had screamed and yelled her way through the match, called the line judges names and questioned every call, who herself had tried to cheat her way through match point, really just said those things?

'It takes a hotshot player to win the point when her opponent's not ready,' Karina said, and then, before Charlie could even react, Karina reached out and yanked Charlie's hand into a viselike handshake. Pumping Charlie's hand up and down until it hurt, she unceremoniously dropped it, plastered on a fake smile, and nearly shouted, 'Great match, Charlotte. You should be really proud of yourself,' before grabbing her bag and walking off the court.

Charlie hit the requisite victory balls into the stands, stood for the trophy presentation and the on-court interviews, and posed for photos with the tournament sponsors, and when she was finished, she was relieved beyond description to find the locker room empty. She stood at the sink mirror, staring at the black skirt with leather trim and bedazzled sneakers and glittering crown, and suddenly felt ridiculous in the very outfit that just hours earlier had made her feel so strong. The tears didn't come, thankfully, until she stood under the scalding hot shower and let her mind revisit all the things Karina had said. Did everyone think she was with Marco because he was famous? Had she cheated to win? Was she the kind of person who would do such awful things?

Charlie stepped out onto a towel and stood in the cool air, allowing herself to drip-dry for a moment. She was in no rush to get dressed for her celebratory dinner at FIG, where at least twenty people from the WTA and the tournament and her whole entourage would be assembled to fete her. Would they all be holding aloft their champagne glasses while thinking they were toasting a cheater? It was humiliating beyond words. Maybe she could claim illness or a leg cramp or something else and retreat to her hotel room? No, whatever it was would draw more attention than if she actually went for two hours, smiled, and begged off early. If she played it right, she could be under her covers by nine.

'Charlie? Oh, sorry, I didn't realize.'

Charlie jumped from the surprise of realizing she had company, but she recognized the voice instantly. Marcy.

'Marcy, hi! What are you doing here?' Charlie asked.

Her ex-coach smiled and Charlie felt a wave of relief wash over her. They hadn't seen each other in many months, and Charlie had often wondered what their first meeting would be like. Marcy looked exactly as Charlie remembered with her straight, super-thick blond hair pulled back at the nape, the kind of all-business ponytail that didn't move a millimeter and could be worn to the gym or a black-tie banquet. As always, she was dressed casually in white jeans and a V-neck Polo sweater that showed off her fit figure and healthy complexion, and she walked with a kind of bounce in her step that made her seem much closer to twenty-five than to her actual age of thirty-eight. It had been eleven years since Marcy retired from playing professionally, and yet it still looked possible she could pick up a racket and beat anyone dumb enough to challenge her.

'Sorry to barge in on you like this,' Marcy said, crossing the distance between them and tossing Charlie a towel.

'Thanks,' Charlie said, wrapping the tiny rectangle of scratchy cotton underneath her arms as best she could. She noticed Marcy's brow, which furrowed slightly. 'Is everything okay?'

'I'm sorry to be the bearer of bad news – well, at least very annoying news – but the doping people are here. I heard them asking where to find you at the player desk. I figured you were here, and I wanted to give you a heads-up. They'll be here any minute.'

'Seriously? Now? Of all times!' Charlie knew she

sounded irritated, as expected, but it was the best news she'd heard in a long time: she'd have to stay in the locker room, within view of the doping official the entire time, until her urine was concentrated enough to test. Which, after a nearly three-hour match where she'd consumed gallons of water, could take an hour. Maybe two. Right after a match was one of the times players most dreaded getting tested, because it could eat up an entire night. Right now it sounded divine.

'I know,' Marcy said, shaking her head sympathetically. 'I hope it goes quickly. You deserve to celebrate.'

'I doubt Karina would agree with you.' Charlie's voice caught.

Marcy understood immediately. 'Oh, Charlie, don't do that to yourself. You and I both know that the game has changed. How many times have we talked about it? A million? You had the mental strength to come back from a first-set loss, you dominated the second-set tiebreaker, and you beat her fair and square in the third. The rest is just noise.'

Charlie knew her ex-coach well enough to know that she didn't mean everything she was saying. Yes, Charlie had shown great mental toughness, and, yes, she had definitely demonstrated impressive strategy and strokes on the court, but she knew in her heart of hearts that she shouldn't have gone ahead with that final serve until Karina was in position. No matter how sleazy her opponent's intention had been. Charlie could have won it anyway – *would* have won it – and she wouldn't be standing there right then, naked in a sterile locker room, too ashamed to enjoy the victory that she really did deserve. And Marcy knew it, too.

The door to the locker room opened. Charlie and Marcy exchanged looks just before the doping official appeared before them, a stout woman in warm-up pants and a pullover that read TENNIS ANTI-DOPING PROGRAMME. 'Charlotte Silver? I'm Theresa Baird, and I'm with the Programme. I am here to advise you that we will be performing a standard urinalysis test to ensure your player eligibility remains intact. Do I have your consent?'

Her consent. As if she had a choice in the matter! And this timing of a post-match test was clearly her punishment for missing that early-morning test the day she'd slept in Marco's hotel room. Once a player missed a test during the hour they had designated as an acceptable testing window, the officials could show up literally anytime and anywhere: a restaurant, a Broadway show, the airport, a friend's apartment, a family reunion. If you didn't agree to take the test at the moment of the tester's choosing, it was reported as a fail and you were immediately penalized as though you were guilty of doping.

Charlie wouldn't argue. 'I consent. But I have to tell you, I'm not sure I can pee right now.'

The woman nodded. She knew it would be the case immediately following a long match. 'Shall we try? Then, if it doesn't work, you can get dressed and we'll wait.'

Marcy raised her eyebrows at Charlie as if to say, *Wow, that sounds like a great time*. Charlie offered her a half wave and mouthed a thank-you. 'Marcy? Would you mind telling my dad and Jake that I might be busy for a little and they shouldn't wait for me? I'll meet them at the restaurant just as soon as we're finished here.' She felt bad asking

Marcy to find her family, to force what would surely be an awkward encounter on her – not to mention the certainty they'd be standing with Todd, waiting for Charlie – but she had no choice: once she officially gave her consent to the test, it was considered in progress, and Charlie wouldn't be allowed use of her cell phone until she'd successfully peed in the cup.

'Of course,' Marcy said, hoisting her tote bag over her shoulder. 'And congrats again, Charlie. You do deserve this.' It wasn't until she walked out that Charlie realized she hadn't asked Marcy anything about her or her husband. It was strange to realize that inquiring about their efforts to have a baby was now definitely off-limits.

'Are you ready to try, Ms Silver?' The woman's voice was gruff, bored.

'Please call me Charlie. I'm sorry, I already blanked on your name. We are about to go into a bathroom stall together, so we should probably be on a first-name basis.'

'My name is Theresa Baird. You can call me Ms Baird.'

The woman was busy unscrewing a wide lid from a plastic cup. 'Got it. Ms Baird it is. And, yes, I'm ready.'

Charlie walked toward the first stall. She crouched over the toilet and faced Ms Baird, who stood just outside of the stall with the door open, and accepted the plastic cup from her. She used both hands to hold it in place underneath the towel that was still wrapped around her chest, but Ms Baird coughed.

'I do apologize, but I must be able to see the cup during the urine deposit.'

Charlie looked up, still half standing and half squatting while holding the cup to her body. 'Really?'

'Yes.'

'Okay, then.' She allowed her towel to drop to the floor. Holding the cup back in place, Charlie tried her best to relax. Finally, after what felt like minutes, she felt the cup warm to her hand. Taking care not to splash either one of them, Charlie held it aloft, victorious. And then she saw: her urine was completely clear. It could have been a container of water.

'Damn,' she said.

'I'll wait out here while you clean up.'

When Charlie emerged a moment later, relieved to be back in a towel, Ms Baird was making notes in a small leather-bound book. 'We'll have to wait,' she murmured, not looking up.

'Still no good, is it?' Charlie asked. 'Is it okay if I get dressed?'

'Yes,' the woman said through pursed lips.

It took all Charlie's energy not to snap back something obnoxious. She tried to remind herself that this woman couldn't possibly enjoy her job, which basically amounted to spending her days in toilet stalls with strangers all over the world, so she took a deep breath and headed toward her locker. Ms Baird followed and watched, but kept a respectful distance while Charlie pulled on a tracksuit. She would put on a real outfit when the whole ordeal was over.

'I'm just going to do my makeup, okay?'

Ms Baird followed her into the sink area and looked through some paperwork while Charlie blow-dried her hair straight. Her stomach rumbled with hunger, but she was careful not to eat anything because then she'd be thirsty, and drinking anything at all right now would only succeed in prolonging the whole miserable experience. She glanced at her watch: she was supposed to be arriving at FIG right then.

Charlie tried again, but to no avail.

'Don't worry, it will happen,' Ms Baird said. It was the first remotely kind or reassuring thing she'd uttered.

Her cell phone rang. Both she and Ms Baird saw *Dad* flash on her screen.

Charlie watched it ring three times, knowing she wasn't permitted to pick it up, but on the fourth ring Ms Baird motioned for Charlie to answer.

'Hey, Dad. I'm still in the locker room. A lady from the Programme is here for testing, and I can't pee, so it might be a while. But she was kind enough to let me answer so you could congratulate me on my big win.'

'Congratulations,' her father said flatly.

'Dad. Come on. We both know Karina was deliberately delaying match point.'

'Mmm.' Whenever her father murmured, it meant he disagreed. Charlie knew this, but as she always did when she knew her father was upset with her, she kept on talking.

'I mean, really. What choice did I have? The ump was completely checked out, and Todd is silently screaming at me to serve the ball, and I know that if the situation were reversed, she would have already hammered a serve at my head. What was I supposed to do? Just stand there like an idiot, getting stiffer and more psyched out every second, and hope she decides to rejoin the match?'

'It's not really for me to say, Charlie,' Mr Silver said.

'Although you probably know where I come down on these things.'

'The old Charlie would have waited and waited because it's the polite thing to do, and I would have lost that match point and then the next one and then the whole thing would have spiraled into a complete shit show. You know it's happened before! And Marcy would have been the first one to tell me that I'd made the right decision and that I'd eventually get mentally stronger with experience and not have it affect me, but I would have lost this tournament. Lost it because I was always trying to make everyone like me. No one else seems to care about that, so why should I? And it's not even like I did anything wrong. I was completely within my right to serve the ball whenever I damn well pleased!'

'Well, it sounds like you have it sorted, then,' her father said.

'Ms Silver? May we try again?' Ms Baird asked, and Charlie was relieved.

'Dad, I have to run. I'll see you at the restaurant just as soon as I'm—'

'I'm on my way back to the hotel for the night,' Mr Silver said. His voice sounded completely neutral to anyone but Charlie, who could hear the disappointment like an electric guitar.

'Already? You're not going to celebrate with us?'

'It's so late already. And I know Jake and Todd are eager to speak with you. Let's touch base tomorrow before my flight.'

Charlie was quiet for a moment. 'Okay, Dad. If that's really what you want.' She could feel the shame in her flushed cheeks.

She hung up and turned her attention to the tester. 'I think I can do it this time,' she said.

This time the urine flowed freely, and after dipping a little paper stick in it, Ms Baird declared it adequately concentrated. 'Thank you for your cooperation,' she said. 'You're free to go.'

Charlie nodded and thanked the woman and headed back to her locker. She pulled a brag book from the pocket of the garment bag that was hanging there and began to leaf through it. This is what it had come to: two outfit choices, both selected by someone else, and still she couldn't figure out how to put them together without a photographic lesson. There were tabs for all kinds of occasions – print interview, player party, television interview, airline travel, family dinners, et cetera – and she flipped to the catchall section labeled CELEBRATIONS. Monique had placed mini sticky notes on two of the dozen or so pictures featured in this section, indicating the two choices that currently hung in Charlie's locker: a spaghetti strap silk romper that gathered at the waist and ankles and a cropped black tee paired with what could only be described as a high-waisted tutu. Figuring she'd spent enough time already both going to the bathroom and wondering how she'd go to the bathroom, Charlie pulled on the second outfit. Standing in front of the mirror, she had to admit that Monique was good at her job. The T-shirt's cap sleeves accentuated her toned arms, and the little swath of skin that showed between the bottom of her shirt and the top of her skirt made her breasts look like they defied gravity. Even the Swarovski-studded black Louboutins gave her legs the illusion of infinity, despite the fact that Monique, at Charlie's repeated insistence, had finally agreed to have the heels cut down from four inches to two.

Her phone bleated with a FaceTime call. Monique's picture stared back at her. Knowing the woman wouldn't stop calling until she answered, Charlie slid the button to the right and held her phone as high as she could with her right hand.

'I like it,' she said, moving the screen to give Monique a full view.

'Where the hell are you? Shouldn't you be at the restaurant by now?' Monique squinted, trying to get a better look. 'I like it, too. I knew that Alice and Olivia skirt would be perfect, and it is. Let me see the Loubs.'

Charlie pointed the phone at her feet. 'They're actually really comfortable at this height.'

Monique made a gagging sound. 'If you ever tell anyone I agreed to having the heels hacked, we're over. Just so you know.'

Charlie laughed.

'Where's the crown? I left a couple extra in a cosmetic pouch at the bottom of the bag.'

'Yeah, I saw them.'

'So put one on. Your choice. How do you like that? Who says I don't let my clients have any creative freedom?'

'They're identical, Monique. One has black stones and one has pink.'

'Yes, well, don't you like that you can choose? Although with this outfit, and in light of the fact that you're celebrating a huge victory, I'd strongly recommend the black.'

'I don't know . . .'

'So wear the pink if you really like it. I can live with that.'

'I just think it's a little much for downtown Charleston, you know? This is like the real-deal South. Home of the cashmere twinset. Am I really going to wear a tiara to dinner?'

'You sure as hell are!' Monique screeched. 'I don't care if all the other girls are wearing every single nauseating pink and green Lilly Pulitzer print ever invented. This is about you and no one else. *You* are the Warrior Princess. And for chrissake, *you* actually just won something! So put on your goddamn tiara and own it. You may as well be at Buckingham fucking Palace right now, because you are tennis royalty and you damn well better act like it!'

Charlie watched as Monique weaved her way onto a packed airport people mover and started barking 'Left is for passing!' to anyone who didn't move as fast as she did. As soon as she stepped off, she turned her attention back to the screen. 'Now!' she yelled so loudly that a family of four all turned to stare at her.

Charlie held her phone so Monique could see and pulled the black tiara from her locker. If she were going to be honest, the cluster of crystals that made up the front design was small and delicate, and their color nearly blended into her hair. From far enough away, maybe it only looked like a sparkly headband? She worked the small clear combs into her hair on either side and adjusted the crown part so it was centered. 'There.'

'Good. Keep it there. Now go put on some mascara and lip gloss and go. I'm making a note to get you some eyelash extensions next time I see you. I think they'd go a long way to—'

'Monique! I can't even wear sunglasses on the court

because they're too distracting. You think I can handle eyelash extensions?'

But the line had already gone dead. She smiled to herself, suddenly feeling better, and gathered up her things.

14

the grand master plan

CHARLESTON, APRIL 2016

Another FaceTime call came through as soon as she'd settled into the back of the tournament car, and she swiped it without looking. 'What, are you stalking me? I'm wearing the damn crown, okay?'

'Charlotte? Hello?' Marco's sexy Spanish accent caused her head to whip around.

'Marco?' She squinted at the screen. He was sitting on a carpeted floor somewhere, his back against an ottoman, wearing tennis clothes and smiling at someone offscreen. A man she didn't recognize sat in a chair behind Marco with an ice pack taped to his shoulder. She waited for Marco to turn his attention back to her but instead he offered someone off camera that killer smile. *'Gracias,'* he said, lisping the *s* sound in the classic Spaniard way. *'Volver a verme pronto.'* When he finally did turn back to Charlie, he stared at the screen blankly as though he'd forgotten whom he had called.

'Hey,' Charlie said, reaching up to turn on the overhead backseat light so he could see her more easily. She was elated to see he'd been following her tournament. Charleston was women only, and usually the men took little notice: they were competing in Monte Carlo at the Rolex Masters, and since Marco was not only the tournament favorite but also the current face of Rolex, he was undoubtedly busy. She ran a quick calculation and figured it was nearly midnight in Europe. His match must have run seriously late.

'Charlie? What's up? What's going on there?'

'What's going on here?' she teased, working harder than she thought to sound casual. 'Oh, just the usual. Winning is exhausting, you know.'

Again he glanced off camera and winked. Where was he? The players' lounge? His hotel room? Someone else's? Then he turned back to look at her. He either hadn't heard her or didn't catch the reference.

'Charlie? Listen, I only have a second. Can you do me a huge favor? Babolat just called that my new set of rackets are ready. If they ship them over, they could get held up in customs. If I have them meet you at JFK, can you fly them over to Munich?'

'Your new rackets?'

'You're playing Munich, I thought you said. And you're coming tomorrow, yes? Or the next day?'

So he remembered she was flying the next day, which logically meant either he knew she'd won and wasn't bothering to mention it, or he didn't even care enough to ask how she'd done. Both options sucked equally.

'Yes. I'm going out to *celebrate* tonight, and then I fly out tomorrow.'

'Connecting in JFK? Or Atlanta? They can get them to either one if I let them know tonight.'

'JFK.' Her voice was steely cold.

'Great. I'll tell Bernardo to call your people. Thanks, baby.'

'Is that all?'

'Sorry, *amante*, it's late here. I will like to see you when you arrive.' He proffered a kiss to the screen, although his gaze was still diverted somewhere off in the distance. *¡Besos!*'

She jammed the end-call button with her thumb so hard she almost dropped her phone. *Selfish prick,* she thought. *How do you say that in Spanish?*

Almost immediately, the phone rang again. Her heart rate surged at the thought that he'd called back to apologize, but Jake's name came up on the caller ID.

'Marcy told you, right? I'm on my way. The doping people literally attacked me right after the match, and it took forever until I could pee up to the acceptable standards.'

'You are a total rock star! Charlie, you won Charleston! You looked incredible out there. I really don't think the score reflects how much you dominated that match. And how she tried to mess with you at the end and you wouldn't let her? Todd and I were freaking out!'

Charlie allowed herself to smile. Now *this* was how you called someone to say congratulations.

'Do you even realize what this will do to your ranking? Not to even mention the big, fat, number one check?'

'Yeah, it's pretty great.'

'Understatement of the year. This is *career-making* for you. It's *happening*, Charlie, it really is. Between Todd and the new image and the attitude, it's all coming together. You won a Premier! Won it. And if that wasn't good enough, I'm about to make it better.'

'Better? Really? Because I'm feeling pretty great right now.'

'I got a phone call.'

'That sounds exciting.'

'I'm serious, Charlie. You're going to want to hear this. Wait, is that you pulling up?'

Charlie looked out the window and saw Jake standing outside the restaurant, phone to his ear. She ended the call, tossed her phone in her bag, and climbed out of the car.

'Wow. You look gorgeous,' Jake said, holding her shoulders. 'Monique?'

Charlie held out her tutu skirt in a little curtsy. 'What do you think? If it were up to me, I'd be in yoga pants.'

'Great win, Charlie!' an overweight man in a business suit bellowed from across the street.

'We love you, Charlie!' came the call from giggly preteen twin girls who trailed after their parents.

She waved and was delighted to see nearly everyone in sight waving back: pedestrians standing at the crosswalk, a line of people waiting for ice cream, nearly all the patrons of an outdoor restaurant.

'Where's Marco?' called out a woman with a newborn strapped to her chest.

Charlie laughed, although the mere mention of his name sent her nails digging into her palms. 'Monte Carlo!' she called back in what she hoped sounded like a carefree voice. 'Tough life, huh?'

The crowd laughed with her, and in that moment she actually *did* feel freer than she could remember. Light. Happy. The earnings, the ranking, the endorsements, it was all pretty damn terrific, but this had to be the best feeling of all.

Jake guided her into the restaurant, and the maître d' ushered them to the best table in the back corner. An enormous metal candelabra glowed from the middle, casting dramatic light around the entire area, and a small tin bucket held a lush arrangement of wildflowers. This farm-to-table restaurant was supposed to be the best in Charleston, possibly the entire South: a Michelin star and rave reviews from every food critic this side of the Mississippi. And Jake said all he'd had to do was call an hour earlier and use her name. Not Todd's. Not Marco's. *Charlie's.*

'Why is it only set for two?' she asked. 'Where is everyone? I thought the whole crew was here tonight.'

'That's where the better news comes in.'

'Marco's here?' she asked, before she could stop herself.

Jake looked confused. 'Marco's here? I thought he was playing Monte Carlo.'

'No, he is. I just thought for a moment . . . wondered if he didn't . . . Never mind.' She felt foolish. Hadn't she just spoken to him – seen him – sitting in a players' lounge in Europe? There was a greater chance Obama would hop on Air Force One to surprise her in Charleston than Marco would leave midway through a tournament.

'Charlie? Can you focus for a second?' Jake's foot was tapping fast against the floor.

She stared at him. He rarely got anxious about anything. 'What's going on? Why do I feel like you're about to tell me someone died?'

'No one died. It's crazier than that. I got a phone call.' He said this last part in a whisper, leaning in close to her ear.

'People only whisper bad news,' Charlie whispered back. 'Like "It's cancer," or "I'm pregnant."'

'Zeke Leighton's publicist called.'

Charlie raised her eyebrows. 'What does Zeke Leighton's publicist want? Tickets? Wait, probably my player credentials to a Slam? Which one? The Open? Or are they filming something in France? Let me guess . . . she's going to pretend they're really for Zeke, but then he'll suddenly have some commitment he can't cancel and she'll be forced to bring her entire family. Isn't this something your assistant can handle?'

'Charlie!' Jake growled, his lips nearly against her ear. 'Zeke is on his way to have dinner with you. Right now. He should be here any minute.'

Charlie laughed, ignoring him. 'Dad's already told me in not so many words that he's horrified by my unsportsmanlike conduct. God knows what Todd's doing: maybe figuring out new torture methods to work me even harder. And I'm sure Dan is on some horse-drawn carriage tour through the Old City.'

Jake all but pushed her into the banquette seat. He stood directly over her and said, 'I don't have enough time to explain the whole thing. Apparently Zeke is here filming a scene for that biopic he's doing with Steve Carell and

Jennifer Lawrence. He's in town for one night. And for some reason – one that was not made clear to me in any way – he had his people call to set up a dinner with you. He saw your match from his trailer today and insisted. I was planning to make sure it was all okay when you got here for drinks after the match, but then you got held up with the doping people. So he's going to be here, probably any second.'

'Wait. Zeke Leighton – *the* Zeke Leighton – is going to be here? To have dinner with us? Now?'

'Not us. You.' Jake's cell phone rang. He held it to his ear and nodded a few times. 'Okay. We're ready. Thanks.'

'Ready? We're *not* ready!' Charlie hissed. 'What's going on here? Is this a date? Isn't he dating what's-her-name? The Israeli model? What am I supposed to tell Marco? I know we haven't completely defined our terms, but I don't think publicly dating other people is acceptable at this point. This is going to be all over the tabloids! Jake, what the hell is happening here?'

Jake hissed, 'It's not dating, it's dinner. Now, be quiet for one second.' Suddenly, a hush fell over the restaurant. A small bustle of people had gathered inside the front door. All together, like a choreographed dance move that reminded her of the old 'Thriller' video, the crowd started moving toward her. Leading the pack in a pair of leather jeans and a black shawl-collar sweater was none other than Zeke Leighton, the most famous actor on planet earth. What Charlie noticed more than his world-renowned hair (dirty-blond waves that grazed his lashes) or that legendary squared-off jaw, or even the way he walked – exuding confidence, as though every step only confirmed to him that he was as spectacularly gorgeous as everyone claimed – was the way he held her gaze with his own, staring deep into her eyes as he traversed the distance between them, his unwavering eye contact equal parts comforting and unnerving.

'Charlotte Silver,' he said, his voice as familiar to her as her brother's. He was nearing forty and his breakthrough hit had come when he was seventeen, so she'd spent hours upon hours of her life watching him, examining him, reading about him, studying his face and features and every detail she could find. Which made her exactly like every other heterosexual woman between the ages of twelve and eighty, and every gay man alive. It was both disconcerting and supremely comfortable seeing him in the flesh after knowing him from afar for so long, and she wasn't surprised in the slightest when he said, 'Please, don't stand.'

But she wanted to. Why, she wasn't sure exactly. 'Zeke, it's great to meet you. I'm so glad we could do this,' she said smoothly, as though her knees weren't shaking, as if her hands weren't a sweaty mess.

As she stood, she noticed two things immediately. First, she was taller than he was. Which shouldn't have been surprising – she was six feet tall without heels, and she knew from a zillion magazine articles that he was five ten on a good day. Then, as she moved in to kiss his cheek (where had she found the nerve to do that?!), Charlie could see the deep grooves around his eyes and beside his mouth. Onscreen he was bronzed, velvety, perfect, and looked like a cross between a young Leo and a clean-cut Brad, but up close he was huskier, rougher, more masculine. And about a thousand times sexier.

lauren weisberger

He motioned for her to sit and he slid into the banquette next to her, closer than was strictly necessary, and she immediately caught a whiff of him. Oddly, it was an earthy, athletic scent that reminded her of male tennis players: that heady mixture of grass and sunshine and possibly clay that suggested he spent nearly all of his time outside. Again her mind went straight to Marco. What was she going to tell him? she wondered, before banishing the thought. If he'd uttered a single word of congratulation for the biggest win of her career, perhaps she would have declined dinner. Perhaps.

She looked around. Jake had disappeared.

'You're smiling. Share the joke with me?' Zeke asked, his own smile causing the slightest dimple below his left eye. How had she never seen that before?

'Oh, it's nothing.' She coughed. What were they supposed to do now? What was going on? She saw a light flash out of the corner of her eye.

'Sorry,' he said, not really sounding it. 'I try to fly under the radar, but it's not so easy with the big guy I have to drag around now.'

Charlie followed his gaze to the restaurant's front picture window, where she saw a gaggle of passersby gathered with iPhones poised, video cameras filming, flashes all on. There were at least two dozen crowded together, looking in, and they were jockeying for position as an enormous bald man in a sport coat and chinos kept them corralled. 'Aren't they too far away to see anything?'

Zeke nodded. 'Definitely. But that won't stop them. I'm sorry to tell you that the paparazzi probably aren't far behind them, and their flashes are way more disruptive. Hopefully the restaurant will handle it.'

250

'How do you deal with that? It must get so oppressive.'

'It's the same for you, I'm sure,' he said graciously.

Charlie laughed. 'Not exactly.'

'Well, for years I had a system down: in and out of back doors, baseball caps, the whole thing. But then there was all that stuff with the psycho woman, and now I have the bodyguard. Which, as you can see, does not exactly lend itself to discretion.'

Charlie vaguely remembered something about a stalker with a golf club breaking into Zeke's pool house.

The waitress came over and tried not to stare at Zeke. 'Hello, Ms Silver and Mr Leighton. We are so pleased to have you with us this evening. May I start you off with a drink?'

'I'll have a club soda and lime,' Charlie said reflexively.

Zeke turned to her and raised an eyebrow. 'Aren't we celebrating tonight? Last I checked, someone won a huge tournament. Doesn't that entitle you to something a little more festive?'

'May I recommend the Seelbach?' the waitress said. 'The recipe was lost during Prohibition and only recently rediscovered. It's made with whiskey, bitters, Cointreau, and a splash of champagne. It's our most popular.'

'Sure,' Charlie said with a shrug.

Zeke held up a finger. 'One for the lady please.'

There was a moment of awkward silence after the waitress left, and before she could even consider it, Charlie blurted out, 'What are we doing here?'

'Having a drink? And hopefully some dinner?' When Charlie didn't smile, he reached across the table and took her hand. 'There's no agenda, Charlotte. I'm shooting in

Charleston tonight and I saw on TV that you were here, too. I'm a big fan of yours. I think you have a gorgeous game, and I admit I've read everything on you I can find. So I called to see if I could take you out tonight because, hell, it's not every night I get to sit across from a beautiful woman who also happens to be very talented.'

Charlie gave him a disbelieving look. 'Seriously?' she asked. 'You expect me to believe that? It's your job to sit across from beautiful women.'

Zeke held both hands above his head in surrender. 'You really want to make me say it?'

'Say what?'

'That it's my grand master plan to get you into bed tonight? That I'm hoping you'll overlook the douchey bodyguard and your handsome tennis player boyfriend and the fact that six hundred people are going to follow us back to my hotel, and you're going to sleep with me regardless? Because I will. I'll say it.'

Charlie felt a quickening in her belly. 'I think you just said it.'

'Did I?' Zeke asked with a mischievous grin. Never had she met someone with so much confidence. Marco suddenly seemed like a boy-child compared with the man sitting across from her. She never imagined there could be a brasher, more openly confident category of men than professional athletes, but clearly she hadn't met an A-list movie star.

The waitress brought their drinks and they toasted. Charlie drained hers in nearly a single sip, and Zeke took a sip of water. And then she remembered all the headlines from years earlier. A messy divorce from his second wife, who was also his publicist and the mother of his two children. The deliciously salacious claims she'd made in court while arguing for full custody. The fiery car crash involving a Maserati, two beautiful women, and the Pacific Coast Highway at four in the morning. The judge-ordered thirty-day inpatient stint at Promises in Malibu. The ensuing rumors of cocaine-fueled orgies at his Hollywood Hills manse. A CAA agent who had supposedly overdosed at one of the parties before a phalanx of A-team crisis managers quickly reworked the story to suggest previous heart troubles. The drinking, the drugs, the womanizing, all left behind in either a brilliant PR coup or a genuine effort to turn his life around and keep his kids, Zeke's fame being well-enough established that he could not only survive but even flourish with a crushingly boring, squeaky-clean lifestyle. Tomes were written on whether the turnaround was sincere or merely for show, and every week it seemed like both camps had further proof. No one knew for sure, but it didn't really matter. Zeke Leighton was worth talking about.

'Has anyone ever said no to you before?' Charlie asked, leaning toward him on both elbows. Flirtatiously, were she being honest.

'Of course, more often than I care to admit. But I'm hoping you're not going to be one of them.'

When the waitress reappeared, Zeke asked her for recommendations. He raised a questioning eyebrow to Charlie, who nodded her assent. He ordered for them. Gun to her head, she couldn't have remembered a single dish he had requested. Nor would she be able to recall, when pressed by Piper, exactly what they'd discussed for the next two hours. There was a story that involved an overzealous fan and his mother that had her in tears, she was laughing so hard, and another about his crushing fear of flying (something she'd never read anywhere). He asked her questions about tennis, the tour, the rigorous travel schedule she maintained eleven months a year, and then asked even more in-depth follow-up questions when she answered. Surprisingly, his fan claim wasn't mere flattery: he knew the game inside and out, knew all the players, followed her closely. Charlie remembered from some article she'd read in *People* or *Entertainment Weekly* that he had a court at his house in LA and played often, and she found it charming that he didn't mention it. In fact, he didn't name-drop a single celebrity with whom he socialized (despite a well-documented visit with George and Amal at Lake Como the previous month and a high-profile week aboard the Sultan of Brunei's yacht, pictures Charlie had pored over when they were published) or try to impress her with all the homes she knew he owned. He was funny and self-deprecating and a good listener, and somehow – although she couldn't really explain it, to herself or anyone else – by the time they shared a lemon sorbet, she actually forgot he was famous. Forgot she'd been at least partially obsessed with him since she was a tween. Forgot that a crowd a hundred-deep had gathered outside the restaurant to catch a glimpse of him. Forgot she was sitting next to arguably the most recognizable man alive.

When Zeke looked her straight in the eye and asked, 'Would you like to get out of here?' Charlie didn't really think about Marco or the media frenzy that would surely ensue or the not-inconsequential fact that she'd had gym sessions that lasted longer than the total time she'd known Zeke. Thinking, for the first time in so long, didn't really factor in at all. She'd been a good girl. She followed the rules everyone else laid out for her. And to what end? She'd missed so much fun over the years with the training and traveling, the practice and tournaments, that she almost felt as if she *couldn't* say no. That she'd be letting herself down if she did – that is, her eighty-year-old self who would remember the night she'd had a sexy affair with a movie star in far greater detail than ten full years of tennis grind. She couldn't blame it on being drunk (she wasn't), or on being starstruck, or even on being angry at Marco. No, the truth was far simpler, and not something she would admit to Piper when they were hashing over every detail or Jake when he feigned disapproval because that's what big brothers do: she was doing it *because she could*.

Charlie looked him straight in the eye and grinned. 'Let's go.'

15

the morning after

CHARLESTON, APRIL 2016

Her fellow players often complained of not knowing where they were when they first woke up in a strange place: all the travel messed with their heads and left them feeling confused and displaced, like nowhere was home. Charlie usually nodded in agreement, but the truth was she always knew exactly where she was, whether it was a hotel room in Singapore or a short-term sublet in Wimbledon Village or a cramped seat on a flight across the Pacific. Today, though, for the first time in possibly her entire life, she understood what they meant. Despite the fact that Zeke Leighton lay next to her in bed – or maybe because of it

– for the briefest moment she couldn't remember where they were or how they'd gotten there.

'Hey,' he murmured, setting down his phone. 'You're up.'

She self-consciously pulled the duvet up to cover her chest, but he reached over and gently pulled it back. He kissed her breasts as though they were highly breakable objects of art.

'What time is it?' she asked, although she could clearly see the bedside clock read 9:12 a.m.

'It's a little after nine. I've been watching you sleep forever.'

'Forever?' She rolled over and, encouraged by his smile, kissed his mouth. 'Didn't we, like, only go to sleep a few hours ago?'

He rolled on top of her, and she could feel that he'd been waiting for her. She moaned.

'We can't,' he said, teasingly pulling her bottom lip in his teeth. 'You have a flight to catch, apparently.'

Munich. Had she already missed her connecting flight to New York?

'How bad is it?' she asked.

'Well, the hotel manager finally knocked. It sounds like your people *really* want to get in touch with you . . .'

'Where should I look?' Charlie asked, grabbing her phone. Immediately she could see that her home screen was exploding with messages: two from her father, two from Jake, one from Todd, four from Piper, and even one from Natalya.

'Take your pick. They all probably say the same thing. And just so you're not surprised, there's pretty much a riot outside the hotel right now. They know you're here.'

'They know I'm here?' Her voice was shrieky, panicked.

'Of course I'm here! I'm staying here! We're in *my* room! I didn't know until we left the restaurant that *you* were staying here, too.'

Zeke held his hands up in self-defense, but he couldn't disguise his amused expression. 'Don't shoot the messenger.'

She bypassed the screen of text messages without reading any of them and clicked open her *NY Post* app. Instantly, a photo of her and Marco appeared. There was a jagged red line running down the center and the headline screamed at her in a massive red font: 'CHEATERS!'

She closed her eyes and took another breath. It was a hideous thing to be called, perhaps even more so as a professional athlete – there was something about that word that just cut her legs right out from under her. *Cheater.* Only the most spineless actually cheated – in sport, in love, or in life. And now here she was, being accused of it in bold print for all the world to see.

Charlie forced herself to pick up her phone, but Zeke clamped his hand over it. 'Maybe you shouldn't read it right now. Not much to be gained.'

She wrested it away from him and quickly read the first two sentences:

No love in this game! It looks like even their close friends got it wrong: despite reports the couple were hot and heavy, it appears that tennis phenoms Marco Vallejo and Charlotte Silver each scored – with other people.

She looked up at Zeke, who was watching her closely. And then it occurred to her: the 'CHEATERS!' headline was plural.

> The first-ranked men's player is competing at the Rolex Open in Monte Carlo and has just advanced to the semifinals. Vallejo's love interest is still a mystery, but multiple sources confirm he was seen kissing a blond beauty at the official player party before departing with her. The cute couple was spotted later in the evening sharing yet another kiss on the balcony outside the gorgeous Spaniard's hotel room – this time while she straddled his lap wearing what appeared to be a men's T-shirt! Not to worry, Silver hit her own winner with a romantic dinner à deux with none other than Zeke Leighton. Not only did the steamy new couple share multiple champagne cocktails and nibble on truffle risotto, but his bodyguard also made a drugstore pit stop (safety first!). And it doesn't look like they kissed good night at the door . . . Hotel staff report the gorgeous duo are still holed up in the movie star's room. Check back for more details!

And if that weren't bad enough, there were pictures. Four of them, to be precise. In the first, Charlotte and Marco shared their first public kiss on the red carpet in Miami. Right after that was a zoomed-in shot of what appeared to be a blond teenager wearing an oversized, collared Nike shirt that ended halfway down the same perfect thighs that were firmly wrapped around Marco's midsection. He was laughing as she kissed his neck. The third photo in the series featured Charlie and Zeke at dinner the previous night, both leaning in toward each other, making obvious, flirtatious eye contact. The last was, thankfully, a bit grainy, but not so much that you couldn't clearly recognize Zeke's bodyguard handing a small red box to a cashier.

259

'Oh. My. God.'

Charlie didn't realize she'd said it aloud until Zeke pulled her closer. 'Come here, this is all crap. Worthless gossip crap. Don't even look at it.'

'Oh. My. God. I'm so humiliated, I don't even know where to begin.' Immediately a thought struck her: her father. It was quickly followed by another: her mother. 'Nooooo,' she moaned, as though physically ill. Which was exactly how she was beginning to feel.

She looked back to her phone and began to scroll through everyone's texts.

Call me ASAP.

C? Where are you? Call me before you read anything.

911! 911!

He's not a sicko secret rapist, is he? You're fine, right? Just not like you . . .

Want to know every delicious detail!!! Call me the second you come up for air!!!

Your flight to Munich has been changed to tonight. Check your email for details.

Charlie, please call me the moment you receive this text. Thank you.

The last text she opened was Natalya's. It was a picture. The subjects were clearly unaware they were being snapped, probably by someone's cell phone. Although she couldn't clearly see the man's face, she could tell by the hair and the distinctive purple check button-down that it was Marco. His head was buried in a woman's neck – or rather, a girl's – but her face was unobstructed. The only caption that accompanied it was 'Look familiar?'

The misspelling distracted her, but only briefly. The girl

did look familiar. She wasn't a player, not even a junior or an amateur, Charlie knew that much. Perhaps she was another player's girlfriend's friend? Or someone who worked at the tournament? The simplest answer was usually the correct one: most likely she was a pretty local girl, one who waited all year for the men's tour to come to town, who looked familiar because she looked like every young, attractive tennis groupie everywhere. As Charlie was squinting at the screen, trying to place her, another text popped open on her screen. It was also from Natalya, and it featured a screen grab. Charlie spread-zoomed the photo and saw that the girl's profile was featured on the homepage of the website Au Pair in America.

Charlie remembered then. Elin. That wasn't her name, of course, but that's what all the players jokingly called her because she could have been a clone of Tiger's ex-wife – the other hot nanny. This girl's name was Sofie Larsson and she was an au pair working for a male player's coach. She was Swedish, eighteen years old, and experienced with children from toddlers to teenagers (she didn't really know newborns but was sooooo excited to learn). Her fluent languages included Swedish, German, English, Italian, and some Dutch, and she planned to attend university one day to study communications. Naturally, she lovvvvvvved to travel.

And screw tennis players, Charlie thought, closing out the text. Little Miss I-Love-Kids-and-Speak-Everything didn't think twice about throwing down for Marco Vallejo. *Better add Spanish to the repertoire.*

'I'm going to head back to my room.' Zeke's voice snapped her back to reality. When had he gotten up and dressed?

'What? Sorry. I, uh . . . This is all kind of new to me.'

He walked around the bed to sit beside her and didn't stop her this time when she yanked the covers up to her armpits. 'Try not to worry too much, okay? These things never last more than a news cycle or two.'

When Charlie didn't respond, Zeke reached out and took her chin between his thumb and forefinger. 'Hey. My people have already put out a statement that while I am a huge fan of yours, we are nothing more than friends who enjoyed a dinner together. That we shared a ride back to the hotel together is hardly noteworthy. It's not much of a coincidence we'd be booked at the same place, considering it's the nicest in Charleston. When there is no new information beyond that, it tends to fade quickly.'

Charlie realized he hadn't yet seen the Marco part of the story. Or he had and he didn't care. And why should he? Like he said, they were consenting adults and she was mature enough to have predicted at least some of this was going to happen. Truth be told, she'd known it would and had done it anyway.

'Okay. Thanks.' She smiled and accepted a kiss from him. At some point during the night, he'd morphed from Zeke Leighton, Movie Star, to Zeke, the sexy older guy who was funny and complimentary and had the slightest paunch and knew his way around a damn good full-body massage. Maybe it was when she caught the briefest glimpse of his self-consciousness when he'd gotten naked, or when he'd peed with the bathroom door ajar, or when he'd made that face in bed. She wasn't sure when, exactly, she'd realized he was just a person, but it had been both a relief and a disappointment.

'What's your number?' he asked, typing it as she told him. Her phone rang.

'There, we have each other's numbers now. Keep in touch? I know we both have crazy schedules and the whole thing, but I had a great time last night, Charlotte.'

'Charlie. Call me Charlie.'

They both laughed.

'Charlie. You're headed on the European swing now, right? Clay season?'

She nodded, slightly impressed.

'Well, I'm off to shoot in Sydney after here, but I'll be back in the States after that for a long stretch. Maybe we'll link up sometime this summer?'

She lowered her lashes and batted them. 'I'll have my people send your people some tickets to the Open. Come if you can.'

'I go every year, did you know that? We have great box seats in the—'

'You ever go as the guest of a top-seeded player? No? Well, the player box seats are the best ones of all.'

He grinned. 'You're the real deal, Charlie Silver, you know that?' Before she could answer, he kissed her once more on the cheek and walked to the door. A moment later, after one last delicious Zeke Leighton smile, he was gone.

Charlie didn't remember dialing Piper's number until her friend started yelling.

'Is it true? I mean, I saw the pictures with my own eyes, but is it really true?'

When Charlotte cleared her throat, Piper literally screamed.

'Oh my god. You had sex with Zeke Leighton. *Zeke*

Leighton! There's some publicist-issued bullshit about you guys being just friends and trying to turn a box of condoms into a tin of Sucrets, but I knew it. I just knew it!'

Charlie glanced at the condom wrappers on the floor and smiled. 'Yeah. It was pretty fun.'

'I wish you could see me right now,' Piper said breathlessly. 'I'm pacing. It's six in the morning here, by the way. I woke up to go to the bathroom at three and glanced at my phone, and Jesus *Christ*, Charlie. Zeke Leighton?'

'It's strange, but he's just kind of a regular guy.'

'Yeah, and just kind of not! If that's some BS move on your part to keep from telling me every fucking detail, well, it's not going to work. Can you imagine if I just happened to fall into bed with Matt Damon and then claimed it was no big deal?'

'I'm not saying it wasn't a big deal, just that—'

'How many times? What positions? Is he a generous lover? He always plays such sensitive roles, I imagine he'd be amazing in bed. Let's start with that. You can tell me about your dinner after the good stuff.'

Charlie laughed. Part of her felt ridiculous sharing the intimate details with her friend, but it was too much fun to keep it to herself. This was what girlfriends did, right? Growing up, she'd missed it all: the games of spin the bottle and the movie theater make-outs and the sneaking out at night to meet a boy. She'd never had a best friend before Piper, never really shared her secrets with anyone besides Jake. It was too delicious to resist.

'Oh, you know. It was pretty much what you'd expect,' she said coyly, smiling in anticipation of Piper's reaction. It didn't disappoint.

'I'm hanging up. Seriously, I'm hanging up right this second if you don't start talking!'

'Okay, okay. We got back here a little after ten. He went to his room first in case anyone was watching and then came down to mine a few minutes later. He brought a little speaker and his phone and a candle he found somewhere and—'

'He's a total pro. I bet he brings, like, a sex kit everywhere he goes. Did he have little airplane bottles of vodka to mix drinks? They're always doing that in the movies.'

'He's recovering, remember?'

'I thought that was for show? For his kids? Or his image? That can't be real . . .'

'I think it is. He didn't have a drink at dinner, and I only had one.'

'You had *sober sex* with Zeke Leighton? Is that what you're saying?'

Charlie held the phone away from her ear. 'Can you stop screaming? You're killing my ears.'

'Let's just be clear on this: you were both stone cold sober?'

'Yes.'

'Oh my god. You're getting married! Charlie! You're marrying Zeke Leighton!'

'Piper, come on. Except for that very first time with Marco in Palm Springs, I don't think I've ever *not* had sex sober. I go months at a time without having a single drink. You did it once, too. Remember?'

Piper shuddered audibly. 'Worst hookups of my life, hands down. I am, in fact, actually marrying Ronin – literally agreeing to spend my entire life with him and have his babies – and we both still want to split a bottle of wine before doing the deed. It's human nature, Charlie.'

'Well, I don't know what to tell you. I had sex with Zeke Leighton sober. Three times. One of those was in the shower. Well, technically in the shower, although we ended up on the floor . . .'

Piper moaned. *I can barely breathe.* You remember his shower scene in *Around the World*? Where he goes down on Rachel McAdams and there's all that steam and water and it's pretty much the sexiest thing you've ever seen? Because that's what I'm picturing right now.'

Charlie glanced toward the shower, which was still wet, and felt herself blush. 'Yeah, it wasn't too far off from that.'

'That is soooooo insanely hot! Okay, okay, let's start from the beginning. You win Charleston – congrats, by the way – and you get a call from him? His people? Take me through the whole thing from the very first moment.'

Charlie knew she should get up and face the mayhem. Her father and Jake had both been calling nonstop since she'd been on the phone. Emails from Todd were popping up on her screen every three minutes. The maid had knocked twice. She still needed to straighten out her travel plans to Europe. There was the small matter of having her one-night stand plastered all over the place. And there was Marco, her semi-boyfriend on whom she'd publicly cheated, and who had cheated right back. And whose tennis rackets she was supposed to shuttle from JFK to Munich, on a flight she wasn't sure she was going to make. But the pull of Piper's interest and the pleasure of reliving the night was too strong. Screw it. The world wasn't going to fall apart if she took another few minutes to talk to her best friend. She collapsed back into the tangled mess of cottony-soft sheets and fluffy down and stretched her legs. Toes pointed like a ballerina, she began slowly lifting each leg high into the air.

'I knew the second I walked into the restaurant that something was up,' she said, feeling calmer than she had any right to feel. Not thinking about what it meant, for once, to be the bad girl. Not thinking about how good it was to break a few rules. There would be fallout to deal with for sure – Marco, the tabloids, her family, just for starters – but Charlie told herself she'd think about it all later. Right now, there was a story to tell.

Charlie grinned. And then she talked and talked and talked.

16

better in bed?

PARIS, MAY 2016

Charlie spotted her father on the escalator before he saw her, but something about the way he stood kept her from running toward him. She hung back for a moment and watched as he stared off into space, looking barely aware of his surroundings. He wasn't slumped, exactly, but he hunched forward in a way that made him look older. The worry lines looked permanently etched into his face – she could see them from where she was standing.

He shuffled off at the bottom and glanced around, clearly unsure of what to do next. When his eyes found Charlie's, his entire expression changed. He instantly stood taller and his mouth turned into a deep, genuine smile, but his eyes remained distant.

'Charlie! What are you doing here?' Mr Silver asked, although his joy was apparent. He wrapped his arms around Charlie and she immediately smelled the smoke.

'What, I can't hang with my dad a little?'

He pressed his hands on her shoulders and kissed both her cheeks. 'Don't you have something better to do than meet your old man at the airport? It was nice enough you bought me a plane ticket. I was planning to take a taxi.'

His embarrassment at accepting the ticket was obvious, and Charlie did him the courtesy of ignoring it. 'What, you don't remember French taxi drivers from your player days? Because they haven't changed at all. And I wouldn't wish that on my worst enemy.'

Her father laughed and offered her his arm. Together they weaved through the crowds gathered at baggage claim. He didn't have a suitcase so they headed outside, where a tournament car waited for them. They climbed into the backseat and her father shook his head.

'I can't believe your mother never got to see this,' he said, his voice cracking just the smallest bit. 'The car service, the awards and accolades. The French Open. You.'

'I've been thinking about her, too,' Charlie said quietly. In moments they'd exited Charles de Gaulle and were whizzing through the farms that surrounded the airport. It always surprised her how rural the land was around one of the busiest international airports in the world. 'Today's her birthday.'

Her father nodded. 'She would have been forty-nine today. My god, I can't even imagine it. Almost fifty. She's frozen in time at thirty-five, a beautiful young mother. She'd already had both you and Jake at your age.'

Charlie stared out the window. He hadn't said any of it, but he didn't need to: her mother had dedicated her life to Charlie and Jake and their father. She had sacrificed her career to be home for all of them; she had cooked and driven carpool and helped with homework and thrown surprise birthday parties and cheered from the sidelines every chance she had. And what had Charlie done to honor her? Excelled at her sport, yes. But also fired her coach and mentor, who'd always stressed the importance of honesty and integrity. Gotten accused of winning tournaments by cheating. Become embroiled in a very public scandal involving two men she had slept with but didn't love. 'Agreed to disagree' with her father, who was clearly struggling with something that she couldn't even name. Charlie noticed her father had not said in ages how proud her mother would have been. It was something he used to say frequently, almost reflexively. *Your mother would have been bursting with happiness to see the woman you've become. She would have been so proud of the person she helped raise. You remind me so much of her.* He had said the words so often they'd almost lost their meaning, but now she would have done anything to hear them again.

Charlie coughed. 'Thanks for coming all the way here, Dad. I know it can't be easy to miss that much work.'

Her father looked at her, surprised. 'What are you talking about, "come all the way here"? You think it's every day your daughter is seeded fourth in a Grand Slam? Charlie, you won Charleston and Munich. You have a very real chance of winning the French Open. The *French Open*. How can you even suggest I wouldn't be here to see it?'

Munich. Perhaps the strangest tournament of her entire life. Fresh off her win in Charleston, feeling alternately exhilarated and terrified by the Zeke Leighton media frenzy and the out-of-body strangeness of Marco and the hot au pair, Charlie was convinced she would be too distracted to do much of anything in Munich. She'd actually spent the entire flight to Germany berating herself. Forget about the sleeping with a stranger and having the whole world find out – that was bad enough. Not to mention embarrassing. But the all-nighter was too physically taxing on an elite athlete, even if she hadn't been drinking. That sleepless night combined with jet lag would make her feel like she was slogging through mud on the court. She would be lethargic and slow and mentally distracted. Just when so many other things were coming together, she was doing her best to sabotage herself. By the time she had checked into the Mandarin Oriental in Munich, she was a mess: exhausted, achy, humiliated. Todd greeted her with an insane workout and the advice *Steer clear of Marco. All tournament. No distraction. You hear me?* And somehow she had managed it. They texted once – *good luck at tomorrow's match, so busy, see you soon* – but nothing else. The awkwardness of the non-reckoning was even worse than the shame of actually putting it all out on the table and acknowledging that they'd both 'cheated' on each other.

Charlie had been certain she would lose in the first round to a wild-card player. And she had stumbled, no doubt. It took her three dicey sets of some of her worst tennis ever to win the first round, and the second round wasn't any prettier. Charlie was better rested by the quarters but still feeling emotional and off balance, and she surprised herself when she stayed focused enough to win that in two clean sets. When it came time to face Natalya in the semis, Charlie was certain she would lose, but Natalya had gotten a horrible case of food poisoning the night before and had to withdraw from the tournament. And just like that, Charlie advanced to the finals. There she once again faced Karina Geiger, who'd been ranked number two under Natalya for the third-longest stretch in history, but, as Charlie had been earlier in the tournament, Karina was off her game. She couldn't get a first serve in, and her net game quickly fell apart. She rallied briefly toward the end of the second set and forced a tiebreaker, but Charlie was still able to capitalize on Karina's mental breakdown at that point to close it out 6–4, 7–5. She'd stood on the court, motionless, for nearly a full minute before the realization set in: she'd won not just one but two major tournaments. Back-to-back. That win would bump her worldwide ranking up to the top five and give her great seeding going into the French Open. It was happening, all of it, and happening fast. Still, she could barely believe it.

'Charlie? Charlie? Tune in, Charlie . . .'

She turned back to her father. He was staring at her, brows furrowed.

'What? Why are you looking at me like that?' She knew it had everything to do with the fact that his daughter was involved in a very public love triangle, but she also knew he would never bring himself to say it.

He smiled. 'Just your old man being concerned. That's all.'

The car exited the highway into the city limits, hurtling

alongside the Seine, the Parisian buildings growing taller and more condensed.

'I just won Charleston and Munich! Are things really so grim?' She tried to keep her voice lighthearted, but she knew exactly what he meant.

'You're looking thin.'

'That's a good thing, Dad. Todd has been saying from the beginning that losing ten pounds would make me faster on my feet. He's right! I was exhausted in the first round – and if it had been last year, I definitely wouldn't have been able to see it through – but I rallied this time. Got over it. And I think it's because I slimmed down overall while still building lean muscle. Who knows? Maybe the Achilles' never would have happened last year if I'd been at fighting weight.'

'It's just that . . .' He appeared to be choosing his words carefully. 'I'm worried that he's pushing you too hard. Your fitness regimen alone sounds excruciating. And that's not taking into account your actual tennis training.'

'It's not *that* much more than what I was doing with Marcy,' she said. A total lie, and they both knew it.

'Take me through it.'

'Come on.'

'I'm just curious. Indulge me.'

Charlie sighed. 'Mondays, Tuesdays, and Wednesdays are full days. That's three hours of tennis, an hour and a half of fitness, lunch, a break, and then two hours of tennis and another hour of fitness. Thursday is a half day, which is only the morning tennis and fitness. Friday and Saturday are full days. Then Sundays are off. It's really not so bad.' Charlie cleared her throat, hoping her lie sounded more believable. The truth was, the regimen felt even more grueling than the description suggested.

'Sweetheart . . .' His voice was low, as though he found this information heartbreaking.

'Dad, I mean this in the nicest possible way, but you're a little out of the loop. Everyone says that fifteen years ago women could get by with solid strokes and strategy alone. If you went to three sets, the winner was the woman who could just stay standing. But now? After all these crazy physical girls have come up? Where they train every bit as hard as – if not harder than – the men? There's no choice anymore. I have to train like that if I want to compete.'

'I guess it's a different game these days,' he said quietly.

'Yes. I've seen old footage of Martina and Chrissy back in the day. Martina won her first tournament when she was downright fat! Can you even imagine?'

They were quiet the remainder of the ride. When the car pulled up in front of Le Meurice, Jake was waiting for them on the sidewalk. He looked adorable in a fitted Moncler puffer vest over a chunky ribbed long-sleeved T-shirt and jeans. The cashmere beanie he wore was the exact shade of blue as his eyes, and for the thousandth time Charlie wondered why he wasn't dating anyone. He was handsome and put together, and seemingly confident. She'd met a handful of his dates in the past, and they were all a lot like him: neither overly effeminate nor hyper-buff gym Nazis whose arms and chests could barely be contained. Charlie knew Jake had had a slutty period in his early twenties when, according to him, he'd 'gone on a tear of gay bars and clubs straight through Hell's

Kitchen, Chelsea, and Brooklyn,' but a hepatitis close call had scared him back to serial monogamy. Now, as far as she could tell, Jake would only date one person at a time – and after insisting on the full battery of tests – but none of them seemed to last longer than a couple of months. Only one Thanksgiving had he brought someone home, a frustrated electrical engineer named Jack who spent his nights trying to break into the stand-up comedy circuit and had cracked them all up with smart, irreverent jokes about politics, current events, and his own unfortunate red hair. Mr Silver had surprised them both by being relaxed and welcoming; Charlie raved on about how much she loved Ginger Jack, how cute 'Jake & Jack' would look on a wedding invitation, how they could name their first-born Jon or Jill, or Jamie if they were feeling oppressed by gender stereotyping. Yet, when Christmas rolled around, Jake showed up alone, and with the exception of a few murmurs about 'schedules' and 'priorities,' they'd never heard another word about Jack.

Her father and Jake wrapped their arms tightly and unabashedly around each other and remained that way for some time. When they finally broke apart, Jake examined Mr Silver as though he were a lost son who had finally returned home after a long and arduous journey.

'What's going on here?' she asked, staring at them both.

Mr Silver smiled, but it was forced. 'Nothing, sweetheart. I'm just always happy to see you two.'

'Seriously, you're looking at each other like someone died. What am I missing?'

Identical expressions washed over both Jake's and her father's faces, but Charlie couldn't identify the emotion before Jake grabbed her arm. 'Come on, you've got an interview with French *Elle* right now. Dad, do you want to go to the room or join us?'

'What do you think?' her father asked with a grin, and followed them. Charlie felt guilty for wishing he would have chosen otherwise.

'Shouldn't I change? I thought the deal was I had to have at least some visible bedazzling for all interviews.'

Charlie nearly had to run to keep up with Jake as he traversed the marble lobby. She heard at least three people stage-whisper her name to their companions as they passed.

'Here,' Jake said, handing her a crystal-encrusted cosmetic bag with her initials in black rhinestones. He pushed her toward the ladies' room. 'Pick a few things from there. We'll meet you in the hospitality suite on the second floor in five. Go!'

She walked into the carpeted bathroom with intricate wood paneling and a three-wick Diptyque candle wafting out the most delicious scent. A quick glance in the mirror confirmed the dark under-eye circles and the dry, peeling lips she already felt. Her usually shiny hair looked dull and heavy; her complexion managed to appear waxy under her omnipresent tan. No wonder her father was so concerned: she looked like shit.

Digging through the duffel-sized cosmetic bag, she pulled out a round brush, her favorite Oscar Blandi dry shampoo, a cordless flat-iron, a bronzer, some mascara, and two lip glosses. Natalya's traveling hair and makeup people were finally understandable. It took close to ten minutes, during which Jake texted her five times, but she definitely made improvements. There was an entire entourage set up in the hospitality suite when she entered: Jake, Todd, her father, an impossibly chic French woman who must have been the reporter, a photographer, his assistant, and a twentysomething guy they introduced as the translator.

'To catch all my mistakes,' laughed Sandrine, the reporter, in what sounded like flawless English.

Charlie greeted everyone and tried not to feel nervous: she still wasn't accustomed to interviews much beyond the usual post-match Q&A about point play and mental focus. But *Elle* didn't really care about her strategy going into the French Open. Not with the current headlines about Zeke Leighton and Marco Vallejo.

'Darling, sit where you are comfortable,' Sandrine said, waving her elegant manicure toward the suite's living room. 'We will talk and then take the photos. *Oui?*'

Charlie nodded and settled into one of the tufted armchairs. She forced herself to smile when really all she wanted was to check into her room, take a hot shower, and order an early dinner. The next few days of training were going to be more intense than they usually were at the start of a Grand Slam, and she needed to start focusing on her routine.

There was a knock at the door and a small commotion as a waiter wheeled in a tea service. With a great flourish he placed plates of intricate pastries and delicate teacups and saucers on the table between Charlie and Sandrine, and when he poured the tea from a heavy silver pot, he quietly assured Charlie that it was '*sans* caffeine.' When Charlie thanked him, he bowed and murmured, 'Mademoiselle.'

'Charlotte, darling,' Sandrine said, managing to make

Charlie's name sound chicly French. 'Tell me how it feels to be a favorite for the Roland-Garros this year?' She pronounced 'favorite' like 'fah-vo-reet.'

She hesitated and out of the corner of her eye she saw Todd twitch like some character in a horror movie. 'It feels fantastic. I've worked a long time for this opportunity, and I'm feeling really good about my chances.'

'Do you think you can win here in *Paree*?'

Charlie wanted to talk about the confidence she felt playing on clay, how it was rare for an American to be so comfortable on the surface, but she'd grown up on Birchwood's Har-Tru courts and had learned how to use the slide and the slower pace to her advantage. She may have even mentioned her new fitness regimen and how working with Todd was giving her an edge, but another glance in his direction revealed more twitching, so instead she said, 'Yes. I know I can win. Now I just have to get out there and do it.'

You won't be winning any awards for being articulate, that's for sure, Charlie thought, but she was pleased to see that Todd's twitching had been replaced by a satisfied smirk.

'What do you think has changed? Less than one year ago you were injured in the first round at Wimbledon – and some even claim that was a . . . how do you say it? A questionable injury. How do you explain your return to the top?' Sandrine pursed her perfect pink lips in a way that made Charlie want to pinch them. Not nicely.

'Questionable injury?' Charlie turned to the translator, thinking there must have been some misunderstanding, but he merely nodded his confirmation. 'I tore my Achilles' tendon and broke my left wrist. The foot injury required

surgery and months of rehab. I'm not sure how that qualifies as a "questionable injury," if that's what you're
suggesting . . .'

Sandrine waved her hand as though these were the
silliest of details. 'Yes, you are right, of course.' Wide, sharky
smile. 'Let's talk about more fun things, yes? Romance! I
know all our readers would love to hear about your trysts
with various beautiful men, *oui?* Tell me, is it Zeke or
Marco? Or both?' Sandrine's laugh rang out in the suddenly
silent room.

'Ms Bisset, as you undoubtedly remember, we agreed
before the interview that Charlotte's personal life beyond
the details of her travel and training schedule would not
be discussed.' Jake's voice was firm, but Charlie could detect
concern.

Sandrine laughed again but her gaze remained fixed on
Charlie. 'Charlotte, darling, surely you don't mind clarifying
a bit for us, do you? Women the world over – myself
included, of course – would love to share the bed of just
one of these men. And to think you have had them both.
Well, we cannot just ignore it, can we?'

Jake jumped to his feet. 'Ms Bisset, I think that's quite
enough.'

'Well, it is true, no?' She had the self-satisfied look of
a cat who'd just devoured a helpless baby bird.

'Either we'll have to redirect the conversation back to
Charlotte's upcoming French Open appearance or that will—'

'Are you asking me which one is better in bed?' Charlie
innocently batted her eyelashes. 'Or just who I prefer in
general? I'd like to better understand your question.'

'Charlie!' The way Jake barked her name instantly

reminded her of her mother: the surprise hurt, the emphasis on the second syllable when most people stressed the first. In that instant, she was transported back in time twenty years. Perhaps it reminded her father as well. He was so appalled by the interview's turn that he strode out the suite's door without a word to anyone.

Sandrine returned Charlie's steady gaze, and Charlie saw a newfound respect in the woman's expression. The reporter reached over to choose a biscotto from the plate, but when she placed it next to her teacup without taking a single bite, Charlie knew she was just buying time.

'Well, either topic is most interesting, darling. Please share whatever it is you're thinking.'

'Charlotte . . .' The warning came from Todd now. Charlie glanced toward him and was surprised to see Dan sitting to his right, staring at his feet. When had he sneaked in?

'Whatever it is I'm thinking . . . hmm, let's see. I'm thinking that I have never felt better prepared for a tournament in my entire life. As you know, I came up playing primarily on clay courts, so I'm super-comfortable with the surface. Thanks to my incredible team' – she stopped here and waved in Todd and Dan's general direction – 'I'm fitter than ever and confident in my new approach. My injuries are healed entirely. I've never felt better.'

If Sandrine noticed that Charlie had redirected the interview, she didn't let on. 'What do you say to the folks out there who point out that you've never won a Grand Slam? Actually . . . wait, I think I have it right here.' Sandrine rifled through her notes. 'Natalya Ivanov was quoted last week as saying, "Charlotte has shown great improvement over the last few months. Of course she has good strokes and an overall strong game. But I think everyone knows you're really just an amateur until you win a Slam." What do you respond to that?'

Charlie forced herself to laugh, but she really wanted to leap out of her chair and snatch the notes away from Sandrine. Natalya had said that? When? 'What would I say to that? I actually don't have to say anything to that. I think my win here in two weeks will speak for itself.'

'So you're feeling confident?'

'Very. And until then, I have nothing more to say. It sounds like Natalya might not agree, but words don't mean much: wins do.' Charlie stood up, clearly catching Sandrine off guard, and reached over to shake her hand. How many interviews had she sat passively for, enduring probing and offensive question after question, always too timid or insecure or polite to do anything but suffer through it? *No longer,* she thought, turning her attention to the camera crew. 'I'm hoping fifteen minutes will be enough to get the right shot. I'm afraid with my schedule today, it's all I can spare.'

Charlie glanced over at her entourage while the translator addressed the camera crew. Jake and Todd wore dumbfounded expressions, but Dan was grinning at her. When she caught his eye, he gave her a subtle thumbs-up. As Jake chatted with Sandrine, making sure she was happy, Charlie scrolled through her news alerts. It was amazing how good it felt to control the interview. So long as she didn't wonder how she'd feel when it was in print.

The first two days of practice in the Stade Roland-Garros were textbook. Charlie moved through her fitness and hitting sessions like a machine, taking care to stretch both before and after every workout and to carefully follow the tournament physio's instructions on how to continue strength training without depleting energy. Todd had arranged for Skype sessions with a prominent nutritionist who specialized in professional athletes (while only using the phrase 'big girl' once, which Charlie felt was a notable improvement), and although none of the information the woman shared with Charlie was earth-shattering, it felt good to have someone making recommendations for each meal. The ratios of carbohydrates, protein, and fat were complicated and important: when you burned a few thousand calories every day merely doing your job, it was crucial to refuel properly. She was supposed to eat every two hours, so after finishing her final practice on the second day, Charlie turned to Dan.

'Want to come to player dining? I'm supposed to get a protein smoothie and some yogurt parfait thing that apparently the French do better than anyone else, surprise, surprise.'

Dan shifted his weight between his feet. 'Sorry, I can't right now.'

'What? Don't tell me you have a riverboat cruise reservation? No, we've been here two days, I'm sure you've done that already.'

He laughed.

'Private tour at the Louvre? A stroll through the Left Bank? No? You must be shopping, then. Not that you strike me as an Hermès kind of guy. Don't you just love a store that makes you stand in line for an hour before they'll sell you a two-thousand-dollar wallet? I know I do.'

Dan reached into his racket bag and pulled out a tattered

trifold wallet made of vinyl and a strip of Velcro. 'Hermès all the way, baby. The ladies love it.'

It was Charlie's turn to laugh. 'Come on, it'll just be for a few minutes. I swear I won't waste much of your sight-seeing time.'

Dan clicked on his phone and stared at the time. He hesitated but then said, 'Okay, I think I can do ten minutes. But only if we go right now.' He threw his racket bag over his shoulder and leaned over to pick up Charlie's.

'What, have you got a hot date?' Charlie said teasingly, but she could see instantly by Dan's red cheeks that she'd guessed right. 'Oh my god, you do. You have a date! When on earth did you have time to pick someone up in Paris? We've been putting in twelve-hour days!'

'It's nothing,' Dan said, his voice cracking just the tiniest bit. He coughed. 'Just some girl from school. She's traveling through right now and so am I. We're meeting up for coffee later.'

'Sounds seriously sexy,' Charlie teased, nearly racing to keep up with him as he strode through the grounds on the way to the player area. They each showed their credentials and took the elevator up to player dining. 'Nothing like coffee to say I want to sleep with you.'

'Classy,' Dan said.

'Dan's getting some!'

She sang this refrain on repeat until he stopped in his tracks and turned around to face her. 'Seriously?'

He waved toward an empty table that overlooked an exhibition court. 'What do you want? I'll get it.'

'Will you get the wrong idea if I say coffee?' Charlie asked flirtatiously.

He returned with two yogurt parfaits plus an espresso for him and a green juice for Charlie. He slid into the booth across from her and devoured his parfait in three bites.

'Seriously, Dan. This girl is in town – in Paris! – for, like, one night and you're taking her to *coffee*? Bad move. You can do better.'

'Ah, the Charlotte Silver school of romance. Where should I take her? Straight to my hotel room? No date required?'

Charlie must have visibly flinched, because Dan immediately looked repentant. 'I'm sorry,' he said. 'I didn't mean it like that.'

'Don't apologize. I haven't exactly been a pillar of morality lately.'

'Well, it's certainly none of my business.' Dan sipped his coffee cup and kept his eyes on the table.

'Do you realize that I spend more time with you on a daily basis than almost anyone else in my entire life? I think we're pretty much each other's business.'

Dan grinned. 'Well, in that case, inquiring minds want to know . . .'

'What? Who's better in bed? Zeke or Marco?'

'I was just going to ask what's going on with either one of them, but, hey, if you want to go there, consider me officially interested.'

Charlie sighed. 'There's really not much to report. Zeke was definitely a onetime thing. I'm going to put it in my scrapbook and look back on it when I'm old and decrepit – and in the meantime try to remind myself that I have nothing to be embarrassed about.'

Dan nodded and for a second she regretted her own honesty – who was *he* to judge?

There was a moment of silence before Dan asked, 'And Marco?'

'Marco, Marco, Marco. It's great having someone to hang out with at tournaments, someone who understands the lifestyle. But he was kind of a jerk before the whole Zeke/ Nannygate drama even started, and since then, well . . . we haven't really talked about it.'

Dan's eyes widened. 'You haven't really talked about it? The entire world has talked about it and you two just haven't bothered?'

'Not exactly.'

The first time Charlie and Marco had seen each other after the whole situation was in the lobby of the Sofitel in Munich. He was on his way to practice and Charlie was en route to her room.

'*Hola*, beautiful,' Marco said with a kiss on her cheek, as though nothing had happened.

'Hi. Did you get your rackets? The front desk said they'd put them in your room.'

Marco peered at her through squinted, questioning eyes. 'The movie star, Charlie? He is really old, no?'

Charlie tried not to smile. So he did care. And he had brought it up first.

'The nanny, Marco? She's a child.'

'She didn't mean anything to me. She was there, you weren't. But you are now. And I missed you.'

They looked at one another. Almost hating herself, Charlie agreed to meet him later that night . . .

The sound of Dan's voice snapped her back to the present.

'So let me get this straight. You're both just going about your merry business?'

'Tell me what you really think, Dan. No, please, don't hold back.'

'You want to know what I think?' He finally brought his gaze up to meet hers. 'I think you're settling for some asshole because it's easy. And that kind of sucks.'

Charlie could feel her color rising despite herself. 'I was kidding. I don't want you to tell me what you really think.'

He gave a half smile. 'You're the one who said we're each other's business.'

'Then at least get your analysis right. I'm settling for some asshole because it's easy, yes. But also because he's really, really hot.'

'Lovely.'

'Well, clearly neither of us thought we were so committed that we couldn't date someone else.'

'Date? Is *that* what you people are calling it these days?'

'And it's kind of a weird, fortunate coincidence that we both got publicly busted for being naughty at the exact same instant. Because neither of us can really give the other one any grief, can we?'

'So you both just pretend the whole thing never happened?'

'Yes.'

Dan looked up at the sky. 'It's like I'm talking to someone who hears voices.'

'Look, I'm working hard, and I'm winning, and I would hardly be the first one who tried to fit in just the smallest bit of fun along the way. Wasn't Agassi doing meth a few years before his French Open win? I mean, let's put this in perspective.'

'Hey, no judgments here,' he said, holding his palms up.

Charlie laughed. 'Yeah, not at all.'

A blond-haired child of four or five streaked past their table. Charlie watched the little girl's pigtails bounce as she made her way around the room. Then, just as she was about to turn back to Dan, a taller but equally energetic blonde raced past them in pursuit of the child.

'Oh my god, it's Elin,' Charlie said, her eyes taking in every detail of the girl down to her adorably funky high-top sneakers.

'Who?'

'Marco's au pair!'

'Wasn't Elin the name of Tiger Woods's ex-wife?'

'I can't believe she's here.'

'What are the chances that they would both be drop-dead-gorgeous blond au pairs named Elin?'

'Her name is not Elin!' Charlie hissed. She watched as the nanny grabbed the squealing little girl and hugged her close. The child wriggled with joy.

'Didn't you just say it was Elin?'

'I can't believe she's here. Of course I can. She nannies for Raj's coach – where else would she be?' Charlie sneaked another peek, and Sofie must have sensed someone looking at her, because she lifted her head and looked directly at Charlie. And smiled.

Instantly, Charlie turned to Dan, who had just stood up. 'She looked right at me. She smiled! Do you believe the nerve? This barely legal babysitter screws my boyfriend and then has the nerve to *smile* at me? And of course I have to be wearing sweaty tennis clothes, while she looks like a supermodel . . .'

'Charlie, you're delusional. I can't even begin to—'

'Here she comes. Oh my god, she's walking over here. Dan, where are you going? *Sit down!* Don't leave me here!' she hissed without moving her lips.

'As fun as this promises to be, I have to go now. I'll see you tomorrow at eight, Court Ten. Bye, Charlie.'

But she hadn't heard a word he said. Sofie was barreling toward her with her pigtailed charge by the hand, and it was clear she planned to say hello. Despite being certain this would happen, Charlie still nearly collapsed from the surprise of it.

It made sense Sofie would recognize Charlie – she was ranked fourth in the world, for heaven's sake – but Charlie wasn't about to admit that she'd spent hours googling this girl and knew not only her name but also that of her favorite fifth-grade teacher.

'You're Charlotte Silver, right?' the girl asked. She looked even younger in person. Fresher, somehow.

'Yes.' Charlie, suddenly convinced she had food stuck in her teeth, was also acutely aware of exactly how her hair was plastered to her head after a long training day. There wasn't a stylist-chosen article of clothing or a crystal in sight . . . nothing but wide expanses of spandex and Drymax and caked-on clay. It was so unfair.

'You must hear this all the time, but I just wanted to tell you that I'm a huge fan!' The girl's smile seemed genuine and her accent was adorable.

Charlie cleared her throat. 'Thank you. That's so nice to hear.'

'I just think it's so cool for a woman to be tough and confident.' Sofie dropped to her knees, and of course

Charlie instantly thought a thousand uncharitable things about how expertly she did so until Sofie turned to the little girl and said, 'This lady is a famous tennis player. She's not just a princess, she's a warrior princess! And she might win this whole tournament!'

The little girl's eyes widened. Sofie sounded so genuine that Charlie was willing to overlook the 'lady' bit. 'She's a pwincess?'

Sofie nodded. 'A real-life one. This is Anabelle, and Anabelle is in love with princesses.'

Charlie stuck out her hand, which Anabelle stared at, and then, feeling like an idiot for not even knowing what to say to a four-year-old, she said, 'It's very nice to meet you, Anabelle. I actually have to go now. I'm meeting, uh, someone.' Charlie had thrown in that last part merely to offer a logical excuse for her speedy departure, but she realized immediately how it sounded.

Sofie must have as well, because she blushed in the most charming way. No wonder Marco couldn't resist her.

'Oh, of course. We don't want to hold you up, do we, Anabelle? Besides, we must go rescue your brother from the day care. Come, darling. Say good-bye to Ms Silver.'

Ms Silver? She looked at Sofie, but the girl gave no hint at being anything but polite.

They all waved good-bye, and Charlie had to admit that she seemed to be the only one feeling strange about the whole thing. All Charlie had to do was recall the photo of Sofie wearing one of Marco's T-shirts and straddling his lap to be able to envision exactly what the rest of their night looked like.

She made her way back to the locker room and texted Jake on the way.

Dinner at the hotel tonight? Need to be asleep early.

His reply came back instantly.

Sorry, I can't tonight. Just order to your room and relax a little. You've been training so hard.

Why can't you? Hot date?

Something like that.

?????????

No one you know.

Don't care, tell me anyway!

Charlie tossed her phone in her locker while she showered and picked it up again the second she returned. Jake had replied three times in a row:

He's cute.

He's not appropriate.

I will tell you on a need to know basis and right now there's nothing to know.

Charlie rolled her eyes. She looked at her phone again.

If Jake had a date tonight, it meant her father was eating alone. She dialed his number and he answered on the third ring.

'Hey, Dad.'

'Oh, Charlie. Hello.'

'I just got back to the hotel. Are you here?'

'That was some interview today, huh?' Charlie could hear that he was trying to mask the disappointment in his voice but wasn't succeeding.

'Yeah, she was pretty out of line. Asking all those questions about my, uh, personal life wasn't really fair.'

'I know I'm no altar boy, but when you're in the public

eye and you give people a lot to talk about, you can hardly blame them for asking.'

Charlie was silent.

'Was all of that Todd's idea? From his No Publicity Is Bad Publicity playbook?'

'No, Dad. I got into trouble all by myself on that one. You can't blame anyone but me.' If he was trying to shame her, it was working. Brilliantly. On second thought, she figured she should eat alone.

'Do you want to join me for dinner with some of my old tour friends?' her dad asked, as if reading her mind.

'No, thanks. I'm going to order something to my room and watch tape. Todd left me a whole bunch of film from last year and I want to review it. We can do dinner tomorrow.'

Her old dad would have said something like 'After your big win tomorrow,' or 'We'll have a victory celebration,' but her father simply assured her he'd be sitting front and center in her player box the following morning and wished her good night.

Charlie took the elevator to her room and found a padded envelope of DVDs waiting for her on the desk. The note attached was scribbled rapidly on hotel stationery.

> *Watch Acapulco first, Singapore second, and*
> *Stuttgart third. Make note of her increased willingness*
> *to take risks on game points and her stunning*
> *second serve. Car will pick you up at seven*
> *tomorrow. – Todd*

Sighing, Charlie inserted the first DVD and waited for it to load. She called room service to order the grilled salmon with a side of steamed vegetables. When the woman on the phone asked her if service was for one or two people, it occurred to her how often lately she ate alone in her hotel room. Marcy had always joined Charlie for room service dinners. The two of them would ask to have the table arranged in front of the TV, and they'd alternate between *Love It or List It* and *Property Brothers*, with the occasional *House Hunters International* thrown in. Clad in sweats and fuzzy travel socks, Marcy would drink wine and Charlie would sneak bites of whatever dessert she'd ordered, and they'd make fun of everyone who had the nerve to appear on the screen in front of them. Jake used to say he could hear the evil cackling from down the hall. The thought of doing any of that with Todd was equal parts laughable and repulsive, and she could feel herself missing Marcy even more than usual.

The three sets of match highlights lasted nearly an hour; when they were over, Charlie looked at her empty plate and could barely remember eating. She picked up her phone to check the time and a text message popped right up.

Hey, grabbing dinner with a few of the guys now. Come? Marco.

She reread the message three times before realizing she was holding her breath.

It wasn't exactly an invitation to a romantic dinner for two, but it was also the night before play began in a Grand Slam tournament and no one would be doing much more than eating early and retiring to their rooms. He certainly didn't need to invite her. She already knew the hot nanny was in Paris and probably perfectly willing to meet him.

And if not her, there were dozens, if not hundreds, of others. The fact that he'd even thought of Charlie counted for something.

Hey! Would love to but can't right now . . .

Charlie had replied no reflexively. She'd already eaten, and she had a surprisingly tough first-round match early the next day. The last thing she needed was any Marco-related distraction.

A text came right back: *So come whenever you can. Eating at patisserie around the corner from hotel. Heading back to Rinaldo's room afterwards to play the new Madden. Everyone to sleep early, just come say hi. Missing you.*

She set her phone down without replying and did a little dance. *He missed her, he missed her, he missed her.* Without even thinking about it, she scrolled through her phone to find 'Blank Space,' mounted it on the bedside speaker, and blasted the volume. Taylor Swift's cotton candy voice filled the room and Charlie started to dance. *I can make the bad guys good for a weekend.* She grabbed a bottle of water for a microphone and hopped up on the bed, shamelessly gyrating her hips to the rhythm, until there was a knock on the door and she jumped down, breathless and not nearly as embarrassed as she should have been. The front desk guy standing in the hallway looked sheepish, as though he'd known Charlie was having a solo dance party to a tween hit, and he couldn't meet her eyes when he conveyed another player's request to turn down her music. It wasn't even seven, but quiet time was enforced on player floors twenty-four hours a day. Charlie nodded solemnly, apologized as sincerely as she could manage, and then cracked up the moment she shut the door. Was this what going crazy felt like? She grabbed her phone and headed to the bathroom.

There in 30, she wrote, her fingers flying across the keyboard. She'd stop by for an hour just to say hello. No harm in that whatsoever.

17

how do you say 'flameout' in french?

THE FRENCH OPEN, MAY 2016

Her heart was beating so fast that she couldn't catch her breath. As slowly as she could, Charlie walked toward the baseline. The perspiration was streaming down her neck into her black tank, and the clay stuck to her sweaty calves in the most uncomfortable way. Todd's instructions reverberated in her mind over and over again, a mantra that brought her no calm, no mindfulness: *Attack and draw. Attack and draw. Attack and draw.* Attack her backhand, which was weaker than it should be, and draw her into the net, which was out of her comfort zone. Eleanor

McKinley also preferred to play quickly, opting to put the ball back in play as fast as possible and not waste a lot of time between points. Charlie had read the interviews Todd's office had collated for her. Eleanor didn't like having the time to dwell on past points – either winners or losers – because it allowed her to get too much in her own head. She preferred to hit hard and take risks and end points rather than endlessly rally back and forth, merely waiting for either her or her opponent to hit an unforced error. Already she would be uneasy playing the French Open's slower courts. Todd was always elated when a player went on the record with such crucial preferences, since he kept a dossier on every woman on the tour.

When she reached the back of the court, Charlie lifted her gaze to the ball boy and offered him the slightest nod. He trotted over holding two balls, one in each hand, and held them aloft as though they were precious jewels. Charlie shook her head and immediately he tucked them in his pocket and pulled out a towel. She accepted it and methodically patted down her forehead, cheeks, and neck, and then, for good measure, her forearms and palms as well. As soon as he had put away the towel, the boy again proffered the balls. Charlie nodded, almost imperceptibly, to his right hand, and he placed the ball on her outstretched racket head. After securing it under the spandex of her black, crystal-encrusted skirt, she held her racket out for the second. This one she bounced as she made her way back to the baseline, preparing to serve. It occurred to her that she was doing precisely what Karina had done to Charlie in the final of Charleston – essentially, stalling for time in order to challenge her opponent's toughness – but she brushed the thought away. It was different now. Instead of being one point away from winning the entire tournament, she was one point from a devastating loss in the very first round.

A glance across the court revealed Eleanor bouncing patiently on the balls of her feet. Her lithe body was almost as tight as her severe bun. She wore a fitted gray tennis dress with an attached pleated skirt that barely moved, and she was as flat-chested as a boy. Altogether it gave the odd impression that she was a wooden figure, a statue carved from lifeless materials that could bounce up and down and right to left without moving anything in between.

Charlie tried to calm her breathing. A snapshot from the night before appeared in her mind like an IMAX film: her legs draped over Marco's proprietarily as they lounged on a couch. Her exhales now, on the court, were similar to those of the night before, only now there was no long, seductive smoke trail streaming from her lips and hanging in the humid air of the hotel suite, just the quick and shallow breaths of someone who knew she was seconds away from big trouble.

Charlie realized there were no possible ways left to procrastinate. This was it. Match point for what could be the single most disappointing match she had ever played. *No! That's no way to think. Entertain that horrid thought and you are as good as done. Attack and draw. Get a first solid serve in, attack her backhand, and if she is still able to return the ball, take advantage of what will surely be its relative weakness and hit a drop shot to draw her into the net. Then watch as she crumbles, because she has no net game.*

Charlie took her position behind the baseline, bounced

the ball three times, and tossed it in the air. It was a perfect toss, she could tell right away, and she was grateful to the muscle memory she'd developed from tens of thousands – hundreds of thousands? millions? – of practice serves when her hips and arms worked in perfect synchronization to connect her racket with the ball. It was a hard, fast, nearly perfect serve, and Charlie was so thankful for it that she wasn't as quick as she should have been returning to position. Eleanor seemed to read exactly where the serve was going to land. She was there, ready and waiting, as though she had received a map showing the exact intended path, and she pounced on it while the ball was still rising, smashing it back to Charlie with a shocking swiftness. Caught unprepared, Charlie ran four steps into no-man's-land and propelled her body into an immediate lunge, taking instinctive advantage of the clay to slide the remaining few feet. She got there in time but was too disoriented to do much with the ball other than get her strings on it and pop it up into the air, and it didn't matter that she got back to position quickly because Eleanor moved in on the weak lob, turned her body sideways, planted her feet, and smashed the overhead so cleanly and with such power that Charlie didn't see it coming until she felt it strike her neck.

The impact alone would have been enough to ensure an angry red welt and a good amount of follow-up bruising, but the exact location of where it hit – dead center of her windpipe – left Charlie literally choking for air. She was hunched over, her head between her knees, gasping for breath. Intellectually, she knew exactly what had happened, knew it would subside in a matter of seconds and she would be able to fill her lungs normally if she could just slow her breathing. But the panic set in, made no doubt worse by the realization that she had just lost her very first round match at the very first Grand Slam tournament she had any real chance of winning, and, well, she continued to choke. She felt a hand on her back and looked up to see Eleanor crouched next to her, rubbing her palm in strong, comforting circles between Charlie's shoulder blades.

'Just try to slow your breathing,' the girl murmured, continuing to massage Charlie's back. 'I'm so sorry.'

Because of Charlie's high seeding in the tournament and two consecutive wins, there were more fans watching their match than might be expected at a typical first round. Everyone wanted to catch a glimpse of the black-haired, black-clad, tiara-wearing phenom as she crushed the relative newcomer on her march to French Open victory. And now all of those same spectators were cheering like crazy and calling out Eleanor's name. She began to feel the embarrassment more acutely as her breath returned to normal. And suddenly, the feel of her opponent's hand on her own sweat-soaked shirt – not to mention that maddening expression of sympathy plastered on her face – well, it was just too much. Charlie twisted her body out of Eleanor's reach and pushed herself to stand. 'I'm fine,' she hissed under her breath. 'As fine as someone can expect to be when her opponent tries to win by clocking her.'

Eleanor's eyes opened wide in surprise. Neither girl seemed at all aware of the cacophony surrounding them.

Charlie couldn't stop herself. 'You got lucky today. Don't think for a second it was anything more than that.'

The girl stared at her for what seemed like a very long time. Then, clearly deciding to take the high road, she looked Charlie straight in the eye, held out her hand, and said, 'Good match.'

Charlie shook Eleanor's hand limply, the shame of it all settling on her like a weight, and made her way to her chair. She packed her bag quickly and ignored the shouts from the fans and the requests for autographs. Leaving the court quickly so Eleanor could enjoy her moment of victory was the very least Charlie could do after her own humiliating loss and even more shameful behavior. She planned to hide in the locker room as long as she possibly could, stand under the shower and let the scalding-hot water pelt her clean. But as soon as Isabel intercepted her in the tunnel leading from court to tennis center, Charlie knew her torture wasn't over yet.

'I need a shower first,' she told Isabel in her best clipped, authoritative tone.

'Sorry, Charlie' – Isabel coughed – 'I'm sorry, but we must do the post-match interview right now.'

'It's a first-round loss, for chrissake,' Charlie grumbled, continuing to walk. 'No one cares.'

Isabel placed her hand firmly on Charlie's arm. 'I'm afraid when a player who is favored to win gets upset early, they do care. I know this is a terrible time. I promise I'll make it as short and as painless as possible. But we must go now.'

Charlie followed her a few paces to a sort of anteroom with a podium and microphone in front of a French Open step-and-repeat. Waiting for her were a handful of reporters and photographers talking among themselves, but they all grew silent the moment she entered the room.

The quiet lasted for exactly six seconds before the questions started firing.

'How does it feel to be eliminated in the first round of a tournament you were favored to, if not win, then at least make it to the second week of?'

'Was it a particular aspect of McKinley's game that you couldn't handle? Or was it something in your own game that felt off?'

'In the last few months you've had quite the image overhaul. How much of the Warrior Princess was on the court today versus the old Charlotte Silver?'

Although the questions were hardly original – if she hadn't heard them before, she certainly could have predicted their being asked today – she found herself stumbling through her memorized, media-trained answers. 'That's the thing about the Slams: you never really can tell what's going to happen.' 'At the end of the day, image doesn't mean a thing if you're not winning.' 'I'll need to revisit some things with my coach and regroup.' 'Of course I'm disappointed, but I plan to be ready to start fresh at Wimbledon in a few weeks.' Charlie repeated these canned answers blandly, almost without inflection, biding her time until they grew tired of her and she was permitted to escape to the shower. *Only a few more minutes*, she told herself, and felt her throat start to close. She took a couple of deep inhales and was grateful when the sensation of imminent crying subsided.

'Did Eleanor beat you today, or did you beat yourself?' Shawn, a longtime reporter on the tennis beat, asked. He traveled with the women's tour and had a reputation for hitting on the younger players.

'Well, of course Eleanor played well today, I think we can all agree on that. She played a beautiful match. And, unfortunately, I don't think I played my best. Clearly not.'

'And why do you think that is?' There was a glint in his eye, a little glimmer of amusement that made Charlie instantly uneasy.

'A lot of reasons. I had too many unforced errors in the first set, including an inexcusable amount of double faults. And my mental focus wasn't where it should have been in the second. I've certainly come back from a set down before, but I couldn't make it happen today.'

Shawn cleared his throat.

Charlie's entire body went on alert: she knew, just instinctively *knew*, that something horrible was about to happen.

He reached into his canvas briefcase and pulled out a huge iPad, the one that was the size of a laptop. It was already turned on, and from somewhere behind her she could hear Jake murmur, 'Oh Christ no.'

'Charlotte, would you say that your less-than-stellar performance on the court today had something to do with this?' Shawn asked in the most sickening self-congratulatory tone.

Jake stepped forward and clamped his hand around hers. 'It's bad, Charlie,' he hissed into her ear. 'Let's cut this off now. Follow me.' He tried to yank her away from the small press conference, but Charlie couldn't stop herself from turning back.

'I'm sorry, I haven't exactly had time to read the news yet today. I don't know to what you're referring.'

Shawn held the screen toward her so she could read the headline. It was unmissable, in what felt like a five-hundred-point font: *Dethroned? Tennis's Warrior Princess Flunks Drug Test.*

Flunked a drug test? What are they talking about? Charlie's mind bounced about, trying to make sense of what she'd just read. She'd gotten the results from her test in Charleston weeks earlier and of course they had been 100 percent clear. Doping? It was an insane suggestion. Every few years a rumor would surface here or there concerning a couple of the women on the tour, especially the ones who were inordinately muscular, but by and large nearly everyone agreed that the constant testing and conversation about doping was excessive and unnecessary. Tennis was a far cry from cycling or baseball: doping might occur in the rarest of circumstances, but it was hardly a sport-wide pandemic.

'I have no comment on that other than to say that there is no truth to it whatsoever.' Charlie said this in a strong, confident voice that made her feel immediately proud of herself. She knew for a fact that the paper would have to print a retraction.

This time Shawn held up his phone. The screen was too small to see anything clearly, but the room had gone eerily quiet. A video was playing. It was difficult for Charlie to make out at first, but after a few seconds she could tell that it was from the hotel suite the night before.

'Charlie.' Jake's voice was low, gravelly. A warning.

Something about the way he said it reminded her of

Marco, how he almost growled her name when they were having sex, his mouth pressed right up against her ear. *Charlie*.

When she'd knocked on Rinaldo's door last night, she had been prepared to stay for exactly one hour. Just enough to flirt a little with Marco, get a feel for where things stood between them, visit a little to take her mind off her match the following morning. She had trained flawlessly for three days, eaten and slept and worked out exactly according to schedule, even watched the tapes Todd had assigned her. It needed to be an early night, of course, but there was no reason she couldn't sip some Pellegrino and hang with Marco and his buddies and unwind a little.

She'd been surprised by the size of the group. As he'd described earlier, Marco was sitting in front of the TV with Rinaldo, a doubles player from Argentina, and two other male players. They were all shouting at the screen and frantically moving their football player avatars around with giant gaming joysticks. A group of long-legged, wavy-haired clones wearing short dresses and high heels giggled together near the windows, each sipping identical flutes of champagne. Every minute or two their collective laughter would ring out, but no one seemed to pay them much attention. Natalya had her legs draped across Benjy on the couch. Her head was thrown back dramatically as Benjy massaged her bare feet. Another cluster of female players – all American and Canadian, all under twenty years old – stood around the kitchen in leggings and hoodies, looking decidedly less glamorous than the model contingent; they were staring at Natalya like she was Katy Perry. Someone had ordered a huge room service spread of various salads, fruit platters, grilled chicken breasts, heaps of steamed broccoli, and an assortment of still and sparkling bottled water, but no one seemed to be eating it.

'Hey,' Charlie said to no one in particular, feeling instantly awkward.

Marco glanced up and broke into the most delicious smile. 'Hey, babe,' he said, his eyes back on the screen as his avatar tackled someone. 'Come on over here. I'll be done in a minute.'

Charlie nodded to Natalya, who nodded in return, and headed toward the kitchenette. The young players who had been gathered nearby took a collective step back to let her pass.

'Hi, Charlie,' said one of them, a sweet seventeen-year-old from Florida. 'Good luck tomorrow.'

Charlie smiled at her. It was so strange to feel like one of the village elders at twenty-five. 'Thanks. You too. Who are you playing?'

The girl blushed. 'I'm not on tomorrow, but my first-round match is against Atherton.'

She waited for Charlie to react, to say something about what a tough match that was going to be, but all Charlie said was 'She's a terrific player, but she can be erratic. I think you have a great chance.'

The girl beamed. Her friends smiled. 'You do?'

Charlie nodded. 'Just don't stay here too late tonight!' she admonished like a den mother. She leaned in close to whisper, 'Besides, those boys are all idiots. Cute, I know, I'm not denying it, but still just boys.'

'Easy for you to say,' laughed one of the other girls. Charlie recognized her as an up-and-coming phenom from

Montreal. She'd recently won the Orange Bowl and had immediately turned pro, but word on the street was she didn't have the emotional maturity yet to match her very adult strokes. 'You have the hottest one.'

They all laughed and Charlie wondered what they said about the whole au pair situation when she wasn't around. No one could accuse the tennis world of discretion – it must have been some very juicy locker room conversation.

As if on cue, Marco came over and enveloped her in a bear hug from behind. He buried his face in her neck, kissing it, and whispered, 'I'm glad you're here.'

Charlie wriggled away but couldn't hide her pleasure. Marco gallantly introduced himself to the young girls and did an expert job of pretending not to notice that each of them was blushing and giggling. She hated that she felt flattered merely because he'd chosen her.

He took her hand and led her back to the couch. The suite's door opened and more people streamed in, a mix of players and their friends and girlfriends plus a few whom Charlie recognized as hitting partners. Behind this group of five was Jake. He looked just as surprised to see her.

'Hey, shouldn't you be in bed now?' he asked, standing over her and Marco. The two men slapped hands hello.

'It's not even nine,' she said, resting her head back against Marco's shoulder. 'Look around. Half the room is scheduled to play tomorrow.'

Jake raised his eyebrows. Charlie gave him the finger. Marco laughed.

One of the model types sidled up to Jake and handed him a beer, which he accepted with a huge, flirtatious smile.

'Really?' Charlie said.

'What? *I* certainly don't have to play tomorrow.'

It didn't take long for the impromptu get-together to turn into a full-fledged party. Soon someone had turned the suite's lights down low and switched the video game to a station playing some sort of European lounge music. A few of the non-tennis girls had begun dancing near the windows, clinking glasses and smoking cigarettes, while the male players hovered nearby. Not a single one of the players, male or female, was drinking anything other than water, but a few of them were taking quick drags off e-cigarettes and laughing as they pressed the electronic lit end to their palms. Charlie had been so wrapped up with Marco, literally cuddled into him on a single armchair, that she hadn't noticed much of anything. When she finally stood up to use the bathroom, she couldn't find Jake anywhere. All of the younger female players had left, too, and most of the people who remained now – maybe a dozen or so – were drinking and dancing together. She knocked on the bathroom door, and when no one answered, she tried the doorknob.

It took a moment to understand what was happening. Natalya was hunched over the sink and Lexi, the phenom from Montreal, stood pressed against her in the small powder room. Neither girl seemed to notice that the door had opened. She could have – should have – just pulled it shut, but she was confused by what she saw: nothing sexual per se, but it wasn't quite platonic either. Natalya finally sensed they weren't alone and turned toward the door. It was only then that Charlie saw Natalya was holding something rolled up tight in her left hand and wiping underneath her nose with her right. Lexi hadn't noticed Charlie yet, and she was reaching around Natalya with a credit card, where she concentrated intently on pushing little piles of white powder into neat, orderly lines.

Charlie's and Natalya's eyes met and Natalya's entire expression filled with a rage so pure, Charlie was certain the girl would kill her. 'Get the fuck out of here,' she snarled, her accent all but disappearing. 'And if you tell anyone, I will make sure you regret it.'

The last part got cut off when Charlie yanked the door closed. She stumbled back into the living room, where a group had begun playing a drinking game that involved poker chips and cereal bowls, and walked into the bedroom to find another bathroom. There she found Marco, Rinaldo, and a model huddled together. *Not them too*, Charlie thought, but she soon saw they were watching a funny video on the model's phone.

'Charlie! Come here, baby,' Marco said, holding out his arm to her. Once again she felt instant pride and then hated herself for it.

The model took a long drag off the electronic cigarette she was holding in between her perfectly manicured fingers and held it out to Marco. None of the players would have ever, under any circumstances, smoked a regular Marlboro, but clearly there was a contingent of them that thought the vaporizers had no harmful side effects. She had assumed everyone took extra-good care of themselves the night before a match, but that was before she walked in on the number-one-ranked woman on earth doing lines off a hotel sink.

Marco took a long drag and the electronic end glowed

brightly, as though it were actually burning. The languorous stream of vapor that Marco exhaled looked exactly like smoke but had no smell at all.

Someone stuck his head in the room and called the model away. With a squeeze of Marco's forearm, she made no effort to disguise her look of disappointment before she scampered off.

'She seems nice,' Charlie said, because she wasn't able to stop herself.

'Who?' Marco asked, pulling her close. He kissed her hard on the mouth. 'Here, take a drag. It'll relax you.'

'I'm feeling great already,' Charlie said, nibbling his bottom lip. She felt his hand slip under the back of her shirt and begin to rub her shoulders. Before she knew what was happening, he was grinding himself into her as he kissed her neck.

'Get a room!' someone called from the living room.

They broke apart and looked at each other, laughing. Marco said, 'Maybe we should go back to my room.'

He held out his hand and helped her off the bed. Charlie followed him into the living room. Everywhere she looked, people were drinking, smoking, and making out. A group of appreciative guys watched as Natalya danced with abandon to Beyoncé, but Benjy wasn't one of them. Charlie glanced around the room and realized he was gone.

'Here,' Marco said, handing her the vaporizer. 'Take this.'

'I don't want it,' Charlie said.

'Just hold on to it for me. I'll be right back.'

She watched as Marco walked into the kitchenette area. All around her, people were laughing and chatting, and she suddenly felt awkward standing there alone. For no other reason than needing to look busy, she put the vaporizer to her lips and took a long, deep drag. It burned the back of her throat, but she was grateful to have something to do with her hands. *It's just water vapor,* she thought as she slowly exhaled.

Almost immediately she felt all her muscles relax. Her shoulders lowered and her neck loosened and her mind quieted. She did it again. And then once more.

It could have been five seconds or five minutes – Charlie had instantly lost track of time – but she knew that whatever had been in that cigarette had affected her mind. Everything around her had softened and grown quieter. A group of guys were laughing raucously, but their voices barely registered with her. Nearby, Charlie could see Marco calling to her from across the room, but she was more interested in the movements his mouth made than in the words he was speaking. A flash went off, and then another, but it felt like it was happening in slow motion.

'Hey, not cool,' someone said in the general direction of the camera.

Natalya shrugged. Her cheeks were the color of sherbet, and a sheen of perspiration along her collarbone only made her more gorgeous. She was holding aloft a phone with a supersized screen. 'Whatever,' she said, waving her hand.

Charlie hadn't seen him approach or heard a word he had said, but suddenly she was aware Marco's hands were around her waist. She turned around and saw him grinning.

'You okay, love?' he asked, crinkling his eyes with a mixture of amusement and concern.

'I feel a little weird,' Charlie managed, not quite sure if she was calibrating her own voice to an appropriate volume.

'You feel a little high is all.' Marco drained half a water bottle and handed the remainder to Charlie. 'I didn't think you'd actually smoke it.'

Charlie meant to take a small sip from the bottle, but the water tasted so delicious that she couldn't stop herself from finishing it. The instant it was gone, she was thirsty again.

'Smoke what?' she asked, trying to shake the last little droplets into her mouth.

'That was THC oil in there.'

'What?'

'It was weed. We were vaping it. I only ever take one drag, just to take the edges off – is that how you say it?'

'I just smoked *weed*? The night before a match?'

'One drag is only like a glass of champagne. It will not affect your play.'

'I smoked more than that!' Charlie could hear her own hysteria.

Marco's brow furrowed and he pulled her in close. 'Shh. I'll take you back to your room; you're going to be fine.'

'I'm not going to be fine!' Charlie whispered in a voice that must have been loud, because the group sitting nearest them turned to look. 'I'm all fucked-up, Marco! I need this to stop. I need it to stop right now!' Where there had been waves of relaxation moments before, there was now only panic. In her twenty-five years, she had never, ever smoked pot. It seemed almost inconceivable, this lapse in ordinary teenage experimentation, but it was true.

'Charlie, try to relax. There's nothing to worry about.'

Marco had her tightly by the wrist and was leading her to the door. When he pulled her into the hallway, she was shocked at how bright everything looked, and how normal. There was a young father carrying a sleeping child back to their room while the mother followed behind pushing an empty stroller; a waiter balancing a tray with what looked like the most delectable ice cream sundae in all the world; a couple dressed to go out, waiting for the elevator.

'Let's take the stairs,' Marco said, pulling her along.

The couple turned and stared at them. 'They recognize me! They know I'm high! It's going to be everywhere tomorrow!'

'*Shut up!*' Marco hissed directly in her ear. Charlie was stunned into silence. It was the first time she had heard him get upset. He was a mental monolith of steady mood and no excessive emotion, both on and off the court. Entire articles had been written on Marco's mental toughness – and, beyond that, his admirable poker face – and Charlie had never, not once, witnessed a chink in the armor. Until now.

As she followed him toward the stairwell, something caught her eye. One of the doors on her left opened just as they were walking past it. It was dark inside the room, and Charlie thought she could see two men standing just inside, whispering. The voices were familiar. She stopped for a closer look, but Marco pulled her along. Was that Jake? It sure sounded like him, but there was no time to investigate. They hiked down two floors to her room, where Marco dug in her back jeans pocket and pulled out her room key. He murmured comforting things the entire time, always reassuring her that the high would wear off soon, that she should just go to bed as planned. After making sure she had water and confirming her alarm was set for six-thirty, he kissed her on the cheek and left. 'I'll order a wake-up call from Reception as well,' he said as he walked out. 'Good luck tomorrow; you'll be great.'

'Charlie? Charlie? Can you hear me?' The voice that called out now was male, but it wasn't Marco. It was Shawn, and she was still standing at the podium, answering questions after her first-round French Open loss.

'Yes, of course I can hear you,' she said.

'Can you clarify this report stating that you failed a drug test?' Shawn asked, once again waving the offending paper.

Charlie's eyes shot to Jake. He seemed to consider his options before stepping in front of her to take the microphone.

'I will state unequivocally that Charlotte's so-called failure on the drug test is in no way relevant to her performance this morning. It was a technicality, nothing more.'

'And this video that was posted to YouTube late last night? Can you comment on this?'

The room had quieted enough that now Shawn's phone was sufficiently loud for everyone to hear. Charlie couldn't see what was happening on the small screen, but she could hear a woman's voice – undeniably her own – shouting, 'I'm all fucked-up, Marco! I need this to stop. I need it to stop right now!'

Jake cleared his throat and leaned toward the microphone. 'Charlotte has no comment right now. Thank you for understanding.' And while the voices came in from all directions, Jake gripped Charlie's arm in the exact same way Marco had the night before and pulled her out of the room.

18

the lindsay lohan of tennis

TOPANGA CANYON, JUNE 2016

'I'm so humiliated,' Charlie moaned. 'Do you even know what they're calling me now?'

'The Delinquent Princess? So what? It's not that bad.' Charlie could hear a spoon scraping against a bowl and then Piper, through a full mouth, said, 'It actually sounds kind of chic. Pot is legal in a whole bunch of states. I don't know how many, but it's a lot.'

Charlie snorted. 'Jake is annoyed, but at least he sort of understands how it all went down. Todd is irate. Listen to this.' She pulled out her phone and scrolled to find the text.

'"I never even thought it possible for you to do something so epically, indescribably, undeniably DUMB." He capitalized "dumb." Just in case I missed it.'

'That's just Todd being Todd.'

'Don't kid yourself. That's not the last he'll have to say on the topic – there's going to be hell to pay with him. And that's if he doesn't fire me first.'

'*You* pay *him*, Charlie, not the other way around.'

'Details.'

'You'll apologize and tell him how much you've learned from the experience, and he'll get over it. Just like everyone else.'

'Maybe. But there's my father, too. He's so disappointed he won't even speak to me.'

'Your father misses the sweet little girl in braids who always said "please" and "thank you," even as people walked all over her. He'll get over it.'

Charlie lowered her voice. 'Sometimes I catch him looking at me with this expression like *Who is this person in front of me?* It's awful, it truly is.'

The walls in her father's new cottage were wafer-thin, and he was reading right outside her door. His door, actually. He had insisted on taking the living room pullout and leaving Charlie the bedroom, an argument that had grown heated quickly. It brought together so many different issues, none of which either of them seemed ready to address: his new accommodations and what they implied about his financial situation; her fall from grace; Todd's involvement; the great distance they both felt now that they weren't discussing anything substantive. When she had instinctively bought a nonstop ticket from Paris to Los Angeles after her humiliating first-round loss, she hadn't thought about anything other than getting home. *Home*. It never made sense for her to have her own place when she was on the road forty-eight weeks out of every fifty-two. She thought about it every now and then, how it could be nice to have her own apartment somewhere – but whenever she got serious enough to consider it, she changed her mind. Why pay rent and utilities and furnish something for a few weeks a year? Especially when she had enough frequent flier miles saved up to fly or stay anywhere on earth, at any time, virtually free of charge? And for those times when she needed a day or two to decompress, to rest and relax and have someone take care of her, she had her family home. Until now. She felt guilty admitting it, but had Charlie even remembered her father had already moved into this depressing, on-property guest cottage, one deemed to have fallen too deep into disrepair to house the club's actual guests, well, she probably would have stayed in a hotel. Or not come home at all. Which of course made her feel even worse.

'You'll deal with it, and so will he. You didn't get arrested for prostitution, did you? Because that would be hard to recover from. Heroin would be a big problem. And as far as I know, you didn't kill anyone. So, all things considered, I think the world can get over you smoking a joint.'

'I didn't smoke a joint!'

'You think I give a rat's ass whether you vaped it or smoked it or snorted it? Charlie, you've got to relax. No one cares.'

'No one cares? Did you happen to notice the video of

me proclaiming how epically fucked-up I am currently has a hundred thousand hits?'

'I admit, the video was a bit of a setback. But those who love you know what happened.'

Charlie muted ESPN, on which she'd spent the few days since she'd gotten home watching endless, torturous coverage of the French Open. Once it ended – and Natalya inevitably won it – there would be a mere three weeks before Wimbledon began.

She watched the final point of Marco silently and methodically destroying a young American opponent in three easy sets before she said, 'I blew a shot at a Grand Slam for some stupid hotel room party with a bunch of people I don't even really know. What does that say about my commitment?'

More bowl scraping. 'I'm not one to talk about commitment. I bailed on tennis the first chance I had. But you're different, Charlie. This is your life. For better or worse – and sometimes it's both – this is what you do. And you do it really freaking well. But maybe you can cut yourself a little slack for living a little? Enjoying yourself just a tiny bit? Is it the worst thing on earth if you're not number one? If you don't win a Slam? Is all of that really too horrible even to fathom?'

Charlie stared at the framed picture her father kept on his nightstand. It was from before her mother's diagnosis, maybe a couple of years earlier, when they'd tried to go camping for a night. The Silvers had driven hours into the Redlands and set up camp in the most beautiful clearing near a river. Jake had patiently showed Charlie how to construct the fire using kindling and then thicker logs while their parents tried to fix the finicky camp stove. She remembered so clearly the four of them balancing the camera on a boulder and running around front to pose for the family shot, and how they never managed to fix the stove but the fire-cooked hot dogs were the best she'd ever tasted. Even the terror Charlie felt that night as the hyenas began their frightening screams now made her smile: she had scampered out of the tent she shared with Jake and into her parents' tent, where she'd wedged herself between their warm bodies and spent the entire night cuddled between them.

'They just sacrificed a lot to get me here.' Her voice was a whisper. Charlie could feel a knot forming in the back of her throat.

'I know they did, sweetie. But so did you. This isn't your father's dream, and from everything you told me, it wasn't your mother's either. This is all *you*. So the way I see it is, you need to decide if this is what you still want. It's okay to change course, you know. At the risk of sounding like some armchair psychologist – which, now that I think about it, might actually appeal to your new, crunchy, pot-smoking self – you only get one shot at it. At any of it. And if being the best in the world is what you want, then fucking *own* it. I know you can! And we'll all support you. But if you've hit a point where you're ready to give the finger to this lifestyle and all it entails, well, you know what? That might be okay, too. We'll all just put on our big-girl underwear and deal with it. Only you can make the call, Charlie.'

'Why is everyone always pushing me to quit?' Charlie didn't even try to hide her irritation. 'The slightest obstacle and the whole world is suggesting I retire. I love tennis, Piper. I know you didn't, but I love this sport. And I've worked really freaking hard to be the best. So, yes, I want that to happen.'

'Well, you're not acting like it. There, I said it. Hate me for it. But someone needs to say it.'

There was a moment of silence before Charlie said, 'Way to talk to the Lindsay Lohan of tennis. Show a little respect, please!'

Piper's laugh came in a staccato burst. 'Yeah, I read that, too. Amazing. You have to know how fun this is for me, don't you?'

There was a knock at the door. 'Charlie? Can you come out for a moment?' Her father sounded tired.

'Sure, Dad, I'll be right there,' she called. And then quietly into the phone, 'What time tomorrow?'

'Festivities commence at the Stockton residence at noon. I'm warning you: it's mostly my mother's friends and their daughters. You will hear a great deal about the newest Range Rovers, the benefits of SoulCycle, and how damn impossible it is finding decent cleaning help these days. Don't judge me.'

It was Charlie's turn to laugh. 'I'll be there! Nothing like a WASPy, day-drinking, racist crew of lunching ladies to make me feel better. Thanks, love. See you at noon.'

'Screw you. And thanks for coming. I'm really glad you blew the French Open so you can now be at my wedding shower.'

'You're welcome.' Charlie put her phone down and climbed off the bed. Her father had removed his sheets and replaced them with the new high-thread-count ones she'd purchased for her room, but it still felt strange beyond description to be sleeping in his bed. For the first time she noticed how worn his old wooden dresser was, how threadbare the bath towels looked. She hadn't ever noticed as a kid.

'Hey, are you going out?' Charlie asked, flopping down on the ugly plaid couch that had come with the cottage. When she had asked after their overstuffed velvet sectional, Mr Silver said he had sold it. Almost none of their things from home fit in the new place.

Her father had changed from his usual coaching uniform into a pair of khakis and a short-sleeved polo shirt. His hair was wet and combed neatly and he was wearing obviously new Docksides. 'Yes, I'm meeting . . . a friend. For dinner.'

Charlie had assumed they'd be eating together. After all, she was back home only a handful of nights a year at this point – ordinarily her father would jump at the chance for dinner together.

She forced herself to say brightly, 'Oh, I didn't realize you had plans. I was thinking I would make your favorite fillet and the twice-baked potatoes. An orgy of carbs and red meat, just the way you like it.' She smiled but instantly regretted using the word 'orgy,' especially since she knew what her father was thinking.

Her father seemed to be struggling to decide something, but then he said, 'So about this whole . . . pot thing.'

Charlie stared at the floor. 'Dad, I'm sorry. I know this must be super-humiliating for you. I never meant . . . I didn't think . . . Well, anyway. I've explained how the whole thing went down. I just wish it hadn't happened at all.'

He walked over and sat beside her on the couch. 'Sweetheart, I was going to say that you shouldn't be so hard on yourself. Everyone makes mistakes. God knows I did.'

'Oh, come on. I've googled you a thousand times. Aside from dating every female player in the top fifty, there's nothing there. Clean as a whistle.'

Her father cleared his throat. He twisted his hands together and then, without looking at her, said, 'I had an affair with a married woman once,' he said quietly.

Charlie forced herself to remain completely still. She didn't even take a breath.

'I was twenty. A kid. An idiot. She was twenty-six and married to my friend's coach, a much older guy – he was probably forty at the time. She was unhappy with him, of course. And we thought we were in love. I told myself I wasn't doing anything wrong because *I* wasn't married to anyone.' He coughed. 'Anyway. As you might imagine, it didn't end well.'

'What happened?'

Her father sighed. 'We were caught together in Wimbledon Village. A borrowed apartment . . . Anyway, it was awful. Her husband went crazy, threatened to kill me and divorce her. Not quietly. The whole tour knew everything. It was all anyone could talk about for weeks. She never spoke to me again – they're still married, by the way – and I felt like the biggest piece of shit ever to live. Probably, I imagine, a little how you're feeling right now. But I'm telling you this, Charlie, so you know that I understand. I know what it's like to be on the road day after day, in and out of anonymous hotels, grinding

321

through practice after practice. And now, with Todd and your intensified training schedule? It's a lot. So cut yourself a little slack. We all know you're not some pot-smoking idiot, just like I wasn't some asshole home-wrecker. We all screw up. We hopefully apologize and make it right, but life goes on.' He nudged her chin up with his finger so she would meet his gaze. 'Okay, kiddo? Can you do that for me?'

She reached up to kiss his cheek, feeling an intense wave of gratitude. 'I'll try. If you tell me where you're going.'

'Me? I have a date.'

He couldn't have surprised her more if he'd announced he'd joined the CIA. Not that it was unreasonable – everyone knew he was hardly celibate when Charlie and Jake were traveling – but he never, ever went out with women when one of them was home. Or if he did, they never knew about it. Clearly this was something more substantial.

'A date? Who's the lucky lady?'

Her father coughed. 'It's, um, someone you know, actually.'

'Someone I know?'

'You probably haven't seen her in a while. I hadn't either. After your mother . . . It was too painful. But we've gotten—' He coughed again. 'We've gotten reacquainted lately.'

'Reacquainted? So this is not a first date?'

'No, this is not a first date. She's, uh, an old friend.'

'This is like a riddle, Dad. Are you going to tell me?' But she suddenly knew. She didn't know how, but she knew she was right. She could feel it.

As she watched his mouth form the words 'It's Eileen,' she said it in her mind at the same time. *Eileen*. Of course it was. Her mind cycled backward, remembering the hints that had been there all along. The time when her father had told her that Amanda, Charlie's oldest childhood friend, had met a guy and followed him to Australia. When Charlie asked how he knew such a juicy tidbit about someone she'd lost touch with forever ago, he'd murmured something about running into Eileen. When was that? Could that really have been almost a year ago? Longer? Or the time she was last home and having lunch with her father at the club and Howie had begun to ask after someone – a new friend – but Mr Silver had cut him off with that look. And what about the time earlier that year, on the anniversary of her mother's death, when she and her father had visited the grave? Although they'd both gone together and Jake was out of town, there was a gorgeous peony arrangement resting in front of the grave-stone and a carefully arranged handful of smooth river rocks – her mother's favorite – resting on top. Mr Silver hadn't seemed surprised when he brushed off Charlie's questions. And of course there was Eileen's unexpected appearance at Charlie's exhibition match at UCLA. How had she been so clueless?

'You're dating Eileen? *Mom's* Eileen?'

'It's complicated, Charlie. I know it sounds . . . strange, but some things are difficult to explain.'

'Wow. I don't know what to say. Just wow.'

Jake Tapper's voice droned on in the background. Something about a sharp increase in oil prices and OPEC. Neither she nor her father looked at each other.

'Charlie? There's something else you should know. It's more serious than that.'

'More serious than what?'

'We're not just dating. We're, uh, actually planning to marry.'

She had no idea why, but her very first thought, despite the fact that her own father was telling her he was marrying her dead mother's best friend, was: *Why is everyone in my life getting married?* In quick succession she thought of the wedding – when it would be planned, how it would conflict with her schedule, what she would wear – and immediately considered the thought that Amanda and her little sister, Kate, would now be her stepsisters. Then she cycled to Jake. Had he known and not told her?

'Charlie?'

She heard his voice somewhere in the background, but her mind was in overdrive, first considering all the possibilities and then feeling guilty for being so selfish.

'Charlie? Can you say something?'

He sounded plaintive, nearly desperate for her approval, and Charlie knew that a kinder, more sensitive daughter would recognize his worry and try to set him at ease. Especially after how he'd just let her off the hook for her own epic mistake. After all, it wasn't like her father was marrying some bimbo younger than his own daughter, a woman who would push for more children, or one of those hyper-controlling types who would try to micromanage all of them into a living hell. No. He was choosing to spend the rest of his years with someone Charlie knew to be kind and generous and filled with endless energy and concern for other people. A woman who had spent twenty-four months shuttling Charlie's mom to chemo appointments and wig consultations and spirit-lifting shopping trips. Someone who had arranged a spontaneous long girls' weekend in Barcelona because Mrs Silver had always dreamed of going, and who had worked out all the details of traveling internationally with a terminal illness. Eileen had driven Charlie to weekend tennis tournaments when her father had to work and her mother was too sick to get out of bed; she had tutored Jake, first when he fell behind in geometry and again in trig; she had often put the needs of her own children second in the weeks and months after Charlie's mom had died in order to be a constant presence in the Silver home, cooking French toast and tuna casseroles and folding laundry and holding Charlie and Jake as they woke, weeping, in the middle of the night. She had been the closest thing to a mom they had in the darkest months, so why did it feel so strange that she would now be their stepmom? Most of all, why couldn't Charlie set aside her own feelings for ten seconds and give her father the smile and hug he so obviously needed?

He father stood up and began to pace. 'I know this must be a bit of a shock,' he said quietly.

'You haven't so much as mentioned Eileen's name in nearly fifteen years after she totally vanished, and now you tell me you're *marrying* her?'

'She was there for this family when no one else was.'

'She dropped off the face of the earth when her husband got upset that she was spending so much time at our house. We, like, practically never saw her again.'

Her father sighed. 'It's hard . . . no, it's impossible, to understand what goes on in someone else's marriage. Eileen gave her time and energy for this family when we needed her most. She did it selflessly and out of love for your mother. Who, by the way, would have done exactly the same thing for her. But she still had two young daughters at home and a husband who needed her. Now, clearly there were problems already – I don't know if you remember they were divorced a couple of years later – but I don't think we can fault her for hearing Bruce's dissatisfaction and trying to be more present for her own family.'

'Is that the story now?' Charlie hated how nasty she sounded, especially after the kindness and understanding he'd just shown her. But she couldn't help herself.

Her father looked at her and squinted. 'I'm sure I could have handled this better. You know I'm not great at these conversations. But I think you could have, too.' He stood up and took his keys from the little mounted hook by the door. 'I won't be too late. Good night, Charlie.'

He closed the door quietly behind him, and Charlie must have stared at it for nearly five uninterrupted minutes, tears rolling down her face, before an email beeped on her phone. Her heart beat a little faster when she saw it was from Todd.

Charlotte,
Let's consider this incident your first fuck-up and your last, at least if you wish to retain my services. Your brother has explained in depth to me the series of events. I most certainly understand that you did not intend to smoke marijuana, and I am also aware that merely missing a testing window with the doping officials results in a failed test, nothing more. That's the good news. The shit news is that no one else

understands either of these two points. Jake and I have been in touch with Meredith to get to work on the optics of this situation. For your part, you will:

1. *Issue an approved apology via Instagram, Facebook, and your website to your fans.*
2. *Explain the doping test 'failure.' Again, this will be approved first by all of us.*
3. *Convince me that you will never again attend 'room parties' or any other such nonsense at any point during a tournament.*
4. *Commit to training and practicing an additional extra hour per day to prepare for Wimbledon.*

I'll pick you up at Heathrow so we can review this. I'm assuming I need not remind you how to conduct yourself on Bono's yacht this weekend. If I catch even a whiff of pot smoke or scandal, you and I are over. Happy travels.

Todd

Charlie read it once more before clicking it closed. She'd had more than enough for one night.

19

bono on a boat

MEGA-YACHT IN THE MED, JUNE 2016

Todd was waiting in baggage claim for her after she cleared customs. He had arranged for all of them to stay in a flat in central Wimbledon Village for two weeks before the tournament began. She would train on the courts, get herself reacquainted with grass courts, and acclimate her body to the time change and food differences. It was almost impossible to believe it had been an entire year since the injury, and she still didn't have a Grand Slam to show for another twelve months of training and traveling. But first there was the yacht.

'Hey,' Charlie said awkwardly, unsure whether to extend a hand or offer a hug.

Todd barely glanced at her. 'You got everything? Only one racket bag? Where's the rest of your crap?'

'I brought six rackets as carry-on and checked the clothes I'll need for the boat, but I sent the rest of my rackets and gear directly to the address you gave me in the Village. Has Nike delivered the outfits yet?'

Todd grunted. 'They're with Monique.'

'Monique?'

'Yes. She's going over every lousy sock and sweatband with a fine-tooth comb to make sure it conforms to all Wimbledon standards. There will not be another wardrobe malfunction this year. Not on my watch.'

'That's great, thanks. I appreciate it,' Charlie said, nearly racing to follow him out to the sidewalk after he grabbed her bags.

'That's about the only thing you *don't* have to worry about. Everything else is definitely your problem.'

Charlie was silent as they walked out to the curb. A driver would be taking her from Heathrow to Luton, one of the smaller airports on the outskirts of London, for her flight to Naples, and Todd was along for the ride. The charity event was a last-minute invitation after Venus Williams had come down with the flu. But to pull out would be effectively admitting a drug problem. Or, as Meredith said, 'Might as well head to Hazelden.'

Todd held the door open for Charlie and motioned for her to climb into the back of a waiting Audi station wagon. She didn't even notice Dan sitting beside the driver until he turned around to say hello.

'What are you doing here? You know I won't be back to hit until Monday,' Charlie said, not intending to sound quite as rude as she had.

Dan shot a look at Todd, who cleared his throat.

'What's going on?' Charlie asked.

Todd climbed in next to her. The driver shifted into gear.

'Dan is accompanying you to Italy,' Todd said.

'Pardon?'

'You heard me.'

'You're sending me with a babysitter?'

Dan averted his eyes.

'What, isn't that what you are? My minder? So I don't humiliate myself and—?'

Todd interrupted. 'Call it whatever you want, Silver. Now, I understand why this trip is necessary from a public relations standpoint – Meredith was insistent you accept this invitation – and because of that I won't fight your attending. But don't think for a single fucking minute that you're there to do anything except pose for cameras, look happy and *sober*, and wave to your adoring fans. Because that would be a huge mistake.'

'I'm not some degenerate teenager, Todd.'

'Could've fooled me.'

'I don't think that's really fair. There have been—'

Todd held up his hand for silence. 'I've spoken with Jake and Isabel from the WTA and they've drafted both your apologies and your explanations. We'll be sending those to you shortly. She'll also provide a media script with approved answers for questions that will inevitably arise about all of this. *Do not deviate*. Under any circumstances. You do *not* have permission to go off script. Understood?'

Before Charlie could answer, Todd's phone rang. He slipped in his earbuds and flipped open his laptop.

The car was quiet for a few minutes as Charlie fumed. Then Dan said, 'I'm not going to cramp your style. Don't worry.'

'I'm headed to a private jet that's going to whisk me off to a mega-yacht for a few days of cruising the Amalfi Coast. I'm not worried about you cramping my style,' she snapped.

Dan nodded.

They were quiet the rest of the drive to Luton. When they arrived, the driver flashed some identification and the car was escorted directly to the runway, where a British immigration official checked their passports from the back-seat. Then a uniformed porter removed Charlie's and Dan's luggage and stowed it carefully in the rear cargo hold of the idling Gulfstream V.

Todd wordlessly tossed her a backpack.

'What's this?' Charlie asked, unzipping it. Inside was a portable DVD player – the kind children used on planes – and a stack of discs. She thumbed through the titles scrawled in Sharpie: 'Munich Semis '14,' 'Sharapova Kicks Ass March '15,' 'Geiger v. Atherton Singapore '15.' The names went on and on.

'You will find the time to watch every last one, and be ready to discuss them. I'll send a car to pick you up here on Monday,' Todd said, barely looking at Charlie. 'I expect you'll be prepared to work. Unless, of course, you want to flush Wimbledon down the toilet like you did Roland-Garros. In which case, you can do it alone.'

Charlie just stared at her hands.

'Good, I'm glad we understand each other.' He turned to Dan. 'I'm holding *you* personally accountable. No drinking, no smoking, no drugs. No fucking *chocolate*, for chrissake. SPF fifty. Eight hours of sleep. Am I making myself clear?'

'Crystal,' Dan said.

Todd pulled the car door shut and the driver peeled away.

Dan glanced at Charlie. 'You okay?'

'Fine,' she said through clenched teeth.

Dan's phone rang as they walked toward the plane's lowered staircase, but he quickly silenced it.

'Is that the Paris girl?'

He remained quiet.

'Things went well, then?' Charlie asked.

Dan blushed.

'Good for you. About time you got a girlfriend, isn't it?'

'Don't take your Todd shit out on me,' he said quietly, motioning for her to walk up the stairs ahead of him. 'He's the jerk-off, not me.'

They reached the top of the stairs and a beautiful black flight attendant in a crisp white uniform greeted them both by name and invited them to sit wherever they'd like. 'Except the two seats in the middle of the plane. Those are the owners' favorites.'

Charlie took one of the forward-facing plush leather armchairs toward the back and motioned for Dan to sit facing her. They were the first ones on board, but the other passengers would arrive momentarily.

The flight attendant held out a silver tray with flutes of champagne and glasses of water. Charlie looked at Dan pointedly and accepted one of the waters.

Charlie cleared her throat. 'I'm sorry. I don't want to have tension.'

'Nothing going on with the girl in Paris,' Dan said. 'I think I just haven't gotten over a past relationship.'

'Name?'

'Katie.'

'Of course it is. How long were you together?'

'Three years. We met senior year at Duke in a creative writing class.'

'Creative writing?' Charlie asked incredulously. 'I had no idea you were interested in writing! I thought it was always tennis for you. And business.'

Dan sat up in his seat a bit straighter. 'I've actually written a novel. Nothing published yet, but I'll hopefully be ready to shop it around soon.'

'For real?' Charlie asked, genuinely shocked.

'Yeah. I'm almost finished with the rewrite. I try to fit it in during off-hours on flights, in the hotels, the downtime. I mean, when else will I have this kind of time while I'm also earning a living? Thanks to you, I can actually take a stab at this.'

Charlie thought about this. 'That makes me happier than you know.' She shook her head. 'Are your parents supportive?'

'Depends. I was the first kid in my family to go to college. They wanted me to study econ and learn how to take the family business from a mom 'n' pop to something that might actually support our family for another generation.' He coughed.

'How did tennis fit in? First singles is hardly just a hobby.'

'I love playing – and I love working for you – but in school, I was doing it for the scholarship.'

'And you never thought of taking it further? You can beat me handily any old time you want.'

Dan laughed. 'As Todd would say, you're still just a chick.'

Charlie kicked him.

'No, seriously, I didn't have that driving will to succeed at tennis. I couldn't seem to give up everything else in my life, like writing or college.'

'Or girls.'

'Or girls. I definitely could not give up girls.'

'The male players don't do badly in that department, I'll remind you,' Charlie said.

'No, they don't, do they?' Dan raised an eyebrow. 'But anyway, I'm just not cut out for the schedule and the training and the single-minded focus.'

Charlie sipped her water. 'So you were telling me about Katie. Lovely, sweet, Southern Katie.'

Dan laughed. '*My* Katie was a born-and-bred New Yorker who thought her nanny was her mother until kindergarten. She was one tough chick. Knew her mind. Knew mine, too. I'd never met a girl like that before, I guess. Private schools and Hamptons houses and French tutors, the whole nine. I was totally seduced by it. It's kind of embarrassing to admit.'

'I get it,' Charlie said quietly. She, too, had been awed by the families her father taught at Birchwood. It was more than their wealth: it was as though they had internalized their privilege at birth and moved through life with such a relaxed, graceful ease. The world was theirs for the taking, so they took.

'Katie stood up for me when her family disapproved of

us, and even though she didn't need to work, she's a kick-ass photographer these days and it was all her own doing. She's pretty impressive, actually.'

'So why aren't you with her?'

Dan turned to look at her. 'Because at the end of the day, there was no way that Katherine Sinclair of Park Avenue and East Hampton was going to marry Dan Rayburn from Marion, Virginia, whose parents owned a hardware shop and who didn't have a passport until he'd graduated from college. Duke or no Duke, she knew who I was.'

Charlie was quiet for a moment. 'Her loss,' she murmured, careful not to meet Dan's eye.

His smile was tinged with sadness. 'Yeah, I'm sure. Anyway, I can see from Facebook that she married Lachlan Dobbs III in Bermuda six months after we broke up. Had two boys in two years, both with Roman numerals after their names. They are currently building a home next to her parents' in Amagansett, and they just moved from Gramercy to a modest little ten-million-dollar townhouse on Seventy-Fourth between Park and Madison. Not that I keep track.'

Charlie laughed, and it was all she could do not to reach across the aisle and hug him. 'I can see that. Very restrained. I'm impressed.' Before Charlie could remind him that he was, in fact, sipping Evian aboard a plush private jet en route to spend a few days aboard one of the world's most luxurious mega-yachts, voices rang out from the stairs.

'Well, well, look who made the cut!' Natalya trilled out, holding the gathers of her maxi dress in the crook of her elbow as she gingerly stepped aboard in four-inch platform espadrilles. Benjy, following behind her, smashed his head into the doorframe. His hands were the size of Ping-Pong paddles.

'Natalya,' Charlie murmured, determined not to let herself get ruffled. 'And Benjy. How are you? No training camp for you?'

'Still officially the off-season,' he said, lowering his enormous body into one of the seats across the aisle from Dan. 'I've been told this little sailboat we'll be visiting has quite the gym, so I'll still get my workouts in.' He looked up and met Charlie's gaze. 'I didn't know you were coming this year. Terrific. Anyone traveling with you?'

Charlie motioned to Dan and introduced them. Natalya was busy staring out her window and yakking in Russian into her phone.

'Anyone else?' he asked.

'Marco is meeting us tonight at the port. They're sending the plane back to London for him and a couple of other people.'

'Mmmm, got it,' Benjy murmured.

'Marco's coming, huh?' Dan said quietly. 'I've got my nannying work cut out for me.'

Charlie turned to him and feigned indignation. 'Really?'

'You heard Todd. There won't be any middle-of-the-night visits, let's just put it that way. Coach's orders.'

'What, are you standing sentry outside my door?'

'Whatever it takes.'

Eleanor McKinley, the young Canadian who'd beaten Charlie in the first round of the French Open, walked onto the plane and nodded to everyone.

Charlie forced herself to wave. The girl's mother, wearing an elegant pantsuit and carrying a Louis Vuitton tote, sat next to Eleanor and began whispering in her ear. As soon as they were settled, Rinaldo, Marco's biggest on-court nemesis and closest friend on the tour, strode aboard.

'Hey, Rinaldo,' Charlie said, standing up to kiss both his cheeks. 'No Elena today?'

He shook his head. 'Home with the baby.'

The flight to Naples was short, under two hours, and the chauffeured Suburban that took them to the marina was sumptuous. Still, nothing prepared Charlie for the sight that awaited them when they approached the dock where *Lady Lotus* proudly floated. She was a sleek, two-year-old, 280-foot mega-yacht that was commissioned by a wealthy entrepreneur from China who was reputed to hate both boats and water. Supposedly he had bought the yacht because he understood it was a Western status symbol, but rumor was he had done little more than sit on the sparkling new decks, barefoot and clad in a designer suit and tie, as the boat bobbed in the marina. Only guests who chartered the yacht – nearly all celebrities, due to the $750,000 per week rental fee – ever actually left the harbor. This week Bono had chartered the boat and invited aboard six of the highest-profile tennis players and another dozen or so uber-wealthy tennis fans for a charity tennis competition. Aboard the yacht. On a floating tennis court that doubled as a helipad. These guests were paying three hundred thousand dollars each to spend two days aboard the yacht, watch the pros play a few games, and, if they wanted, pull out their own rackets and have a hit with the world's best. All the money went to AIDS prevention and treatment in Africa. It was an annual Bono tradition and, naturally, one of the most coveted invitations in both tennis and philanthropy circles.

'Jesus Christ,' Dan muttered under his breath as a tall blond deckhand in a short-sleeved polo and navy shorts held open the car door.

At least two dozen crew lined up shoulder to shoulder across the hull, hands crossed behind their backs and smiling as the group made their way to the gangway. There, after removing their shoes and placing them in individual woven baskets that already bore their names, Charlie and Dan filed onto the main deck, where a steward offered them cool, citrus-scented towels and a Crest-ad smile. Her white polo was embroidered with LADY LOTUS, and she wore a crisp navy skirt that showed off her deeply tanned legs. Everywhere Charlie turned, another matching deckhand or steward with dazzling teeth and shiny hair smiled back at her.

'Welcome, Ms Silver. Mr Rayburn. My name is Johanna. We are so happy to have you aboard,' a girl no older than nineteen or twenty said to Charlie and Dan. 'I just wanted to ensure you are aware that we have you assigned to bunk together? Due to space considerations?' The girl looked momentarily concerned.

'Yes, of course,' Dan said, silencing Charlie's anticipated protest. It was hard to imagine there wasn't an extra room somewhere on this floating city.

'We have taken the liberty of making up separate beds for you,' Johanna continued. 'The accommodations are large. And during our tour I will point out where there are additional guest bathing facilities, should you not wish to share the head.'

Maybe Charlie would protest more if she weren't so dumbfounded by their surroundings. Johanna led Charlie and Dan through automatic sliding glass doors into a behemoth salon, richly upholstered in white leather with walnut accents. There was a sectional that seated twelve and additional armchairs and love seats for at least another dozen, specially commissioned sets of classic board games, an entire wall of first-edition novels, hardcover photo books of past celebrity cruises, and a mounted projection screen. Opposite the television were two Warhols and a Lichtenstein. They continued through the salon and outside to a staircase that led them to a lower sundeck featuring a gym with enough equipment to rival an Equinox, a spa locker room complete with two massage tables, steam, sauna, and hot and cold plunge pools. Adjacent to that was a sort of miniature beauty salon with a stylist's chair, mirrored vanity, and equipment for providing facials and manicures. Somewhere around the third teak sundeck that was outfitted with a resistance lap pool, Charlie lost track of where they were.

'Charlie, are you seeing this?' Dan shouted when Johanna allowed them a peek into the storage unit at the bottom of the boat where the owner kept his 'toys': four jet skis, water skis, wakeboards, snorkel and scuba gear, and two tenders that would ferry the groups to shore or take them out to play on the water.

'I see it,' she said, a little embarrassed that Dan was acting as excited as she felt.

'Incredible. Just incredible,' he murmured, taking it all

in. Charlie knew he must be thinking of his parents back at their home in Virginia, just as she was picturing her father in his one-bedroom guest cottage that could most kindly be described as 'rustic.' The whole thing felt so surreal.

But even she could barely mask her awe when Johanna escorted them into their cabin. A king-sized platform bed with a leather headboard mounted to the wall sat atop a white silk area rug. A single handheld remote controlled the cabin lights, temperature, window shades, window tinting, and bathroom floor heat; a separate command unit with its own touchscreen could summon the drop-down television from its hiding place in the wall and offer a menu of more than a thousand movies and nearly two hundred TV series. The music selection included over twenty thousand songs and could be played overhead, in a pillow speaker while sleeping, or in the shower. One of the walls contained a hidden handle that pulled down to create a twin-sized bed. It was already made up exactly like the king, and it included a push-button panel that could be raised or lowered for privacy, creating a nearly separate sleeping nook for Dan. Charlie relaxed.

'Please feel free to take the afternoon at leisure,' Johanna said, sweeping her arms. 'Lunch is a cold buffet on the third-floor aft deck, available whenever you please. We are still waiting for guests to board this afternoon, so we won't be launching immediately. Should you need anything at all, please don't hesitate to pick up any phone extension and you'll immediately be connected to a steward. Is there anything I can do before I leave you?'

Charlie glanced around. 'I'd love to fit in a workout

before everyone else gets here. Would it be possible to have my luggage brought down?'

'It's already been unpacked. Folded clothes have been placed in drawers, shoes are in the storage units under the bed, toiletries in the bathroom, and hanging clothes are currently being pressed and will be placed in your closet. Which reminds me, just leave any laundry in the basket and we'll collect it each morning. I do apologize that we are unable to offer daily dry cleaning, but if you have something that requires it, we're happy to bring it ashore whenever possible.'

'Thank you,' Charlie managed.

Johanna smiled and closed the door behind her.

'What a dump,' Dan said, sitting down on the edge of his pull-down bed.

'No dry cleaning? What kind of shitty yacht is this?' Charlie said.

'I want a refund.'

The two of them convulsed in laughter. Charlie had to wipe the tears from her cheeks a full minute later. She couldn't remember laughing that hard in weeks. Or had it been months? Each individual muscle in her stomach ached and she could feel the makeup smeared across her face, but she didn't care at all.

Their eyes met for a single moment before Dan quickly looked away. 'You're going to work out?' he asked, grabbing a book.

'Yeah, I think I'll get that in now. Then probably shower and grab some lunch.'

'Sounds good. I'll see you later.' Charlie tried not to stare at his exposed abs when he pulled his sweater off.

She looked away the moment his T-shirt came down to cover the skin, but his eyes caught hers.

'Have fun,' she called out, ducking into the bathroom to change into workout clothes. She shut the door firmly behind her and waited to come back out until after his footsteps had receded into the hallway.

There was a collective inhalation among the women – especially the middle-aged wives of the billionaire philanthropists, the ones who had yet to see him in the flesh – as Marco joined the group, barefoot, on the aft deck for sunset cocktails. He was freshly showered, his hair still wet and swept back off his face, his pink button-down casually untucked over a pair of tight-fitting navy chinos. His teeth and toenails looked like they were glowing against his intensely tanned skin. Charlie glanced around at the women – all freshly scrubbed and tanned and turned out themselves – and could see from their expressions that there wasn't one among them, married or otherwise, who wouldn't fall into bed with Marco if given even the smallest window. It took him nearly ten minutes of being admired and courted and flirted with before he made his way to Charlie.

'Hey,' he said, leaning over to allow her to kiss his cheek.

'Hey, congratulations on Stuttgart,' she said, trying not to notice that his greeting was no warmer or more affectionate than he'd given any of the women. And then, because she couldn't help herself: 'I don't think I've spoken to you since then.'

'Thanks, love.' He looked around. 'So pretty, isn't it?'

Charlie was just about to ask him how the flight in with

Bono had gone, when Dan materialized beside her. He, too, had just showered and looked handsome in a blue linen shirt and white pants. He had nowhere near Marco's sex appeal, but he cleaned up well.

'Can I talk to you for a minute?' he whispered, leaning in close.

'Who's your friend?' Marco asked, appearing vaguely interested for the first time.

'You know Dan,' Charlie said, looking at Marco with a surprised expression.

'Dan Rayburn. Charlie's hitting partner. We've met probably a dozen times before,' he said neutrally.

Marco squinted, trying to place him, and laughed. 'Sorry, man. I did not mean to offend. You know how it is with these women – they're all so . . . how do you say it? Change their mind all the time? Fickle. That's it. I know you seem familiar, but the hitting partners, they come and go all the time.'

Charlie could see the flash of irritation on Dan's face, and she pulled him off to the side, telling Marco she'd be back in a moment.

The sun was just beginning to get low in the sky; the city of Naples looked far prettier in the hazy glint of dusk than it had driving through it at high noon.

'What is it? Marco? Don't let him bother you,' Charlie said, noticing the way Dan's knuckles were almost white from gripping the railing.

'Bother me? You've got to be kidding. He doesn't *bother* me, I just hate the fact that you're dating such a douchebag. There. I said it.'

Charlie was shocked by Dan's outburst, and she hated

the way she sounded, but she couldn't stop herself. 'You had something to tell me? Presumably something other than criticizing my romantic life?'

Dan's whole neck and cheeks had reddened. 'Jake called to tell me he'll be joining us tonight.'

'Wow, Todd must be really worried his little Delinquent Princess is suddenly going to go hog wild and start blowing heaps of cocaine while doing a striptease for the whole boat. I get *two* babysitters? And the great irony is that Natalya may very well go down on every single male on this boat, NFL boyfriend or not, and no one seems to care about that. *I'm* the slut. I just love it.'

Dan coughed. 'Jake said that the charity people had an extra spot for someone from Elite Athlete Management, so he's taking it.' He paused. 'I don't think there's any more to it.'

Charlie was quiet.

'They were going to put him in the crew quarters, but I had Johanna move my stuff there so Jake can stay with you. He'll be more comfortable.' What he didn't need to say was: *I'm sure we both will be, too.*

Charlie softened. 'Thanks,' she said. It had been weeks since she and Jake had had a face-to-face conversation. He hadn't even texted her about his arrival. Just Dan. He'd stayed in Europe to smooth over her public relations nightmare at the French Open, and she hadn't seen him since.

'No problem.'

A steward walked over and handed a glass of Pellegrino with lime to Charlie and a beer in a frosted mug to Dan. Despite not even being offered a drink of choice, it was impossible to remain in a bad mood. Especially as the sky turned purple over the ocean once the sun set and dinner was served. Jake joined them mid-meal and flashed Charlie a *Do you f'ing believe this* look, making her laugh. Across the table and down a few seats, Dan was doing his best to feign interest in one of the billion-aire wives, and Marco was doing the same but looked to be enjoying himself a whole lot more. Natalya was practically curled up in the lap of an oil magnate while Benjy talked with Jake. Everyone was drinking except Charlie.

Before dessert and aperitifs were served, Bono stood at the head of the table to welcome everyone. Even these world-famous CEOs appeared awed by him. 'You all know how strongly I feel about our work in Africa,' he said as the group applauded politely. 'Each and every one of you – whether a player donating time or a business leader donating funds – is contributing enormously to our AIDS treatment and prevention efforts.'

Charlie filed every detail away, preparing to text everything to Piper when she got back to her cabin. When Bono and the rest of the band left during dessert to set up for a jam session in the screening room, Jake sounded like he might pass out.

'A jam session? How can they even call it that? It's U2, for god's sake. U2!'

When they'd made their way to a banquette on the outermost part of the deck, another steward materialized to bring Charlie more Pellegrino and Jake a martini.

'I could get used to this,' she said, taking a sip. 'Do you think they'll help me shower?'

'Definitely. Just ask. Actually you probably don't even have to ask. Just think it and it'll happen.' They laughed together.

They both watched as Benjy pushed back from the dinner table and made his way to the stairs. He looked like he was going to hit his massive head on the ceiling, but he ducked at exactly the right time. He rubbed his elbow as though trying to work out a muscle kink.

'Nice guy,' Charlie murmured.

'Who?' Jake asked, although he, too, had been staring at him.

'Benjy. You were talking to him during dinner.'

'Oh. Yes.'

'He seems okay. I don't know what on earth he sees in her. He doesn't seem as dumb as he could be, being a football player and all.'

Jake's eyes squinted and his lower jaw jutted out. 'She's a vile human being. And she certainly doesn't deserve *him*,' he said heatedly.

'I've been telling you she's awful for the last ten years. You're just getting it now?'

Jake shook his head. 'Dad said he told you about Eileen.'

'Uh-huh.'

'They seem really happy together.'

'How long have you known?' Charlie twisted her fingers in her lap. She had apologized and told her father that she was happy for him and that of course she'd support any decision he made. But things were still strained when she left.

'A while now, I guess.'

'Really.'

'Don't be mad, C. He specifically asked me not to tell you because he didn't want to distract you.'

'Distract me?'

'It was just never a good time. You were always right in the middle of, or right about to start, or en route to a major tournament. It's been a big year for you, with the injury and the surgery, the new coach, the image overhaul, and, well, I just think he—'

'You've known for a *year*?' Charlie knew she sounded angry, but more than anything, she felt so detached. Her own father was in a serious relationship – now ready to get married – and she hadn't known a thing. He hadn't told her, but she hadn't noticed either.

Jake sighed. 'He kept it from you for your sake, Charlie. Because he knew you'd be upset.'

'Well, this feels worse than if he'd just treated me like an adult in the first place.'

It was Jake's turn to say nothing. He didn't have to: Charlie knew exactly what he was thinking.

She stood up. 'I'm beat. Still not used to the time change. I'm going to turn in.'

Jake held out a hand and Charlie helped pull him up. 'Sure you are,' he said with a wicked grin.

'What? You think there's room in Marco's bed tonight? You don't have to worry about that. Judging from dinner, his cabin is going to look like a deli counter: Take a number and get in line.'

'Lovely,' Jake said, laughing. 'You taking a number?'

'Good night, Jake . . .'

'You're seriously missing the jam session? It's *U2*, Charlie.'

'I'm on probation, remember? Todd probably has the yacht on a live feed. Besides, they're doing a real concert for everyone tomorrow night. And I'm tired. I'll be asleep when you come in, so be quiet, okay?' She kissed his cheek and waved to Dan on her way to the staircase that would lead to her cabin. As she walked by, she thought she could sense Marco watching her, but when she glanced back he was smiling at a woman draped on his shoulder. As she changed into a nightshirt and brushed her teeth and washed her face, she must have checked her phone a hundred times, but there was nothing. Radio silence from the hot Spaniard. She was more surprised at the depth of her disappointment than anything else.

Charlie didn't remember falling asleep, but when she awakened, the cabin was pitch-black. The yacht's motor hummed from somewhere belowdecks as the boat rocked gently. Her phone read 4:58 a.m. She knew from the printed card next to her bed that sunrise would occur around 5:30 a.m. and that they were due to anchor in Capri a half hour later. It was immediately obvious she wouldn't be able to fall back asleep, so she stretched for a bit and made her way to the bathroom. It was only then she noticed that Jake's bed was still untouched.

Charlie pulled on a T-shirt and workout leggings and threw her hair into a messy bun. She tied a Nike hoodie around her waist in case it was windy and, as an after-thought, took some headphones. Grabbing a bottle of Evian from the basket on her desk and the backpack with the DVD player Todd had given her, she headed for the stairs. It was perfect: she'd be able to find Jake and save him the embarrassment of getting caught passed out on a couch somewhere, and after she'd sent him back to the cabin, she could enjoy the peace and quiet of watching the sun rise over the Mediterranean. Afterward she could fit in a workout with the onboard trainer, watch some tape, and still have time for a quick breakfast before she was expected on the helipad tennis court for her scheduled hit-around.

The uppermost deck was like a perch, with a sunken hot tub overlooking the boat's bow. It was dark and deserted, as was the area just below it. The captain and one of his mates stuck their heads out from the lit bridge to inquire if she needed anything, but she merely waved and walked back toward the stern. The aft deck that held the tennis court was empty, and so was the one below it. Was it possible everyone was still partying? It seemed unlikely, but who could predict what a jam session with U2 aboard a luxury yacht looked like? For all she knew, the entire lot could be engaged in some drug-fueled orgy, far away from the paparazzi. She picked up the pace. She berated herself for being such a loser, but at least Todd would be happy.

When Charlie reached the screening room, she saw that all twenty leather armchairs and ottomans had been stored in orderly rows and the band's instrument cases were neatly stacked in a corner. She stood in the dark and silence and tried not to worry: Jake was a big boy, and besides, what really could have happened? For all she knew, he could have made his way back to the cabin at some point in the last twenty minutes she'd been roaming the boat. She'd decided that was the likeliest scenario and started back upstairs when she heard a noise. As she moved to the back of the screening room, it became a loud, steady snore.

It took a moment for her eyes to adjust to the darkness once she opened the door, and to realize that she was in the projector room with a panel of electronics elaborate enough to rival an air traffic control tower. A classic director's chair stood in front of the panel, and a three-seater leather couch sat against the back wall. The room was no more spacious than a small bedroom, but it featured a half dozen framed movie posters on the wall (no doubt original) and a built-in cabinet that contained hundreds of DVDs. Charlie was so fascinated by the obsessive DVD filing system that she almost forgot why she was there until a particularly loud snort brought back her attention. By then her eyes had fully adjusted, but she still didn't believe what she saw when she squinted toward the couch: Jake, lying on his back with his mouth open, his steady breathing rattled by snores. Not alone. Curled up right alongside him, with his head tucked into Jake's neck, was Benjy. *Natalya's* Benjy. Both men were dressed from the waist down, but their shirtless embrace left little doubt of the extent of their familiarity.

Charlie froze. Should she turn and leave as quietly as possible and confront Jake about it later, in private? That left the distinct possibility that someone else would find them first. Should she shake them awake and tell them to go back to their rooms before the others awoke? Jake would be embarrassed, no doubt, but Benjy would be mortified. He was one of the most famous quarterbacks in the NFL, someone who practically earned a living capitalizing on his alpha-male straightness. He was portrayed as an aggressive, testosterone-fueled womanizer who moved from model to singer to actress with exactly the ease and frequency one might expect of a successful, good-looking athlete. Like Marco, she thought before she could stop herself.

'Charlie!' Jake's voice was urgent.

He must have sensed someone else in the room and awakened, his face registering an expression Charlie didn't recognize. Embarrassment? Or was that relief?

'What are you doing?' she hissed, carefully calibrating her whisper so as not to wake Benjy.

'What does it look like I'm doing?' Jake said. He hadn't moved a muscle, but Benjy stirred.

They both remained motionless until Benjy settled again and his breathing became steady.

'We're going to be at shore soon, Jake. You have *got* to get out of here. Get *him* out of here.'

'What time is it?'

Charlie looked at her phone. 'Almost five-thirty in the morning. I can't even. Ohmigod. The irony of this is killing me!'

'Charlie, please.'

She couldn't help but smile. 'Who's the big scandalous slut now? Huh? Who is it?' she stage-whispered.

Jake looked like he wanted to kill her but he couldn't move an inch.

'I'm going to the gym. I suggest you leave separately. The crew is definitely up by now. And don't think you'll get away without giving me every single solitary sordid detail. You owe me at least that for saving your ass right now. And his!'

Charlie turned to leave and quietly pulled the door closed behind her. She waited for just a moment until she heard

Jake shaking Benjy awake and urging him to remain quiet. Making her way back to the upper deck, Charlie began to feel queasy. As excited as she was for Jake's postgame recap, she knew nothing good could come of this.

En route to the gym – she needed a workout now more than ever – Charlie pressed her ear directly against Marco's door. How low was the bar set when you were eavesdropping on your sometimes hookup's room? It was too pathetic for words. *She* was too pathetic for words. All of which was confirmed moments later when she had rounded the corner and nearly crashed into Dan, who was already dressed in shorts and sneakers, also clearly headed to the gym before he was due to warm her up on the afterdeck court.

'I won't tell Todd,' he had said, looking at his feet as though trying to save her from her unspeakably humiliating walk of shame.

'Tell Todd what?' she snapped, all of her surprise and hurt and anger pouring out.

His head popped up when he heard the nastiness of her tone, and his eyes widened in surprise. 'He just, uh, he wanted to make sure—'

Charlie felt instantly guilty when she saw how miserable Dan looked. 'Forget it. Just so you know, it's not how it looks.' *I didn't even rank for a late-night sex call.* For some inexplicable reason, she found herself wanting to tell Dan everything, but before she could say another word, he backed away.

'It's none of my business,' he said, holding his hands up as though he were worried she might strike him.

Charlie kept her mouth shut. Dan was in a lousy position,

wedged in between Todd, who had given him this opportunity, and Charlie, who paid his salary. And she was still reeling from what she'd just seen with Jake.

It wasn't until almost eleven that she was able to corner Jake on a sundeck near the breakfast area.

'Sit down this *second*!' Charlie hissed, sidling up to her brother as he helped himself to a plate of sliced fruit.

'Charlie . . .'

She held a coffee cup in one hand and gripped Jake's arm with the other, but he refused to look at her. 'Jake? Look at me! What happened?'

He looked at her and motioned for them to move toward two chaise longue chairs.

'Did you have sex with him?'

Jake's silence said everything.

'Like, full-on penetration sex? The real deal?'

'Charlie.'

'It wasn't just that you both had a few too many drinks and he may have been slightly bi-curious and you guys had a little make-out and then fell asleep? Maybe that's what happened?'

This time Jake met her gaze. 'I'm in love with him.'

In an effort not to spit her decaf coffee across the table, Charlie inhaled sharply, causing the coffee to go down her throat the wrong way. She began to cough violently.

'Charlie? Grow up.'

'No, I'm not making fun of—' She coughed a few more times and then finally managed to clear her throat as her eyes streamed. 'I . . . I just don't know what to say.'

'You don't have to say anything.' Jake pushed his chair back.

'No, wait. Please don't be mad at me. You can understand that this is a little surprising. I mean, he's a *quarterback*.'

'So?'

'So it's not like the NFL generally runs around wearing rainbow ribbons and shouting for LGBT equality, you know? Their mission is to hit each other as hard as possible.'

'Ben is different.'

'"Ben"?'

'He hates Benjy. It's just how the public knows him.'

Charlie refrained from making a snarky comment. 'Can you take me through the night?' she asked slowly. 'How did it happen? Have you been getting a vibe from him for a while now or was it a complete surprise last night?'

Jake twisted his fingers. He seemed to be debating what to tell her.

'Tell me whatever it is you're thinking right now.'

'Last night wasn't the first time.'

Charlie's hand flew to her mouth before she could stop it. She quickly pretended to pick something from her teeth. 'It wasn't?'

'We've been together for months.'

'"Together"?'

'Well, sleeping together. But it's more than that.'

'For *months*?'

'Since Australia.'

'Oh. My. God.' Australia. Five months earlier. Charlie had been so consumed with her own triumphant return after surgery and her brand-new Todd-created image that she had no idea what Jake was doing at the time. 'There was that night at the restaurant in Melbourne. The first night Dad met Todd. Weren't Natalya and Benjy at the player party?'

Jake nodded. 'Exactly. That was when we first met. But nothing happened until the night after the tournament was over. You and Natalya had both already left for Dubai, and we ran into each other in the hotel gym. One thing led to another.'

'Oh my god,' she said again. 'Were you surprised? How could you not tell me! I can't believe how long this has been going on! I won't even comment on the fact that you gave me *hell* for keeping quiet about Marco.'

For the first time all morning, Jake relaxed visibly. He smiled enough that the cute crinkles appeared around his eyes. 'I wasn't surprised. I got a vibe, you know? As soon as all the tennis people had left and we were the only ones around, it was the most natural thing in the world.'

Suddenly, it started to make sense: the frisson she always felt when Benjy and Jake were in the same place; Benjy inquiring who might be traveling with Charlie on the private jet to the yacht; Jake's naked hatred of Natalya. Now she looked at her brother as he described all the different ways he and Benjy had carved time out for one another, all the places they'd secretly met and stories they'd shared, and she felt a surge of intense love for him.

'You're so happy,' she said quietly.

'I'm so happy,' he agreed. 'This is it, Charlie. He's the one.'

'He is? You really think so?' The familiar knot appeared in Charlie's throat before she could help herself.

'Don't cry, C. This is a good thing. A really good thing, I swear.'

Charlie wiped her eyes. 'No, I'm thrilled for you. For

both of you. It's just . . . It's going to be really hard. You must know that.'

Jake nodded. 'Yes. Really freaking hard. We agreed to keep it quiet and first see what happens, see if this is the real deal or not, before we did something stupid and blew up our lives unnecessarily. But we love each other. And we don't want to hide anymore.'

Charlie ached for her brother. Why did everything have to be so complicated? The difficult part should be meeting someone terrific, not wondering how the whole rest of the world was going to feel about it. But Benjy and Jake were so much bigger than just the two of them, and the road ahead was going to be difficult.

'So. Not just an NFL player, but a quarterback. And not just any NFL quarterback, but second only to Tom freaking *Brady*. How am I doing so far?' Charlie asked.

'Yeah. Keep going.'

'And this very straight athlete is also thought to be one-half of a very straight couple. Does Natalya know anything? She must suspect something.'

Jake shrugged. 'I'm not so sure. She's pretty self-obsessed. So long as Ben shows up for photo ops, she doesn't seem all that concerned with what else he does.'

'Sounds lovely.'

'Charlie, I need your promise that you won't say anything. Not to Natalya, no matter how much she pisses you off. Not to Marco. Not to Piper.'

'Please, Jake, you have my word. I promise.'

'Ben and I just need a little time to figure it all out. See what the best way of handling it is.'

'I promise.' Charlie put her hand on her brother's

shoulder. 'Jake? I know this whole situation isn't . . . ideal, but I'm really happy for you.'

An enormous smile spread on his face. 'Thanks, C. He's amazing.'

Charlie wrapped her arms around him and inhaled his familiar smell. She couldn't remember seeing him so happy. Giddy, almost.

Charlie's phone buzzed. They both looked at the screen when she pulled it from her bag. *Let's meet later.*

'He loves you,' Jake said, reading over her shoulder. 'Who would believe it? We both scored gorgeous guys.'

Her heart had raced a little faster when she saw Marco's text, but she quickly remembered the humiliation of pressing her ear against Marco's door, wondering where he was and what he was doing.

'Yep,' she quickly agreed, setting down her coffee. 'Come on, I can't be late.'

20

over it

'Move your ass!' Todd screamed from the sidelines. Charlie managed to get her frame on the ball before it went flying off to the side. 'Stop being so fucking hesitant! You're not going to die if you *move* a little.'

I know I'm not going to die, Charlie screamed silently. *I'm worried about ending up in surgery and rehab again for six more months. Grass is slippery, you jerk. Remember?*

But she knew Todd was right: the moment you feared falling or injury was the moment you fell, hurt yourself, or lost the match. People loved talking about focus, staying mentally strong and present, and everyone assumed it only mattered when you were on the court and you were down a game or a set or a match point. But more often the mental focus was about consistency. The ability to squash the insistent, horrible thoughts in your mind: the slippery grass; the opponent's faster-than-expected serve; the raucous crowd; the twinge in your elbow; the lame line umpire; the idiot in the stands in a neon shirt who won't sit down; the sweat in your eyes . . . On and on the mind went, cycling through all the assaulting sights and smells and sounds that competed for a player's attention. Only a select few of the players – through practice, experience, and sheer determination – ever developed the mental toughness to tune it all out. It was why hundreds of them had the strokes and the game to win, and so few were actual winners.

Dan slammed another ball down the line, which Charlie reached, but he finessed the next shot to fall right over the net, leaving her scrambling to reach it in time. 'Move!' Todd bellowed. Charlie didn't even get close.

'That was cheap,' she muttered.

'Nothing cheap about it!' Todd yelled, beginning to pace up and down the sidelines. 'You're six feet tall and the fourth-best girl player in the whole fucking *universe*. YOU NEED TO GET THERE!'

This continued for another twenty brutal minutes until their court time was up. Dripping in sweat and exhausted from the practice, Charlie braced herself for Todd's assessment.

After a few seconds of mopping her face with a towel, she glanced up toward Todd, who stood a few feet away, staring at her with what could only be described as naked hatred.

'What?' she couldn't stop herself from asking.

More staring. Then a slow, disgusted shake of his head.

'You're afraid. You're fucking *afraid*. I can't even believe what I'm seeing. After all we've done – after everything I've done *for* you – you're still dancing around out there like a goddamn amateur.'

'Todd, I really think that I—'

'You either figure out how to get over whatever fucked-up mental problem you have going on, or pack it in. Because there is no in-between.'

Thankfully, his phone rang before he could continue. He swiped the screen and barked, 'What?'

'Well, that was lovely,' Charlie said as she collapsed onto the bench.

Dan handed her a cup of watered-down Gatorade. 'Don't beat yourself up. You were hitting well. It's natural you're a little hesitant back on the grass, given what happened last year.'

'Yeah, but Todd's right: I need to suck it up. Grass isn't anyone's favorite surface. I need to get over the fear. It just feels like playing on ice.'

He mopped his own neck with a towel. 'You're playing Gretchen tomorrow?'

Charlie nodded. At thirty-six, Gretchen Strasser was the oldest player on the women's tour. She'd taken the prior year off to have a baby, and although she'd won three Slams and been ranked number one in her late twenties, it was generally agreed that her best days were long over. The announcers thought she should have retired instead of taken maternity leave, but Charlie understood why she couldn't let go. How easy was it to walk away from your lifelong identity? Like most professional athletes, chances were you didn't have the time or inclination to do anything else. Once you stopped playing, you had to reinvent your entire life. It was terrifying for most players, and Charlie wondered if some part of that fear didn't push her to get up and play every day, even when she didn't particularly feel like it.

'You're going to beat her easily. I know you are. Just forget everything about last year – the grass, the slip, the sneakers, the whole thing – and focus on hammering your return-of-serve and forcing her to come in. Her service game is weak, and yours has never been better. You'll break her early and often, I'm sure of it. You've got this.' Dan's tone was urgent, and when Charlie looked up, he was death-gripping his racket like he might break it in half.

'You really think so?'

'I *know* so. You're hitting great, Charlie. Better than I've seen you hit all year.'

Charlie was about to thank him when Todd hung up the phone. 'Do an hour in the gym before you break for lunch. Then I want you back out here with Dan and that chick – what's her name? The young one? Eleanor. And her hitting partner. You're scheduled to share the court at three. None of us have time for stupid mental shit now, so we're going to beat this anxiety right out of you. Got it?'

Charlie and Dan nodded. Todd strode off the court.

Before Charlie could feel sorry for herself, Dan reached over and gently placed his palm atop her forearm. She froze. Had he ever touched her before? It felt so strangely intimate. 'Charlie? Just so you know, I think—'

'Ah, look who it is!' A voice rang out. Dan yanked his arm away as Marco strode onto the court. He looked beautiful: strong, tall, and tan in his tennis whites, and he was smiling at Charlie as though she were the best part of his day. In a flash he was standing in front of her, pulling her up from the bench, and kissing her on the mouth while Dan, Marco's coach, and another men's player and his coach all tried not to watch.

'How lucky am I?' he asked, and Charlie wanted to hate him, but of course she didn't.

'Hey,' she said.

'Whoa, someone is a little sweaty, no?' Marco said, backpedaling, his hands held up in an exaggerated stop motion.

'She just hit for two hours. What do you expect?' Dan asked, his tone openly hostile.

Everyone was quiet for a moment before Marco laughed. Not nicely. '*Amigo*, can I ask you a huge favor? Can you run my rackets to the stringing room? They need to be there before one, but I'm on the court now until two. Cool?' He flung his racket bag toward Dan, kissed Charlie again, and trotted to the baseline while the others followed.

Charlie watched Dan flush red as he packed up his own bag and slung both his and Marco's over his shoulder.

'I'm sorry,' she said, moving quickly to keep up with him. 'That was uncalled-for.'

'It's fine,' Dan said, although his voice suggested otherwise. 'Come on, I'll walk you to the gym. It's on the way to the stringing room.'

Maybe it was seeing Dan treated so badly but after walking in silence for a bit, Charlie blurted out, 'What are you doing tonight? I have lights-out at nine but do you maybe want to come with me to Austria House? They have some celebrity chef cooking dinner tonight. Have you ever heard of Andre Alexander?'

'Seriously? He's there? Tonight?'

'Yes, and only for, like, twenty people, but I'm sure they won't mind if I bring you. What do you say?'

Dan appeared to consider it.

'What, will you miss the hop-on hop-off tour of London? Or an organized pub crawl of all the best fish 'n' chips places? Or maybe it's a visit to the set of *Downton Abbey*? Come on, fess up, I know you have some culturally enriching plan for the night . . .'

Dan laughed.

'Tell me!' she squealed, and poked him in the side.

'I was just going to make a quick visit to the Lawn Tennis Museum. They have late hours tonight. But a meal from Andre Alexander sounds way better.'

'The *Lawn Tennis Museum*? Please tell me you're kidding.'

Dan blushed. 'I know, I know. It's a stretch, even for me.' They had reached the entrance to the gym when Charlie's phone began to ring.

'Hello?' she answered, once again cursing the lack of caller ID.

'Charlie?' Marco's voice boomed through the phone. Dan looked at the ground but didn't make a move to leave.

'Yes?'

'I have to get back to practice. Just wanted to tell you that we're going to Austria House for dinner tonight. Andre Alexander's cooking. It's going to be incredible.'

'Marco, I, uh . . .' She could feel her face get hot, but

before she could say anything, Dan leaned over and whispered, 'Go with him, Charlie. Seriously, don't think twice. I actually forgot about other plans I had for tonight, so I can't make it anyway. I'll see you at three, okay?'

Charlie watched as he jogged away.

'Charlie?' Marco sounded annoyed. 'Meet me there at six. *Ciao, ciao.*' And the call disconnected.

When Charlie opened her eyes the next morning, she woke with a fire she hadn't felt in months. *Wimbledon.* She was proud of herself for skipping the Austria House dinner the night before and staying in bed – she'd had nearly eleven hours of sleep and she felt great. Marco's text wondering where she was hadn't hurt either. Two hours later, she put Strasser away in straight sets. Efficiently, and with intention. Even Todd had praised her.

Next up was Veronica Kulyk, a Ukrainian girl who'd only recently started playing professionally and was currently ranked twenty-fourth in the world. Charlie met Veronica in the locker room, where they watched the match that preceded their own on overhead screens.

'I cannot believe I am playing the semifinals of Wimbledon!' Veronica said, not bothering to hide her excitement. 'It is something I have thought about for so long, it is so strange to think it is happening.'

Veronica's blond bun was secured so tightly to the back of her crown that it pulled the skin around her eyes taut. It made her look even younger, Charlie thought.

'Don't worry, the crowd is lovely here. All golf claps.' Charlie wanted to be polite, but she was also going through her own pre-match checklist. No fear. No hesitation. No worries about the grass.

And then Veronica began to cry. It began with a few small tears and some delicate sniffling, but soon Veronica was convulsing with sobs. Charlie fought the urge to hug her. She could hear Todd in her head: *No mercy! This is not your friend. Focus on your own goddamn game!*

Finally, Charlie got up and put her hand on the girl's back.

'I am sorry,' Veronica said in careful English, the crying causing her accent to become even stronger.

'It's fine,' Charlie soothed, not exactly sure why the girl was crying. 'Before the first time I played Wimbledon, I was puking in the locker room for at least—'

'You don't understand,' Veronica interrupted. 'If I don't play well, my family does not keep their home. My brothers will not eat.'

The crowd on the television politely cheered above them. The men's match currently unfolding on Centre Court had just entered a third-set tiebreaker, which, depending on the outcome of the next few points, meant the women had either seconds or hours before their match began.

Charlie heard more enthusiastic applause from the television but wouldn't allow herself to glance up.

'My parents, they give everything to me,' Veronica continued. 'All the work, the little money they earn, it all goes to me. I am their hope for everything.'

Charlie didn't know what to say. She wasn't surprised that Veronica supported her entire family. It was a common story among girls in certain areas of the world. Sometimes a girl became an entire family's – or even an entire community's

– hope for the future. Every last dollar and bit of energy had been poured into her training and coaching, and now she was expected to pay it all back with interest. So few ever made it to the big leagues – it was nearly impossible to get to that level, whether from privilege or poverty, it almost never mattered – but the ones who did make it to the top, and who had great financial and emotional debts to repay, well, they had it the hardest of all.

A purple-suited female official walked into the locker room and startled at Veronica's obviously tearstained face. 'Is there a problem?' she asked in that clipped British tone they seemed to teach them at Wimbledon school.

'No, no, there is no problem,' Veronica said, leaping to her feet. She did a few high knee jumps and bent over to place her flattened palms on the floor. 'Is it our turn?'

'Yes,' the woman said, still sounding suspicious. She glanced at Charlie. 'Ms Silver? Are you sorted and ready for your match?'

'I am,' Charlie said, her adrenaline beginning to surge.

Both girls grabbed their enormous racket bags and followed the official out of the locker room and into the hallway, where they were immediately flanked on both sides by the purple-suited security people who would escort them to Centre Court. Tennis fans clad in crisp button-downs and well-tailored suits and fresh floral sundresses smiled at them and cleared a path. A few called out 'Good luck!' or 'Go Charlie!' or 'Wishing you both a great match,' but that was it. Charlie almost laughed: compared with the US Open, where fans preferred screaming to talking and dancing to cheering – where barely a match went by during which a group of drunk fans didn't flash some cleverly worded home-crafted placard – this place was downright sleepy. If the US Open was a two-week trip to Ibiza, Wimbledon was a meditative hike through a scenic national park.

The girls walked out onto the court. Charlie immediately turned to her bag ritual: Gatorade and Evian bottles lined up just so, backup rackets unwrapped and ready, towel slung over the back of her chair. As she pulled out an extra bobby pin to secure her miniature crown a bit more tightly, the laminated picture of her mother fell facedown on the grass court. Charlie had looked at that picture no fewer than a thousand times – it had been with her from the very first professional match she'd ever played. Now she could feel her mother's presence in a way she hadn't since the days right after her mother's death, when Charlie would bolt awake in her bed, convinced her mother had been lying next to her. It was exactly like that, right there on the tennis court, for the first time in so many years: her mother there, watching her, knowing her. *With* her. Charlie stood rooted to the spot next to her chair, unwilling to move an inch, and allowed the entire rest of the world to fade into the background, remembering only the smell of her mother's moisturizer and the feel of her cotton night-gown and the way her hair would tickle Charlie's face when she bent over to kiss her good night.

Charlie looked to the cloudless sky and smiled. She had this.

The warm-up felt lightning fast. Almost before she real-ized it, Charlie was up three games to love in the first set. She caught a glimpse of Veronica's face on the changeover: teeth gritted, shoulders proudly pressed back, looking fierce and determined. But some part of her looked scared, too, and Charlie couldn't help but feel a wave of guilt wash over her. What did it mean if Charlie lost that day? Who would really care except her? Todd, the man she paid exorbitant amounts of money to push her, but who truly cared nothing about her as a person? Nike? Swarovski? The other giant corporations she had courted so determinedly to win their endorsements? Jake? Her father? Charlie thought of all she had missed during her childhood, all the movies and camps and boyfriends and – the biggest sacrifice of all – college. What did any of that really mean when it had been entirely her choice? Her own pressure and expectations? Not only had neither of her parents pressured her to play, but at times they had actively encouraged her not to. How many times had her mother begged Charlie to compete only if she truly loved it? How often had her father literally *pleaded* with her to stay in college, to study, to pursue a different passion – one that could last a lifetime, something that she wouldn't age out of by her thirties, a career that wouldn't rob her of the opportunity to have a family or take a vacation or be defined by something other than a ranking or a win?

Charlie felt deeply for Veronica, for all the pressure the young girl had to bear: she hated that Veronica might play tennis despite loathing the sport, the travel, and the pressure, resenting the physical toll it took on her body and the way it stole her childhood. Charlie felt guilty that she could choose her own path – to play, to walk away, or anything in between – and do it with the confidence that her family and friends would support her. She felt all of this more acutely that day as she beat Veronica in a quick, efficient two sets. She hadn't done anything wrong – in fact, by everyone's assessment, from the television announcer to the cheering fans, she had done everything right – but nothing about that win felt good. Thoughts of Veronica and her mother and Marcy swirled through her mind as she went through the motions of humbly accepting the crowd's appreciation. And as overwhelmed with vying emotions as she was in that moment, Charlie had a stunning realization: for the first time in her entire career she had made it to the finals of a Grand Slam tournament, and about that fact in particular, she felt very little at all.

The first thing Charlie saw when she walked into Elite Athlete Management's hospitality tent was Marco leaning in close to Natalya, whispering something in her ear that made her laugh. He looked coolly casual in tight-fitting pants and an untucked linen shirt, his longish hair so perfectly in place it was impossible not to wonder if he'd had it blown out. It was annoying to admit, but he was only the second-most-attractive person in the room after Natalya. The girl looked stunning: white Hervé bandage dress, four-inch pink patent pumps, legs so long and lean and gorgeously bronzed that it was hard to look away. Charlie looked down at her own strapless dress and sparkly gold sandals – both of which she'd loved mere moments earlier – and felt like a teenager headed to prom.

'Stop staring,' Jake said, pulling her around by the upper arm.

'Did you see how he's flirting with her?' Charlie hissed.

'He's like that with everyone. He's Marco.'

'She wants him, I know she does.'

'You're probably right. But what do you think the chances are that they haven't slept together yet?'

Charlie turned to look at Jake. Why had she never even considered that? Of course they had – maybe even currently *were*. It made perfect sense. It would almost be insane to think otherwise.

'Do you think so?'

Jake sighed. 'I don't know. Probably. Ben says she doesn't seem to care much that *they* barely sleep together.'

Charlie knew Benjy wasn't at Wimbledon because of the start of training camp, but Jake told her they'd been FaceTiming every day. Jake was headed to Miami to visit him the following week, and they were going to work out a plan for going public. The NFL had seen only one openly gay player before, and the news of one of the most famous and accomplished quarterbacks of all time being in a loving relationship with another man was going to generate a media shitstorm. Charlie was so happy for Jake – for them both – but she felt sick even imagining what they still had to face.

'Where's Dad?' Charlie asked, glancing around. 'Didn't you say he was meeting us here?'

'Yeah, he was on the phone with Eileen when I left. He should be here any minute.'

Charlie followed Jake's gaze toward the door leading from the rented villa to the enormous outdoor tent and saw an Elite intern leading a half dozen reporters and cameramen toward them.

'You ready for this?' he asked.

'Do I have a choice?'

Jake didn't answer but steered Charlie toward the area

near the white lacquer bar where Marco and Natalya were flirting, or fake-flirting, or whatever it was they were doing.

'*Hola*, gorgeous,' he said, leaning in to kiss Charlie tenderly on the lips. Anyone who happened to witness that kiss would swear they were soul mates.

'Sooooo,' Natalya said, drawing out the word to make it sound like a song. 'Congratulations on *finally* making it to a final.'

If anyone else caught the sarcasm, they ignored it.

'I first got to the finals of Wimbledon, what, six years ago? Yes. I was only eighteen. A baby. And won four Slams since then. You must be so *relieved* you finally scored one. It was getting embarrassing, no?'

Shocked by Natalya's brazenness, Charlie almost laughed. She felt Jake beside her and heard Todd in her ear: *Focus. Win. Distraction is for losers.*

'Too bad you won't win this one. Maybe next time,' Natalya hissed. Under her breath, so only Charlie could hear. She stared straight into Charlie's eyes and then turned to walk away. Charlie watched as a group of wealthy-looking businessmen parted their circle for her in an elated welcome.

A panel of flat screens hung over the bar. Tonight they featured great matches from the past, and some highlights of the previous two weeks at Wimbledon. When she glanced up, Charlie saw herself put away an overhead in her match against Veronica.

Marco whistled. 'That was a very nice shot. I remember that one,' he said, placing his hand on the small of her back.

A photographer approached. 'It's been decades since we

had a couple where both people were in the finals before,' the photographer said.

'Wait until we both win,' Marco said, tightening his grip around her waist and pulling her toward him. Just as his lips met hers, Marco squeezed Charlie's ass. Hard. And not nicely. She yelped a little and wrenched away, but then she remembered the cameras recording everything. Right behind them stood her father, watching the whole thing, an inscrutable expression on his face.

'Don't do that again,' she whispered into Marco's ear, but he merely laughed.

'Come here, Charlie. Smile for the cameras.'

The photographers snapped away as Charlie and Marco stood arm in arm with enormous plastered-on smiles, their piles of wavy dark hair pressed together. It occurred to her she couldn't remember when they'd last slept together. Being seen together as a couple was mutually beneficial, but when had all the flirtation stopped? When had they stopped sneaking around to each other's rooms late at night and texting each other racy things? Wasn't a casual hookup supposed to at least be *fun*?

Charlie headed over to her father when the photos were complete. 'Will you walk me back to the flat?' she asked.

'You're ready to leave?'

'Very. And I'd love it if you wanted to take a walk with me.'

Mr Silver nodded, and Charlie could see he was happy to be asked. She made her way across the tent and excused herself for interrupting Jake while he spoke with a group of other agents.

'You okay?' Jake whispered. 'It hasn't even been an hour.'

'I posed for all the pictures and drank my Pellegrino, and now I want to take my nervous self home and watch TV before bed. Dad's coming with me.'

'Okay,' Jake said, kissing her cheek. 'Remember, tonight is like any other night. Try to zone out and relax a little, and then stick to your routine. You're ready for this final, Charlie. I know you are.'

Charlie inhaled sharply. *Final. At Wimbledon.* The first Grand Slam final of her career was happening the next day. 'I can't believe my first final is against *her*.'

Jake looked over at Natalya, who had found her way back to Marco. She'd perched herself on the arm of his chair, where her already minuscule dress rode up so high that the entire party could confirm that Natalya wore a black lace thong. She was laughing delightedly at something Marco had said.

'Is it weird that we are both potentially sleeping with someone who—?'

Charlie held up a hand. 'Just don't.'

'Okay, I won't. But for the record, it is super-weird.'

'I can't even.'

'Night, C. I'll see you first thing in the morning.' Jake waved to their father, who was patiently waiting near the tent's entrance.

Charlie didn't bother telling Marco she was leaving, and he didn't so much as glance in her direction when she took her father's arm and walked out onto the street.

'Everything okay?' her father asked, and Charlie could tell he was carefully calibrating his voice to sound interested but not overly pushy.

'Yes, why wouldn't it be?' She followed as her father

led her to the leafy residential street, where they started walking uphill back to the main village.

'Just because you didn't seem to say good-bye to Marco.'

'It's over between Marco and me,' Charlie said quietly. She hadn't planned to say it, but the moment she heard the words, they felt right.

'I'm sorry, honey,' her father said, sounding surprisingly sincere.

'He doesn't even know yet,' Charlie laughed. 'But I think it's safe to say that the only one who's going to lose any sleep over this is Todd. And maybe the publicity people at the WTA. I don't think you have to worry about Marco's feelings.'

Her father hugged her. 'Of all the things that keep me up, I assure you that Marco Vallejo's feelings are not one of them.'

Charlie laughed. 'You must be happy to hear he's getting the ax.'

Mr Silver stopped walking and turned to look at her. 'I'll say it again. I'm only happy if you are, Charlie. You know that, don't you? With Marco, with tennis, with everything – I only want you to be happy.'

Charlie could feel her throat begin to tighten. 'Thanks,' she managed. 'You've always taught me that. I'm sorry I haven't been able to say the same. I've been awful about the Eileen thing.'

'I wouldn't exactly put it—'

'No, it's true. I have. Like an immature brat who can't think about anyone's feelings except her own. I owe you an apology.'

They looked at one another; her father's smile was tinged with sadness.

'I know it's not easy, Charlie. All these years it's been just us, and now there's someone else. And not just anyone, but Mom's best friend. It must feel . . . bizarre.'

'It does. But not the part about you finding someone – I'm so happy about that. Eileen just brings back so many memories of those horrible days right afterward, you know? And I know it's crazy – like, grounds for institutionalization crazy – but I guess there's always some small part of me that thinks Mom might come back one day. With you married again, and to Eileen, well, where would Mom go?'

'I know exactly what you mean, sweetheart. That crazy thought is part of why I've only ever dated, and never really committed. But I've come to think your mother didn't want me to stay frozen in time, unhappy and alone. Now, don't get me wrong – if I had been the one who died first, I would've been very happy for your mother to remain a chaste and devoted widow for the rest of her life. But she was a better person than that. Before she died, she must have told me a thousand times that she wanted me to have a full life. To fall in love again. After making sure I was all set up to take care of you and Jake, it's what she wanted most.'

They crossed the main street and walked down a cul-de-sac toward their rented townhouse. Mr Silver unlocked the front door and immediately plugged in the electric teakettle.

'I'd like Eileen to start coming to tournaments,' Charlie said. 'And not just local ones, like UCLA. If she wants to, that is.'

Mr Silver looked at her. 'I think she'd like that,' he said, his voice catching. 'I know *I* would.'

Charlie crossed the kitchen and hugged her father. She allowed herself to relax into the embrace, resting her head on his shoulder and inhaling his familiar smell. She squeezed as tightly as she could and thought of how long it had been since they'd done this.

'I'm going to go up,' she said, suddenly exhausted.

'No tea? I made you the herbal mint just how you like it.' He handed her a steaming mug.

'I'll take it upstairs with me. Thanks, Dad. I love you.'

He wiped the counter with a dishrag. 'I love you, too, sweetie. Regardless of what happens tomorrow, I hope you know how proud I am of you. Finals of Wimbledon . . . I can barely wrap my mind around it.'

Charlie couldn't help but smile.

'Oh, and, Charlie? I was lying before.'

She stopped and turned around. 'About what?'

'I really am happy that you're ditching Marco. I think he's an ass who is completely unworthy of my daughter. There, I said it.'

Charlie laughed. 'I never would have guessed.'

'Well, you've got to give me credit for keeping my mouth shut as long as I did. Not easy for a dad. You'll see one day. But, yes, he's . . . a total douchebag.'

'Dad!'

'What?'

'Good night . . .'

Charlie walked into the bedroom that was decorated in muted shades of gray and ivory, all very soothing and inoffensive – like all of England – and finished her tea. She changed into a tank top and PJ shorts and had just crawled under the covers when she heard a knock on her door.

'Dad? Come in,' she called out, relieved that she wouldn't have to be alone with her thoughts quite yet. How was she ever going to sleep the night before the Wimbledon final? Or, worse, what would happen if she didn't?

'It's me,' Jake said, looking especially handsome in the blue blazer he'd worn to the party. 'You're not sleeping yet, are you?'

'Yeah, right. Come in, close the door,' she said. He threw himself in a heap at the end of her bed, the same way he'd been doing since they were kids.

'I'd kill for an Ambien. I don't even know the last time I took one, but I remember it was pretty fantastic.'

Jake looked at her.

'What? I'm obviously kidding.' She kicked his ribs from underneath the covers.

'Dad told me about Marco. He was literally waiting for me by the front door. Is it true?'

'Yes. I tried to be super-cool and okay with being casual and not having any titles and just rolling with everything. Clearly he's gorgeous. He's great in bed. He's the guy everyone wants, including me for a really long time. But he's also kind of a douchebag, as Dad so eloquently put it. And while of course parts of it – of him – are fun, I always end up feeling like I'm impersonating someone who is legitimately cool and casual. Which I'm actually not.'

'And you feel like this is a big news flash? That you're not excited to be someone's booty call?'

'Sort of.'

'Oh, well, I hope you don't mind me saying so, but that's just plain idiotic.'

'When did you get so judgey?'

'I'm not judging you, Charlie.'

'Of course you are! You're my brother, that's what you do.'

'Okay, fine, I'm judging you. But for being stupid, not slutty. I thought your little fling with Zeke Leighton was pretty much the greatest thing ever, remember? That's good fun. No expectations, everyone on the same page, a sexy one-off romp. Well played. But this whole Marco thing hasn't sat well with me from the beginning. You're just not that girl.'

'Is this where I point out that you and Todd practically pimped me out to Marco for the sake of "optics"? I mean, let's call a spade a spade.'

'No way! *Todd* pimped you out. I just agreed it was a good strategy when you seemed to be happy and having fun with it. But I can see now why this whole non-relationship relationship isn't terrific, and I entirely support your ditching him.'

Charlie stretched her arms over her head, relieved she was starting to feel tired. 'What about you? How's Benjy? I mean Ben?'

Jake's face was lost in the dark, but Charlie could hear the smile in his words. 'He's great, C. Really, really great. We're . . . We're talking about moving in together.'

Any other night Charlie would have bolted up in bed, run to turn on the lights, and demanded more information. Never before had he declared anything close to that level of commitment. But, for whatever reason, that night it felt like the most natural thing in the world to hear Jake talk about his future with the man he loved. She said, 'Really?

That's great, Jake. How will it work? You'll have to go to Miami, obviously.'

'Yeah. Nothing definite, but once he's officially out and the madness has settled down, I'll probably move into his place on Palm Island. I can work out of Elite's Miami office and I travel so much with you anyway that there's really no reason I have to be based in New York. So that's tentatively the plan.'

'It sounds great, Jake. It really does. I've never seen you like this before.'

'Me neither. He's just . . . I don't know how to describe it.'

'You love him. Plain and simple. Nothing else really matters.'

They were quiet for a moment.

'I'll let you get some sleep,' Jake said, hauling himself up.

Charlie could only make out his shadow in the darkness, but she smiled anyway. 'I don't even resent you for getting the husband, the kids, and the white picket fence before me,' she said.

'Yes you do,' Jake said, leaning over to kiss her cheek. 'But I can live with that.'

'Yeah, you're right. I do. But I'm so happy for you, too. Just don't make me wear a bridesmaid dress to the wedding, okay? That'll put me over the edge.'

'Deal.'

''Night, Jakey.'

He opened the door and light flooded in from the hallway. 'Hey, C? Just one more thing. Kick that bitch's ass tomorrow.'

Instead of feeling agitation and anxiety like she always did when someone mentioned Natalya, Charlie laughed. Then she luxuriated in the cool sheets and the thought of Jake's happiness and she drifted off into a deep, dreamless sleep.

21

go time

THE FINALS, CENTRE COURT, JUNE 2016

The day of the finals, Charlie had her ritualistic grilled salmon and vegetables for lunch. One by one her family and team offered advice at the table in their rented Wimbledon Village flat.

Todd: 'You set the pace. Drive to the net. No fear. Own this match. This is your chance to prove to the entire world that you've got what it takes, so don't fuck it up!'

Jake: 'Play your own game. Don't let Natalya get inside your head. You've got this, Charlie.'

Dan: 'You've made it to the very top and this is the final hurdle. You can do this!'

Dad: 'This is a once-in-a-lifetime opportunity, and you alone have made it happen. Your mother would be so proud of you, and so am I.'

After eating, Todd moved everyone into the living room to view the tapes he had assembled from Wimbledon finals past. Together they watched colossal blowouts while Todd warned, 'Don't let this be you,' and triumphant upsets where he kept repeating 'This is the goal' while waving his arms with urgency.

Now, a few hours later, Charlie wiped a rivulet of perspiration from her eyebrow with a white wristband that featured a single delicate amethyst crystal – her mother's birthstone. She was careful not to rub the stone near her face, but each time after she wiped away the sweat, she'd press the stone to her lips. It was a new ritual, something of an oxymoron in the tennis world, but it was helping Charlie keep calm and focused. Steady.

She had felt nearly out-of-body during the walk to Centre Court and the ensuing introductions, but by the time warm-ups began and she and Natalya could actually start hitting the ball, the decades of muscle memory kicked in. Charlie settled instantly into her smooth and steady strokes. After the warm-up, when the women had three minutes to sit and prepare for start of play, Charlie could feel Natalya glaring at her from the opposite side of the net. The media, the WTA, and tennis fans everywhere had gone crazy with this final, which was a true marketing and publicity bonanza. The two women shared millions in endorsements between them, had graced the covers of fashion and sporting magazines, were both dating famous male athletes at the very top of their games, and each was, at least according to the press, 'gorgeous in her own way.' One breathless headline had called the final 'The Battle of the Beauties'; another had read 'Cold War Heating Up on Centre Court.' There was Charlie, the underdog all-American with the wavy dark hair and muscular legs and the easy smile, pitted against Natalya, the angular, sexy, blond ice queen with a confident jaunt to every step and an attitude that made people love to hate her. If Charlie could eke out the win, it would be her first Grand Slam title. Natalya had won four Grand Slams – two US Opens and two Australian Opens – but this would be her first-ever Wimbledon. Who wanted it more? the announcers kept asking each other. It was agreed the women were closely matched – Natalya clearly trumped Charlie in serving and overall fitness, but with the exception of Roland-Garros, Charlie's net game had been flawless lately and her backhand was the best in the business. The Wimbledon trophy and nearly $2.7 million were at stake, and the tension and excitement inside Centre Court were palpable.

Charlie did a quick scan of the Royal Box: Elton John and David Furnish, Anna Wintour, Bradley Cooper. Then she turned around to check out the player box. Only at Wimbledon did two opponents share one box among their guests. To the left sat Natalya's parents, coach, physio, hitting partner, hair and makeup artist, and a couple of Russian girlfriends. Benjy was nowhere to be found, but Charlie knew from Jake that he couldn't get away: the Dolphins had just drafted a new backup quarterback, and Benjy was helping to train him. Next to Natalya's crew, Charlie saw her own entourage watching her intently.

Todd, Jake, and her father sat in the box's front row, and they all waved when they caught her gaze in what could have been a choreographed performance. Behind them, Piper and Ronin sat in the first two seats on the aisle. Piper gave her a double thumbs-up and blew a kiss. In the third seat was Dan. He looked handsome in chinos and a button-down and was chatting animatedly with Ronin while they waited for play to start.

Dan had been waiting for her in the kitchen earlier that day, showered and dressed and ready to go. He had handed her the amethyst wristband on their walk to the site, and she had had to press her arms into her sides to keep from hugging him. He had also shown her the hats he'd asked Nike to make for the guests in Charlie's half of the player box: all white with a subtle white swoosh on the back and a decidedly unsubtle TEAM SILVER in enormous black print across the front. Every one of Charlie's entourage was wearing them, except the one who sat sullenly to Dan's left: Marco. Nearly every time Charlie sneaked a peek, Marco was staring at his phone or checking the crowd to make sure people recognized him. Once, his eyes had even been closed. *I won't wait another day,* she thought to herself as she walked out onto the court before serving for the first time. *I will end it tonight.*

One of Charlie's secret fears was not just losing but losing so badly that the first set – or, shudderingly, the entire match – would be a shutout. She wouldn't fully exhale until she had logged at least one game on the scoreboard, which she did, easily holding her serve to lead in the first set, 1–0. The women stayed on serve the rest of the set until the score was 6–5 in favor of Charlie, and Natalya won the next game to force a tiebreaker. Natalya had a massive 5–1 lead in the tiebreak, but Charlie battled back to win it on an ace and take the first set, 7–6. When Charlie pumped her fists exultantly and nearly collapsed to the ground, she could feel the crowd cheer with her. She could sense their desire for her to win, and for the first time that day she felt certain she *would* win.

The second set was grueling but much less linear than the first. Natalya broke Charlie's serve early, and although Charlie was able to break her back, it set a strangely uncomfortable pace for the next few games. The wind had picked up a bit, making the bounces a little less predictable, and the temperature felt as though it had dropped a few degrees in minutes. A slew of neatly uniformed ball kids appeared on the sidelines during a changeover to prepare for possible rain: they would quickly unfurl a specially fitted cover to keep the grass court dry and, if necessary, begin the process of closing the infamous Centre Court roof. It was enough of a distraction to both players that each of their games seemed to suffer: Charlie couldn't get a decent first serve in; Natalya hit too many easy unforced errors. They both quickly rebounded with a string of strong winners until the final game of the set. Charlie literally gave it away at deuce with two astonishing double faults in a row. The crowd groaned. She couldn't look at her box. The second set went to Natalya, 7–5.

Charlie sat in her chair on the sidelines after losing the second set and breathed. She wasn't panicked, but she was angry at herself. Nearly two hours had elapsed already, and she was proud that she still felt strong and energized without the sickening adrenaline surges that had haunted her past matches. But now there was a whole set ahead. On the positive side, with the exception of the double faults, Charlie had played beautifully. If anything, Natalya was the one who, despite eking out the second-set win, looked piqued and annoyed. Charlie could see her inspect her racket's grip and fiddle with a new roll of grip tape, which she tried to pry open with her teeth. Natalya's frustration grew more obvious every moment as she bit and chewed and stabbed at the packaging, and Charlie couldn't look away. No doubt Natalya had six identical rackets in her bag with freshly wrapped grip tape already in place, but for some reason she kept wrestling with the one in her hand. When the chair umpire called time and the women were expected to begin the third and final set, Natalya chucked her racket so hard into the side court that it left a small divot. Technically she could have been called for unsportsmanlike conduct, but the officials were no doubt wary about penalty calls during a Slam final. Charlie bounced lightly on the balls of her feet and sidestepped along the baseline to keep loose while she waited for her opponent, who had finally pulled a new racket from her bag. A frisson of hope surged through Charlie as she pressed her Swarovski amethyst to her mouth. It was obvious Natalya was beginning to unravel. It was time to pounce.

Once again, they each held service and then broke one another at exactly the same times, bringing the score to 4–4. Charlie felt a momentary stab of panic when Natalya moved ahead to 5–4 with consecutive down-the-line winners, but she was able to even it out on her next serve. After holding their own serves once again, the women were tied at 6–6. Todd had hammered into her the danger of not closing it out early in the third set: Wimbledon scoring didn't allow for a tiebreaker in the final set, so Charlie needed to win by two full games no matter how long it took. As Charlie sat on the sideline, trying to slow her breathing after a particularly grueling twelve games, she tried not to remember Todd's warning: *Don't let it drag out in the third. You're fit, but you're still only a year into recovery. And Natalya's record in long matches is the stuff of fucking legends.* The match clock already read three hours and six minutes: Wimbledon history, Charlie knew, and most certainly the longest match of her professional career. Her legs were beginning to cramp, although not horribly, and she was more winded than she would have liked, but all things considered, she felt good. She had been playing her absolute best tennis. Regardless of what happened, she would be able to be proud of how she played.

When the umpire called time, Charlie jumped to her feet with more energy than she felt and did a little jog next to the chair to loosen her hamstrings. She glanced up at the player box and saw Dan on his feet, his hands folded around his mouth to create a little megaphone, literally screaming her name while the hordes of quiet and polite fans who sat around him looked on in equal parts amusement and disapproval, when she felt Natalya sidle up next to her.

'You see your boyfriend up there?' Natalya asked, calibrating her voice perfectly so that only Charlie could hear her.

A glance to the player box revealed Marco sitting calmly and quietly, watching Charlie and Natalya.

'Marco?' she asked, more out of surprise that Natalya was speaking to her than a genuine interest in engaging. These were the very first words the women had exchanged since walking onto the court.

'Yes. Our Marco. I just wanted to thank you for lending him to me last night,' Natalya said, a smile spreading slowly on her face.

'Ms Silver and Ms Ivanov, please take your sides. Play will commence now.'

Charlie was stunned. Natalya had the audacity to try to rattle her points away from the end of their epic match. *Our Marco.*

Before jogging to the baseline, Natalya quickly leaned toward Charlie once more, and in a husky whisper said, 'I certainly don't need to tell you this, but he was good in bed. Like, *really* good.'

'Ms Ivanov? Ms Silver?' the umpire inquired.

As Charlie walked to her own side, a visual of Natalya hovering naked over Marco flickered into her head. Only the feeling of her own fingernails digging into her palms brought her back to the present.

Focus! Charlie screamed at herself. *This is the Final. Of. Wimbledon. You are going to break up with him anyway. She could be lying just to upset you. You don't even like him, so don't throw the Wimbledon Final for him! Focus. Focus. Focus!*

She placed her toes directly against the baseline, bounced the ball three times, and tossed it into the air. *Perfect toss*, Charlie thought as she launched her entire body upward to attack the ball while it hovered at its highest point. It went smashing across the net and into the far corner of the service box, where Natalya got a racket on it but could only send it careening into the alley.

15–0, Charlie.

Charlie's next serve was also perfect, landing straight and hard in the middle of the box. Natalya's return was weaker than normal, and Charlie pounced on it for a blazing crosscourt winner.

30–0.

Natalya bent over to adjust her socks and flashed Charlie – and the entire audience – a view of her perfect butt. Charlie couldn't help herself: she looked over at Marco and, sure enough, caught him staring directly at it. When Natalya served for the next point, Charlie mis-hit the return with the frame instead of the strings.

I hate her, Charlie thought, feeling a surge of anger and adrenaline course from her stomach to her throat. *I hate her, I hate her, I hate her.*

Charlie lost the next point. She came in on a short ball by hitting an excellent approach shot but then flubbed an easy overhead and missed the line by at least a foot.

30–30.

Something about missing that last shot shook Charlie in a way she hadn't felt for the last three hours. If she continued like this, she would lose the match – the whole tournament – over an unethical opponent and a man she didn't even like. And if that happened, she would have no one to blame but herself. *It will not go down that way,* Charlie told herself as she sliced a backhand short and watched as Natalya scrambled to reach it.

For the next four points, Charlie played the best tennis of her life. Her focus was laser-like, her strokes and footwork impeccable. She set aside Natalya and Marco and the cramping and the winded feeling and pushed herself to run for everything. No ball was too fast or far to reach, no shortcuts were acceptable: each point got 100 percent of her effort and strength. Natalya, too, played beautifully. Both women ran and slid and stretched in a show of incomparable fortitude and determination, and the crowd clapped their excited appreciation.

Despite it all, Natalya broke Charlie to win the game and make it 7–6. The rules called for the players to switch sides on odd-numbered games. Charlie was so focused on how much the next game mattered that she didn't notice Natalya had sidled up next to her.

When they met in front of the umpire's chair, Natalya deliberately led with her shoulder and bumped into Charlie – taking great care to make it look like an accident. Instantly a thought popped into Charlie's head.

'Natalya?' Charlie asked quietly, making sure no one could hear, keeping her mouth still so no one watching on TV could read her lips.

'Mmm?'

'There's something you should know, too. About Benjy.'

Natalya met Charlie's gaze. Charlie could see instantly her opponent had no idea what Charlie was about to say. 'What's that?'

Charlie opened her mouth and searched for the perfect way to deliver the sucker-punch news she so desperately wanted to share, but nothing came out.

'I'm waiting.'

'Ladies? Please take your sides,' the umpire said, his hand over the microphone.

The scene from the boat a couple of weeks earlier popped into her head: Benjy and Jake, both beautiful and shirtless, sleeping peacefully next to each other. Charlie could see Jake's obvious joy and happiness as clearly as if he'd been standing in front of her.

Natalya leaned in so close Charlie could feel her breath. They were an identical height and their noses almost touched. 'Did I mention that Marco said I have the best ass he's ever seen? No? You would be surprised how often I hear that,' Natalya said, shaking her ponytail with a laugh.

Natalya turned her back to Charlie, and in that moment Charlie remembered how it felt to win Charleston when she'd served before her opponent was ready. She imagined what her father would say if he knew the tactics she'd resorted to; she wondered what her mother would think of the woman she'd become. But most of all she thought of Jake and what it would do to his relationship to have it broadcast all over the world before he and Benjy were ready.

'Good luck,' Charlie said, because that's all she could think to say. She would win or lose this point based on any number of factors, but betraying Jake's confidence wasn't going to be one of them.

Natalya rolled her eyes and returned to the baseline. She did side-to-side jumps that caused her ponytail and skirt to do the most adorable little flips.

Charlie watched as Natalya extended her racket out to the nearest ball boy and grinned at him when he placed two balls on the strings. Natalya tucked one neatly under her skirt, approached the baseline, and placed her feet. Charlie bounced on her toes, ready to receive service, but despite her readiness, Natalya's first serve hit the corner of the box and Charlie couldn't even get close to it. Charlie took the next point by hitting a perfect lob over Natalya's head, where it hit the back of the line, but then Natalya won the next two. 40–15. Charlie could almost hear the television announcers tell their audiences in dozens of languages all over the world that this was match point for Natalya. Tournament point. Charlie already knew the predictable headline if she lost: 'Another Silver for Silver.'

Charlie filled her lungs with air and exhaled slowly, feeling her shoulders lower and her gaze steady. She returned Natalya's serve perfectly and then followed it up with a forehand and a backhand. Both were flawlessly executed, sailing hard and fast over the net, landing exactly where she had intended them. Quickly she worked her way to the net, where she felt confident, and hit an excellent volley deep to Natalya's backhand. For the briefest moment Charlie stopped to admire her own shot – it had grazed the line and would be very difficult for Natalya to return well – but in a split second Natalya's return came flying over the net with a surprising amount of power, and Charlie lunged toward the ball. Her racket never even connected with it. She turned around just in time to see it land behind her, an inch or two within the baseline, an impressive and definitive winner.

Natalya fell to the ground. The umpire announced the win, Ms Ivanov's first at Wimbledon, to thunderous applause. The entirety of Centre Court rose to its feet, cheering both women in what had to be one of the most exciting finals in Wimbledon history. The cameras on the sidelines clicked madly. The various officials began preparing the winner presentation. As Charlie glanced to the player box, she caught Natalya's friends embracing. Jake and her father looked crestfallen. Todd raked his hands through his hair. Marco bowed to both girls. Piper and Ronin stood and clapped politely. Only Dan seemed to be proud of her and willing Charlie to look at him. When she caught his eye, he pointed at her and mouthed, 'You played a *great* match.'

A surge of realization followed, almost as though Charlie hadn't understood until right then: it was over and she had lost. The disappointment that followed was swift and stabbing, and yet, she could walk off Centre Court with her shoulders back and her head held high. She had played honestly. She had played with integrity. It hadn't been good enough to win a Slam – at least not yet. But it was good enough to give the finger to the bedazzled sports bras and nasty opponents and cheating boyfriends and abusive coaches and all the other noise that she'd allowed to seep in and poison her for so long. It was good enough to end all that.

Charlie suffered through the post-match interviews with grace and dignity, pausing often to thank her family and her team and to congratulate Natalya on a tournament won well. She raised her runner-up trophy high, waved her thanks to the crowd, and left the court quickly so Natalya could enjoy her moment. Charlie had given 100 percent, and although she'd made some errors with the double faults – and who didn't have a couple of errors in a record-setting final? – she had performed to the very best of her ability. Natalya had simply played better. She deserved to win. It didn't make Charlie's disappointment any less acute, but this time it wasn't commingled with regret or anger or second-guessing herself. Whether it was the adrenaline or the relief or the coursing endorphins, Charlie felt no pain on the walk toward the locker room – no muscle aches, no soreness, no lingering discomfort from her previous injuries. It would all come, of course. You didn't set the time record for a final match at Wimbledon and not pay the price, but at that moment she felt oddly at peace: she had competed at the very highest level, had given the match everything she had, and hadn't resorted to disgusting behavior to get an edge. For the first time in longer than she cared to remember, Charlie had nothing to apologize for.

Perhaps it was the commotion in the Hallway of Champions, or the exhaustion beginning to settle into her body, but Charlie almost didn't notice the feeling of a large hand around her upper arm until it tightened its grip so hard she nearly yelped in pain. Alarmed, she whipped around to see Todd glaring at her with a look of pure hatred.

'What the *fuck* did you do out there?' he said in a whisper-scream so loud the entire area went instantly silent.

Charlie was so shocked she didn't say a word.

'Do you hear me? Hello? Hello, Wimbledon *loser*? Want to explain how anyone in her right mind could possibly throw away an entire set by double-faulting? Please, give me your brilliant analysis, because I am at a *total fucking loss.*'

Any of the officials or line judges or coaches or journalists who hadn't heard the first part of Todd's tantrum had noticed him now. The hallway was so absolutely silent that

Charlie wondered if the crowd back on the court could hear him. Still, she was so surprised she couldn't speak, couldn't even ask him to let go of her arm, which he was squeezing uncomfortably hard.

'Not one but *two* double faults! What, were you smoking weed again before this match? Out screwing around with your boyfriend? What was it, Silver? Because, for the life of me, I can't figure out what the *fuck* happened out there.'

It was the sound of Dan's voice that finally shook her out of her shock.

'Let go of her arm,' Dan growled, quietly enough that only she and Todd could hear, but with an edge that caused them both to look up.

'Get the fuck out of here, I'm not talking to you,' Todd said. He dropped Charlie's arm but moved his face even closer to hers.

Dan was on him in a flash, his own hand clamped over Todd's shoulder. Somewhere behind her, Charlie could hear others gasp as they drew the same conclusion: there was going to be a fight. Quickly, Charlie turned to Dan and gave him a look: *Thank you, but I've got this*. Dan hesitated for a moment but then moved a few steps back.

'I was going to do this in private, but since it seems like you prefer putting on shows, let's get this over with now. Todd, thank you for your time and expertise, but I will no longer be needing your services.'

For a split second Todd froze, his hands suspended in midair, his mouth hanging open. Then he licked his lips once, twice, three times and snarled, 'Yeah, right. You're lucky I ever agreed to coach you in the first place. You can't fire me.'

'I just did,' Charlie said.

'Get showered and meet me in the lounge. You and I have a lot to talk about. First on the list is your shitty attitude.'

'I tried to be polite, but I'm not sure how else to say it. You're fired. Finished. You and I have nothing left to say to each other. Not now, and not ever.' Charlie turned to the small crowd of people who had gathered to listen while pretending not to listen. 'Feel free to spread the word: I fired Todd Feltner. And I loved every minute of it.'

22

grovel, plead, beg, and bribe

NEW YORK CITY, AUGUST 2016

Wrapped in a waffle-weave robe with a towel twisted around her head, Charlie peered through the telescope on the windowsill of her suite. From the twentieth floor, the treetops clustered together to make Central Park look like a continuous field of green, with only patches of water and miniature ant people biking or strolling or riding through. Each day for the last two weeks Charlie would watch the sun cast distinctly summery shadows on the trees. Whoever claimed there was nothing bucolic about New York City had clearly never stayed in a park-view penthouse suite at the Ritz-Carlton in high summer.

A knock at the door caused her to glance at the clock. Nearly eight a.m. She padded to the door, looked through the peephole, and threw it open.

'I thought you were breakfast!' Charlie said, launching herself at Piper, who stood in the hotel's hallway looking slightly rumpled but still glamorous in wide-legged jeans and a tucked-in silk button-down. Oversized sunglasses held back her wavy hair.

'Oooh, does that mean you ordered something? I'm starving.' Piper kissed Charlie's cheek and pushed right past her, unaware that her gigantic shoulder bag smashed Charlie directly in the chest.

'Yes, and I got a lot, so you're in luck. Come in,' she said, although Piper had already dropped her bag in the suite's marble foyer and beelined directly for the picture windows.

'Spectacular,' she declared, glancing at the park for a brief second before swiveling the telescope in the direction of the nearest high-rise. 'Have you seen anyone naked yet?'

'I can't believe you willingly took a red-eye just for me. Wait, come here. Let me see your ring!'

Piper held up her left hand and shrugged. 'We went plain gold bands, just because it pissed off my mother. Is that ridiculous?'

'Yes, totally. But so is eloping, and that didn't stop you.'

Piper looked directly at Charlie. 'Do you hate me? You know we only did it because we couldn't stand our families. The idea of our mothers hashing out a menu for some hideous seated luncheon for all their friends . . .' She shuddered. 'We just couldn't. But you know I missed having you there, right?'

Charlie smiled. 'I know. I was devastated not to wear a floor-length dusty-pink gown. And how I regret not having to write a speech and google "wedding toast jokes." It was heartbreaking, really it was.'

'Yeah, when you put it that way, you definitely do owe me. I am happily married and on my way to a vineyard in South America, and you and I never needed to have a single conversation about up-dos or strippers dressed like policemen. It was a win for everyone.'

'Where is Ronin?'

'Probably asleep already. He went to check in. Fourteenth floor, I think? No view like this, that's for sure. This is reserved exclusively for number-two-ranked players in the world.'

Charlie laughed.

Piper flopped onto a couch in the sitting room. She picked up a folded copy of Page Six from the coffee table and held it up for Charlie.

'Please tell me you're not reading this.'

'Of course I am. But I give you my word, I really don't care.' The New York papers had gone crazy covering Marco and Natalya frolicking all over the city together. In just the past few days since each had been knocked out in the semis, they'd been photographed at restaurants, shops, nightclubs, and even an upscale sex toy boutique on the Lower East Side. From the pictures, it looked like they did nothing all day long but spend money, make out, and grope one another, but Charlie could all too easily imagine the reality behind the cameras.

Piper pulled the cap off a bottle of Fiji water and took a long slug. 'You nervous?'

'You could say that.'

'Arthur Ashe, prime time, women's final. Pretty big stage,' Piper said, dabbing her lips with the back of a finger. 'The biggest, actually.'

Charlie's heart beat a little faster. 'I almost can't believe it's happening.'

There was a knock at the door at the same time that Charlie's phone rang. 'That'll be breakfast. Can you just get it and sign the bill?' she said to Piper as she swiped open the call. 'Hello?'

'How are you feeling?' Jake's voice came through the line in a rush: panicked, excited, thrilled.

'Hanging in there. Piper just got here. Where are you?'

'I'm on my way to Flushing Meadows to meet with the American Express people. We need to work out who's sitting in your box tonight and who's in their suite.'

'Charlie! Visitor!' Piper called. Charlie could tell from the tone of her voice that it wasn't a food delivery. Then, a beat afterward, she heard Dan's laugh.

'Jake? I'll call you right back.' She clicked off the phone as he protested and felt a brief stab of guilt, but as soon as she saw Dan dressed for practice with a racket bag slung over his shoulder, Charlie forgot instantly about her brother.

'Hey,' he said, his voice revealing nothing. 'I, uh, I didn't realize you had company.'

'I'm hardly company, *Dan*,' Piper said.

The suite's bell rang again.

'That has to be the food,' Charlie said.

Dan flashed Charlie a quick smile.

'Why don't I get that?' Piper said, looking between the two of them.

The moment she disappeared into the foyer, Dan crossed the room to Charlie and pulled her into a hug. His US Open T-shirt smelled of laundry detergent and deodorant and sunblock. It felt so good to nuzzle her cheek into the warmth of his neck that it was all Charlie could do not to collapse into him. Neither of them noticed Piper's return until she pushed the food cart into the living room. Charlie and Dan yanked away from each other as though a parent had just caught them making out in the basement.

'What? You think I didn't see the writing on the wall for this one?' Piper said, pulling a chocolate croissant from the bread basket. She took a bite, swallowed, and poured herself a cup of black coffee. 'Another reason to elope.'

'Elope?' Charlie sputtered, her cheeks already flushing. 'Piper, we're not even – it's not like—'

Dan merely stood, arms crossed awkwardly, staring off through the windows into Central Park.

'I meant me. Another reason for *me* to elope. The croissant. To not have to starve myself for a year to fit into some princess wedding dress, that's all. Is there something you guys want to tell me?' Piper's widened eyes were all faux innocence.

'Not the time for this . . .' Charlie knew she wouldn't keep anything from Piper, but it certainly wasn't a conversation she was ready to have in front of Dan.

'I'm, uh, going to head to the site in a few. I just stopped by to, um, see if you wanted me to take anything. Your racket bag?'

With this, Piper began laughing. 'Her racket bag? You two are adorable, you really are. Whatever is going on here isn't my business. At least, not until later tonight, when we're all toasting a US Open win or drowning a loss in rivers of vodka – and, yes, you are having a drink one way or another, Charlie. Then I will want every sordid detail. But until then, suffice it to say, I think you two look adorable together.'

'Piper . . .' Charlie warned with a stern look.

'Thanks?' Dan said. He turned to Charlie, who realized she wasn't the least bit self-conscious standing there in a bathrobe with wet hair. 'Do you want me to wait for you or meet you there?'

Charlie turned her face to him and looked directly into his eyes. How had she never noticed their unusual shade of gray before? Or the way he read a book, a real, actual book printed on old-school paper, during every meal he ate alone? Or the way he cracked his knuckles when he was nervous but stopped the moment he noticed someone watching him?

From her tiptoes, Charlie pressed her lips against his. 'Go ahead. I'm here for another hour and then I'm supposed to meet Marcy in player dining. I'll text you when I'm on my way.'

He nodded, kissed her again, waved to Piper, who was busy feigning indifference to the whole scene on the couch, and left. Charlie couldn't help but smile. Months ago she was skulking around, desperate for Marco's erratic attention. She marveled at how surprised Marco had been when she ended it. He, like Todd, had shown her she was making exactly the right decision.

Charlie looked at Piper but said nothing.

'What?' Piper shrugged. 'You think this is remotely surprising? It was a matter of when, not if.'

'Oh, come on!' Charlie said. She sat down next to Piper and pulled a pillow into her stomach.

'You and Dan? Please. Anyone with two eyes could've seen that one coming.'

'Am I really that predictable?'

'Yes.'

'Thanks.'

'Charlie! A little self-awareness, please. Marco Vallejo? Zeke Leighton? Not what I – or anyone else – would exactly describe as boyfriend material. But doe-eyed Dan with the puritanical work ethic? Who also happens to be tall, kind, and very cute? He's a no-brainer.'

'We're taking it slow,' Charlie said, forking a piece of honeydew from a bowl of fruit salad.

'How slow?'

'Exceedingly.'

Piper tilted her head. 'You haven't slept with him yet?'

'Yes.'

'Yes, you're telling me that, or yes, of course you have?'

'We just both think it's better not to rush into anything. We acknowledge we're . . . I don't know . . . into each other. We just don't need to dive into bed yet.'

'Really.'

'It's not like it's been *so* long. A month. We didn't even kiss for the first time until Toronto. Four weeks ago. Things progressed a little in Cincinnati, a little bit more in New Haven, and now here we are.'

'So where does that get you now? Second base? Third?'

Charlie gave Piper the finger. 'Laugh all you want. You're married now and destined to a life of sexless boredom forever and ever. At least I have something to look forward to.'

'Fair point.'

Charlie took a sip of her fully caffeinated coffee – the very first change she instituted after firing Todd – and said, 'He's a pretty great guy, P. Smart, loyal, kind, the whole nine. But you know the best part? Things are just easy when I'm with him. He has a way of boiling the most complicated things down to what really matters. No games, no drama, no *Is he going to text me? Does he like me?* bullshit. It's really refreshing.'

'Sounds it. I'm happy for you, Charlie. You deserve to date a non-asshole.'

'I'm blushing.' Charlie checked her phone and saw the time. 'I have to run. We have a very abbreviated practice today, but I'm meeting with Marcy beforehand.'

Piper stood up and slung her enormous bag back over her shoulder. 'I hope you're going to grovel, plead, beg, and bribe her to coach you again?'

'That about sums it up.'

The two women hugged. Piper took both of Charlie's hands in her own and said, 'Kick some ass tonight, Silver. It's about f'ing time you won one of these things.'

Charlie placed her racket bag at a table near the windows, which offered an expansive view onto the stretch of empty practice courts. The hundreds of players who'd already been knocked out in the earlier rounds had left Flushing Meadows. Some took a break and went home; others traveled to wherever their coaches were based for a few days' intensive work; still others trudged on to the next tournament in preparation for the grueling Asian swing of the tour, the final stretch before they had six or eight weeks off at the end of the year. Everyone who wasn't injured or retired would begin again in January in Australia. And although there had been weeks this summer when Charlie thought she might not be among them, she had decided that no matter what happened in this final match, she wanted to give herself one more year.

Player dining, like everywhere else at the Open that day, was nearly empty. Normally it bustled with players and their entourages of managers, coaches, hitting partners, agents, families, and friends. The flat screens hanging from the ceiling usually showed all the live matches happening around the site while mothers and nannies chased young children around the tables, plying them with chocolate milk and cheddar bunnies. You couldn't walk two feet without hearing at least three languages. Everywhere people jostled for space and called to each other in Spanish, Croatian, Serbian, German, Chinese, Russian, French, and every imaginable accent in the English language. People were busy typing into laptops or iPhones as all sorts of business deals were negotiated and schedules were tweaked and travel plans were booked, canceled, and booked again. She loved the energy of player dining – especially at a Slam – knowing that after so many years on the circuit, she could walk over to pretty much any table and recognize at least a dozen people. But today it was unnerving to see it so quiet.

Doing a quick calculation of what she had already eaten for breakfast (egg white veggie omelet with rye toast, fruit salad, cottage cheese, and coffee) and what time she would be practicing (three o'clock) and competing (seven that evening), Charlie chose a Greek yogurt parfait with a side of protein-enriched granola and a banana.

'Good luck tonight,' the cashier, a woman who also looked to be in her mid-twenties, said to Charlie as she handed her the receipt.

Charlie smiled and thanked her. When she returned to the table, Marcy was already seated.

'What can I get you?' Charlie asked, placing her tray down. 'You want your usual turkey wrap with a Diet Coke?'

Marcy shook her head. 'I'm good, I don't need anything. I already have a tea.' She wrapped her hands around the steaming take-out cup the way someone might if they were enjoying their après-ski hot chocolate, despite the fact that the outside temperature was pushing ninety.

Charlie took a seat directly across from her old coach.

Marcy took a sip of tea. 'Charlie, I can't even begin to describe how proud I am of you. Last year at this time you were in a rehab facility. Now you're hours away from playing a Grand Slam final. It's truly incredible. You deserve this so much.'

'*You* deserve it,' Charlie said. She could feel a lump forming in her throat. 'Todd did a lot of work on my image, and having Dan travel with me made practices more productive, but *you* are the one who taught me everything. You picked up right where my father left off and brought my strokes and game to the next level. You taught me to how to eat well without being a lunatic about it, how to get fit without being totally obsessive, how to conduct myself on and off the court. Can you even imagine what you would have done to me if Charleston had happened on your watch and I'd gone ahead to win the match by serving before my opponent was ready?'

Marcy smiled. She knew exactly what Charlie meant. 'Are you kidding? I would've made you give the damn title back.'

'Exactly. Todd encouraged that strategy.'

'I'm not surprised.'

'I hated myself after that match. Hated him, too.'

'I'm sorry to hear that, Charlie. You have what it takes to win it fair and square. You didn't need to pull a stunt like that.'

'I know that now. Which is one of the reasons why I fired Todd. Go on, say it. You told me so.'

'I told you so. But don't be so hard on yourself, Charlie.'

'Well, anyway. All of this was my really long, convoluted way of saying I'm sorry.'

'You don't owe me an apology. We worked together almost ten years. Taking you from juniors to the pros was one of the most rewarding things I've ever done – even better than when I went through it myself. It's okay you wanted a new perspective. It's healthy.'

'In theory.'

'Sometimes in reality, too. It doesn't sound like Todd was the right fit, but there are plenty of terrific coaches out there.'

'I want you,' Charlie blurted out, although she had planned an entire pitch, even written it out so she said exactly what she meant and didn't forget anything. 'I want to work with you again.'

Marcy was quiet.

'I know you must hate me, Marce, or at the very least

think I'm an idiot, which I completely was for ending what we had. But is there any way you would consider coming back to my team? *Just for a year. One year.* I'm going to go back to college after that. And in this next year, I want to work my ass off and try to win tournaments I haven't won yet, but I also want to take the time to check out these incredible countries I visit every twelve months but have never really seen. I know it's a lot to ask, especially after everything, but . . . will you join me?'

When Marcy smiled sadly, Charlie knew it wasn't going to happen.

'I miss watching *Love It or List It* with you,' Charlie said.

Marcy barked her short, staccato laugh. 'I miss it, too. Have you been watching *Fixer Upper*? Chip and Joanna used to annoy the hell out of me, but I'm kind of into them now.'

'Me too! I'm a little sick of her obsession with light cabinets and dark countertops, but I can forgive her.'

'Charlie?' Marcy cleared her throat, then took a sip of tea as if to fortify her willpower. 'I can't come back to coach you.'

Charlie felt her cheeks redden. Of course Marcy didn't want to come back after the way Charlie had treated her. She felt stupid for even asking.

'I'd love to work with you again. It hardly even felt like work, did it? But I'm taking some . . . personal time. I'm pregnant.'

Charlie felt a wave of relief. 'You're *pregnant*? For real?'

'Fourth round of in vitro was a charm. I'm just past the twelve-week mark. I'm due next February.'

'Oh my god. Congratulations! I know you've been trying

for so long, and I didn't want to ask how it was going . . . I'm just so happy for you guys!'

Marcy's entire face lit up. 'Thanks. We are thrilled! But as you can imagine, Will's keeping me on a short leash for the next six months. No international travel at all, and no travel anywhere after the seventh month. So as you can see, I'm not cut out for tour work right now.'

Charlie laughed. 'No, I would say not.'

'But, Charlie? I would if I could.'

'You mean that?' Charlie asked.

'I do. I'd be back in a heartbeat. Those were some of the best years of my career.'

'Mine too,' said Charlie, wiping a stray tear.

'Hey! No crying on the day of a final. This is all good stuff. How are you feeling about tonight?'

Charlie smiled through her tears. She knew only part of the emotion was connected to Marcy, that so much of it was being overwhelmed with the reality of making it to the finals of the US Open. As an American. And the favorite. She'd be playing under the lights that evening on her home turf, the crowd of twenty-three thousand screaming her name over and over and over again. It was almost too much to understand.

Charlie took a drink of water. 'I don't even know where I'm at. Physically, I'm feeling strong and ready. Emotionally, I'm a nervous wreck. I guess I'm also relieved to be playing Karina and not Natalya.'

'I was in the Emirates Suite for the semis against Natalya. You just *undid* her game. Took it apart point by point. You controlled the pace of the match and didn't give her an inch. You were focused, methodical, and entirely in control.

I don't need to tell you that winning straight sets in a Slam semi is pretty damn impressive, and if you can do it there – against Natalya Ivanov – you can do it tonight, too.'

'Thank you,' Charlie said. She sat up straighter and pushed her shoulders back. 'Thank you for everything you've done for me. Always. Your baby is so lucky to have you as her mom.'

'Her?'

'It has to be a girl.'

'She *is* a girl.'

'You know already?' Charlie asked, eyes wide.

'They have a blood test now for old moms like me. Yes, a girl. Maybe one day you'll help me teach her to play?'

Charlie walked around the table, slid in the banquette next to Marcy, and gave her a proper hug. 'I'd be honored.'

23

charlotte silver ready to play

US OPEN, AUGUST 2016

Charlie watched as Karina Geiger fielded the questions from the ESPN reporter. The two women were standing in the long hallway that led from the locker room to the court at Arthur Ashe Stadium. Surrounding them both were framed black-and-white photos of all the champions who had played that court, either a year or a decade or a half century before them: Steffi, Pete, Andre, Roger, Stefan, Jennifer, Marco, Chrissy, Martina, Rinaldo, John, Serena, Jimmy, Natalya, Venus, Rafa, Andy, Maria. Otherwise it wasn't fancy or particularly impressive – just a windowless corridor that felt dark and a bit industrial if it weren't for the legends staring down from every direction.

'What do you hope to accomplish at this match today?' the woman reporter asked Karina, thrusting the microphone under her chin.

Karina, normally friendly, couldn't keep the look of disdain off her face. 'Accomplish?' she asked in accented English. Karina looked at the reporter pointedly. 'Well, I'm not here today to work on my backhand,' she said, and pulled back on her oversized headphones.

'Good luck, Karina!' the reporter called, but Karina had already slung her racket bag over her shoulder and proceeded to the door, where she would bounce and pace, waiting for Charlie to do her interview so both women could be formally announced onto the court.

'And here we have Charlotte Silver, number-two-ranked woman in the world and clearly the crowd favorite here in Flushing Meadows today. Charlotte, how are you feeling right now?'

Reporters loved this question, and every player in the history of the game gave a variation on a theme: 'I'm feeling really confident in my game right now. I'm ready.'

Which is exactly what Charlie said. She was surprised, as she always was, when the reporter nodded enthusiastically, as though Charlie had just shared a great revelation.

'It must be quite the experience to be standing in the company of such legends,' the woman stated, her lipsticked mouth hovering centimeters from the microphone.

Charlie waited for the question, but as is often the case, there wasn't one.

'It sure is,' Charlie said, looking directly into the woman's eyes. She could see the cameraman zoom in for a close-up over the reporter's shoulder. 'And this is an especially poignant night for me. It will be my second-to-last US Open ever.'

Charlie could feel the quiet descend on the hallway before she could hear it.

'Does that mean . . . Are you saying . . . Is this a retirement announcement?' the reporter sputtered.

Charlie leaned forward and caught Dan winking at her. He and Jake already knew her plan, but this would be the first her father was hearing about it. She took the microphone and, rather than answer the reporter, looked off to the side, directly at her father. 'Yes, it is. Regardless of whether I win or lose here tonight, I'm only going to play professionally for one more year. Next year's US Open will be my last major tournament.'

The surprise on Mr Silver's face was second only to the reporter's, who was clearly not prepared to deviate from the usual pregame script. She coughed for a minute, began to ask a question, and then stopped. Finally, she said, 'It's unusual, no, for a player who's only twenty-five and by all accounts at the peak of her career to retire? Any further explanation of your decision? What will come next for Charlotte Silver?'

Charlie only said, 'Please excuse me, but I have a match to play.'

'Yes, yes,' the reporter murmured, obviously having forgotten all about the reason for the interview in light of her breaking news scoop. 'We wish you the best of luck today. And always.'

Charlie immediately felt her father's hand clamp over her shoulder. She turned to face him and threw her arms around his neck. 'It's time,' she said into his neck.

'You're certain?' he asked so only she could hear.

She pulled back a bit and nodded. 'Yes. One more year. It finally feels like enough.'

Her father's eyes crinkled as he smiled. 'It's more than enough; it's incredible what you've accomplished. How hard you've worked. But the best part of all is that you feel that for yourself. It's all I've ever wanted for you.'

'I know, Dad. And I appreciate it, more than you know.'

'Charlotte? Karina? Time for the introductions,' Isabel called out, checking the giant digital clock that was counting down the seconds from its perch above the court entrance.

Her father kissed her cheek. Behind him, Dan grinned at her and gave her a knowing look while Jake flashed her a thumbs-up. A tournament official motioned for Charlie's and Karina's entourages to follow him through another exit, where he would escort them to their respective player boxes. The door to the court was for players only. The women would have to walk through it alone.

Charlie listened as the announcer called out Karina's career highlights and accomplishments: ranked as high as number one in the world; made it to the finals of a Grand Slam six times and won three of them; youngest woman in the last ten years to win two consecutive Slams. The screen showed the rowdy American crowd cheering, as they would for any final contender, but it was obvious they were anxious for Charlie. By the time the announcer began calling Charlie's stats, the crowd drowned out his voice. Charlie tried to listen to his biography of her, to hear how he encapsulated the last twenty-odd years of her life into a single paragraph, but the noise and the emotion were too overwhelming. When it was finally time for her to take her first steps on the legendary court, she was so overcome that Isabel had to give her a firm push.

The applause was thunderous. It sounded like it began in the sections closest to Charlie's entrance and rolled from box to box, section to section, and side to side with the strength of a hurricane. There wasn't a person seated in the entire stadium: it seemed as though each and every one of the twenty-three thousand people who had come out that gorgeous August evening was on his or her feet, whooping and clapping. When she raised her hand and waved to them, they roared their response. Charlie could feel the reverberations in her chest, the sounds of excitement that almost bordered on hysteria.

As Charlie lined her rackets up against her chair and cracked open the first of her Gatorade bottles, she glanced toward her player box. In the very front row were Jake and Benjy, sitting side by side. No doubt the stadium cameras were having a field day with those two: *Sports Illustrated* had just released their new issue, the first time in history they featured an openly gay athlete on the cover. Benjy was pictured in his Dolphins uniform and helmet, war paint under his eyes, staring straight at the camera with his bulging arms crossed over his massive chest. The headline above the photo read 'DEAL WITH IT' in a massive white font and just underneath, in smaller lettering: 'Football's Favorite Quarterback Comes Out and Couldn't Care Less What You Have to Say About It.' As expected, the media had gone crazy when Benjy first made the announcement earlier in the summer, but after a few weeks of nonstop coverage and carefully scripted statements of support from the NFL, the story was beginning to fade. Charlie had never seen Jake happier. Next to them sat her father and Eileen. A small, family-only wedding ceremony was planned for the following month, and Charlie already had her gift picked out: two round-the-world tickets for them to explore, relax, and hopefully visit her in far-flung cities.

In the row behind them were Piper and Ronin, who would be leaving on a middle-of-the-night flight for their honeymoon in South America. Piper caught Charlie's eyes and opened her own so wide that Charlie burst out laughing. Charlie nodded. Piper gave her a look that said, *Seriously?* and glanced furtively to her right where none other than Zeke Leighton sat, waving cheerily to Charlie and mugging for the cameras. Every time a camera found him and splashed his image over the huge screens papering the stadium, the crowd went crazy. From the third and last row, Dan sat alone. She knew her father and Jake and probably Piper, too, had invited him to sit with them, but he liked to watch from his seat behind the others and examine every point with the focused attention of a surgeon at work. He would calculate and analyze. He would *will* her to win. And when it was over, whether she'd won decisively or lost humiliatingly or something in between, he would wrap his arms around her and ask if she wanted to try the new Korean noodle place he'd read about. Charlie saw him massaging his forehead in nervous circles, but she smiled at him anyway.

The warm-up went by so quickly that the coin toss nearly caught Charlie by surprise. When the chair umpire indicated that Charlie had won, she automatically elected to serve. Karina flashed her a single hard look and began to retreat back to her chair. The women would have a final minute of quiet before official play commenced, but Charlie called her name.

The ball boys and girls, the line judges, the chair umpire, and the thousands of fans all watched as Karina slowly turned around. Her enormous frame, all muscle, was surprisingly agile, and she covered the distance to the net in three long strides. She raised a single eyebrow.

Charlie moved toward the net and stood closer to Karina than either of them liked: she was acutely aware of the cameras and wanted to avoid being overheard. Leaning in, Charlie's lips nearly touching her opponent's ear and her heart beating fast, she said, 'I'm sorry for what I did at Charleston. It was a shitty way to win.'

Karina took two steps back and looked Charlie in the eye. They held each other's gaze for a few seconds before Karina nodded. 'Thank you.'

Back at her chair, Charlie took a sip of Gatorade and a bite of banana. Thirty seconds to start time. She took a final look at her player box and felt an enormous rush of gratitude for the people in her life, and then, with her last remaining seconds, she pulled the laminated photo she had kept in her racket bag for as long as she could remember and propped it against her chair's armrest. Today, her mother would watch from the best seat in the house.

Charlie jogged to her spot on the baseline as Karina strode to hers. She bounced on her toes, waiting for her nerves to settle, for the familiar and addictive feeling of calm to settle over her. Across the net, her opponent took deep, gulping breaths, obviously trying to control her own adrenaline overload. The chair umpire leaned forward and in a commanding voice announced, 'First set. Charlotte Silver ready to serve. Play!'

She took a deep breath and tried to exhale as slowly as possible. It was happening. Charlie planted her feet, bounced the ball three times, and, with a clear mind, tossed it into the air. The ball disappeared into the stadium lights, and Charlie felt a momentary stab of panic and uncertainty, but still she launched her body upward, a combination of muscle memory and faith and fervent hope, knowing she was ready for anything.

acknowledgments

This book wouldn't have been possible without the help and guidance of both Ari Fleischer and Micky Lawler, two people who so clearly love tennis and the players who dedicate their lives to the sport. Thank you, Ari, for giving me a crash-course education on professional tennis and for tapping into your vast network of contacts to point me in all the right directions. And Micky: you have generously offered your time, expertise, humor, ideas, and friendship in so many ways I'm not sure I could even list them all. One of the best parts of writing a new book is getting to meet new people, and that has never been more true than with you.

Thank you to Daniela Hantuchová, a player I admire so much, for sharing the details of your career with me. You gave me an inside glimpse into what it feels like to compete at the very top level – the fitness and nutrition regimens, the travel schedule, the joys and difficulties of life on tour – and you awed me with your grace both on and off the court. I'll always be cheering for you (often too loudly – GO DANI!) from the sidelines.

I owe an enormous debt of gratitude to all those in the tennis world who took the time to meet with me. At the Women's Tennis Association, thank you to Ann Austin, Laurence Applebaum, Catherine Sneddon, Stacey Allaster, Megan Rose, Jeff Watson, Amy Hitchinson, and Kathleen Stroia for your invaluable assistance with my research. Thanks to Kelly Wolf for helping organize my phenomenal trip to Wimbledon and to Peter-Michael Reichel and Sandra Reichel for your generosity while I was there. Elizabeth and Michael Byrne, thank you for opening your beautiful home in Wimbledon Village and welcoming me so warmly – I only hope I can be a repeat visitor soon. Thank you to Anne Worcester and Rosie Rodriguez for your hospitality at the CT Open, and to Dr David Cohen, orthopedic surgeon and adored brother-in-law, for your medical advice and fact-checking. Finally, an enormous thank-you to Jared Pinsky for answering all my questions about hitting partners, and Yana Soyfer and Carrie Lubitz for helping me understand both the benefits and drawbacks of a childhood spent playing tennis at the very highest levels.

To Sloan Harris at ICM, my friend and agent – thank you for your (by now finely honed after eight years together) ability to talk heel heights and tennis bracelets with the same fluency as contracts and other boring business things. Heather Karpas, thank you for being a sounding board and a trusted adviser and, on more occasions than I want to admit, a lifesaver. Kristyn Keene, I'm sending you a huge hug and a thank-you for always being enthusiastic and helpful and for having all the right answers.

Thank you to my entire family at Simon & Schuster. It's been twelve years now I've had the honor of being published by such a terrific team. Carolyn Reidy and Jon Karp, thank you for believing in and supporting not only my books but also my entire career. Thanks to Richard Rhorer, Sarah Reidy, Zack Knoll, Ebony LaDelle, Jackie Seow, Emily Graff, Lisa Silverman, Katie Rizzo, Elizabeth Breeden, and Samantha O'Hara for all the work you do each and every day to help craft and launch my books

– and all the others we love to read. Most of all, to Marysue Rucci, who is so much more than an editor. Thank you for being a cheerleader and an adviser and a teacher. From the first hints of an outline straight through to publication, you have overseen this book with both a loving and careful eye, and I am so grateful to have you as my trusted publishing partner and friend.

I'm so lucky to work with the best team in the UK. To Lynne Drew at HarperCollins, thank you for your astute editorial comments and your ongoing support for all my books – your friendship means the world to me. Enormous thanks as well to Charlotte Brabbin, Elizabeth Dawson, Jaime Frost, Heike Schüssler, and the entire HarperCollins teams in both the UK and Australia. At Curtis Brown, thank you to Vivienne Schuster and Sophie Baker for the myriad ways you guide me year after year.

Thank you to all my friends, whether new or lifelong, I adore you all. Ika and Alexander Green, thank you for providing inspiration and an enthusiastic early reading. Thanks to Kyle White and Ludmilla Suvorova for your endless support, and to Jenn Falik for helping me navigate a whole new world. Oddette Staple, you hold us all together. Thank you for all you do.

I'm so grateful for my family, near and far. To my mother, Cheryl, for your love and support, and to my father, Steve, for introducing me to tennis at a young age and sharing my love of the sport. Judy and Bernie, thank you both for your kindness and help. To Jackie and Mel: not everyone is lucky enough to have a second set of parents, and I'm proud to say I love mine. To my siblings and closest friends: Dana, Seth, Dave, and Allison, thank you for being such a huge part of my life in all the best ways.

Most important, thank you to my husband. Mike, you make it all possible. You were the one who insisted I write about something I love, and who helped me shepherd this book from a rough first draft to a polished final edit. I am forever grateful for all you do for me, for us, for our family. I love you.

And finally to my sweet and dazzling R and S, you are my everything.

THE DEVIL WEARS PRADA

THE BOOK THAT INSPIRED THE HIT MOVIE

When Andrea first sets foot in the plush Manhattan offices
of Runway she knows nothing. She's never heard of the world's
most fashionable magazine, or its feared and fawned-over editor,
Miranda Priestly – her new boss.

A year later, she knows altogether too much:

That it's a sacking offence to wear anything lower than
a three-inch heel to work.

That you can charge anything at all to the Runway account, but you
must never, ever, leave your desk, or let Miranda's coffee get cold.

And that at 3 a.m. on a Sunday, when your boyfriend's dumping
you because you're always at work, if Miranda phones, you jump.

But this is her big break – it's going to be worth it in the end.

Isn't it?

EVERYONE WORTH KNOWING

CAN SHE SURVIVE THE WORLD OF PARTIES, PRADA AND PLAYBOYS?

Bette gets paid to party. And she can hardly believe her luck. Gaining VIP access to Manhattan's hottest spots and meeting 'everyone worth knowing' is a million miles away from her old job. Overnight, New York has become her sexy late-night playground.

But quicker than you can say Chanel, Bette turns up in the gossip columns as girlfriend to a notorious British playboy. It's news that delights her new boss – but her friends want to know what's happened to the girl they love, who always had time for nights filled with 80s music, junk food, trashy rom-coms and her mates.

Can Bette say goodbye to the parties and the Prada and step back into the real world – and find a prince who's got a heart to match his charm?

CHASING HARRY WINSTON

THREE BEST FRIENDS. TWO RESOLUTIONS.
ONE YEAR TO PULL IT OFF.

Emmy has just split with her boyfriend of five years. A serial monogamist, she suddenly realises how much she's missed the thrill of single life. A new job travelling across the globe could offer her the one thing she is craving, so she vows to find a man on every continent for some pure no-strings-attached fun.

Adriana is stunning and can have any man she desires. Yet all she wants is an eligible bachelor who'll slip a five-carat Harry Winston diamond on her finger.

Leigh has a doting boyfriend that most girls would kill for. But when literary bad boy Jesse Chapman asks to work with her and more, she just can't refuse.

Over cocktails one night, the three friends make a pact – come hell or high water, they must change one thing in their lives by the end of the year...

LAST NIGHT AT CHATEAU MARMONT

HEARTBREAK, HEADLINES AND HERMES...

Brooke and Julian live a happy life in New York – she's the breadwinner working two jobs and he's the struggling musician husband. Then Julian becomes an overnight success – and their life changes forever.

Soon they are moving in exclusive circles, dining at the glitziest restaurants, attending the most outrageous parties in town and jetting off to the trendiest hotspots in LA.

But Julian's new-found fame means that Brooke must face the savage attentions of the ruthless paparazzi. And when a scandalous picture hits the front pages, Brooke's world is turned upside down. Can her marriage survive the events of that fateful night at Chateau Marmont? It's time for Brooke to decide if she's going to sink or swim...